VINTAGE

ZÎN

Haritha Savithri is a writer, freelance journalist, human rights activist and translator. She has translated İskender Pala's *Tulip of Istanbul*, Samar Yazbek's *The Crossing* and Ahmet Ümit's *The Cry of a Swallow* into Malayalam. Her book *Murivettavarute Pathakal* received the 2022 Kerala Sahitya Akademi Award for best travelogue. *Zîn* won the Udya Sahitya Puraskaram 2023. Savithri lives in Spain and is pursuing research in English philology at the University of Barcelona.

Nandakumar K. is a Dubai-based translator. His co-translation of M. Mukundan's *Delhi Gadhakal* (Delhi: A Soliloquy) won the 2021 JCB Prize for Literature. His other translations include *A Thousand Cuts*, the autobiography of Professor T.J. Joseph, which won the Kerala Sahitya Akademi Award; *The Lesbian Cow and Other Stories* by Indu Menon; *In the Name of the Lord*, the autobiography of Sister Lucy Kalapura; *Anthill*, a novel by Vinoy Thomas which won the Kerala Sahitya Akademi Award, and the children's book *Elephantam Misophantam* by the same author. Nandakumar is the grandson of Mahakavi Vallathol Narayana Menon.

HARITHA SAVITHRI

Translated from the Malayalam by
NANDAKUMAR K.

VINTAGE
An imprint of Penguin Random House

VINTAGE

USA | Canada | UK | Ireland | Australia
New Zealand | India | South Africa | China | Singapore

Vintage is part of the Penguin Random House group of companies
whose addresses can be found at global.penguinrandomhouse.com

Published by Penguin Random House India Pvt. Ltd
4th Floor, Capital Tower 1, MG Road,
Gurugram 122 002, Haryana, India

First published in Malayalam by Mathrubhumi Books, 2022
Published in Vintage by Penguin Random House India 2024

Copyright © Haritha Savithri 2022
Translation copyright © Nandakumar K. 2024

All rights reserved

10 9 8 7 6 5 4 3 2 1

ISBN 9780143461661

Typeset in Adobe Garamond Pro by Manipal Technologies Limited, Manipal

www.penguin.co.in

To Ivan

Foreword

By N.S. Madhavan

Malayalam literature has rarely ventured into territories alien to it. We can't really find fault with that. Ordinarily, the green shoots of self-expression sprout only in very familiar environments. At the same time, literature also reminds us that life and human condition have a universality that transcends geographical and temporal boundaries. This explains how Thunchaththu Ramanujan Ezhuthachan and Shakespeare affectionately rub shoulders with each other on our bookshelves. Human emotions are the same, everywhere and in every era.

Zîn, Haritha Savithri's novel reminds us of this universal truth. This novel takes Malayalam literature—which has never stepped beyond north India or the Gulf nations at best—directly to Diyarbakır.

This Turkish town was the epicentre of Kurdish people's struggle for their homeland. Who are Kurds? Malayalis have been aware of these people for some time now; however, this knowledge was born with a sense of shock and outrage. The name of that guilt which has racked Malayalis—and other helpless people around the world—was Aylan Kurdi. The innocent

face of that three-year-old—seemingly asleep on the beach of a
Turkish resort in Bodrum with his face half-buried in the sand—
made it impossible for the world to turn their faces away from the
Kurd problem. Aylan, his mother Rehan and his older brother
Galip lost their lives while fleeing to Greece via sea to escape the
genocide unleashed by Syria and the IS (Islamic State) against
the Kurds.

Aylan's photos also remind us of the nine-year-old Vietnamese
girl Kim Phúc, known as the Napalm Girl, whose clothes had
been vaporized in the US Army's napalm bomb attack. The 1972
photo lit the fuse of anti-war sentiments in the US, turning the
tide against the Vietnam War. It was because the enormity and
immorality of the biggest superpower in the world carpet-bombing
a small country in the faraway Asia was seen as simple and
straightforward as the Biblical story of David vs Goliath, that
the one photo was able to influence the course of the war with
such ease.

However, as heart-rending as little Aylan's picture was, because
the complicated and complex history of the Kurdish-majority
regions was not as simple and straightforward as the David vs
Goliath story, it could not be assimilated as easily. Why? Because it
did not epitomize what the Kurds were undergoing. The persecution
that Kurds undergo cannot be captured by one photo.

This makes Haritha's *Zîn* an important novel in Malayalam.
Very little has been told of and read of the Kurds. Among the few,
but widely read, books is the autobiographical work, *The Daughter
of Kurdland* by Dr Widad Akreyi. She is perhaps the most famous
Kurdish writer and activist and has written other popular works
too. When the boundaries set by a memoir are breached in a novel
with its greater freedom, matters, especially reflections, can be
presented with greater clarity. Haritha uses this possibility to the
hilt in this novel.

Kurds, who follow Islam, are a race who inhabit the region that shares borders with Iraq, Syria, Armenia and Turkey. They have no country of their own. The Jews got their Promised Land before the Second World War and before the State of Israel came into existence, because of the vice-like grip they had on the world of capitalism and the support they wrangled out of the West. Kurds had, or have, no one to speak for them.

The concept of Kurdistan, by joining the Kurd-majority regions within the geographies of Iraq, Turkey, Syria and Armenia, gained ground at the beginning of the twentieth century. Kurds were minorities in each of these countries. They became the victims of racial prejudice and extermination.

The defeat of the Central Powers—the Ottoman Empire of Turkey was one of the constituents apart from Germany and Austro-Hungary—in the First World War presented the best opportunity for a homeland for the Kurds. The Treaty of Sèvres in 1920 allowed Britain, France and their allies to carve up the Ottoman Empire between them. At that time, the Kurd-majority area of Turkey and the present-day Mosul of Iraq were declared as Kurdistan. But it did not turn into a country. The Kurds chose to hold a plebiscite at first. It was, anyway, incomplete—Armenia's Kurd regions were missed out.

In 1923, the Treaty of Lausanne annulled the Treaty of Sèvres and gave birth to the Republic of Turkey. Kurdistan, which existed only on paper, became an empty dream and Kurds were again a minority in Turkey. What followed was a massacre in 1925, in which some 20,000 Kurds were killed in military action. In 1932, in Dersim, 40,000 were slaughtered. Next what we know is that the pogroms had spread to all the countries where Kurds lived.

If the US had wanted to prevent the Kurds' extermination in Iraq, they could have done it. Between 1975–90, the US had a complete hands-off policy in Kurdish matters. Taking advantage of that, Saddam Hussain killed thousands of Kurds. In 1998, in the closing days of the Iran–Iraq War, Saddam used chemical weapons in the Kurdish village of Halabja; thousands including women and children died a horrible death.

After the defeat of Saddam Hussain in the 1991 Gulf War, the Shias raised the flag of revolt in the southern provinces of Iraq. Drawing inspiration from this, the Kurds in the north provinces went on the warpath. Of the eighteen provinces of Iraq, fifteen fell into the hands of Shias or Kurds. However, the US did not back the rebels. The backlash from Saddam Hussain was cruel and terrifying. Where Kurds had helped the US against Saddam when he turned on them, the US chose to turn a blind eye to his heinous acts. It was only in 1999 that the US declared that attacks on Kurds would not be pardoned. The US had cited crimes against humanity as the reason for hanging Saddam. But the truth remains that the US was as complicit and culpable in the case of Kurds killed by Saddam as he himself was.

The help that Kurds had given to the US was the reason the Syrian Army and the Islamic State had unleashed their brand of terror and annihilation on the Kurds. Unable to resist these depredations, hundreds died in their attempt to flee, including little Aylan.

The miseries of Kurds in Turkey have already been touched upon. For over a century, the Turks have been hunting down Kurds who once made up 20 per cent of the country's population. Turkey denied the very existence of Kurds. The words, Kurds and Kurdistan, were banned. Until 1991, they were officially called Mountain Turks.

From the time the movement for a Kurd homeland started in the 1980s, Kurds and the Turkish government have been on a collision course. The resistance took an organized form only after the communist-inspired Kurdish Workers Party (PKK or Partiya

Karkerên Kurdistan) was formed in 1978 under the leadership of Abdullah Öcalan, who is, even today, rotting in a Turkish jail. The response from the Turkish government was ghastly. From 1978, some 4000 Kurdish villages have been evacuated, displacing their entire inhabitants. More than 40,000 Kurdish people have been killed in various ways. Although after the 2012 peace talks, there was a de-escalation of the violence, from July 2015, skirmishes between the Turkish Army and Kurdish freedom fighters have started again.

Haritha's novel takes the readers through times of death and distress. I have touched upon the long history of the Kurdish people's miseries only to provide a prologue to this novel. And to remind the readers that these pages bear the weight of centuries of history of these forlorn people.

Diyarbakır, a Kurd-majority city, is marked to be its capital, if at all a Kurdistan would come into existence. The novel begins in this crucible of resistance. The narration follows a group of Kurd freedom fighters. Into this mix, a Malayali girl, who is the lover of and carrying the baby of one of the militants, is thrown in. However, the novel is not written from the viewpoint of that girl. Our journey is mostly with the Kurds. Leaving aside those engaged in the fight, when the war zone is viewed through the eyes of this girl, it attains a mordant poignancy and neutral honesty.

The action takes place in one of the biggest combat zones of our times. The novel succeeds not only because of the subject Haritha has chosen, but its credible assimilation that she has achieved through her clear writing style. When the aroma of coffee spreads from the coffee shops in those troubled lands; when the morning light bounces off the blueness of the Tigris which has borne countless corpses to the sea; when desperate for refuge, the Kurd fighters knock on doors, invariably there are only brave women to open them—the novelist is telling us that in times of utmost strife and endless battles, life is not left unlived.

A story set in unfamiliar locales or unfolding during fraught times in history does not necessarily make it great literature. It has to have an element that touches everyone by transcending the confines of time and space. There are no signs of Kurds winning their battles anytime in the near future. Yet they are arrayed on the war front. Why? As Antonio Gramsci says, though intelligence makes one a pessimist, willpower makes one an optimist. *Zin* celebrates the ultimate truth of this will to live and to love.

Sur

The fruits of the red cotton tree had started to pop and fall from its needle-like tip that scored the sky. Fluffy cotton balls floated down as if the clouds were shedding. Within seconds, they covered her like a fleece blanket. She freed her hands, flapped them and tried to shake off the shroud to escape from being smothered. The diaphanous cotton balls continued to swirl in the whistling breeze and hovered above her like a shroud. She was being pulled into the soft depths and kept surfacing again. She could not breathe. Kicking up from the depths, she came up gasping for air. Try as she might, the downy cotton balls, still snowing down on her, pushed her down into the bottomless depths of an abyss.

'Ammae . . .' With a scream, Seetha leapt out of her bed. In a panic, she threw away the soft, heavy duvet covering her face. The humming of the old room heater sounded like a wild animal's growl. Still breathless, she gulped in the thin warm air in the room hungrily. When Seetha's hyperventilation abated, her room with its furniture and the 'Lilies of the Valley' painting on the wall returned into focus.

She sat blinking at the large, metal-frame clock in the room. Six o'clock. She was unsure if it was morning or late evening. The curtains that blocked the sights and the light outside made the

1

darkness linger inside. Though she was famished, she languidly slid back into the warmth under the duvet.

Moments later, she woke up with a start from her half-asleep state to the sound of tinkling bells. Where was the phone? By the time she found it under her pillow, it rang again. It was Timur. He had managed to get her a SIM card from the Turkcell store across from her hotel.

'Are you not up yet?' Timur's serene voice echoed in the room from the phone's speaker. 'If you are tired, go back to sleep. I shall go and find out.'

Seetha rose from the bed. Her legs were feeling weak from exhaustion.

'Timur, I need a shower. I will be at the reception in twenty minutes.'

'No hurry. Take your time.'

He cut the call.

The hot shower energized her. After wrapping her hair—that she had blow-dried in a hurry—in an orange Rajasthani dupatta and donning a loose, long-sleeved red tunic, she looked at her reflection in the mirror. Dressed in this droll fashion and with a swollen face and puffy eyes, she could not recognize herself. She recalled how Dewran had once kissed her wet forehead with his warm lips and hugged her tightly as she came out of the bath when they used to live together. She now broke out in goose pimples at the memory of his hard muscles that had pressed against her.

A short while now. Not far to go. To get rid of the flush, she rubbed her cheeks hard.

The mobile phone rang again as if to remind her that she had ran out of time. Seated on a black sofa in the well-appointed reception, Timur looked up from what he was reading and gave her a warning stare as she hurried towards him.

'Take it slow!' He rolled his eyes.

That brought a smile to her lips. What if she were home, back in Kerala? How her amma had bustled about when her older sister was pregnant. There was a constant stream of savouries being cooked in the kitchen. The house reeked of herbal medicines and concoctions that amma had made with Janakiamma's help. She recalled the lassitude in her sister's face as she was made to rest after her oil-anointed bath and consuming the medicinal *kanji*.

And instead, where . . . God, is she herself at this moment . . .?

She suppressed her sigh so that Timur would not see it.

'Don't worry. We're not late. It's a little less cold now. People are coming out only now,' Timur said as he watched the melancholy spread across her face.

Although she had tried to emulate Kurd women's style of dressing, people still stared at her quizzically. Kids followed her carrying freshly baked circular breads that resembled big bangles strung together hoping she may buy a couple. The aroma from the golden-coloured breads sprinkled generously with roasted sesame seeds gave her hunger a new edge. She dropped the idea of buying a piece when she realized that Timur was getting uncomfortable in the presence of those shabbily dressed kids, whose cheeks were ruddy from the cold. He kept admonishing them in harsh-sounding Turkish, probably asking them to stay away.

The market was not crowded at that hour. In front of their curved doors, the shops that were open, had stacked high multi-coloured sweetmeats and toffees, dates and almonds coated in chocolate. Targeting the tourists that come to see the fort that ran round the town, holding up plastic bottles, the urchin helpers in those shops shouted at the top of their voices, 'Su uuu . . . one lira. Su . . . uu . . . pure as rainwater. Su . . . uuu . . . one lira!'

Seetha and Timur passed roadside vendors of dried apricots, pushcarts topped with powdered spices, fabrics and garment sellers, old-timers selling sliced watermelon and fruit sellers inviting them from behind heaps of shiny, violet cherries.

'Have a coffee,' some people invited Seetha solicitously. She hesitated as she was perplexed and unsure how to respond. Timur took over and politely kept refusing the offers.

'Do not worry, Kurds are the most hospitable people. They can see you are a foreigner. They believe it is their duty to serve you,' he told her, laughing.

They reached a street that had started to bustle and was redolent with the smell of coffee. Pedestrians, bicycles, pushcarts and vehicles at crawling speed moved side by side with great camaraderie. Women flocked around shops that sold coffee beans from tall, colourful, carved wooden containers. The pleasant aroma and the rhythmic sounds from the shiny, brass mechanical coffee grinders stationed by the roadside tarried in the cool air.

The sounds and the smell transported Seetha thousands of kilometres away to the backyard of her own home in her native land. Her mother's sweet smell. The memory of the rice balls that her mother used to make with pounded golden-roasted rice, jaggery and coconut, to have along with the coffee, made her salivate.

She noticed that across the street, beyond the shops that sold dried chillies, tomatoes and vegetables strung like garlands, there was nothing. It looked as if someone had sliced off the city, leaving behind only a row of buildings opening out in the street they were walking on.

Blocking the lanes that snaked between the buildings, like the roots of the main street, were concrete slabs that were about the height of three men. As Timur walked ahead reading the name boards of the shops, Seetha tugged at his shirt, pointing them out to him. 'Don't point your finger,' warned Timur. 'It's only been two years since there's been an uprising here. You'll see many things here. Walk as if you've noticed nothing. Don't draw attention to yourself.'

On the granite slab paved street, parting the pedestrians, a large, dark, armoured Vuran was being driven slowly towards them. The sight of the gun turret and the rifle-toting soldiers watching them from behind the barred, bulletproof glass windows sent a shiver through Seetha. Ignoring their probing looks that scanned every face in the crowd, and the gun barrels that poked out of the vehicle, she stuck by Timur who was deep in conversation with someone.

He was using the word 'Bedew' repeatedly. His interlocutor, a young man with tired eyes and a long beard, was listening intently and appeared to be thinking. He kept pulling at the hair that peeked out of his nostrils and scratching his head framed by unruly locks. After being lost in thought for a little while, he seemed to murmur something apologetically to Timur and walked away.

Timur looked at Seetha in desperation. A shoe store in this small town! In which unknown corner was it located? They kept walking. Kabab vendors with their cart-mounted, charcoal-fired clay ovens, and their helper boys lugging buckets filled with water, were finding unoccupied spots by the roadside. The air started to fill with smoke and the smell of roasted mutton.

'Are you hungry?' Timur asked suddenly as if he had remembered it only then. After a look at Seetha's tired face, he murmured apologetically, 'I should have asked you earlier.'

They took the seats in front of an eatery in one of the lanes, away from the smoke. Small, colourfully decorated mats were placed on the seats for comfort of the customers.

A minaret supported by four round pillars stood in the centre of that by-lane. Lugging heavy shoulder bags, tourists were going around it and posing for photographs. The lane ended abruptly beyond the minaret. Seetha's astounded eyes were locked on the heavy metal plates and thick concrete slabs that blocked the way.

Proffering the menu card, the owner of the eatery pottered around them anxiously. Following Seetha's gaze, the man pointed at the minaret and said with obvious pride in broken English, 'Old . . . five hundred years . . .'

Taking his eyes off the menu card, Timur said, 'It's true.' Then turning to Seetha and handing it over he asked, 'What would you like to eat?'

Seetha felt that Timur was uncomfortable having the man hover around them. 'Can I get some rice?'

'You want rice?' Timur's eyes widened in surprise. After a little reflection he spoke to the eatery owner in Turkish.

'You may like pilaf. It's made with rice, meat and vegetables is what the man said.'

'Is it pulao?' Seetha asked, pleased.

'No, pilaf!' Timur said emphatically.

Still gazing at the pillars holding up the minaret, Seetha tried to find the connection between pilaf and pulao.

'Have you seen such a minaret anywhere?'

'No.' Seetha, still lost in thought, turned and looked at Timur. 'Such thin legs!' she continued to show her surprise.

'The legs of this four-legged minaret represent the four tenets of Islam and the minaret, the oneness of Islam. The people here claim that if one passes between the pillars seven times, his or her wishes will be fulfilled.'

'In that case let me have a go,' Seetha said, laughing. 'But then, why do you have such high walls that remind one of jails? And closed-circuit cameras! I've never seen such security even in holy mosques.'

Timur leaned forward as if to share a secret.

'If you take a close look, you'll see that the minaret is pockmarked with bullet holes.'

'How do you know? You're here for the first time?' Seetha could not control her curiosity.

'Haven't I told you that my father is a lawyer? Tahir Elçi was his friend. He was assassinated here.'

Seetha blanched. 'Why?' Her voice quavered.

'These are bad times, Seetha. Elçi was not only a good lawyer, but an excellent politician too. Four or five years back, he held a press conference beneath this shot-up minaret. His aim was to prove with examples how political fights undermine and destroy the cultural tradition of a land. After the press meet, when he and his bodyguard were approaching the car, they were attacked and killed.'

A jolt of fear passed through Seetha.

'Who, who killed them?'

A disquieted Timur turned away as if to check if the food was coming.

'I don't know. Such killings are commonplace here.'

'Timur, I'm sure you know. Tell me the truth. Who killed him?'

'Shush! You shouldn't say such things aloud.'

'Why are you not open with me?' Seetha was getting angry.

Timur sighed in his helplessness.

'After the press meet was over, there was a shootout between the police and the rebels here in Yenikapı Street. The official version is that he was caught in the crossfire and an unintended victim,' Timur whispered.

'You don't believe it, do you?' Seetha asked in wonder.

'Elçi had always maintained that Kurdistan Workers' Party[1] was not a terrorist organization. His argument was that to brand an organisation that believed in the ideal of resistance and acted accordingly as terrorists was unfair. He had received many death threats following this.'

'What are you driving at? That it was a planned assassination?'

'The food is here.' The visibly uneasy Timur tried to change the subject.

The owner brought a colourfully etched copper platter with a variety of food items. Timur pushed towards her a bowl of labneh, and a plate of salad comprising green leaves, tomato and cucumber.

It looked as if Timur had decided to ask the eatery owner about Bedew, who replied enthusiastically to his questions. He discussed the route at length and using a stubby pencil borrowed from him, Timur drew a small map of the route on a paper napkin.

When the man tried to explain to Seetha that leather bags and sandals of Bedew were of top quality, Timur peremptorily ordered him to get the pilaf as if to dismiss him from there. The man went away with a scowl on his face.

'Such curiosity! Strange fellow! I don't like him.' Timur muttered below his breath.

'Did he explain to you where Bedew is?' Seetha was anxious.

'Yes. Actually, it is a teashop. On the ground floor they sell leather items made by cobblers from the countryside. Since the teashop is on the upper floor, people here refer to it as Terrace.'

'Shall we go there?'

'You have your food first. We have walked around enough for the day. Let's get back to the hotel, take some rest and then go in the evening.'

Seetha had no appetite. Nevertheless, afraid that Timur may scold her, she ate everything that was placed before her.

The owner came with the bill. When Timur went up to the cash counter to pay, the man showed a streak of rustic inquisitiveness and started to pump Seetha with questions.

'Madam, where are you coming from?'

'India.' She smiled as was her wont when answering this question.

'My name is Alibek. I own this place.' As if to prove that it all belonged to him, he vainly waved his arms in all directions.

'How did you land up here? Normally tourists all go to Istanbul.'

'Some of my friends are here.'

Alibek pondered for a little while.

'Are you staying with them?'

She was familiar with such inquisitiveness from villagers. Nevertheless, she did not like the piercing look in his cunning eyes.

'I am staying in Hotel Diyarbakır.'

When he saw Seetha conversing with the man, Timur hurried back after paying the bill.

'Don't ever discuss anything with strangers,' he said harshly.

'He only asked me where I am from and where I am staying,' Seetha sounded like a culprit.

'And then? Did you tell him where you are staying? Seetha, you are an idiot.' Timur shook his head in exasperation.

'If Bedew is near, let's go and have a look,' Seetha said, trying change the subject.

'Not possible. In your state, don't tire out your body any further. We'll go at 6 p.m.'

His tone was sharp. He was silent till they reached the hotel. His uneasy silence filled her with gloom.

'Whoever knocks, don't open the door. Whatever is the matter, you should call me.'

Timur saw her safely into her room and said before heading to his own, 'We'll meet at 6 p.m. at the reception.'

Pressing herself against the door that had shut behind her with thud, Seetha took stock of the situation. There was fear in his voice. I must keep my big mouth shut, she cautioned herself, overcome by guilt.

With the thought, that in the evening they would be going to Bedew, Seetha calmed her fears and anxieties. She even started to hope that she may run into Dewran there. Tossing and turning in an excitement tinged with anxiety, she could not find sleep.

Where should I look for you? Streets redolent with the smell of coffee? Dark alleys behind shops selling spices and sweetmeats? Deserted courtyards of mosques?

She sighed when she remembered the hint of a mischievous smile beneath the thick, slightly upturned moustache. The smile seemed to convey that it would not be easy to find him. If he had decided to go into hiding, there was no one better than him who could do it. Overcome by frustration and cussedness, she paced around the room. 'I'm no less than you, Dewran. Till the moment I get to stand in front of you, you may hide in your hole,' she muttered.

Seetha was back at the reception before 6 p.m. Yusuf, a boy in his teens and with sparse facial hair, was the receptionist for the evening. He smiled shyly and enquired solicitously how her stay was. In the mornings, he attended classes at a university in Mardin, about 100 km away, and worked as the night receptionist. Seetha felt that his statement, that he was getting to sleep more in the nights because tourists had dwindled after the recent clashes, came out of relief more than anything else.

Timur, when he emerged, was happy to see a calm Seetha seated on the sofa. He seemed to have recovered from his choler. He proudly showed her the map which he had faithfully and neatly transferred to an A4 size paper from the paper napkin. Going by the map prepared with the help of Alibek, the Terrace did not appear to be far from their hotel.

The street was crowded with people out for a stroll and others who were hurrying back home after buying food. The street vendors were having a good day. As she wended her way between women who were haggling with cloth sellers and urchins who were darting around selling savouries, Seetha was trembling with anticipation and stress.

'That is Bedew,' Timur pointed to small shop that had a coffee-grinder in front. Ahead of the door that had been painted blue, leather sandals were arranged neatly on a small bench. A narrow flight of steps along the side of the shop suggested to them it was the way to the Terrace. Noticing the glint in her eye, Timur, with a smile, let her lead the way.

As she climbed the steps with effort, a wild hope rose in Seetha's mind that Dewran may be waiting for her there. Realising that she was in a flap, Timur patted her shoulder gently to calm her down.

The Terrace was bright and airy. Panting, she looked around expectantly. There were some small plants in wooden barrels, three or four tables and a few chairs under the multi-coloured, applique-work awning. Seetha looked around again to make sure that Dewran was not hiding there to tease her. Swaying in a light breeze that had sprung up suddenly, the plants in the barrels shook their heads as if denying his presence. The place was empty. The angst and dismay that had been reined in till then burst out in a cascade of tears. Helpless, Timur plonked down on a chair. The unending search and apparently unending wails and tension that it was creating had exhausted him.

'There was no reason to believe that Dewran would be here,' feeling helpless, he tried to console Seetha. 'We'll certainly find a way to get to him,' Timur reassured her, gently stroking her hair as she cried with her head on the table.

From a room on the side, a man emerged through a door that had a picture of a lady plucking coffee beans. He was astonished to see a tearful Seetha and Timur with his fingers caught in her hair.

'Who are you? What happened?'

Placing the vessel in his hands on a table, he walked up to Timur. Rising from the creaky wooden chair with alacrity, Timur introduced Seetha and himself. Taking sidelong glances at the still-sobbing Seetha, Timur made enquiries about Dewran in low tones. The man's face brightened when he heard Dewran's name. As Seetha tried to control her sobs to listen in on their conversation, holding her shoulders, Timur eagerly pulled her up and spoke excitedly, 'He is the manager of this teashop, Esat! He knows Dewran and his friends too. Stop crying!'

He introduced Seetha to Esat.

'Seetha, Dewran's girlfriend.'

Esat took her hands in his own affectionately.

'Don't be sad. I shall do all that I can. Can you tell me everything that happened?'

Timur narrated the events until then in detail. Seetha, now with her tears under control, kept filling the gaps in the story and replying to Esat's questions in broken English.

After he had listened to everything, Esat told them what he knew of Dewran. He was a member of a group of youth which, on most days, fuelled by countless cups of tea and ignited by chain-smoked cigarettes, held heated political debates on the Terrace late into the evening. Apart from the hearsay that Dewran had been missing for some time, Esat did not know much. Now that he was aware of what had happened, he made a phone call.

'I called a very good friend of Dewran. He'll be here in few minutes. You can wait here,' Esat tried to comfort Seetha.

He gave them an iced drink of pomegranate syrup mixed in water boiled with cinnamon bark and then cooled. Seetha could hear the voices of women from the ground floor, haggling over the prices of sandals. Esat went down telling them apologetically that there was only a young boy to look after the sales.

'If you wail like this and unnerve me, what will I do? Are you still not convinced that come what may, we will not return without meeting Dewran?' When they were alone again, Timur started to complain with a scowl on his face. Her crying had shaken him that much.

She smiled at him sheepishly. She felt ashamed when she recalled her daftness.

Once the sun went down, the regulars started to turn up at the teashop for their cuppa and gossip. They looked at Seetha curiously and tried to engage her in conversation. Timur had instructed her that her standard reply should be that she was researching the similarities between Indian and Kurdish cultures.

To most of them, this sounded credible. Impressed by her coming to study their culture, many of the men offered to buy Seetha tea. They also volunteered to render any help she needed.

The emptiness that could be seen from where she was seated had grabbed her attention. Beyond the rooftops of the teashop and some houses adjacent to it, nothing remained standing. The remains of the destroyed buildings were more disturbing question marks than structures. Some distance away, as part of some ongoing construction, the rising and lowering arm and bucket of an earthmover could be seen. Beyond the scattered ruins and detritus lay the desert-brown land—fallow, unyielding, vast in size and frozen in time.

When she saw that whenever she tried to get his attention to bear on that desolate sight, he was trying to evade the subject, she gave it up in annoyance. She tried to understand whatever everyone seated around them were conversing about, slurping tea and smoking endlessly. She watched curiously as the carelessly dressed young men with long, uncut tresses and untrimmed beards took out paper and tobacco from their small, colourfully embroidered bags and rolled their own smokes.

As time passed, her anxiety returned. Each footstep she heard on the stairs made her crane her neck and check who the new arrival was. Eventually, Esat arrived. He came to her ostensibly to serve another cup of tea.

'A young man in a blue dress will arrive now. He will also enquire about the purpose of your trip like others did. He's the friend of Dewran's we have been waiting for.' Esat left after collecting the empty cups.

A tall young man arrived. He looked very tired. Like other people before him, he also showed surprise at Seetha's presence, greeted her and asked the same questions. After introducing himself as Akbar, in a loud voice, he held forth on the innocuous subject of Kurdish music. He was probably trying to ensure that others around them were not getting attracted to their conversation. He continued to talk enthusiastically about the most uninteresting, tedious things.

When the crowd thinned, Esat came to them in a hurry. 'I have closed the door to the Terrace. Assuming the shop is closed, no one will come now to have tea.'

He pushed a twelve- or thirteen-year-old boy towards them. 'Ask Ramzan if you need anything.' He hurried down. From the time the shop opened, Seetha had noticed the boy running around tirelessly running errands for Esat. Smiling politely, and without hanging around, he disappeared into the small kitchen on the side.

Akbar, who was till then boring them with a long-winded babble on music, turned towards Seetha. His sleepy eyes suddenly lit up.

'Dewran's lover!'

He grabbed her hands, held them tight and looked into her eyes.

'I didn't know he had returned.'

'Please don't smoke so close to her,' Timur pleaded when he saw that Akbar had lit a cigarette.

Akbar gave Timur and Seetha an astonished look. When he understood the reason, he threw the cigarette down and ground it underfoot. 'Please forgive me. I hadn't realized.'

'Damn!' Akbar scratched his unruly hair as if in a dilemma. 'Why did you come here in this state? It's dangerous here now.'

Chewing his nails, he kept his gaze on Seetha.

'Dewran doesn't know I'm pregnant,' Seetha said softly. When she said the word, she wondered why it felt so heavy. 'If he's getting into any trouble, you should dissuade him. I've no one else. My family has already abandoned me.'

'He will of course end up in trouble. The police have come to know that Arman is alive. They have intensified their hunt for him. In such circumstances, will anyone with any sense return?'

'Who's Arman?' Timur was anxious.

'Hasn't he told you about Arman?' Akbar looked askance at Timur and Seetha.

'He hasn't mentioned anything about these troubles. He used to talk about his family always.'

'Arman is Dewran's elder brother. If you couch it in the government's language, a violent, homicidal criminal wanted by the Turkish police and the Interpol.'

He looked repeatedly at Seetha and Timur's faces that had turned paper white out of fear.

'Arman was a student like you. His interest was only studies and his family. He lived in a small flat in Sur, along with Gul and Dewran . . .'

Holding their breaths, Seetha and Timur listened to the unfolding story . . .

'Isn't it better that you go back?' After his narration, Akbar asked Seetha, seated with her head bowed.

'No!' Her dark eyes shone with both tears and determination. 'The chances are that I will lose in the end. I know well that the odds are stacked against me. But I'll not go back.'

Akbar looked at Timur in dismay.

Sounds of loud pounding on the ground floor door reached them. Ramzan came out of the kitchen in a flash. After gesturing to Akbar, who had leapt to his feet, to sit down, he went near the stairs and cocked his ears. Along with things being dropped and sent crashing, harsh interrogative voices and loud bleating-like answers from Esat could also be heard. He turned and looked at them, his face ashen with fear.

'It's the police. They are looking for you, sister,' he said looking at Seetha.

From his demeanour it was clear to them that he had been trained how to act in such exigencies. In one easy yank, he pulled up a long plank—the tabletop of a folding table—that had been kept leaning on the side of the terrace. He placed it firmly across the parapet walls of the terraces of the teashop and the neighbouring house and called to them.

'They will come up soon to check the Terrace. Make good your escape while you can.'

Without a second thought, Akbar crossed to the neighbouring building. As a numbed Seetha stood with disbelieving eyes watching his form disappear beyond the rooftop, Timur caught her hand and pulled, 'Rush, the police!'

He pulled a chair close to the parapet wall so that she could step on to the plank. Even after he—almost dragging her—brought her to the parapet, she stood frozen, unable to move. Timur caught hold of her shoulders and shook her roughly.

'Seetha, for God's sake, please! Didn't you hear what Akbar told us? If you fall into the hands of the police, they will use you as bait to catch Dewran.'

He shook her by her shoulders again. She seemed to wake with a start. She stared at him.

'Quick!'

Trembling with fear, Timur pushed her up, on to the chair, and from there on to the plank. He followed her close behind making sure she did not miss her step or fall. The moment they crossed over, Ramzan pulled the plank back. When Seetha looked back, she could see him struggling to shove it under the stack of table legs.

They crawled over the tiles where both roofs met. When they reached a flat space, invisible from the Terrace, Timur stopped. Lying flat on his back, he asked Seetha to follow suit.

Still panting, she sat beside him. She felt the coolness of the tiles singeing her skin. She pulled out the dupatta that she was using like scarf, bunched it up, and lay down with her face resting on it. When Timur saw tears streaming down her cheeks, he turned his face and gnashed his teeth.

'Someone has surely betrayed us. When I saw you shovelling all that information into Alibek I knew this would happen. I'll smash in that sonofabitch's face.'

Loud voices were carrying to them from the Terrace.

'They are checking out the place since they don't believe Esat. This place would have been under their surveillance.'

Timur stood up slowly.

'Let's go.' He helped her up.

Stooping and crawling on their stomachs, they reached the last rooftop. When she saw the ruins of the next building, Seetha felt a hollow in the pit of her stomach.

'See here, it's easy to get down. Step on the top of the wall, then on the windowsill beneath it and slide down to the heap of rubble below.' He tried to embolden her by sounding as if climbing down was the most facile act.

'Don't slip or fall,' he looked into her eyes nervously. She could see his fear. Timur was already standing on the broken wall. She took his hand and stepped down. Lowering herself on to the windowsill, she slid down to rubble below without much trouble. She extended her hand towards Timur who stood with a look of disbelieving amazement on his face.

'That was smartly done,' he complimented her and leapt down.

'All the lanes from here to the main street have been blocked.' Looking at the buildings that seemed to stand shoulder to shoulder, barring their way, he was lost in thought for some time.

'There has to be a way through them.' He started to part the bushes and shrubs and walk ahead.

'Be careful; there could be creepy-crawlies here.'

It was getting dark. They had to walk over the relics of houses where once generations had lived, loved, dreamed and cherished. They walked through a space which, with its scattered remains of flowerpots and planters, appeared to have been someone's courtyard. Seetha tried to imagine how that small garden, tended to by some loving housewife, would have looked with its flowers, fragrance, butterflies and fountain.

The bushes and rubble made for slow, painstaking progress. The outline of the slim minaret framed against the dark sky could be seen at a distance. Seetha felt as if the burnt and cracked walls were closing in on her, trying to crush and smother her. The place was noisome; the stench was overpowering. The ground was littered with broken tiles, clods and shattered timber.

While trying to keep up with Timur, she tripped over something, lost her step and was propelled forward. To stop herself from falling, she grabbed the nearest broken wall, causing a couple of tiles and a lot of dust resting on the rafters overhead to get dislodged and rain down ahead of her. Disturbed by this unusual racket, the permanent residents of that site, a few bats, registered their displeasure by flapping their wings loudly and zooming over their heads.

'What happened?' an agitated Timur asked.

He lifted and removed the window frame that was blocking her path. She pulled herself up slowly, holding the hand he had offered. She felt her long dress had got caught in something. She turned and looked down. A bone! A human bone. Seetha screamed involuntarily. She extricated her dress from the curled bones of a human hand.

Timur helped a severely trembling Seetha to come out of the detritus of fallen rafters and beams. The sight of the bone had shaken him too.

'This was like a war zone. Do you have any idea how many people were disappeared? Beneath this rubble will be many more skeletons.'

He put his arm around her, and they walked side by side. Tiredness and fear had sapped the strength in her legs. Timur was almost dragging her sagging form along. He tried to see if he could enter the street through a breach at the end of the ruins. However, as if with the intention to prevent anyone from visiting this wrecked part of the town, every hole, every doorway, every fracture had been meticulously sealed off.

'We can't go farther than this. The police would be watching this area,' he said despairingly.

He seated Seetha on a plank nearby and tried to push open an old, decrepit door. It appeared to have been locked or shored up from the other side with something sturdy. Every time he smashed his shoulder and upper arm into it, it creaked but held firm.

He took a few steps back and tried to ram the door with his full body weight. Cursing and swearing, when he sat down in pain, he saw that one of the panels of the door had come loose; he called out to her cheerfully.

The door led to a large room. The light from the street was streaming in through the ventilator. Small heaps of merchandise scattered here and there made them believe it had been a warehouse of some sort, now gone derelict. The musty smell of rotten grains and dust hit them through the broken door.

Forcing the now loose panels, they entered the room. The sight of rats scurrying along the floor covered in litter and dust nauseated Seetha.

'Look, the light is from a streetlamp. We should find a way to get out.' Easing his hand out of her grip, he started to explore the room. The door to the street had been locked on the outside using only a hook-eye latch. Using a nail, he found by groping around on the floor, he flicked it open through the gap in the door.

'You wait here. Let me check how it is outside.'

He kept the door ajar and watched the alley through the gap.

'It's deserted, come, let's go . . .'

Taking her hand in his, he stepped out. He did not forget to close and latch the door. They were relieved that the alley led to the main street.

Seetha used the dupatta to cover her face, head and shoulders. Though far away, the neon sign of Diyarbakır Otel energized them. Timur had given up the habit of walking in the front and started to walk in step with Seetha. That way, the attention she drew from passers-by reduced. As if waiting for them, Yusuf stood at the door of the hotel.

'The police were here.' When he said that, his voice quivered with fear.

Taking the pale-faced Yusuf to the side, Timur spoke to him in whispers. Anxious and trying to catch what they were saying to each other, Seetha seated herself on a nearby sofa.

Timur came and knelt beside her.

'Listen carefully. We are leaving this place. We can go to Istanbul and stay at my home. You can rest there. I will use my connections to keep the search on.'

She sat like a statue for some time. It took some time for it to sink in that Timur's plan was to get away from there. She was on the brink of tears.

'But didn't you say that we'll go back only after finding him?' She started to weep as if her last hope had been dashed.

'For me your safety is the most important thing now.' His tone was uncompromising.

Sobbing, Seetha shook her head to indicate she was going nowhere. Timur looked at Yusuf helplessly.

Yusuf came and sat beside them.

'Madam, the police were here. I was so scared. For some reason, I felt that I should tell them you had left. Luckily, they did not make further enquiries or look at the register. I've been told to inform them if you ever came back. You must leave immediately. Or I will also be in trouble.'

He took them to a small room near the kitchen, where the employees took their bath, changed clothes and rested. Egg trays for the next day's breakfast were stacked on a steel table. From an ante room for storing gas cylinders and other things, Yusuf pulled out their bags.

'My apologies. When they left, I brought these down and hid them. They've gone crazy. If they had returned and decided to search your room, that would've been my end.'

'Don't worry my friend, you've been a great help!'

'You may use this room for now.' Yusuf left, closing the door behind him. Timur held Seetha, who had turned numb, close.

'We don't have time. The police will be back any time now. Get ready quickly. Let me see if I can hire a car.'

Seetha lifted her welled up eyes and tried to say something as if she was beseeching.

'There's no other way, Seetha.'

He went out ignoring the pleading look on her face. 'I'll be back soon,' he mumbled. After trying hard to think where he could find a car, finally, he decided to go back to Bedew.

Like that of the shops on the way, the door of Bedew was also shut. The red coffee grinder stood near the door. After lingering there for a little while, he decided to knock on the door and try his luck.

Taking care not to disturb the silence that hung heavily in that place, he tapped very softly on door one . . . two . . . He waited for a few seconds and tapped again one . . . two . . . He heard some murmurs from inside. A small single-panel window by the side of the door opened and a face peeped out.

'Who's it?' Esat was in a flutter. When he saw it was Timur, he opened the door and pulled him inside.

'Why did you return? The police wrecked my shop.'

Timur could see it was true. The floor was littered with leather bags and sandals. One side of Esat's face was red and swollen. Timur looked around in distress.

'You don't worry about all this. But why did you come here at this time? There are spies everywhere.'

'If we go to the airport, she could be arrested there. I can give you whatever money you want. I need a car. I have to take Seetha away from here without any loss of time.'

'I don't have a car,' Esat said mulling things over. 'There's an old van here which is used to fetch goods from the leather workers in the countryside.'

He pointed to an old van parked a little away from the shop.

'This's enough. Will it get to Istanbul?'

'Why not? Though it's old, the engine is in good condition. Only I use it.'

Timur pulled out some money from his pocket and handed it to Esat.

'My friend, I'm not sure when I can get this vehicle back to you. I'll send some more money soon.'

Esat shoved the money back into Timur's pocket, 'Return it when your use is over. That's enough. I have friends here to help me; and they have vehicles. Keep the money with you. You'll need it for this trip.'

When he saw the determined look on Esat's face, Timur quietly put the money back in his pocket without trying persuading him further.

Although the van started only after a little protest, once it started to roll, Timur felt that it was good enough to get them to Istanbul. He parked it a little away from the hotel. Yusuf appeared to be busy in the kitchen. It seemed that one of the vacant rooms had been taken.

The aroma of fried mutton arose from the kitchen. Without disturbing Yusuf, Timur knocked on the door of the room that had been given for their use. Although he hesitated at first thinking Seetha might be taking a shower, realizing how each moment was precious, Timur pushed the door open. The room was empty. The bathroom door was open. Timur could feel the jolt in his body.

'Yusuf . . .' he shrieked, 'who was here?'

Yusuf came running with a spatula in hand.

'No one!'

'Where's Seetha?' Timur barked.

Yusuf stepped back in alarm.

'Sir, I don't know. No one has come here. Maybe madam left by herself.'

Holding his head in his hands, Timur sat on the bed. His head was throbbing. He did not feel capable of taking another step.

'Sir,' Yusuf called him softly, 'this looks like a note left by madam.'

Timur grabbed the piece of paper. It was Seetha's note. He was familiar with her cursive handwriting and clarity of style.

'Timur, the police are looking for me. They don't know you. You should leave for Istanbul without getting into any more trouble. I'll not return without meeting Dewran.'

The paper slipped out of Timur's hand. He cried openly, unaware why he was doing it. Chewing his nails, Yusuf stood by, nonplussed. He walked back to the kitchen, leaving Timur to cry in peace.

Timur

Why was the granite-paved street making such a racket? His laboured breathing, thumping heartbeats, and the clippety-clop of the leather soles seemed to be out of place in the cold, congealed silence of the sleepy street. He had parked the van and was running towards Bedew. An old, brown mongrel was sleeping in front of the shuttered doors. After taking a lazy look through its half-open eye at the bounding lunatic who had appeared in front of him, the dog pushed himself off the ground unwillingly and slowly walked off on unsteady legs.

As if he no longer cared who heard him, Timur repeatedly banged on Esat's door. The street that was buzzing and busy like a beehive during daytime, was in peaceful, if tired, repose now, enjoying the cool breeze that wafted over it. The sounds of someone trying to batter down the fragile shutters woke up the Syrian refugees, sleeping by the roadside, who raised their heads to find out the source of the disturbance. Startled, one or two children started to whimper. The men, in order to assess the situation, sat up and started preparations to have a smoke.

A half-awake Esat opened the door. His face showed his displeasure. However, the sight of Timur vaporized his sleep. He once more pulled Timur in, as he stood holding the door, panting and his face flushed.

'Why? What happened?'

'Seetha . . .! She's missing.' Timur managed to blurt out, still fighting for breath.

'Missing? I had thought you'd have left Diyarbakır by now.' Esat pulled up his pyjamas that were slipping down.

'Esat! She's missing. When I returned, this note was all that was there. Here . . . look!'

Esat looked at both sides of the note and held it up against the light.

'Are you sure this is her handwriting?' Esat's expression was grave.

'It's her handwriting all right. My only doubt is if she was made to write it,' Timur's voice was quavering with fear.

After handing back the note, Esat appeared lost in thought. His frown became more pronounced, and his gaze was fixed at some unseen point as if in a trance.

'They'll not hesitate to do it,' he growled.

When he saw the despondent look on Timur's face, Esat forced himself to regain composure. He donned his serene look once more.

'Don't worry. We'll search for her.'

Ignoring Timur, he took off his sleepwear and wore a pair of jeans and T-shirt that were hanging on a chair's backrest.

'Oy, Esat, any problem? Do you need any help?' asked the head of the refugee family in a sleepy but loud voice that showed concern. He had seen them locking up the door as he was sleeping on a heap of old clothes in the front of the adjacent store.

'Huh, no, nothing. My aunt isn't well. We'll just go to the hospital and return.' Esat spoke in firm tones. As if satisfied with the reply, the man pulled the rags back on top of himself and readied to return to sleep.

By the time he started the van, Esat had informed Akbar of the new developments. He repeated what Timur had told him and kept looking questioningly at Timur for affirmation. He kept nodding gravely as he talked.

'Don't worry. Akbar and his friends will help us.' Although Esat tried to reassure him, Timur remained silent. The sense of precariousness and uncertainty had rendered him powerless.

'You reached only yesterday. How did you manage to rouse the police's suspicions within such short time?'

'I don't know. I have my suspicions about the owner of the restaurant where we had food. Maybe your teashop was already under surveillance. Even ordinary people may wonder what an Indian lady has to do with your shop.'

'Seetha doesn't know that in this country, people even breathe with the Intelligence's permission.' Esat's voice was full of dismay.

'Let's check at the bus terminal. Not that it would be of any use. Still, let's try.' He accelerated.

There were few cars on the road. Esat stopped near a terminal where minibuses were parked in rows. The staff were in deep sleep after a long day. Esat was hesitant to wake them up. However, they did not have to think too long about the next step. A giant dog that seemed to have been guarding the buses woke up, stood and shook itself off. After looking at the intruders in silence for a short while, let out deep-bass barks. Some others followed suit, their mutt heads emerging slowly from underneath the parked vehicles.

The dogs, in a show of gratitude to their benefactors—the bus terminal workers who fed them a portion of their own meals every day—now arrayed in front of Timur and Esat. Although Timur, spooked by their shining eyes, minatory barks, and their attack-ready crouch wanted to flee, his legs refused to obey him. A man poked his head out through a bus window and stared at them. In a voice slurred by sleep, he asked them who they were.

'Man, drive these dogs off first!' Esat told him crossly.

After a few seconds a young man with a full beard emerged from the bus. He shushed and drove away the dogs and apologized to Timur and Esat for the inconvenience. Esat was careful of revealing nothing more than that a girl who had come with Timur for research had disappeared. After giving a description of her, he requested the man to check with other staff if they had any news about her.

'An Indian girl! How can she disappear without anyone noticing it?'

He kept looking at them suspiciously as he scratched his head. However, when he saw the pleading look on Esat's face, without further ado, the man started to slap the side of all the vehicles to call out to people inside.

A few members of the staff came out, swearing. When they were told the reason, they gaped at one another, huddled and spoke in whispers. After a little while, one of them, who appeared to be their leader, called Esat to his side. The man kept rubbing the sides of his face as if to get rid of his sleepiness.

'Look here, none of us has seen a girl like that. If she's travelling with her face covered, how would anyone recognize her? And if she has left by any of the late buses from here, we can only find out tomorrow,' he said, stealing a look at the exhausted-looking Timur.

Esat and Timur thanked the men and walked back to their van. The eventful day and Seetha's disappearance had taken their toll on Timur.

'Don't worry. If a girl like Seetha has travelled out from here, she would have been noticed. We'll get some information by the morning,' Esat again tried to reassure him. The words made

Timur's eye burn; he was on the point of breaking down. Esat put a hand around his shoulder after recognizing his state.

'Timur, women are not like us men. They can survive adverse circumstances by keeping their wits about them. Especially Seetha; she is no ordinary girl.'

'It's not just that. She's physically weak . . . wish I knew where she was, all by herself.' He spoke dolefully, trying not to recall her pale, swollen face.

Timur did not have the heart to even ask where they were headed. He curled up like a drenched bird next to Esat, who was driving silently. The sky had turned cloudy, presaging rain. Streaks of lightning flashed occasionally. The atmosphere, heavy, sullen and without even a light breeze, appeared to be holding its breath.

'It's going to rain,' Esat spoke to no one in particular. They were driving at a good speed through the dark, winding roads. Esat stopped the van after some time.

'Timur, enough of sleeping! Let's try to meet Akbar.'

Timur followed as Esat walked briskly in long strides. Even in the darkness he could make out the state of the decrepit street. Ugly, multi-storeyed buildings with tiny rooms and tinier ventilation stood on either side of the pot-holed street. In their broken, barred balconies, clothes flung carelessly on clotheslines fluttered above their heads. Timur felt that they may float down any time.

Akbar's house was old, keeping with the character of the street. Removing a plank of wood that served as a door, Esat entered without knocking. Timur could make out he was quite familiar with the place.

The musty air within—composed of cigarette smoke, mildew and dirty clothes—made Timur gag and cough. A candle stood in the middle of the room, its flame sickly and flickering. It looked as if it may be extinguished any moment. Indeterminate forms of people could be discerned on the cane chairs in the dark corners. The chairs too had heaps of clothes, which did not seem to particularly deter the men curled up on them.

A sharp clap of thunder seemed to shake the building. Rain drops started to play tattoo on the roof tiles. Timur could hear things toppling outside the room because of the strong wind that had started out of nowhere.

'Seetha is not in any police station of Diyarbakır,' Akbar's voice rose from one of the corners. 'Timur, sit down. We have our people in the police stations here. If they have any information, we'll be informed.'

'Could they have taken her to Istanbul?' Esat asked.

'Nothing's certain. We have to wait till we receive some information.'

Timur collapsed into a vacant chair near him that had a piece of cloth carelessly thrown on it; it received him like a cradle would. In that moment, he realized how much the stress and tension had sapped him.

'What if, on being tipped off, Arman and his men shifted her to a safe house?' one of the men asked.

His hope rekindled, Timur tried to locate the speaker. Someone who was curled up like a bundle of clothes stirred in his chair.

'I know Arman well. We are like brothers. He'll pluck out his own heart and give it to those dear to him.'

A thousand unasked questions choked Timur.

To no one in particular, the man continued in a deadpan voice. 'It's not him alone; everyone in that family is like that. Arman invited me home the first time to eat dolma made with vine leaves grown in his father's vineyard. The stuffing of rice, meat, spices and I don't know what else made by Gul was delicious.'

The name Gul sent a fresh shiver through Timur's mind. No one seemed to be worried about where she was. He had an inkling that this man may be aware of her whereabouts.

'It had been days since I had had home-cooked food. When she saw me gobbling it up—after surviving on the tasteless food at the hostel and hating it—Gul invited me to join them for lunch every Sunday. That was the beginning. Gradually I became like a member of the family.'

He stopped and lit a cigarette. Timur kept his eyes peeled on the cigarette's glow.

'Where's Gul now?' Timur asked, with studied disinterest in his voice.

'I don't know. She was studying in Barcelona. Aren't you all together? Isn't she there?'

'No! After Dewran, she also left Barcelona.'

'Ya Allah! What to make of these children!' The man sat with his head lowered into his hands.

'Could Gul be with Arman?' Timur asked again, not to let the man stray from the subject.

'She must be in their native place. In the village of Çiçika. Arman is underground; she can't possibly be with him.'

'Shall I go there?'

There was moment's silence. Timur could see two glowering animal-like eyes from behind a veil of cigarette smoke boring into his own.

'You had come with Seetha, right? The police would be looking for you too. Try to get home soonest! We'll take care of Gul.'

The voice was cold and sharp like a knife blade. Timur realized that he should not have shown his concern. To be surrounded by these curt men was discomfiting. Although there were five or six men inside, a cold silence pervaded the room. The quietude was punctuated by sounds of filling and rolling of cigarettes and munching of peanuts.

Esat and Akbar, who had been conferring in undertones inside the kitchen, returned to the front room. Glass jars with sugar, honey, tea, ince belli glasses, reminiscent of women's waists, and spoons appeared on the dusty and fraying carpet. Everyone sat down around the candle and started to drink tea. The young man who had ordered Timur to leave the place at the earliest was throwing him sidelong glances. It appeared as if he was feeling guilty about what he had said. Timur, avoiding to look at anyone, focused on the steaming tea in his hand.

'Timur, I wasn't trying to be nasty,' he started softly. 'I saw you asking about Gul with a lot of keenness. That family has suffered enough. None of them was in active politics. Arman had no interest in politics except that he had collated old Kurd folk songs, set them to tune and sung them. I don't remember seeing him in any political meeting. Yet, see what's been done to that family now.'

Timur remained silent. He could well understand their anger. However, their promise to keep Gul safe only inflamed Timur's purely selfish interest in her and his love for her. He remembered the Sunday on which he had gone to the house where Seetha and Gul put up together. She was standing on the balcony along with a bucket-load of washed clothes. Perhaps because she had been rinsing them for a long time, her slim, long fingers, that Timur was besotted with, had turned deep pink. The fragrance of the morning was flowing from her as if she had just stepped out of the bath.

Contrary to her usual habit of scrapping with him like a fighting cock, she presented him with a coy smile and invited him to share their simple breakfast of whole-meal bread and jam made from freshly picked cherries from the tree behind their house. Her well-moistened, healthy skin glowed when she smiled. He found it hard to control the impulse to embrace this girl who resembled nature drenched by fresh rain.

Timur decided he owed those loud-mouths no explanation about his concern for Gul. To take the heat off her, he decided to divert the conversation towards Arman. To learn more about it, he spoke of the days when Arman had been pulled into the vortex of violence.

'Akbar said that Arman had attacked the police and provided the leadership for bomb attacks.'

'That's rich! Did you not ask him what led Arman, who wouldn't hurt a fly, to do such things? Did you not enquire into why he—brilliant in studies—would throw away his future and jeopardize his family by choosing the path of rebellion?'

'Because his lover was killed by the soldiers.'

Timur was troubled by the direction in which this interrogation was headed.

'Did Akbar tell you how she was killed?'

The man's tone was unsympathetic. He turned to look at Akbar who was gathering the empty glasses and putting them on a tray.

'How could I have told them? That girl was already overwrought. And to make it worse, pregnant. I narrated these things briefly without scaring her further.' Akbar was indignant.

The man turned towards Timur. 'You would have seen the TV reports on the attacks that happened here?'

Timur bowed his head in some kind of unnamed guilt.

'I was in Barcelona at that time. The TV channels there completely ignored this news. They may have made passing references that my mind possibly failed to register. Or they didn't say enough to attract my attention.'

The man laughed raucously.

'That's how it is. Here we are set on fire alive. We are beaten to death and thrown into ditches. And that too using the soldiers whose pay come from the taxes we pay! With no idea of what matters, you earn top degrees in foreign universities.'

A worried Akbar intervened, 'It's possible what he says is true. The news may not have reached the outside world. They would be taking care that such news does not get leaked. You know that, don't you, Mustafa?'

Mustafa remained silent for a little while. His eyes, still boring into Timur, were gleaming in the flickering candlelight.

'You are a Turk, aren't you? If we're killed like flies, our women are raped, our babies are set on fire, what does it matter to you?'

'That's not true. Whenever I used to call home, my father would tell me bits and pieces about the carnage. I'm very sorry about all that happened.'

His voice broke. He remained silent for a short while.

'Shouldn't care be taken that such clashes do not take place? Other parts of the country don't have such problems. From what I understand, the loss has been all yours.' Timur said this reluctantly. He stole glances at the others to see their reactions.

'It's futile talking to guys like him. They are all blind and deaf.'

A despairing Mustafa leaned back in his chair.

Akbar placed the tray down. He shifted forward to watch Timur's face clearly.

'Just now, you said that all the losses are of Kurds. Aren't we the most conscious of this? With every riot we lose our men. Our women are raped and humiliated. Our property is destroyed. When people are conscious of that, will they create trouble?'

Timur looked at Akbar suspiciously.

'Then who's creating the trouble?'

'Whoever gains from it, they do.'

'I don't get it.'

'Think a bit. If there were no clashes in Kurd regions, what would have been the outcome of the referendum held a few months after that? Would they have won? I believe the riots were the tilling of the field for the ruling party to harvest.'

Timur remained still.

'How many objectives did they meet in one fell swoop? Apart from political victories, they butchered a bunch of worthless Kurds like exterminating worms.' Mustafa laughed mockingly.

'I never thought that way.'

The knowledge that whatever he had believed till then was wrong defeated Timur. Akbar and Mustafa did not miss the desperation and bafflement in his face as if he had been slapped when he was least expecting it.

'It's not just you. Blinded by racism, the majority of the people in this country didn't think that way.'

Mustafa spoke dispassionately, his words filled with apathy. An uneasy silence filled the room. Timur was assailed by guilt.

'Don't doubt my blood. I am with you all. I can be only on the side of the disenfranchised, poor and oppressed people.' His voice, though tired, was firm.

'Are you a communist?' Mustafa asked scornfully. Someone among them sniggered. Timur nodded his head equivocally, which could have been interpreted either way.

'People from your kind of privileged families can have such romanticized ideals. However, we do not have that luxury. In the government's books, we are born extremists. Hapless people who have to take every step and say every word carefully and in fear in order not to die on the wrong side of a gun.'

'Mustafa, haven't you realized yet that he's with us? You've been at his throat from the time he arrived here,' Akbar lost his cool and railed.

'It's okay. I've no complaints,' Timur tried to calm Akbar down.

'Since you were close to Arman, can you please at least tell me in detail what happened to him? Maybe that'll help me in finding Seetha and Dewran,' he said in order to change the subject. Possibly due to the excitement and tension of the past few hours, he had turned febrile, and his body was shivering. He was warming his fingers over the candle flame.

Mustafa looked at the others. Their sullen faces showed that they were on the same page as Akbar. He gave up his petulance and decided to remain mute. Although he slurped his tea and chewed mouthfuls of roasted peanuts noisily, no one paid him any attention.

Mustafa realized that his behaviour had been over the top. Although he tried to say something in an apologetic tone to Timur, he had to give up the attempt halfway with the bemusement of someone doing an unfamiliar act. After cursing himself, as if to compensate for his churlish behaviour, Mustafa started to answer Timur's question.

'I did tell you that Arman and I were the best of friends . . .'

Timur paid him full attention. Outside, the strong winds had died down. The historical Kurdish earth's petrichor, which gushed in through the recalcitrant windowpanes that refused to close, overwhelmed Timur gradually.

Çîçika

The floodlight from the watchtowers streamed into the car. They were more platforms on stilts than real watchtowers. Soldiers holding guns ostentatiously stood on those platforms. Seetha shivered at the sight of them peering into the car. The mechanized gates in front of them slid open slowly. Dadwar let out a sigh of relief and let in the clutch carefully.

'There are more check-posts. At least four more,' he said.

'Four check-posts within a distance of twenty-five kilometres? Who do the soldiers expect to check in these mountains?'

'Why are you talking as if you don't know anything?' Dadwar grimaced. Her ignorance seemed to upset him. Seetha clammed up. Only the engine's growl cut through the heavy silence.

The hills around her were silhouetted against the moonlight. There were few tall trees, one or two flashed by occasionally as they drove along. Seetha thought of the people who survived in that inhospitable land amid the rocky terrain, arid earth, small hardy plants and bushes . . . people in whom life throbbed as if nature had poured her soul into them.

The driver applied the brake suddenly, interrupting her chain of thought. Although she was wearing the seatbelt, the momentum made her slide forward. Another check-post immediately after a sharp bend in the road! She could imagine that whatever was muttered and remained unsaid between the clenched teeth of Dadwar were the choicest of abuses.

Talking loudly and with their guns pointed at the car, the soldiers went around the vehicle inspecting it. They ordered Dadwar to get out of the car. He grovelled before them. The piteous beseeching look in his eyes reminded her of Timur. He must have gone crazy trying to find her. While they were together, he protected her like a guardian angel, without even allowing a scratch on her. When she recalled how she had fled from Diyarbakır Otel by tricking him, she burned in guilt.

'I had no other way, Timur! Forgive me! Please forgive me,' she murmured ruefully. A soldier peered into the car over Dadwar's shoulder as he remained bowed obsequiously, pleading and begging. The soldier rapped Dadwar on his head with his truncheon and screamed at him. After being interrogated and berated for a long time, a drained Dadwar shuffled back inside, hanging his head.

Seetha wanted to cry—how many people were being harassed and in trouble because of her. Her heart was still palpitating as she recalled how she had, only a few hours ago, managed to trick Timur and evade the police to make good her escape from Diyarbakır. The memory of how she ran out of the hotel like a cat on a hot tin roof made her breathless.

As soon as Timur left muttering 'I'll be back soon', she had written a note for him on a piece of paper she found there, picked up her bag and hotfooted out of the hotel. She knew that he would return without wasting time since he was aware she was alone. He may not need much time to hire a car.

When she opened the door, the smell of mutton and garlic being fried in olive oil hit her. She could hear vessels being knocked around in from the kitchen. Yusuf was busy. Luckily, the smiling manager with his yellowed teeth who used to turn up occasionally was missing at the desk. After pulling the dupatta across her face and covering most of it, Seetha walked towards the bus terminal.

Such a beautiful name—Çiçika! When she looked at the route on her smartphone, she realized that it was not easy to reach that village from Silvan. There was only a narrow torturous road through the mountains. No buses plied that route. Even a car would find it difficult to negotiate it. It was no wonder that Dewran had boasted about his old Volvo. She decided she would cross that bridge after reaching Silvan first.

The bus terminal was full of people who could not afford to buy a jacket to keep themselves warm and were making do with three or four layers of clothes. Destitute people, who gave off a strong sweaty odour, kept to themselves, and, impatient to get home, were checking the time and craning their necks to see if the bus was arriving. Each of them was a solitary island in that small sea of humanity. Seetha, in her fully covered-up state, mingled with the crowd and went unnoticed.

She could see no buses to Silvan. In order not to catch anyone's eye, she stood with her head bowed as if she was constantly checking her phone. Her fear increased exponentially with the delay in the arrival of the bus. She knew that the moment he realized she was missing, Timur would start searching for her. One of the first places he would check would be the bus terminal. When she was toying with the idea of getting into the first available bus and going wherever it took her, the bus for Silvan arrived.

Unable to find a vacant seat, Seetha hung on to the overhead hang rail of the bus. An old woman was standing next to her. Short-statured and burdened with a heavy basket, she found it hard to keep her balance in the running bus. Two young men rose from their seats and offered her the seat.

'God bless, my sons . . .' She sat down hurriedly, shifted to the side making space and with a wink and nod invited Seetha to share the seat. Seetha was watching how the men around her were getting up and offering their seats to women. As soon as she lifted her bag to put it on the side rack, hands reached out to help her. Giving them a gratitude-filled smile, she sat down. The granny next to her was talking to herself, looking at sights outside. She closed her eyes and leaned back, enjoying a rare feeling of security.

Swaying, bumping, stopping in between, and speeding up for small stretches, the bus took two hours to reach Silvan.

'Ten o'clock!' agitated and looking around, she muttered to herself. While still in the bus, she had given up the idea of staying for the night in a decent hotel and continuing the journey the next day. She assumed it would be suicidal considering that the police were on the lookout for her. She could see four or five taxis waiting at a distance. Pulling her trolley bag behind her, she walked slowly towards the group of taxi drivers.

A young driver came forward to help her with her suitcase.

'Çîçika?'

When he heard her say that, with a surprised look he put down the suitcase. He discovered only then that she was a foreigner. Other drivers also walked up to them.

'*Inglees?*'

They surrounded her, their interest piqued.

'Dadwar . . .' one of the men called out.

A middle-aged man enjoying his cigarette a little distance away turned and looked at them.

'Dadwar . . . *Inglees* . . . *Inglees* . . .' the young drivers called out cheerfully.

The man threw away the cigarette in a hurry and hastened towards them.

'English?'

Seetha nodded hesitantly. She was amused when she heard his British accent.

His old car could not negotiate the hills. There were too many soldiers on the way. If the car got stalled, there would be no one to give a hand. He tried to dissuade Seetha with many such reasons. He asked her why she didn't stay in a hotel and then leave in the morning.

'If you can't come, ask if anyone else is willing. I have to go tonight.'

She was worn-out by the stress and risks that she had undergone during the last few hours. When he saw the look on her face, as if she would dissolve in a hail of tears, his heart melted.

'Sister, get into the car. If one's fated to spend this night in those forests, so be it.'

He drove a beaten-up old car that was parked behind other cars and stopped it in front of her. One of the men put her bag in the car. As she prepared to get into backseat, Dadwar stopped her.

'The route will be crawling with soldiers. If they see you are a foreigner, they'll surely stop us.'

Seetha got into the passenger seat in the front. Pointing to her dupatta that had by then slipped down to her shoulders, he politely asked her to cover her head.

'Don't think I am an old fogey! I'll have to tell the soldiers that you're my sister. The story I have in mind is—our grandmother in the village is taken sick and that's why, though it's late, we're headed that way. It's lucky that at first glance you can pass for a Kurd woman. If they realize that you are a foreigner, that'll be the end of it. They'll be suspicious about why you are in this part of the country so late in the night. We'll be arrested and taken in for questioning. So, please keep most of your face covered.'

Cognizant of the risk and danger they were facing, Seetha wrapped the dupatta around her face, leaving only her eyes exposed. The jalopy left the main road and entered a dirt road with a growl and squeal. Dadwar switched on the heater and set the temperature at a level she was comfortable with.

'It'll take us about an hour. Push back your seat and try to sleep,' Dadwar told her as he manoeuvred the car carefully.

Seetha did not intend to sleep. Her memories were full of Dewran boasting like a teenager about his feats with his car on this tortuous route. When they were approaching a check-post, she ruefully thought this was one thing he had not told her anything about.

'There are more to come. They keep the roadblocks at a different spot every day,' Dadwar said angrily, as he started the car after the checking.

Seetha was consumed by guilt.

'Forgive me. I had to put you through this trouble because of my dire state.'

Dadwar did not respond.

A dim light on top of a faraway hill made Seetha curious.

'Do people live there?'

'That's a watchtower.' Dadwar spoke impassively.

'Watchtower? For what?' she asked in wonderment. 'Why do you have so much security in this place? No one's living in these parts.'

'You really have no clue, do you?' Dadwar raised his voice. Seetha could see he was cross.

'The Worker's Party has the deepest roots in the south-east of Turkey. The people in power consider them as terrorists. They claim that the Party workers are hiding in these hills and forests.'

A shiver ran down Seetha's spine. She looked around; a range of placid, indigo-coloured gelid hills stood tall in the faint moonlight.

Is he somewhere in there?

Could he be watching her from somewhere?

'Who are you? Why are you going to this remote village at this late hour?' Dadwar asked, interrupting her thoughts.

Although he had controlled his curiosity till then, his innate rustic inquisitiveness could no longer be contained. Although he was not ready to swallow and be satisfied with her claim, that her friends were staying there, the light from another check-post they were approaching stopped him from pursuing it further. He gave Seetha a look as if checking that everything was all right.

They were allowed to go through without scrutiny. The sharp curves and turns and bumps and potholes on the road made Seetha nauseous.

'I'll throw up,' she said in a raspy voice.

Dadwar quickly took the car to the side. Only a bilious fluid came out of her empty stomach. Its biliousness made her retch again.

'Here, drink some water!' Dadwar took out his water bottle.

She liked the taste of the water which had been boiled with some kind of leaves or herbs.

'These curves make even me nauseous,' Dadwar said kindly to console her.

They went through another two check-posts without attracting much attention. Shouting at one another, the soldiers shifted the roadblocks to allow them through.

Since he realized his passenger was not keeping well, Dadwar was driving slow. The cold inside the car and her own weariness made her sleepy.

The only option to stay awake was to keep conversing with Dadwar. 'How's it that you talk such good English?'

'I lived in England for a long time. I was the driver of a wealthy man.' Dadwar did not take his eyes off the road.

'Usually, people will stick around in places like that. Why did you decide to return?' Seetha was curious.

'Life! Daughter, this damned life! What does it not make us do! Look at you! An Indian. Hasn't life brought you to this wilderness in Kurdistan?' Seetha recognized the disappointment in his voice.

'My boss had said he'd get my wife a job too. But some family problems brought me back.'

His smile was full of bitterness.

'You said you are coming from Sur. The sights there would have given you fair idea of our lives.'

'Yes. A part of that city has been hacked away.'

'Bigotry and hatred. They want to destroy the culture and traditions that have been handed down through our many generations. That is why, with the help of battle tanks, they have razed old houses that we have been living in for centuries and whatever history has left behind. They have obliterated the past of our land. Our history!' Pain throbbed in his voice.

'I did feel that. Your streets are like museums. This region is enough to make any history lover salivate. I could spend only one day there. Yet, I could see the place has a beauty and antiquity that I have not seen anywhere else.' Seetha acquiesced with him.

'Four thousand years! People say Sur is that old. It's one of UNESCO's World Heritage sites. Do you know how many tourists used to visit us? Taxi drivers and guides were making money hand over fist. With one siege of Sur, they destroyed everything.'

'Even when I saw the destruction around me, I didn't want to come away from there. Someday, I will stay in Sur for a few days and see everything.'

'What is left there to see now? They've excavated and extracted the relics of so many civilisations and annexations of that land. They didn't even leave a brick of the most beautiful parts of Sur.' He sighed.

'When we drove from the Diyarbakır airport to Sur, we saw a Christian church on the way. It looks rather ancient.'

'St Mary Church! That's worth more than a visit!' Dadwar was enthusiastic.

'I was amazed. I was under the impression that only Muslims lived here.'

'Only Muslims? No way! Among us Kurds you have Christians, Jews and followers of other religions. Our language, our culture and this revered land make us one, make us Kurds!'

'Oh, I didn't know that,' Seetha said, amazed.

'Only Allah knows how long these will survive. Last year, the government took over no less than six churches.'

'Why?'

'They claim they are protecting them.' Dadwar laughed bitterly again.

'They're wiping out history . . .Why are they doing this?' Seetha was incredulous.

'Even if we're all killed, their hatred, their bloodlust will not end. They're out to prove that Kurds as a race never existed on the face of this earth.'

'Is their hatred towards Kurds the only reason for this?'

'If I tell you, you may think I am making up stories. This bloodletting is not of recent origin. Long ago, many Armenians lived in Diyarbakır. They were constantly at war with the Turks and us. About a hundred years ago, they fled the place with literally only the clothes on their backs. Fearing that they may be robbed on the way, they had buried all their gold, money and valuables beneath their houses and in their compounds before leaving. They may have planned to return later and reclaim them.'

When the powerful beam of the searchlight on the top of the hill swept past them a few times and lit up the surroundings, Dadwar clammed up and concentrated on his driving. The searchlight that seemed to probe every inch in its sweep unnerved Seetha.

'And then? What happened then?'

'What could have happened? The Armenians couldn't return. All that money and gold remained buried. When the military operations started, and trenches were dug to stop the army tanks, some of our young men got some of it. That was when the old stories gained currency again.'

'And . . .?'

'By that time, the Turkish Army had captured the city. Since the soldiers knew of these caches of gold and money, they used their tanks to flatten the old heritage houses and historical monuments. They dug up the city using earth movers.'

Seetha fancied she could hear the rumble of the earth-moving equipment as they ploughed through the place and sieved the soil. It was resounding in her ears.

'We'll be there soon, only a little distance left to Çîçika,' Dadwar said, changing the subject. He appeared to relax for the first time during their journey.

'Why did you have to come back from England to this troubled land? You should've stayed put.'

'Sister, I had no other choice. My younger brother Kemal was a student of music. My mother and he lived near Suruç. He used to do some minor social work.'

Before he continued, he emptied the water bottle thirstily.

'Kobanî town close to the Syrian border had been almost destroyed in the attacks. Not a single building was spared. No food, no water, no shelter. Only some scared humans who lived in privation, like rats in their burrows. Unable to stand that sight, some of the young men from this side decided to help in the reconstruction of Kobanî. Even youngsters from Istanbul reached there. My brother went to the town centre to join up with them.'

Seetha sensed Dadwar stifled a sob that rose in his throat.

'Cracking jokes and carrying his guitar he left; what we next saw was his leg-less torso. He was barely alive. The shock turned my mother into a mute.'

'What happened?' Seetha was shocked.

'It was a suicide attack. Thirty-four young men vaporized in the blast. After their body parts were blown away, one hundred and four boys are the living dead, like my Kemal, who still survive to tell the tale.'

'Who did it?'

'The Islamic State had claimed the honours,' Dadwar spoke coldly.

'You say it as if you don't believe it,' Seetha asked, unable to bear the coldness in his voice.

Dadwar laughed deprecatingly.

'What should I believe? This was not the first attack. Every attack carried out by Islamic State in Kurdistan was against the opponents of the Turkish government.' Gazing into her widened eyes, he continued, 'To exact revenge against the attack in Suruç, that same day, two Turkish soldiers were shot and killed by unknown persons. Their reply was to roll their tanks into Kurdish land. That was how the massacre, which the world calls 'clashes', began. The Worker's Party tried its best to protect us. They resisted as much as they could. All for nothing . . .'

Seetha sensed Dadwar's voice was breaking. She realized that he was not willing to talk more. When she tried to make sense of all that she had heard and seen, her own mind felt under siege.

'After we go beyond that bend, we'll able to see the lights from the village.'

The car seemed to surge forward. The bumpy, pot-holed dirt track seemed to have made way for a compacted, flat road. Seetha kept staring through the window. The stories she had been told were burying the remnants of her hope.

Occasional signs of habitation had started to appear. She rubbed her eyes and looked at either side. The moonlit fields that stretched on both sides were full of healthy, shining weeds.

'Haven't they ploughed the land yet?' an uneasy Dadwar asked aloud.

Seetha could lights flickering like fireflies at a distance. They were outshone by the stars in the clear sky that seemed to be taking umbrage at the competition from the lights on the ground. Warned by the sound of the approaching car, some creature that resembled a calf rose from the middle of the road and went to the side.

'That's a calf,' Seetha said.

'That's not a calf, that's a sheepdog.'

'So big!' Seetha turned back to look. She could hear its loud barks warning the residents of the visitors in their midst.

'It belongs to one of the villagers. I have seen it walking around in the night before also.'

'Do you come here regularly?' Seetha was curious.

'Rarely. Since there is no public transport, people summon taxis to come this place.'

Houses, while still some distance away, came into view.

'Okay, so which house do you want to go to?'

She was caught up short and did not know what to tell him.

'Two of my friends are from here. Dewran and Gul. Do you know them?'

Dadwar laughed.

'Must be kids. I don't know them.'

He stopped the car at the entrance of the village.

'Everyone must be asleep. Whom to ask?'

Suddenly, they heard shouting. A donkey foal ran towards them on the straight road ahead of them. Howling and screaming, four or five urchins were chasing it.

'Little devils! They are running around even at midnight!' Dadwar muttered.

He blocked their path. 'Stop, kids! Do you know two people called Dewran and Gul?'

'My brother's name is Dewran,' the youngest among them said.

'My aunt's name is Gul.' Another one piped up.

Dadwar turned to Seetha helplessly. 'These names are very common here. Do you know any other information?'

Seetha, lost in thought, was chewing on her nails.

By then two of the urchins had caught hold of the foal and brought it back. It kicked the ground with its hooves and snorted in protest.

'Yes! Dewran has a dog named Roja. And a Volvo car.'

When the urchins heard the word Volvo, they started to cheer.

'Yes, we know. We have been taken on drives in that car,' one of them said.

'Can you lead us to his home?' Dadwar requested.

'Why not, uncle, follow us.'

With an unhappy donkey and cheering children in front, the car rolled slowly into the village.

Arman

Within a few moments of Mustafa starting his narration, Timur felt as if he had been transported to the place and time of the story. Although this would not be the first time they were hearing these stories, this time around, Timur noticed a child-like frisson of excitement passing through the men around him. They shifted and made themselves comfortable in their seats, refilled their glasses with tea and moved themselves closer to Mustafa.

'We met when Arman joined the university again to study law after he had completed his master's in literature.'

Stubbing his cigarette underfoot and letting out a cough, Mustafa took up the story again.

'Arman's aged parents lived in a remote village among the mountains. After retirement, his father had bought land in his native village for viticulture and settled down there. He had also bought an apartment in the city, spending his savings, for his children to stay to pursue their education. Arman stayed there with his siblings Dewran and Gul.

'Dewran was a good football player. He used to spend the evenings with his teammates and occasionally have a beer in the nights. Gul was an accomplished dancer. She was busy with her studies, dance practice, and the trips that she took along with her friends.

'Arman was different, someone who could be described as a bookworm. His tall, lanky frame, thick spectacle frame, and eyes that seemed lost to this world gave him an intellectual look. Although many girls vied for his attention, his love for Kurdish folk songs that were becoming moribund prevailed. His only hobby and entertainment included travelling to remote villages with his camera during holidays and recording harvest songs and folk tales from old peasants. He was trying to publish a book containing this collection—an attempt to preserve his language and traditions that were being repressed and alienated.

'He had a beautiful voice. During evenings he would sit by the window and play *saz*. It was a sight to behold! That mesmeric voice and those country tunes would transport us to an unknown age. We would leave everything and gather around him to listen to his songs.'

Mustafa took a break to ensure that his friends in the room were listening to him, and to drink the remaining tea from his glass. Gratified that he had everyone's attention, although the story was being repeated, he patted down and stroked his unruly beard.

'Around that time, as Arman tried to get his book published and do his course work, something happened that upended his life. He had returned from one of the literary seminars in a disturbed state. A sprightly girl from a neighbouring university who was in their group had stolen his heart. I was surprised that, though pale and shaking with nervousness, he had managed to ask her telephone number. The mischievous girl could immediately guess his intentions. Although in the beginning she had teased him, something in that besotted young man had attracted her to him.

'In the following days, Arman hovered around the telephone. Finally bowing to Gul's persuasions, he called her. When he discovered that she was also waiting for his call, his happiness knew no bounds. Her name was Dilva—someone who had a tinkling laugh and was witty and mirthful. They grew close quickly. They were an enviably compatible pair of lovers. She started to accompany him on his trips to the villages. Though the town she lived in—Cizîr—was far from Sur, every weekend she turned up at Arman's flat without fail.

'It is true that her visits did create some misgivings in our minds,' Mustafa said in a voice with a smidgen of guilt. Everyone feared that they would lose the liberty that they had in that house and the bosom friendship with Arman. However, Dilva quickly turned into our friend too. She became one of us, ribbing us as if we had been together for years and enjoying our type of humour.

'However, the happy days didn't last long. The peace initiatives by Abdullah Öcalan[1] in 2013, which had given all of us renewed hopes, had been vitiated by then. The political uncertainty in Kurd areas that had been simmering was coming to a boil.

'They started to set fire to our generally sparse semi-arid forests—Silvan, Silopi, İdil, Nusaybin, Yüksekova . . . the sky over Kurds' heads were raining shells those days. The major destructions were in Sur and Cizîr.

'While Arman and Gul were careful not to get entangled in the protests, Dewran was quite active in meetings and demonstrations. He didn't return home on many nights. Without proper food and sleep, dark circles appeared below those sparkling eyes, and he was hit by bouts of ill-health. The strangers who came asking for Dewran unnerved Arman and Gul. The house that had once resounded with laughter was now filled with gloom and doom.

'One day, when Dewran arrived with a deep wound on his shoulder and bloodied clothes, Arman understood that things were now beyond their control. He decided to inform their parents. The hapless elders were perturbed when they heard stories of Dewran's doings. They summoned Gul and Dewran back to Çîçika.

'Dewran protested vehemently. But he was afraid of his father who was strict. If riled enough, he wouldn't hesitate to land two slaps on his grown-up sons. Eventually, after endless muttering and hunger strikes, left with no option, Dewran left for his village along with his little sister.

'On the day of their departure, although Dewran went around with a scowl on his face to let his displeasure against Arman's betrayal be known, by evening when they were ready to leave, his resentment had melted away. Dewran, with his political connections, knew more than anyone else what was going to happen in the coming days. I felt even the thought of Arman being all alone scared him.

'"This place is headed for big trouble. Things are going to get worse. You also come with us . . ."

'He kept pleading with Arman like a child.

'"You know that I can't come," Arman smiled.

'"We can take Dilva with us. Mother is not going to protest," Dewran was adamant.

'"Don't be impertinent, speaking big things with your tiny mouth! You should help father in irrigating the vineyard. Don't loiter around with that dog of yours!"

'Arman suppressed his smile. He was loading Gul's heavy suitcase on to the car.

'"It's curfew time. Don't over-speed. Gul is with you, don't you forget that."

'After such peremptory instructions to Dewran, Arman turned to Gul, "When you're travelling, keep your head fully covered. The police need no excuses to question and dump anyone in the jail."

'Gul was silent. She knew that Arman was staying back because he could not bear to be away from Dilva. The thought of leaving him behind was filling her with a dread that something untoward was about to happen. She was aware it was futile to persuade him to go with them. Uncharacteristically, while they were parting, Gul hugged her brother.

'"Come quickly after finishing up here."

'As he watched her eyes brim with tears, Arman felt a twinge of regret. When he saw the pleading look in Dewran's eyes, for a moment he did wonder if he should accompany them. But what about Dilva . . .? He gave up the idea considering the mischiefs she could get embroiled in.

'Pushing the tarrying Dewran into the car, Arman closed the door with an air of finality. Seething inside, he watched the speeding Volvo disappear into the distance, leaving behind a trail of dust in Dewran's usual style.

'"He's going too fast," Arman said, perturbed.

'He was aware that their parents were very concerned. The situation in Sur and Cizîr was turning dire by the minute. Although the internet connection in the village was patchy, news of soldiers reaching different parts of Diyarbakır and pictures of attacks on Kurds were being seen by his parents. When he considered how Dilva had got into such a hole that he could not stay away even for a day or two—to go and stay with his parents and console them—it riled him.

'Despite his counselling, Dilva was getting increasingly involved with youth protesting the administration. She had stopped coming to Sur. She was more interested in holding demonstrations with her group. Though he had gone to Cizîr twice to meet her, he could not find place or time to sit and talk with her undisturbed. He returned frustrated.

'His mother started to call every day asking him to move to their village. More than a couple of times she called me too, to complain and appeal. Every time, she remembered to instruct me strictly to never leave him alone.

'I was staying with Arman during those days. As the clashes and police threats increased, the hostel staff had fled in fear.'

After sipping tea from the glass that Akbar had filled for him, Mustafa continued.

'Arman looked very disturbed in the days that followed. From the time he heard that the government had ordered all the teachers of the school, where Dilva had a part-time job, to return to their native places, he lost his peace of mind. The army had taken over the control of the schools. He could guess they were being converted into military camps. As he could perceive it was a slippery slope and things were moving from bad to worse, angered by his own helplessness and impotency, he used to pace around the room in great distress.

'"If there's no school, why's she staying back in Cizîr?" mindful of Dilva's obstinacy, I asked Arman.

'"She and her friends are trying to hold classes at home so that the children's studies are not interrupted," Arman said despairingly.

'"But Arman, curfew has been declared in Cizîr. You should bring her out of there at the earliest," I told him, worried.

'On that day I saw another face of the normally serene Arman. When heard me, he kicked a glass-topped occasional table in front of him, sending it flying. Shattered glass littered the floor.

'"Is it a pup or kitten to be carried and brought here? Who's coming just because I ask her to?" He was trembling with anger.

'When I silently took the broom and started to sweep, Arman joined me after a little while. I could see he was feeling guilty about his immoderate behaviour. After mumbling something of an apology, he made me a glass of tea as if to make amends.

'The news from the affected areas was getting worse day by day. Although the fighters of the Kurdistan Workers' Party were putting up stiff resistance, one by one, the towns were falling to the army. They shot and killed people indiscriminately. Tanks knocked down houses. Curfew had been imposed in many places creating a climate of fear. The public was in misery, unable to get food and medicines. The misery was compounded when even drinking water was not available.

'People were desperate as they could not receive information on their near and dear ones in the affected zones. It had been days since we had heard about Dilva. When we were on the verge of going mad with worry, Arman and I tried to go to Cizîr thrice, but the police stopped us every time and sent us back.

'I was afraid that if we tried again, we would be arrested and thrown in jail. If that happened, I knew we would be charged with terrorism and spend the best part of our lives behind bars, I persuaded Arman to bide his time till we had some definite information on Dilva.

'One day, Arman received a call from Dilva's friend who was staying with her. After managing to escape from Cizîr, she was calling from the first phone booth she had come across. Her shrill voice kept trailing off, repeatedly saying, "Save Dilva!" Arman later told us that she spoke like someone who was demented. In between her wailing, sobs and disjointed babble, Arman found it difficult to gather any information on Dilva's current location. Eventually all he could gather from her was that Dilva was, along with some other people, marooned in the basement of a building near their place of stay. The call got disconnected after some more pleas to save her.

'Without losing any time, Arman changed into a pullover and leather jacket to withstand the cold. While he changed clothes, he explained to me what needed to be done in the house. After dropping some bread and a bottle of water into his small backpack, he got hold of the sharpest kitchen knife and packed it.

'Looking at me as if to bid goodbye, he said, "Till I return, you must remain here."

'I needed lesser time than him to get ready. I didn't bother to explain anything.

'"Wherever you are going, I'm going too." After yanking the jacket off the wall hook, I put it on and walked ahead of him. He didn't try to dissuade me. We set off.

'We used his father's old car, a Mercedes that had been left behind. The roads were filled with policemen. Burning vehicles could be seen by the roadside. We were stopped by the police many times, who checked our papers. Though there were threatening looks and obscenities were shouted at us, none of them stopped us from proceeding.

'I was driving, and when we approached Cizîr, he asked me to stop the car. His plan was to search for Dilva all by himself. I was adamant that come what may, I wouldn't let him go alone. When he saw that he wouldn't be able to get rid of me, he changed tack.

'"I'll come back only with her. I don't know what condition I'll be in. Someone should be there who can still drive."

'I thought that sounded reasonable. Support from outside was always good. I knew that when it was only one man it would be easy for him to sneak in and do things unnoticed. So, we decided that it would be better if Arman entered the town alone.

'Before he left, he hugged me tightly, handed over some money and asked me to stay safe. I broke down as I watched him disappear into the distance. Those days Cizîr was synonymous with death.

'I parked the car in a lane and waited. Time seemed to crawl. Far away, I could see military planes flying above the town. Bomb blasts could be heard from various directions.

'The water in our water bottle had already been consumed. I was dying from thirst. Afraid that people inside the neighbouring houses could be watching, I was unable to even pee. I had to find a refuge. When it was dark enough, I parked the car and walked to an isolated house a little distance away. A housewife named Sarya and her four children lived there. Four days ago, her husband had left for the town for some work and never returned. She was weeping while she told me this.

'I had no hesitation in confiding in her that I was waiting for a friend who had gone in search of a girl stuck in Cizîr. When she heard that, despite the troubled times, she said I could stay with them till Arman returned. Though they didn't seem to be well off, she served me a platter full of food.

'For sleeping, she offered a cloth hammock next to a brick-and-clay oven by the side of the house. She provided some firewood to beat the cold outside. She also fetched some old woollens that belonged to her husband. I felt I was back home.

'It was winter; by the time it was night, I started to shiver in the cold. Sarya and her children brought some damp firewood from the pile next to the barn. When they added some coal embers from their fireplace, the flame was rekindled. Though the damp firewood was sputtering and smoky in the beginning, it soon caught fire fully and a pleasant warmth enveloped me.

'"The fire inside the oven is not visible from the outside. We have enough firewood. Don't hesitate to use it," Sarya told me when she left after placing a clay pot filled with water on the table.

'She had forbidden me from smoking and talking loudly. After the clashes had started, electricity connection had been cut in that area. Sarya was afraid even to light a candle.

'My mobile phone had no signal. The landline in that house was not working. She was despondent when she told me the entire telecommunication system of Cizîr had been destroyed. Although the children were not old enough to understand everything, they too seemed to be affected by the fear that hung in the air. Without running around or making any noise, they were seated all the time, bored and lost in thought. Looking at the flock of birds and their unhurried flights above me, I lay in the hammock, trying to recall the topography of Cizîr which I had visited a long time ago.

'The children had moved their play area near to my hammock and the oven which provided warmth all the time. I had to be careful not to trip on their scattered toys whenever I needed to be afoot in my bivouac. Late in the evening, I fancied that the sounds of the faraway explosions outdid the cooing of the pigeons in that yard and noise from the children chasing them.

'Unable to tear away my eyes from the red and orange flames that shot up into the sky with every explosion, and sick with worry, I spent sleepless nights, and made it till dawn broke. The sounds of gunfire were constant and could be heard from one direction or the other. The terrifying sounds of the caterpillar treads of the tanks, that ground their way over the nearby road, became a regular thing. By the third day, with no news of Arman, worry and fear had reduced me to a whimpering mass.

'Since the area where the house was situated was on a rise, we could see the flashes of explosions and columns of smoke rising from Cizîr. The pillars of plumes were black as if someone had made a bonfire of tyres. The small jets kept roaring overhead causing everything below to tremble. Mesmerized by the flames rising from various locations of the town, I, unable to pray, and Sarya, chanting something quietly, waited.

'As days passed, I started to lose hope. On a very cold night, when I had started to doubt if I would ever see him again, Arman returned.

'I was being kept awake by the booming explosions. If I did manage to doze off, either an explosion or the rumble of armoured cars or military trucks startled me into wakefulness. Giant mosquitoes and a blood-sucking insect whined and buzzed around my exposed lower limbs. I tried to get some sleep curling up and covering myself from head to toe to stop the light and sound from entering my cocoon.

'As if the noise pollution till then wasn't enough, a bird with a horrid cry was squawking from a nearby tree. Sarya and her children had been asleep for a few hours already. The embers had died down and the cold was back. Though I knew if I could feed it some more firewood, the fire would burn till the morning, I didn't have the heart to leave the comfort of my cocoon.

'When I was drifting back to sleep, suddenly I got the feeling that someone was standing beside me. Throwing off the clothes that I was using to cover myself, I sat up as if poked with something sharp. Silhouetted against the moonlight someone stood very still, like a statue. I went numb, cold and mute.

'"Mustafa, it's me! Arman!" the statue spoke. The sound emerged with a rasp as if it had come from a throat grown rusty from not vocalizing for a long time.

'"Arman!" When I got my breath back, I scrambled down from the hammock. When I reached out to take his hands in mine, he staggered back and hissed, "Don't touch me!"

'"Why, what happened?"

'When I moved close to him, he again moved back.

'"Quiet! Don't make a noise!" he spoke sharply.

'"I had given you my word that I'd be back. The only reason why I came now."

'"How did you find me?"'

'"I saw our car parked outside."'

'He took the clay pot and drank greedily from it. Whatever was left he poured over his head and then sat down on the table.

'He reeked of stale sweat, putrid blood and acrid smoke. I waited for him to speak.

'"Mustafa, there's no more Dilva. Nor Arman." His voice was cold.

'"What are you saying?"'

'I was afraid that he had lost his mental equilibrium.

'"They have killed Dilva. After gang-raping her, she and many like her were set on fire in a basement while still alive after pouring petrol over them."

'I felt my legs turning into jelly. The words kept echoing in my mind.

'The words "after pouring petrol over them" went on ricocheting endlessly within me. I looked at Arman forlornly. The hard look on his face as he stared unblinking into the darkness frightened me.

'He spoke impassively as if reporting the death of an unknown girl killed by some unknown persons. It seemed like he was reconciled to the fact that she was no more. I was completely shaken—Dilva, whom we thought would one day enter Arman's seventeenth-floor apartment as his bride . . .! The pink-cheeked girl with eyes as deep as the ocean.

'"Mustafa, it was not Dilva alone. Many girls, many babies, old mothers, young men and many more innocent human beings were incinerated inside basements."

'After being silent for a little while, he continued, "Only now I realize what she had been fighting for really. I'll continue that fight."

'"Arman, your mother's waiting for you. Please . . ."'

'The words came out of my mouth with great difficulty. His granite-hard words did not allow me to continue.

'"Mustafa, this land is bigger and greater than any mother. Even when she knew she may get killed, Dilva chose to remain in Cizîr for this land. If I so desire, at this moment I can return to Çîçika and lead a normal life. However, I'll never have peace in my life. Her soul will never forgive me."

'He peered at my face. "Promise me something. No one should know I'm alive."

'"What if they are told?" I spoke mechanically. Cogent thought was beyond me then.

'"It's the best for my family and you. Everyone should believe that I have also perished in this conflagration. You should tell everyone—family, friends and acquaintances—that you have come away after being tired of waiting for me to turn up. If not, they will hound my family to hunt me down."

'I nodded silently. Although I could see he was headed for dire troubles, I didn't say anything against his decision. Suddenly, a sound like a cat mewing rose from beyond the wall. Arman rose to his feet.

'"It's time for me to go."

'He lifted the clay pot, peered into it and kept it down in dismay.

'"Water! There's no water there. I think people will die of thirst," he said as if speaking to himself. He stood there for some time as if pondering over something. When the sound of the cat's mewl rose again, he started and shook his head as if he had been shaken out of a dream.

'It was clear that the time for him to leave had arrived. Although he made as if he wanted to hug me, he held himself back. I had a feeling that I would never see him again.

'"Where are you going?" I asked, distraught.

'"Now?" he laughed.

'"The Turkish Army has a graffiti artist. On my way here, I had read a poem he's written on one of the walls in Cizîr. I need a tête-à-tête with him! I must congratulate him."

'I didn't understand anything. I heard a car engine start up a little distance away. With a wave in my direction, he bounded away, silent as a cat. When I watched him leap over the compound wall effortlessly, I felt I had been dreaming till then.

'Shocking my frozen brain into the present, a bomb exploded not far away from where I was. I could hear the children crying and the hubbub of people trying to assess the damage. An unusual brightness appeared above Cizîr town. The firestorm caught on and spread. As I stood there, looking at the sky turned red from the fires below, all I could think was of the flushed face of Dilva. Her beautiful form was transforming into a glowing ember that was thrashing about begging for its life in the inferno. Scorched by the heat of that flame, a scream got stuck in my parched throat.

'Although emotion had subdued the intellect for some time, I regained my senses shortly. The military action in the town could quickly spread to the suburbs where I was. The bomb blasts and gunfire that had been inching closer presaged that. When I walked towards the house to warn Sarya, who was sleeping inside unaware of all this, I lurched. I seemed to have aged in a matter of seconds; my limbs had no strength to carry me.'

Mustafa stopped and picked up his glass of tea again. The young men who could have been statues in that dim-lit, smoke-filled room while listening to the narration, took out their tobacco pouches. Akbar went inside to fetch more tea. From the now cloudless sky, a wan moon peered at them through the broken window.

Cizîr

'The sky seen through the foliage above us was grey. The scorched smell in the wind that kept blowing and kicking up the dust was getting stronger. There were no signs of the flock of birds that used to fly leisurely in the sky during the initial few days. When I thought there was nothing left for me to do there, I felt a hollowness inside me.'

Although he did not let his mind wander when Mustafa was speaking, Timur's insides burned up when he thought of Seetha. He was aware that, all by himself, little could be accomplished in that unfamiliar place. Since Akbar and his friends had taken the responsibility for finding her, Timur decided to leave things to them. The stream of calls and messages they were receiving was proof that the search was on at a heartening pace. Since it was imperative that under the current circumstances, he understood the lay of the land and the truth behind the incidents till then, Timur decided to concentrate on Mustafa's story.

'I was certain that Dilva and Arman would never return. There was nothing left for me to do there. It was time for me to bid goodbye to that small house, which had provided me food and a roof for three days.

'As usual, Sarya came with my breakfast of home-made cheese, freshly baked bread and a boiled egg. I could make out from her reddened nose, puffy cheeks and tousled hair that she had been crying all night. The sight of the full breakfast caused a lump in my throat.

'When she turned back after placing the plate in front me without saying a word, I coughed lightly to catch her attention.

'"Sarya, I see no reason to prolong my stay here. I was thinking of returning to Sur."

'She turned around. Tears had welled up in her eyes. Adjusting the scarf that had slipped off her head, she sat on the floor and took my hands in hers.

'"Brother, if you have no urgent matter to attend to, can you stay here for a few more days? I am terrified."

'It was more of a whimper than a plea. I didn't know what I should do. In my aimless life till then, I had learnt no tactic to counter women's tears. That teary appeal had the power to tether me to that hammock like a watchdog for lifetime, what to talk of a few days. Without replying, I kept staring at her.

'Although my mind weakened for a second, I quickly regained my better judgement. She may have been a mother of four, but she was still young and bursting with health. If Sarya's or Hozan's families came to know of this help I was rendering—it would not matter to them that I was sleeping in the open on a hammock, suffering the cold—that would be the end of Sarya and myself.

'Deciding that I should leave at the earliest, I pulled out my hand from hers. When she saw my dissenting expression, Sarya started to plead relentlessly.

'"Brother . . . please show some mercy, please help. Stay till Hozan returns. If he comes to know you have been helping us, he will be grateful to you for life."

'"Sarya, while staying here, other than eating up the food meant for you all, what help have I been?" I stammered.

'"That shouldn't be your worry. The store had two sacks of flour. Plenty of potatoes from last year's crop remain. By God's grace, the hens are laying eggs and the cows are giving enough and more milk." She looked into my eyes with forlorn hope.

'"Sarya, that's not the main thing." I was honest with her, "If anyone comes to know of me staying here, forget me, they will finish you off."

'"Both our families were against our marriage. We were exiled from our village. We had to flee from there to save our lives. Both of us have no relatives in Cizîr. Should any of the neighbours get nosey, I shall tell them that my brother has come from the village to help me because of the clashes."

'My mind kept warning me that I was getting into needless trouble. However, I couldn't ignore the tears of that woman who had been so hospitable to me.

'When she saw I was still debating with myself, she started her entreaties again.

'"I understand that it's very inconvenient for you. You have to sleep in the yard in this cold. I was forced to do it because there is no spare room in the house. I shall give you the woollen blanket that Hozan uses. Moreover, if you can bring the car in, it will save you from the dew in the night."

'That was a good idea. If I pushed back the front seats of Arman's old Mercedes car fully, I could sleep in comfort. I went with Sarya's children and pushed the car into the compound. The car crawled in the compound like a giant crocodile. In the process, we broke three or four of Sarya's flowerpots.

'Taking it as their new toy, the children had a whale of time, inside and outside the car. They quickly grew tired of it and went back to their despondent selves. The more I watched their downcast, cheerless faces, the more I felt I needed to do something for them.

'When Sarya came with my lunch, I asked her where Hozan was employed. She only knew he was a supervisor in a construction company. She didn't know where the work site was.

'I noted down the name of his company and an approximate address. Not that I had any chance, but I was hopeful of securing a lead. I quizzed her repeatedly on the location of the work site—I kept asking about the distance or any landmarks nearby. However, I drew a complete blank. Hanging on to her mother's dress, her third daughter who had been listening to our conversation from behind her peeked out and said, "This shop is near where baba works."

'She pointed to a sweets container that was half buried in the sand. I picked up the tin container that lay open amidst the children's toys. It had the name and address of a shop in Cizîr that sold baklava and ice-cream. I sweet-talked the girl into coming out from behind Sarya.

'"Did your baba tell you that he works near this shop?"

'As she tried to disappear behind her mother again, I pulled her back. She kept giggling, showing her decayed teeth in a bid to escape by shaking me off.

'"It's possible! Recently, every evening, he has been coming with sweetmeats in such tins. I've been telling him that he's been spoiling the children like this," said a surprised Sarya, flipping the tin in her hand as she examined it.

'I smiled at her, relieved. "Let me go and have a look."

'This time, her eyes filled with tears of happiness. She sobbed and thanked me with folded hands, unable to say anything.

Watching their mother weep again, the children gathered around
her and looked at me anxiously.

"'God bless you," she said between her sobs.

'I remembered Dilva. Why had God not blessed her? Why
had God wrecked Arman's dreams and life? What blessing was the
God, who stood by and watched even babies being burnt to death
alive in that basement, going to bestow on us?

"'Can you make some bread for me quickly? I'd like to start
without wasting any time."

'Sarya ran to the kitchen. I had a bath and ate a large meal,
since I needed a lot of energy during the next few hours.

'Within an hour, Sarya reappeared holding a cloth rucksack.
"There is some bread, two apples and some chocolate. Use the
water carefully. From what I hear, there is terrible shortage of
water since soldiers are going around destroying water tanks."

'I wore a jacket over the rucksack, which I had flattened first
so that it would not be prominent.

"'Don't you need any weapons?" Sarya asked me with hesitation.

"'No, I don't think they would be of any use."

'I said my goodbyes and started to walk slowly. The sun which
had peeped out for some time in the afternoon had gone back
into hiding. The cold started to creep in. Chiding myself that it
was not cold but my fear, I looked back. The hapless mother and
her four children were still standing in the yard looking at me.
The children waved their hands cheerfully. I assumed that Sarya
would go back to weeping. The thought that I'd never be able to
forgive myself if I couldn't find their father quickened my steps.
The chilly wind made goose pimples break out all over my body.
I felt the loving, gentle warmth of the breads inside the rucksack
seeping into me gradually.

'I had learnt by heart the name and address of the sweet
shop—Şêrîn. I avoided main roads and used side streets and by-

lanes. Away from downtown Cizîr, Hozan and Sarya's house was in a less populated area, where lived low-income families who couldn't afford to buy or rent houses in the town.

'From their house, which looked down on the town, the vast fields abutting the town could be seen. None of the houses on the way had smoke rising out of their chimneys. I wondered if they had been abandoned or whether the residents were huddled together in the basement holding their breaths, awaiting their fate. I thought it would have been good if I could meet someone to ask if there was a shortcut to Cizîr.

'Heading towards the town, a small, low-flying jet roared overhead, deafening me. Two of the three shops on that road were shuttered. After walking a little further, near one of the shopfronts, I saw a form that resembled an old, filled sack. It was an old man wrapped in a soiled, tattered blanket. Passers-by could have taken him for some inanimate thing like a stack of old cartons or barrels in front of the nearby shops. He didn't appear to be aware of what was going on around him. When I went and stood in front of him, his gaze was fixed on something beyond me.

'"Baba . . ."

'Warily, I bowed down to look into his eyes. His bilious, dull eyes stared at me as if he had woken up from a trance. His face was covered in wrinkles. With a sob, his body buckled, and he sat down. As his shaking body listed to one side, I jumped forward and held him with both my hands. There was no one in the vicinity. Yet I shouted for help. "Hey, please, someone help . . ."

'There was no one. Not a single soul.

'An alarmed black-headed pigeon sitting on the half-wall of the next store cocked its head a few times to look at us and flew away in a hurry. I could hear no sounds but the whines of the overgrown Asian Tiger mosquitoes that had flown in from the Tigris, which resembled a silver-thread from afar. A skinny dog peeked out behind a fallen barrel at the other side of road, stared at us disinterested for a short while, and withdrew to continue its siesta.

'Almost three-fourths of the water, which Sarya had instructed to preserve, I poured on the man's head to revive him. He opened his eyes after a little while. He gulped down the rest of the water greedily and desperately asked for more. When I lifted my hands to show my helplessness, he winked at me as if to say it's okay. I could see from his movements that he was feeling better.

'When it appeared that he had gained enough strength to sit up, I placed my tobacco pouch, untouched for the past three days, before him. Those tired eyes sparkled. Sucking in the smoke hungrily, he scanned the address I was trying to reach. Doing some mental maths and knowing that I will have to walk at least seven kilometres, he scanned me from tip to toe as if he was measuring me. "You're young and strong. It's only walking distance." A crinkle appeared fleetingly on one corner of his mouth, which could be described as a smile.

'I had no pen or pencil with me. He smoothened the fine camel brown dust on the ground, picked up a twig and, drew a route map for me.

'"For much of the distance you'll only see fields. You may see single-room structures built for farmers' rest. In all probability, all of them will be deserted. Once you reach the town, follow the Tigris. Otherwise, you'll lose your way."

'He frowned in disappointment. After thinking for a moment, the old man picked up the twig again, scratched his head with it and said, "The place you have to reach is almost at the other end of the town. Somehow manage to reach the Cizîr bridge. It's only another a kilometre or so from there. If you ask someone there, they'll tell the way."

'When I stood up to leave, he took the tobacco pouch and extended it towards me.

'"I don't need it, baba. I've stopped smoking," I said.

'He gave me a surprised look and bowed his head in gratitude.

'"Please don't sit here. It's dangerous." I pointed to the plane that was circling the skies. His face changed. He grabbed my hand with pain evident on his face.

'"I'm waiting for my son. They took him away; said they'll release him after questioning." He started to tremble. "Jiyan, he's the youngest. He's only twenty. They must have beaten him to death . . ." He started to cry bitterly.

'My legs seemed to give out. "Do you have anyone at home?" I spoke up despite my recalcitrant tongue.

'"My wife. She's cried enough for a lifetime. They kicked and pummelled him in front of her. His screams were enough to tell us that at least of few of his ribs were broken." He bawled like a child. I was helpless.

'"Baba, it's not good for you to sit outside like this. What if something happens to your wife? How'll you come to know of it? Let's go to your home. I'll come with you."

'"My son, I am seventy and my wife is fifty. What more than this can happen to us?" He looked at me with pained eyes, overflowing with tears.

'"I can't leave you here and go. Come, I'll be with you till your house."

'I helped him up. He stood up without protest. Watching him struggle to walk broke my heart. I could see that his aged, slight, skin-and-bones body had suffered trauma.

'"What happened with you?" I asked him loudly, fear perhaps adding decibels to my voice.

"'Don't worry,' he said in a comforting tone. "When I was watching him being beaten up, I tried to intervene. I suffered only small cuts. I am old, you shouldn't worry."

'I almost carried him to his house. I found out some details about him during the journey. His name was Hakar. His family had been leading a comfortable life with some farming and a shop in the town. His children had, except for the youngest, married and moved out. The youngest did have some political leanings. But what did he do to deserve to get beaten to death like this— Hakar started to wail again. Unable to find words to console him, I held his weakened body close to me.

'His house was not far off. It was an old house; the lime-washed walls filled with dark ivy climbers and a blue-painted door reminded me of my own house. I felt that my mother with her well-worn scarf tied tightly around her head may open the door and appear before me.

'As soon as Hakar knocked, a woman opened the door. She must have been waiting right behind it, expecting someone to turn up. After craning her neck and looking behind us anxiously, she sat down on the floor and, holding her head in her hands, started to sob. Hakar sat down beside her and tried to console her.

'I looked around. Everything seemed to have been wrecked and smashed. There were no signs of a fire having been kindled to warm themselves or cook. I stood there silently, waiting for their crying to get over.

"'Both of you should listen to me." I intervened eventually. I announced in a voice loud and firm enough to catch their attention and gain their confidence.

"'You should give me two days. I'll certainly return. We can find out where Jiyan is and about his condition. Please understand that you're not alone."

'The assurance I gave them had no basis. The need to keep those two alive and hopeful had become mine too. From the floor, two pairs of bloodshot eyes looked at me unbelievingly.

'"You should start a fire, cook and eat something. I'll be back in two days." I kept my voice firm. I knew I had to leave—if I had to find Hozan, I needed the daylight. The sky had already turned grey and cloudy.

'Before leaving, I examined Hakar's wounds and bruises and made sure none of them was lethal. Controlling her sobs, Hakar's wife promised me that she would cook, clean up the place and apply salve on his wounds.

'"Two days, a mere two days!"

'I mumbled to myself worriedly as I strode ahead. I could feel two pairs of tearful and hope-filled eyes on my back, increasing my disquiet. When I considered how powerless and weak I had turned out to be in the past, vain and often lit up, I had gone about hell-raising, I felt only contempt for myself.

'I left behind the fields that Hakar had described to me. I calculated that I had covered about two kilometres. Although, by sticking to the back lanes and avoiding main streets, I managed to reach the edge of the town without being noticed, sneaking in would be very difficult. There was no guessing where all the soldiers would have stationed themselves.

'A narrow lane stretching into the distance between the buildings gave me hope. The area around that tarred lane was deserted. I assumed that people would have abandoned the houses. Occasional sounds of firing and explosions were heard from different directions, piercing through the silence that had blanketed the town.

'Some distance into the lane, ahead of a curve, loud voices and laughter brought me to a stop. I assumed they were soldiers lying in wait for infiltrators like me. Flattening myself against the wall of the building, I inched forward to do some reconnaissance. A little further down I could see parked military vehicles. Although there had been talk of Cizîr being sealed, I hadn't expected that even small lanes would be barricaded off.

'The soldiers were smoking and laughing, leaning against the armoured cars parked blocking the lane. If they would have seen me, there was no doubt that I would be taken in for questioning. Flattening myself against a closed door, I started to think what I should do.

'"Are you a doctor?" It was as though someone had whispered into my ear. It made me jump out of my skin. A pair of eyes glinted through a very narrow gap in the door.

'"No. But can you allow me in? If I stay here, they will see me any moment," I pleaded.

'The very next moment, someone pulled me inside the house. I had lost my footing in the process, and I hit the cemented floor as if I had been flung down. My eyes could not adjust to the darkness in the room. The cold steel of some pointed weapon caressed my nose and stopped at the centre of my forehead, pressing into my skin.

'"Who are you?" a sharp feminine voice demanded. Gradually forms started to take shape in the darkness. Someone lit a small candle. The well-honed dagger glinted menacingly in the low light. I writhed like a small prey impaled on its sharp point.

'"Don't hurt me. I'm not your enemy," I pleaded in a hoarse voice.

'By then I could make out those around me were all women. Their heavy clothes and the dim light of the room made second guessing rather difficult.

'"Ayşe . . . take away the knife." Someone spoke. After caressing my face down from my forehead with that heavy dagger, the young woman sheathed it. Her stony, impassive face told me that if the opportunity presented itself, she would not hesitate for even a moment before thrusting it into my heart.

'There was a sudden shriek from a woman in pain, as if she was in her death throes. It made me tremble. It was cut short as if someone had gagged her.

'"What's happening here?" I spoke haltingly.

'"Who are you?" One of the woman spoke up.

"My friend had come to the town. There's no news of him. I've come in search of him." I managed to babble.

'I had the impression that all of them were trying not to laugh. A woman who looked older than the others, knelt before my prone body. Looking deep into my eyes, that noble-looking lady asked in a stern voice, "You idiot! Don't you know what is happening in this place? No one has the permission to come in or go out of this town! Consider yourself lucky that you were not seen by them!"

'"Who's crying?" My attention was on the occasional shrieks from the chamber inside.

'"Don't worry. We're not butchering anyone here."

The women around me started to laugh.

'"How can you laugh like this?" I was worried they had all lost their minds.

'"A woman is in labour inside that room. For two days we have been trying to get hold of a doctor." The noble-looking woman sighed.

'"Do you know midwifery?" The laughter that was suppressed till then burst out. I found it unnerving.

'"Throw this guy out." The lady rose up from the floor and commanded.

'"Wait . . ." Slapping away the hands that reached out to me, I leapt up on to my feet. I stood obsequiously in front of the lady who, by then it was obvious, was their leader.

'"Please help me. I can't go back without him. Five lives, with no one to help them, are waiting for him."

'She gave me a searching look.

'"They'll kill you." From beneath a frown brought on by concern, her glowering eyes bored into mine.

'"I shall take care." I gave everyone an imploring look. "I don't have an option."

'When she heard that moaning request, the grand lady took another lady from the group to the side and spoke in hushed tones. The others sat down on the carpet leaning against the bolster pillows. But their cold hard stares were fixed on me. I was scared to even move from where I stood.

'I was troubled by the thought of what could be the final decision. After the secret confabulation, the noble lady took my arm and dragged me along with her. We passed through the kitchen into a small quadrangle, paved with round pebbles and strewn with children's toys around. Plants with desiccated leaves that had survived the cold of the winter could be seen here and there. Grapevines that had been reduced to stiff stems had climbed up the walls, spread and formed a canopy over the quadrangle. Strangely the thought that came to me was that with a potful of strong tea and a book in hand, one could sit there for any amount of time.

'"Hurry up instead of standing and gaping . . ." she scolded me, quickly jumped down into the quadrangle and ran to the other end.

'There was a sudden explosion. The walls of the building shook. A terrified lamb bleated from the other side of the wall on the rear side. Equally shocked and terrified, the explosion sent me sprawling into the ground. Unmoved by all this, the lady was knocking on a door on the other side of the courtyard. Her angry stare made me leap back to my feet, dust myself and panting and reach her side.

'The continuous knocking brought a girl in a headscarf peering out from the door. Relief and happiness spread on her face. She opened her arms to hug the lady who was with me. However, when she saw me behind the lady, she was taken aback, and she instinctively pulled back the arms she had opened out. Pushing the confounded girl aside, the lady barrelled into the room.

"'I'll tell you everything later. First send him out through the garage." Her voice shook with anxiety.

"'How's Karo now?" the girl asked, as we were being led through the dark rooms briskly. I avoided looking at her beautiful eyes that were looking towards me suspiciously.

"'When the ambulance came, the bloodthirsty men started to shoot at it. The driver luckily managed to reverse the vehicle and escape. I doubt if any of the ambulance drivers will touch their vehicles till all this comes to an end. We heard that two drivers have already been shot and injured," the elderly woman said angrily as she walked forward at a pace close to running.

"'Karo still has one month to go. Two days ago, a neighbouring house was hit by a shell. All the excitement possibly triggered her, and she went into labour," the girl told me.

"'What'll we do now?" I said anxiously.

"'There's a nurse in this neighbourhood. We have arranged for her to come. Why are you bothered with this? First make sure that you don't lose your life," the lady told him harshly. She easily lifted the shutter in front of us with one hand. It opened into a garage.

"'Go off . . .!"

'She gave me a push. There was dusty car inside the garage. Hiding behind it, I peeped out. The garage door opened out into a blackened square. The fire-blackened walls, and remains of burnt doors, reminded me of a funeral pyre. I was stunned like a mouse that had fallen into an ash-filled, hot fireplace.

'The sound of the shutter being lowered behind me increased my tension. I turned around in desperation. The descending shutter was like a curtain cutting me off from those two women who were watching me.

'I waited to make sure no was around in that vicinity. A cool breeze was blowing through the square with a low humming sound. The smell of gun powder, and the acrid smoke from the smouldering door and windows suffocated me.

'As per Hakar's map, I had cut across the town for about five kilometres to reach Hozan's work site. I still had the option of retracing my steps. But something inside me declared, "You are a Kurd. Don't back down!"

'Kicking away the scorched wooden debris on the ground, I walked out.'

Mustafa

'I was trying to keep the Tigris in my view through the gaps between the buildings. Hakar had pointedly asked me to follow the river. I had a fair idea how to reach the banks of the Tigris. However, I was also worried that I might lose my way in the labyrinthine alleys and lanes and end up where I started.

'Even if I wanted to ask someone the way, there was no sign of life anywhere. I was weak from stress, fear and thirst. I examined the rucksack. It contained the empty water bottle and apples. I decided that one apple would be enough quench my thirst.

'Something whizzed past my head the moment I brought the apple to my mouth after having seated myself on a broken step of one of the nearby shops. I shot up from there like a wounded animal and started to run. Guns were going off behind me with deafening sounds. I ran through the lanes till I thought my legs would fall off from my body. When it was clear to me that if I tried to run any more, I would collapse, panting like a dog, I tried to hide myself behind the smoking remains of a nearby building.

'Though breathing was difficult, I covered my mouth so that the sound of my panting wouldn't be heard. I sat motionless like a statue. After a few minutes, two soldiers ran past the building. Listening to the fading sounds of their boots, I crawled over the debris of the building. With that attack, I had realized it would be unsafe to move around during the daylight. Listening to the thumping of my heart and waiting for it to normalize, I lay on the cold ground like a thrashed snake.

'I could imagine what had happened. The absence of soldiers in the open had led to my overconfidence and made me indiscreet. How foolish could I be? Distrusting myself, I scanned the surroundings. They might be hiding in any of these buildings.

'Not long ago, children's feet would have pattered over these lanes; women would have gone through them meeting friends and buying groceries; in these burnt houses, families would have once cheerfully sat around the dinner table to have their meals and sing songs about heroes from the hills of Kurdistan; they would have loved and quarrelled with one another, tutored their children and led ordinary, happy lives. It was over the dreams of such innocent people that with their machine guns and sniper rifles, the soldiers were now lying in wait for their prey.

'Tired by my effort to count the bullet holes on the walls, my eyes closed gradually. The stench of rotting human flesh assailed my nostrils. I was lying on top of an ash heap of the corpse of a house. Human corpses too could be buried under all the rubble and be the source of the fetor. Despite all that, I had to lie there for a few hours more. I decided to lie low till nightfall.

'I was woken up by the sound of an explosion. It was very dark. Fatigue had made me fall asleep. Screams of people could be heard from afar. Smaller explosions and their echoes followed. Some other part of the town was under attack.

'"God, what do you have to say about what's happening down here?" I stared at the sky. Oblivious to the enormity that lit the embers on this earth, the twinkling stars looked down and smiled at me.

'The cloud cover of the morning had disappeared. The moon shone generously on the ruined buildings and trees. I should leave immediately. I tried to help myself up using my limbs that had gone numb. The stench around me made me nauseated. I had a splitting headache too. I yearned for some water. I used my tongue to wet my chapped lips.

'I took care to keep myself in the shadows. I worked out that if I travelled to my right, I would hit the Tigris. However, contrary to my expectations, soldiers were patrolling even the inner lanes. Armoured cars passed by occasionally, their huge guns poking out of them and scanning every inch on either side of the streets. Lurking inside buildings smashed by tanks and leaping over remnants of walls, I made tortuous progress towards the banks of the Tigris.

'After some time, I could see the lights of the vehicles zooming past at a distance. I had not accounted for this—to reach the river I had to cross a highway! Although it was night, sounds of gunfire had not ceased. I could see flares going up from many points all over the town. I decided to hide and study the vehicular movements.

'Only military vehicles were speeding in both directions on the highway. I was afraid that vantage points in the tall buildings on either side of the highway might be a lair of snipers. Swathed in complete darkness, without even a spot of light showing, those buildings looked forbidding. To prevent infiltrators from entering the town, I imagined that soldiers would be present where this highway from Nusaybin entered the town.

'My observation of the surroundings assured me that there was no danger in that area. Other than the vehicles passing by, there seemed to be no other movement. I had to cross the highway on a dead run. After making sure there were no vehicles coming from either direction, gathering all my strength, I shot off like a hare chased by hounds.

'Although I crossed the road without loss of life or limb, I didn't stop running for the fear that someone may be pursuing me. I ran till I no longer could. Eventually exhausted and panting like a hare, I leaned against a wall to get my breath back. Suddenly from the corner of my eye I saw some movement in a nearby ruined house.

'I tried to withdraw into myself. Within seconds, I went behind a heap of rubble like a tortoise into its shell. It took a long time for my heartbeats to quieten down. Whoever it was, he or she wasn't making any attempt to hide his or her presence. After watching for a little while, I deemed that the form pacing to and fro in those ruins couldn't be a soldier lying in wait for his victims.

'I could make out that it was a woman. She was pacing, sniffling and mumbling unintelligibly to herself. Announcing that I was not the enemy loud enough for her to hear, I moved towards her side of the ruins. Since a better part of the roof hadn't collapsed, the moonlight did not enter the building.

'"Can I get some water?"

'"Who are you?" her shaky voice demanded.

'"I'm searching for someone, on the way, actually. I'm thirsty."

'She moved out of the shadows to where there was some light. She looked thirty-ish. After looking at me and deciding that I was no troublemaker, she pointed to the rear of the building. "There is a small well. Drink was much as you want."

'I was relieved when I heard that water was available. I found the well with some difficulty since it had been covered with plastic sheets, hessian and wooden planks. I drew water using a rusted, dented bucket tied to a thin threadbare rope. The well was deeper than I had imagined. After drinking the ice-cold water to my fill, washing my legs and hands and filling my water bottle, I walked back to thank the lady.

'She was seated in some dark recess of the building. My effusive words of gratitude were met with silence. My question whether that path would lead to the Tigris was replied with a monosyllabic yes.

'"What are you looking for?" I asked, deciding to throw caution to the winds.

'"My life!" the tremulous voice from the darkness replied. "Everyone has fled. Isn't my life beneath all this rubble . . .? How can I leave?" The tremulous voice had been transformed into a keening shriek which echoed around, piercing the darkness. The woman appeared to be demented.

'I was terrified. I felt she was running towards me screeching. I ran out into the open suppressing my own scream. Her shrieks were most certainly going to attract soldiers in the vicinity. I leapt over a wall and hid behind it.

'Her wails started to taper off after some time. I could hear her plaintive mumbling and muttering from behind the rubble. I jumped over the wall on to the lane. I started to walk towards the river, beyond caring now if there were any soldiers around. I had been reduced to a detached mental state to the extent that sounds of explosion reaching me could have come from another planet for all that I cared.

'When I reached the riverbank, I stopped as if I had walked into a wall. In that cool moonlight, the splendid Tigris, an iridescent blue, was flowing serenely. Although the humid chilly breeze had me shivering, I breathed in the familiar smell of the river. Peace descended on me, as if I were lying on my mother's lap. I broke down completely and dropped on the ground.

'After sitting on that cold ground listlessly for a long time, I suddenly remembered with a start the purpose for which I was there. I had to fulfil my promise to Sarya. I had to send back Hozan to his children who waited for him to return with sweetmeats in the evenings. Finding him the same night may

make the difference between his life and death; mine too. I left
the road and, dragging my unwilling feet, started to walk along
the riverbank. Another five kilometres remained as per Hakar's
calculations. Since there were very few habitations close to the
river, I tried to console myself with the thought that consequently,
soldiers may also be scarce.

'However, that was short-lived. Lights from the approaching
vehicles appeared. I hid behind a clump of reeds. A searchlight
swept the area. Although it went past where I was hiding a
number of times, since it went over my head, I was saved from
being detected.

'I was watching the lights of the receding vehicles and trying
to shake off and squash the biting ants, when I felt the cold
steel of a gun barrel poking the nape of my neck. Shocked and
terrified, a whine started to escape from my throat when in a low
growl, a whispered but peremptory voice warned me, "Silence!"
A stinking dark strip of cloth came around my face, and I was
blindfolded.

'"Walk!" another terse whisper. But this time it was a woman's
voice. When I felt the hand holding me and leading me was a
woman's, I tried to feint and shake her off. A heavy sharp blow
landed on my head in the same instant. The world went dark and
as my knees started to buckle, two strong hands grabbed me and
started to shake me.

'"Don't try anything funny if you don't want to die!" Someone
patted me down to check for weapons.

'"Not even a penknife," the man reported.

'They dragged me over the sand and dry leaves like a sack of
potatoes. As stones and sharp stubs cut and scored my body, I
moaned. I was kicked, verbally abused and warned to stay quiet.
When the sand turned wet, I sensed we were close to the river.
I was shivering like a man with ague out of both fear and cold.

Assuming they were going to drown me, in between my cries, I kept begging for my life and claiming that I was innocent.

"'You moron, pipe down. This place is crawling with soldiers!'"

'They removed my blindfold. When that smelly cloth that was making me gag was removed, I took a few deep breaths. In the darkness, the faces of my captors—three men and a woman—were unclear. AK-47s and large bags hung from their shoulders. I lay on the muddy ground like a miserable worm in front of those powerful figures.

'The girl took sympathy on me and squatting close, asked me gently who I was and why I was wandering around at this time of the night. The compassion in her voice made me weep again. I had understood by then who these young men were. The epaulettes had the insignias of YPG[1] or YPJ.[2]

"'So, you and your friend came to Cizîr in search of Dilva!'"

"'Do you all know Dilva?' I asked expectantly.

"'We know now. We now know everyone who was ripped apart and burnt alive in that basement,' one of the men said mournfully.

"'What's your plan to find this guy Hozan?' someone asked.

"'I have an idea where his construction site is.' I eagerly gave them the address of the sweet shop.

"'That is far from here,' the girl shook her head to convey the hopelessness of my situation.

"'If you end up in front of the soldiers, they'll finish you,' one of the men said.

"'Would you like to come with us? We'll help you to find Hozan,' the girl asked me.

"'What are you saying?' the others protested. We have no authority to take on additional missions like this!'"

"'He is a Kurd like us. Only one of us will go in search of a friend even when we know we may perish in the attempt. For this reason alone, we can't abandon him,' she took them on spiritedly.

'"You shall have to answer Amraz!"

'"I shall!" She helped me up.

'Once we started to walk, the antipathy in their body language melted away. As my panic reduced, I looked at the group from the corner of my eyes. Their thick uniform had dark, damp patches. They must have crossed the river from the Syrian side on rubber dinghies or boats in the cover of darkness. All of them appeared to be in their early twenties. If they were put in a classroom in civilian dress, no one would have said that they were once walking around with guns and heavy bags as wanted persons with a price on their heads.

'The thought that any of the explosions whose sounds we kept hearing could take our lives was enough to wipe away the fear and loathing I had felt in the beginning.

'"We are headed to Cûdî. We need to leave the river and get into the town."

'Berivan, as the girl was addressed by her companions, looked at me. "Are you afraid? One of us will accompany you to where you have to go."

'"I was terrified when I was alone," I confessed. They looked at one another and smiled.

'"You should be more afraid when we're with you. If you're alone and even if you're seen by them, you may still be able to get away with your life."

'"More than death, loneliness terrified me. This was like a ghost town. Blackened houses, where the fire licked them completely, were destroyed in explosions. Screams hit you when you least expect them. The town smelled like a putrefied corpse. I thought I would go mad." I needed to unburden myself after all the pain and stress I had gone through that day.

'Berivan lifted her melancholic eyes and looked at me.

'"This is my land! The land where I was born and grew up in!" Her voice shook.

'"Shhhh! Silence!" ordered the young man who was in the front. We had entered the town leaving the river behind. Shattered glass littered the road. They gave off a mesmeric gleam in the moonlight. After making sure there were no soldiers watching the area, they decided to check out an area where clashes had taken place the previous night.

'Her companions told me to get into a balcony of a destroyed building along with Berivan and keep watch. With the gun at the ready, she took up a vantage position from where she could see in all directions. Forgetting the task I was charged with, my eyes kept flying to Berivan. With intense concentration, as she stood still like a statue silhouetted against the moonlight with rifle in hand, I felt she was more beautiful than any other girl I had met.

'In the murky darkness, one could spot the sandbags with bullet holes and heaps of stone that soldiers had used for their protection. After inspecting them, the men walked towards the bombarded house. As she stared at the skeleton of that house, I asked Berivan hesitantly what had happened there.

'"Two of our comrades were inside. They fought valiantly till the last moment." She sighed. In the moonlight, I could see her exquisite eyes becoming moist.

'Berivan and I went down after the men signalled us after they had done the inspection. They were discussing what had happened during the attack.

'"There are corpses inside. It's difficult to say what these bastards would have done. Taybet's body lay on the street for a whole week."

'"I beg your pardon, I've had no news since the last few days. Who's Taybet?" I asked Berivan in a low voice.

'"Taybet died in the shooting in Silopî. She was the mother of eleven children!"

'I had a feeling that Berivan was reluctant to discuss the matter. As she strode ahead, I asked her again what had happened to Taybet.

'"Huh! You want to know? Turkish soldiers used her body as bait. They knew someone would try to come for her help. After she was shot, she lay there for an interminable six hours, bleeding and fighting death."

'Our conversation was cut short since we had to clamber over the rubble of the houses that bulldozers had brought down. Gathering courage, I again asked Berivan what had transpired later. I could see my questions were making her seethe in anger and sorrow.

'"What could have happened? When her sister's husband, with a white flag in hand, tried to go to her dying body, the soldiers shot him dead. Her husband was wounded in the firing. Seven days . . .! For seven days that mother's body lay on the road and rotted."

'She gnashed her teeth. The man ahead of us stopped. Our whispers were irritating him.

'"Enough of your small talk!" he ordered. "We have to cross the highway. Careful!"

'When I heard I should cross the highway once more, a chill travelled down my spine. Although I was worried, we were taking the same route, I took care to not show my disquiet to Berivan.

'"Look here. This highway has a lot of military traffic. We've to bide our time; make sure there are no approaching vehicles and only then cross it. Watch out for any movements around you. Two of us will go across first. Then the rest," Daryan, their leader, instructed in a whisper.

'We stayed low behind the destroyed buildings beside the highway. The highway was deserted. As we lay flat on that chilly ground for ten minutes daring not even to breathe, we saw no other sign of life, except for two armoured vehicles rolling by slowly with their occupants scanning the sides of the highway.

'Daryan stood up. "Mustafa, you come with me, we'll cross first." He pulled me up. "If you see no approaching vehicles after we have cross, you all must follow immediately. This place is not safe," he instructed the others.

'All of them were holding their guns at the ready. I found it hard to keep pace with Daryan even though I did not carry anything. Despite the heavy backpack and a loaded gun that must have weighed four-to-five kilos, he bounded across like a deer. As soon as we reached the other side, he pulled me down and found a place to hide. While I was catching my breath, he had lined up his gun and was waiting for his comrades.

'Berivan and the others crossed over the next instant, almost as if they had flown across. I was jealous of the ease with which they walked long distances carrying so much weight, and how nimbly they leaped over obstructions, and assumed this was gained through daily practice and exercise.

'"We're entering downtown. Soldiers will be everywhere. Be careful," Daryan warned.

'"We're about to reach Cûdî. It's here that they had burnt alive hundreds of old people, young girls and babies who had sought refuge in three basements by pouring petrol on to them and setting it alight," Berivan whispered in my ear when she was sure Daryan was not watching.

'Since soldiers were on patrol, we concentrated on sticking to the shadows and moving with stealth. I had lost my sense of direction. We must have travelled quite some distance.

'"Hey, stop!" Berivan stopped me with her hand on my arm.

'"Do you see that road?" Where she pointed to, I could see a bigger road which our lane led to.

"'That's Bostancı Caddesi. Dilva and other girls were gang-raped in a basement on that street. And then burnt alive," Berivan whispered in my ear.

'My eyes felt as if they had been set alight. I wished to cry. I recalled how Dilva used to blush when laughing at the jokes cracked by our group of friends, or when she looked at Arman affectionately.

"'Can I see the place?" I asked anxiously. To pay homage to Dilva, I wanted to bow and touch my forehead on the ground that witnessed her sacrifice for the land she was born in.

"'How stupid can you be? That place is swarming with soldiers in anticipation of our retaliatory attacks." Berivan stared at me.

"'Where else are you headed then?"

"'Our people are stationed in these parts. They need help."

'Fighting had broken out somewhere close by. There was continuous gunfire. Daryan drew up, and as he had to wait for us to catch up, he stomped the ground impatiently.

"'Look here, Mustafa. We had promised that we would help you. Berivan will come with you to find your man. You can talk to her as much as you want on the way."

'I could understand that Daryan was not happy with my presence. I couldn't have blamed him. Trying to help me could endanger their own lives. Berivan threw Daryan a displeased look.

"'Can't one of you go?"

"'Can't you hear all the firing? There's heavy fighting. They need all the help they can get. This guy's sweet shop is less than two kilometres from here. You take your time."

He laughed sardonically.

"'Don't forget I can use this more effectively than you can, Daryan!" riled Berivan growled, tapping her gun.

"'I've no objection to accompanying Mustafa. However, I can help Amraz and his group better than you can."

'They faced off like two territorial wild animals crouching to tear into each other. After angrily locking eyes with her, Daryan shook his head as if he had no time to waste and turned around on his heel.

'After looking daggers at him for a few more moments, she turned towards me. "Shall we go?"

'I followed her obediently. I looked back after a couple of steps. The rest of the group had melted into the darkness without disturbing even a leaf. Berivan was waiting for me with a friendly smile as if to comfort me. "Don't fear. I can use this better than all of them," she said, caressing her gun with affection.

'"I have no doubt about that, Berivan!" I said with conviction.

'As was the habit, we used the shadows and moved along ruins of the buildings. In some places, the debris had spilled on to the street, blocking it. I got a distinct feeling that it used to be a densely populated area. The stench of rotting flesh assailed me. I followed Berivan, ignoring my queasiness. She seemed unaffected by it. Keeping in the shadows she made slow progress.

'It was close to daybreak. Since it was winter, sunrise would be late. However, we didn't have much time on hand. Crouched behind a heap of rubble, she gestured to me to hunker down. During our relatively short association, I had realized she was capable of hearing what was not audible and seeing what was not visible to me. The acuity of her animal-like instinct and senses—whetted by life in forests and the time spent in hiding—surprised me.

'After listening closely, I could hear the approaching sound of soldiers' boots. Even after they passed us, the strong smell of tobacco lingered in the air. I crawled on all fours quietly towards Berivan who was seated with her back to a wall. She took out a water bottle from her backpack and offered it to me.

'"Drink up. Water is the most precious thing in Cizîr right now."

'I took a swig and returned the bottle. She also drank a mouthful and returned the bottle carefully to the backpack. "They have destroyed the entire water distribution network. Water tanks have been bombed. They shat and peed in the wells. People are dying of thirst in Cizîr," Berivan said bitterly.

'I recalled the demented woman who had allowed me to drink from her well. I told Berivan of the well which had been camouflaged and of the woman who had lost her mind in her grief.

'"It's a good thing that you told me this. Our people will soon run out of water. It's very important to know where to get clean water from." She was silent for a while before continuing, "Someone dear to her must be buried under the rubble." The agony of loss was apparent in her voice. But who in this place hadn't suffered losses? I suddenly remember Arman.

'"Do you know Arman?"

'"I have come here only today. You mean your friend, Dilva's lover? If both of us remain alive, perhaps we may still get to meet." A fleeting smile appeared on her lips.

'"He had told me that he's going in search of some graffiti artist . . ."

'"Graffiti artist?" I saw her frown as she tried to work it out.

'"Yes, some graffiti artist in the Turkish Army."

'Ah, okay . . . I understand,' she said as she heaved the bag on to her shoulders, preparing to leave.

'"Do you know what he is planning to do?"

'"I can well imagine." She didn't look at me.

'"Please tell me Berivan. I feel it in my bones that he's going to get into trouble," I pleaded.

'"After gang-raping and immolating the girls, the soldiers had left comments on the walls." Her voice was rough.

'"What did they write?"

'"That their holiday in the basement was highly amusing." She turned and looked at me, her eyes were brimming with tears.

'"They were describing the fun they had raping those girls and setting them on fire. Now you tell me, who's going to be in trouble? Your friend or the guy who wrote it?"

'I stood numb, rooted to the ground. Angry, she shook me roughly by my shoulders.

'"Why are you silent? Who's going to be in trouble?"

'"The man who wrote it!" I said mechanically. Blood surged through my veins. My hands balled into fists, and I found it hard to control myself. I cursed myself for not bounding over that compound wall and accompanying Arman to go with those waiting for him.

'"Walk, another five hundred metres and we'll reach your sweet shop." I followed her like a robot.

'A so-called democratic government that finds fun in shooting and killing our babies; shitting in our wells; fouling our drinking water; tearing our girls into pieces like rabid wolves; dunking our live bodies with petrol and setting us alight! You have given birth to every militant that there is! Every corpse that falls on this land sows myriad seeds of revolt here.

'I kept looking at the slim form striding ahead of me, and the gun in her arms which could be brought into play at the slightest provocation.

'It took us about half-an-hour to cover the five hundred metres. Since military vehicles were zipping past, we had to wait behind a half-destroyed house for some time. The sounds of a baby crying could be heard from inside. A woman's voice full of frustration and helplessness was heard in between. She was cursing the soldiers who were camping inside even hospitals.

'"People have to make do with contaminated water. Infectious diseases are spreading," Berivan muttered while we walked. Although we reached our destination, except for the fact that there used to be a street there, nothing more was visible. The heaps of rubble and detritus lay like worrisome question marks about the lives destroyed by the tanks and shelling.

'"Şêrîn, the sweet shop you mentioned, stood approximately hereabouts. We can do a quick recce here," Berivan said to console me. Was Hozan working close by? I thought he couldn't have survived. The place had undergone a horrendous assault.

'"We have no time to waste. In these circumstances, it's impossible to search for the work site you believe is here. We could've asked someone, but I don't think there's anything alive here."

'Berivan looked around desperately. We knocked on bullet-riddled doors, hoping someone may be inside. We were disappointed. We continued to search without giving up hope. I was aware that I was putting Berivan's life at greater risk with every passing minute.

'"Berivan, please leave now. You helped me reach here. Anyone will recognize you in this uniform. It's dangerous," I pleaded with her. She too knew she was playing with fire. In a last throw of the dice, we headed towards a few buildings, a little away, which seemed to be in better shape.

'We decided to check with the first house. It had not suffered much damage. She pressed her ear against the windowpane and tried to listen for signs of people. After shaking her head to indicate no one was inside, she started to walk towards the next house. But she seemingly changed her mind and walked back. Leaving the gun at the door, she knocked at the door with the insouciance of visiting a neighbour's house. There was no immediate response. After some time, a female voice demanded, "Who's that?"

'"We need help. Please open the door."

'When she heard Berivan's voice, the woman opened the door. She was about forty years old and plump. She looked as if she had been sleeping. Perhaps in the darkness she couldn't see Berivan's dress and form; in a voice thick with sleep, she asked, "What do you want?"

'I moved out of Berivan's shadow and asked her if any multi-storey building was being constructed nearby. After a small pause, she pointed in the direction directly opposite to her house.

'"There's a small tailor's shop which has been ransacked by the soldiers. The building is still standing. It belonged to a lady called Salma whose name the shop bears. A building was being built behind that shop."

'To ensure we were not barking up the wrong tree, we asked her about the sweet shop. She said it belonged to one of her relatives and it was destroyed by the soldiers.

'Berivan thanked her. When we were leaving, the candlelight from inside fell on Berivan. The woman made a sound that had equal measure of surprise and happiness in it.

'"Sister, I thought you had come in search of someone missing. Please have something before you go."

'From her reaction I judged that Berivan was accustomed to such displays of affection. She allowed herself to be hugged and fussed over for a little while. Then she said, "We are short of time. If you can, please give us some water."

'The woman went in looking pleased. She returned with a clay pot full of water. Berivan accepted it greedily. After taking a sip as if to taste it, she drank it till she had her fill. While we were filling our bottles, she went inside and returned holding two oranges.

'"There's nothing but these that I can give you," she mumbled remorsefully.

'"Not at all! This is more than enough. It's as if I have had a feast; my belly is full. Here, look . . ." Putting two orange carpels into her mouth, a laughing Berivan said, caressing her tummy.

Her face and laughter bore a childlike innocence. The woman's eyes welled up as she stood looking at Berivan without blinking.

'"Be safe, my child . . ."

'When we started walking again, Berivan was uncharacteristically silent. We headed in the direction pointed out by the woman. It was not difficult to locate the tailoring shop. The name Salma glistened on the red-painted name board that hung askew. The shutters lay open. Very little was left inside. From the road we could see a half-built structure beyond it.

'"We need to be quick. There'll be light very soon." Berivan's voice was edgy.

'One side of the building had taken a shell hit. The smell of rotting flesh which I had grown familiar with was present there too. We moved in only after ensuring that no one was lurking. We searched the ground floor. It was empty. As I sat down despondent, Berivan caught my hand and pulled me up. She suggested that we take a look at the upper floor too.

'Berivan tugged at a rope by the side of the stairs that had no handrail. Suddenly, sounds of something crashing could be heard from the upper floor. She jumped back in shock. I was petrified.

'After gesturing to me to stay silent, with her gun pointed up, she started to climb the stairs. Picking up a piece of wood lying there, I followed her. It was impossible to discern if anyone was hiding in the detritus of the roof that shelling had brought down in part and the building materials that lay scattered around.

'"Is there anyone here? We're not enemies." Berivan spoke loudly. Her voice echoed in the room.

'The place was bereft of people. There were only some wooden carved pillars, mostly broken, timber and cement bags. Berivan gripped and squeezed my hand hard. We looked at each other in dismay in the thinning darkness.

'As we went down, all the travails I had gone through in the past few hours weighed me down. Berivan's face was gloomy as well and showed her disappointment.

'"Shall we leave?" she asked. I nodded. Our prospects were very bleak. I followed her in silence out of the building. She stopped as we emerged from the building. She looked at me as if querying, what next?

'A low moan emanating from a space beside made us jump out of our skins. It was heard again—as if the person was in great pain. The source appeared to be in between a fallen stack of timbers in front of the building. We found a man between the planks and beams. I started to pull out the heavy beams. Berivan put down the rifle and extricated a flashlight from her bag. Shielding it so that the light won't be seen by others, she examined the body.

'"There are no wounds. His entire body is swollen. He may have suffered fractures. Have you come in search of this man?" she asked.

'That's when it dawned on me that I had no idea how Hozan looked like. I said sheepishly that I wouldn't be able to recognise him, even if I saw him.

'Berivan poured water on his face and wet his lips. She let drops of water fall on his lips. He started to run his tongue over them. The water went into him slowly. Within a few seconds, he started to murmur replies to our questions. It was Hozan. When the building was shelled and part of the roof had collapsed, it fell on him. From the first floor he fell onto the stack of timber. Another worker who was standing along with Hozan suffered grievous injuries and died after a few hours. The rest of the workers ran away. Berivan said the overwhelming stench must be from the body of the dead worker.

'Since his bag with his food and water had fallen along with him, he had been able to manage for the first two days. Starvation,

thirst, cold, pain and, above all, the dread that he may die there—
unaided and unknown—had enfeebled and shattered him.

'Berivan and I moved to the side and discussed how Hozan
could be moved from there Carrying him all that distance was
impossible. I was thinking hard when Berivan nudged. She
pointed to a pushcart, visible in the morning twilight, lying on its
side near building materials.

A child's smile displaying decayed teeth flashed in my mind.
With moist eyes, I hugged Berivan. Her eyes also held tears
in them.

'"Don't waste a moment! You must leave this instant," she
pressed me.

'How will I push this cart and go back on the road we came
through? The soldiers will stop me before I go a hundred metres.
They won't let me pass.'

She smiled. She pointed towards the west. I could see the
border of the town and light brown fields beyond that.

'"Go due west from here till where the fields begin. Then
turn south and walk through the fields. You'll reach where you
started from."

'"Arrrghh! Why did that old man send me till the banks of the
Tigris?" I held my head and cursed him.

'"He may have thought that you may lose your way," she
laughed and continued. "How could you have ever found your
way walking through the fields? He had told you to follow the
Tigris and enquire when you reach the Cizîr bridge, right?
For a stranger in these parts, there couldn't be a better route
and landmark."

'We carried Hozan as tenderly as possible till the pushcart. He
groaned with pain every step of the way. He was heavy and it took
a lot out of us to carry him. We were drenched in sweat despite
the cold. Although old, the pushcart was sturdy. We spread gunny

bags on it before loading him on to it. After we covered him with more sacks, assailed by doubt, we looked at each other.

"'I don't know how he will survive the six-to-seven-kilometre journey," my voice was full of dismay and anxiety. Berivan unzipped her bag, as if she had remembered something suddenly.

"'I've morphine with me." She took a medical kit and extracted a syringe and an ampoule. It didn't appear as if Hozan even felt the prick of the needle. "Now he won't feel the pain much," she said while zipping up her bag.

'It was time to part ways. "'How'll you go?" I was quite worried about her.

"Don't worry about me. Now I won't be able to move around till nightfall."

"Why don't you go to that woman's house?"

'She laughed when she saw my anxious solicitude. "For us this is normal. I have water with me and some chocolate bars. That's enough to keep me going till night. My team members are close by. Have no fear."

'I was reluctant to let go of her soft hand. Unable to find words to bid goodbye, I was at a loss. Her face was clearly visible in the strengthening twilight. Her wide eyes held all the warmth in the world. I stood hopelessly lost in those eyes, wallowing in their depths into which I had been dropped. For the first time in my life, I was infatuated like a callow teenager and my heart was thumping in my chest.

"'Go . . . !!!" Berivan whispered. She gently pulled her hand from my grip. With a slight nod of her head as if seeking leave, she hoisted her bag on her shoulder, picked up the gun and walked into the building.

'Slowly I pushed the cart out of the plot. Although Hozan moaned, he didn't appear to be in pain now. The rubber tyres allowed smooth passage over the paved road. When I looked back at the receding building, my head dropped in guilt for leaving her alone till it was night again, with little food and a rotting corpse for company.

'A couple of local residents passed by me. Preoccupied with their own thoughts, they didn't appear to notice me or the pushcart or the wounded man in it covered with sacks. The only one who did was an old woman dressed in rags who sat by the roadside. She stared at me.

"This is my land! How dare you despoil my land and my children?" she screamed at me, wagging her finger. The fire in her deranged eyes frightened me. Keeping my eyes on the road leading to fields at a distance, I walked, pushing the cart as fast as I could.

Narjes

Mustafa sat with his head bowed. Timur felt that Mustafa's mind was still entangled in memories of that devastated city. Timur walked up to the window and looked out. It was close to dawn. The dark intimidating sky of the night was replaced by a gentle blue one. Birds were chittering and singing. It was biting cold. A couple of Mustafa's friends were curled up and asleep in their chairs. Esat, lost in thought, sat with his stare fixed at some indeterminate point on the ceiling and was blowing smoke rings at it.

Timur was agog to find out what had happened next. To get Mustafa's attention, he manufactured a cough and asked for a cigarette from Esat.

'How long did it take you to get Hozan home?' Timur asked, unable to control his eagerness.

Mustafa spoke without lifting his head, 'It wasn't easy.' He lit another cigarette and continued his narration.

'Occasionally, I could see people hurrying on that road leading to the fields. Their faces showed their anxiety of having to be out and about in such dangerous times.

'I had piled sacks on top of Hozan to hide the fact that it was a man I was carrying in the cart. Two soldiers stood by watching the faces of everyone. Covered in soot and dirt and in a torn jacket, the soldiers only thought I was a boorish peasant pushing a cart. But the screams of the lunatic woman unconsciously made me hasten my steps.

'"Stop!" someone bawled from my rear. Flustered, I started to run, still pushing the cart. Suddenly as if a hot spike had pierced me, something went into my leg. With a howl, I went sprawling. The soldiers whose boots pounded the pavement reached me. They started to kick me from side to side to make sure I carried no hidden weapons. I was afraid the searing pain in my leg would make me faint. I bawled and caught hold of their boots pleading my innocence and begging to be let off. The pain made spittle flow out of my mouth when I howled. I must have sounded like a street dog being beaten to death.

Mustafa shuddered perhaps in memory of that pain.

'"Perhaps because I spoke unaccented Turkish, they didn't hurt me anymore. When they realized I was no militant, they abandoned me by the roadside. I was quickly losing my consciousness. The sound of the receding boots and the view of the pushcart, which lay toppled on its side, grew lesser and dimmer, and I slipped into oblivion.

'I kept drifting in and out of consciousness. And there was the agonizing pain like that of a hot skewer stuck into my leg. It was distressing my mind and body. I knew I had no escape from there. I was destined to bleed to death lying on that roadside.

'Someone shook me awake. My voice was stuck in my throat. I wanted desperately to open my eyes. I opened my mouth to talk; all that came out were unintelligible sounds. Someone stroked my head whispering, "It's okay . . . it's okay . . ."

'I blacked out again. I realized later that I was unconscious only for a short time. But, even now, the very thought of that period when I felt I was shut in a coffin, gagged and blindfolded, makes me go into a blind panic.

'Once the soldiers disappeared, some local people on the scene, who had witnessed what happened, saved us. Once Hozan realized there were people trying to help, from between the sacks he started to moan. When they realized both of us were alive, we were carried to a temporary hospital surreptitiously run by the Worker's Party somewhere between the smashed buildings.

'The people who came to our help thought I was a militant,' Mustafa smiled at me as he tapped the cigarette ash onto the floor. 'They valued the lives of the militants more than those of their own children.'

'A house that hadn't suffered much damage had been converted into a hospital. Some inmates had such horrific wounds. Some of the bodies were riddled with bullets. Others had lost their limbs to exploding shells. A girl who lay next to me had both her legs pulverized. I heard them discussing frantically how to get her to a bigger, better hospital.

'When I looked at those eyes, over which death had spread its pall, I was reminded of Berivan.

'I didn't think the girl next to me was able to see anyone. Yet, her glassy eyes seemed to be moving all the time. She was gasping for air like a beached fish. Her body was pale from severe loss of blood. The bottom of her dark olive uniform, from waist down, was soaked in blood. I could see that her stretched outright arm, slim like a schoolgirl's, was not a weak shade of pink; the deathly pallor of the translucent, wilted skin scared me. I thought she would die any moment. I wished to hold that shivering hand and infuse into her whatever little life was left in me.

'Only a youngish looking doctor and helper were present. Possibly in the hope that additional help would reach soon, they were doing their best for the girl. In the meanwhile, an elderly woman bearing a basin of hot water and clean towels entered. Though she showed an initial shock at the sight of blood-drenched girl, she quickly recovered. She kept the basin, et cetera on a table and walked towards the girl's bed. Her lips were moving as if chanting a prayer.

'She caressed the girl's forehead with the tenderness of touching a flower. Suddenly the girl's glassed over eyes looked agitated; as if electrocuted by the hand on her forehead, her body convulsed once.

'"God bless you," the woman said in a kindly voice.'

Mustafa struggled to describe the scene. He took a sip of water and continued.

'The girl died after some time. I lay on a mat next to her corpse. Her wax-like lips were slightly parted. I have been unable to sleep peacefully after that day. Even now, the pale-faced girl with her melancholy demeanour and ill-fitting olive-green fatigues appear whenever I am falling asleep.'

Mustafa covered his face with his hands. Timur thought he was weeping. He seemed to wake up with a start and restarted his narration.

'Unable to withstand the smell of stale blood that lingered in that room, I vomited many times. They had given me a painkiller shot. I can recall them tending to Hozan's badly damaged body. Although the young doctor and helper kept requesting everyone not to cry out, while his broken bones were being set, and strapped, Hozan kept howling in pain.

'With whatever instruments they had, they managed to extricate the bullet in my leg. I bit down on my forearm to keep myself from screaming. When they were pulling out the bullet through my flesh and tissues, I blacked out with the pain again.

'When I came to, the first thing I saw was the anxiety-filled, wide eyes of Hozan staring at me. The girl's corpse had been moved out. I didn't have the courage to ask them where they had moved it to.'

Mustafa let out a deep, sad sigh.

'I knew staying there would be inconvenient to those people. I told the helper that we would leave the make-shift hospital immediately. He came and sat near me. He was solicitous; asked me where we would go and what we were planning to do. I explained to him how I landed up there briefly. Unable to withstand my insistence, the fellow helped me up. The pain from the wound didn't allow me to put weight on my leg. Every step I took elicited a groan from me.

'"You won't get far on this leg," he told me matter-of-factly.

'I decided that I would get out of the town even if I had to drag my foot or even crawl. When I sat pondering over what should be done, I saw the pushcart parked outside.

'"How did this reach here?" I asked the young man in surprise. At that moment I knew I would succeed in my experiment.

'"You were brought here in that," the fellow told me. I requested him to help me load Hozan onto the pushcart. The fellow gave me an incredulous stare.

'"Man . . . you can't even walk. If you try to walk, the stitches will come off with the first few steps. How are you then planning to push this pushcart six or seven kilometres bearing Hozan's weight? Don't even think about it!" He was rather cross. I didn't reply. Resting his head on his hand, he seemed to be thinking.

'"This part of the town doesn't have a high presence of soldiers. They are many houses abandoned by people who have fled in fear. Why don't you stay in one of them for a few days and then leave? I will bring you some food and water," the woman who had come with the water earlier said. She had been listening in on our conversation.

'I didn't have the luxury of time. The tear-stained faces of Hakar, Sarya, Hozan and their sweets-craving children would not leave me in peace. I shook my head in defiance.

'When it was clear that I wouldn't be dissuaded, the fellow called the doctor for help. They loaded Hozan onto the pushcart without much strain.

'"I have no painkillers to give you. There's very little stock in our medicine cabinet." The doctor expressed his helplessness in faultless English. He was a foreigner. I tried to guess his nationality looking at his golden blond hair and hazel-coloured eyes.

'"You are lucky. The wound is not deep, and the bullet missed your nerves. If it weren't so, you wouldn't be able to even keep your foot down," the helper informed me.

'From the cabinet, he had handed over to me three old sheets that smelt clean. When I limped towards the pushcart, I looked back. Those youngsters stood there looking at me without blinking. I could see the faded but colourful scarf of the woman behind them.

'After covering Hozan fully in a way it wouldn't look that a human was underneath, I started to push the cart putting as less weight as possible on my wounded leg.

'"If you go a hundred metres on that lane and turn left, after another five hundred metres you will hit the main road," the helper shouted after me. A few steps and I broke out in a heavy sweat, unable to bear the pain. I decided that once I was on the macadam road, less effort would be needed to push the cart.

'I could hear people running through the lane. I moved to the side giving them as much space as possible. A group went by, carrying a bleeding person. They were sweating profusely and panting even in that cold, indicating that they had run a long way. I stole a glance at the body on the stretcher. I could see no sign of life in that still form except for the spreading blotch of blood on the uniform from some wound below the chest.

'The doctor who had come to the door to bid me goodbye jumped out into the yard and shouted instructions to the others inside. I decided that I couldn't waste any time and started to push the cart again. A shriek from behind from someone in terrible pain startled me. When I recovered from the shock, the thought that struck me was—at least the man is still alive!

'The effort of pushing the cart, relying on one leg and the occasional shooting pain from the other made me groan and hiss at every step. When I swore to alleviate the pain, a concerned Hozan lifted his head to look at me.

'"Keep your head down!" I spoke through my clenched teeth. My eyes stung—I thought scalding vapours were coming out of them. Taking another step felt impossible. I placed the handle of the pushcart on a parapet wall to make sure Hozan's body wouldn't slip off and, completely knackered, sat down on the steps nearby. The wound was throbbing, threatening to explode any moment. Possibly afraid of getting another scolding, Hozan lay unmoving inside the cart. Gazing at the flower designs of the carefully carelessly heaped sheets on the pushcart, I wondered what my next move should be.

'Someone touched my shoulder gently. I looked up. It was the woman from the hospital. Keeping down a large vessel she had been holding, she embraced me, letting my febrile head rest on her chest. I broke down, and crying loudly, embraced her too. Stroking my head as I sobbed like a small child, she waited patiently for my grief to lessen.

'"That's enough," she said with compassion.

'I stopped crying and sheepishly, blowing my nose, I looked at the pushcart. A baffled Hozan, who had been observing the scene, withdrew his head into and under the sheets like a tortoise into its shell.

'"Now, do what I tell you," she said in a low but peremptory tone. "You too get into that pushcart under the sheets. Let me try pushing it for some time now."

'"Hey, no!" I replied without a second thought. I couldn't imagine a woman pushing two men in a pushcart.

'"Look here, I gave birth to seven boys like you and brought them up. Get in there and lie low!"

'This time her voice was not amiable. Trying to avoid the commanding look on her face, I tried to get into the pushcart dragging my throbbing leg. I had my doubts if it had enough room for two adults.

'"There's no room," I declared, in my eagerness to avoid the ignominy.

'"Come and hold one end of this sheet!"

'Pulling the sheet, Hozan was lying on, we carefully moved him to one edge of the cart. I climbed onto the space that was left. Being left with no option but to obey her enervated me further.

'Our bodies were knocking against each other. Hozan's eyes reflected his fear and hopelessness. It was as if he felt we'd never make it out of there. Not wanting to hurt him by touching his bruised body, I tried to shrink myself to one side of the cart.

'"Don't trouble yourself, we've enough room here," Hozan spoke in hushed tones. I could see that he too was mortified that our combined weights had to be hauled by a lone woman. Stout and stocky, with a swaying gait, the woman was very strong. She lifted the heavy wooden handle of the cart with ease. I was afraid that if she lost control, the cart would tip and Hozan would slide out. With a grunt and some effort, she brought the cart under her control and started to push it on to the road. After the initial struggle, she quickly got the hang of it and the cart started to roll smoothly needing little effort from her side.

'"Take the sheet and cover yourself well," she chided us in a low tone, while placing the large vessel on the sheets covering us. Watching her wonder-eyed, I quickly crawled under the sheets and hid myself.

'Hozan seemed to be running a very high temperature; his body was radiating the heat. Even the small bumps on the road caused him pain. Every small jerk elicited a feeble moan through his clenched teeth.

"'Hang on for some more time. Bear up a little more," she said in between her own panting. Her laboured breathing caused me grave concern. Although I could see nothing around us, I could feel that the cart had reached the macadam road.

"Granny," someone called out. "Is Bijar at home?"

'Our cart slowed down and stopped.

"'Why are you alone at this time?" The woman's voice was stern.

"'I'm bored sitting at home. I thought if Bijar is there I could play with him for some time."

"It's good thing that you're here. I am exhausted. Help me push this."

'With one more person to push the cart, our progress was faster and smoother.

"'This is so heavy! What are you hauling, Bijar's granny?"

Suddenly, there an explosion close by.

"'All that I'll tell you later. Stop wasting time talking and push this a little harder."

'After a little while, they turned into some place and stopped the cart. I lifted my head and tried to look. It appeared to be some sort of garage. It was dark, damp and narrow. Things were lying around in small heaps.

'After she pulled down the rolling shutter, the woman switched on the light. A sooty bulb reluctantly gave out a weak yellowish light. She came to us and sat on her knees. I was seeing her face clearly for the first time. She was past sixty years. I peered at the ruddy, sweaty face overrun by wrinkles.

"'What are you looking at?" she smiled and asked. "Tell me where you want to go."

"'I won't let you do this," remonstrating, I tried to scramble up.

'She pushed me back on to the cart.

"'Who told you that I was taking you there?" She smiled displaying her yellow teeth.

'The child who had helped to push the cart stood by with a look of astonishment. To put him at ease, I smiled at him.

"'Is that you, granny?" there was a query from inside the building.

"'Bijar, come here. See who's here." She called to someone affectionately.

'An eleven- or twelve-year-old boy came running, with a ball in hand. Although he whistled at the sight of his friend, he pulled up short when he saw the pushcart, bundle of clothes and two heads sticking out of it. He hid himself behind the woman and peered at us from there.

"'Don't be afraid, they're your father's friends," she said, pulling him from behind her to the front.

"'Father's friends? I've never seen them before!" He was suspicious. She wilfully ignored his misgiving look.

"'Go and fetch Bayan and Adar. I've some work for them." As he hesitated, she tried to bribe him, "I'll make delicious baklava for you." That must have been enticing enough, I should think. He fell for it. After looking at both of us once more suspiciously he called his bewildered friend and took him inside.

"'My grandson," the woman said with obvious pride.

"'What's your name?" I asked reluctantly.

"'Narjes." Then she sang in her sweet voice:

The white, tender Narcissus flower,
That hooked my heart.

'Bijar and his friend came in with two more children. They appeared to be twins. Bayan and Adar whooped when they saw the guests and the droll vehicle that granny had brought in.

'Narjes pressed her hands over their mouths. "Don't you know that you shouldn't make noise?"

Bijar boxed the ear of one of them. "Stop, this's not the time to fight!" Narjes growled.

"'Get the hay bundles from the barn," Narjes instructed. The children raced to carry out the mission. Since it was clear that protest was useless, I explained to her where we had to go. She reflected a little and said she knew the place. Some of her relatives lived there.

'With a stick, she poked and struck the damp, hay bundles that smelt of cow dung which the children had brought in and deposited on the floor to make sure there were no reptiles inside. She tested the strength of the coils of ropes that hung from wall hooks on the smoked-licked dark walls of the garage—part of her hurried preparations for the trip. After that, with the affectionate authority that only mothers have, she inspected our wounds again. To dampen the bumps on the way, she carefully stuffed pieces of old clothes at different places beneath Hozan's body. The apples and water bottles that Bijar had brought from the kitchen were put into small bags and hung on the shoulders of Bayan and Adar.

'A young woman appeared at the door and helped the two boys into their jackets. She said, "There's a lot of trouble outside." She didn't seem to be very pleased about Narjes setting out on an adventure like this and involving the children, too.

"'What if such a thing happens to your husband?" Narjes demanded crossly. "It's been one month since we've had some news from him. Even if we pray the whole day, Allah will not show any mercy on us. For that we need to do good deeds."

'I could see the young woman biting down the sobs rising within her. After inspecting the children's shoes and clothes, the woman went up to her. "Look at me, I'm their grandmother. If anyone has to touch them, it will be over my dead body."

'The young woman hugged her and wept.

'"Don't worry. We have to save these young men's lives. Or else God will not forgive us." She consoled the young woman and did the last bit of preparations for our journey.

'"Drink up enough water," said Narjes, holding the bottle to Hozan's lips and helping him drink. "After this, you can get water only after you reach your home."

'I also drank as much water I could hold and lay down peacefully. The new-found hope and sense of security had quietened down Hozan. It seemed to have alleviated his pain too.

'Narjes was busy arranging the hay on top of us. Although her eyes still held tears, the young woman helped Narjes to do it neatly. She sent Bayan and Adar, who were guffawing at their granny's doings, to have food. She instructed them to eat well.

'"Our stock of flour is almost over," the woman said with a sigh, as if to no one in particular, as she arranged the hay.

'"Don't worry. All that will come. Never fear. Never lose hope either. Always remember the most powerful weapon is your mind. Learn to keep it in control." Narjes' voice was firm.

'After ensuring that we had enough room to breathe, they tied the hay down to the cart. We started almost immediately after that. To any onlooker the group would have appeared to comprise a grandmother and her grandchildren transporting some hay for cattle. Narjes also found time to stop the cart in between and exchange pleasantries with acquaintances she ran into.

'The children were happy to do the pushing and pulling. It appeared that this journey came as a great relief to them from the tedium of the past few days and the fear of death hanging over them. They even found enough cheer to sing a small ditty as they pushed the cart.

'Narjes, at every given opportunity, told her interlocutors that she was taking two days' hay supplies for Laila's starving cows, whoever that Laila was. When two of Bijar's friends joined the group, the pace picked up with more hands on the wheel.

'After some distance, the sounds of an approaching vehicle could be heard. The chattering of the children and Narjes's conversation stopped as if turned off by a switch. I shut my eyes and prayed that it shouldn't be a military vehicle. Hozan reached out and grabbed my hand. I could see that he was also scared. I frantically searched for the gaps between the hay for us to breathe. We may not again be able to enjoy the sunlight trying to peep through the hay and the light breeze that bore the smells of damp hay and dried grass. If found, we would be burnt alive using the same hay.

'From its sounds I felt it was a military truck. As I had expected, the vehicle stopped when it reached us. Hozan's damp hand tightened its grip on mine. I was afraid that fear and stress may make him bawl out aloud.

'"Where are you terrorist runts going with this whore?" someone with a heavy voice demanded. It was followed by raucous laughter of a group of men.

'"The cattle are starving, boss," Narjes said with utmost respect. Along with the vilest of abuses, there was a sound of a slap. I could sense Hozan trembling uncontrollably. The wailing of the children filled the place.

'"Fucking cattle of hers! Nobody should forget that there are basements still in Cizîr waiting to be filled!" someone growled above us menacingly.

'"Ahmet, don't you remember what the colonel said? This is enough, come, let's go . . ." someone shouted above the hum of the engine.

'We lay beneath the hay, helpless and impotent, listening to the receding sounds of the truck.

"Granny, get up . . ."

"Help, there's blood, someone help . . ." the children started to wail.

"'Shut up! Nothing's happened to me!"

'We heard Narjes's tired voice amid the children's ruckus.

"'I was hit on the head with the rifle butt. It's a small wound. Allah saved me." Narjes said loudly so that we could hear her.

'There was a suppressed sob close to my ear. Hozan was crying. My eyes too stung. We could hear the fuss made by Bijar, the most sensible among the children, as he examined his grandmother's wound and her own protestations. After a little while, the cart started to roll again.

'Soon we reached the fields, leaving behind the sounds of gunfire and explosions that were raking the town.

"'The next part of the journey won't be so easy, children," Narjes said more to herself than to the others.

'That proved to be true. It was a dirt track used by tractors, other farm vehicles and farm animals. The itching from the hay and dust was causing me allergies; I wanted to sneeze. The jolts from the potholes and bumps on the track were causing Hozan considerable pain. His moans started again.

"Be careful, children," Narjes begged of the children. The boys who had joined in between were of Bijar's age. I assumed that Hozan's moans would have tipped them off, because they asked the playful Bayan and Adar to move out and started to move the cart with care. Though the speed dropped off, they avoided potholes and stones and made the journey less bone-jarring.

'To distract my mind from the overwhelming feeling of dread, I tried to recognize the smells and sounds of the places we were passing through. We passed fields that had been tilled recently, with its cow dung-manured soil waiting for sowing of the seeds. In between, smells of burnt leaves, possibly to keep away the cold, and wood sap could be discerned. The barking of a dog, possibly some farmer's, was heard and it was shouted down by a stentorian voice. I wished to fling away the hay that was pressing down on us and to take in a lungful of pure air. The journey seemed interminable.

'Narjes and her minions stopped in between to take rest. After drinking water and sharing apples, the procession resumed making stately progress. Despite the extra care taken by the children, Hozan's condition was worsening. By now, his broken body could have been hurt by a feather falling on it.

'When his moans and whimpers became continuous, the children fell completely silent. Although Narjes started a harvest song to keep their spirits up, she too gave up soon. Even the normally chatty Bayan and Adar stopped their babble. The only sound that could be heard was of low-flying aircraft. Since I had no doubts that they wouldn't hesitate to drop a bomb or two on an old woman and some children transporting hay on a push cart, every time a plane passed above, my heart skipped a few beats.

'It was getting to be noon. Although it was winter, the sun was warm. It started to get extremely stuffy under the hay. I thought I might get roasted in there.

'"It's not far now, sons. Be patient," Narjes's tired voice said, seemingly close to my ear. After ten minutes, Narjes whispered, as if telling me a secret, "Is there a green, massive car standing in front of the house?" I thought I would faint from happiness. That was Arman's father's car, the one the children and I had pushed into Sarya's yard.

'"Yes! That's the one!" I said loudly. Hozan was lying motionless. I thought he had fainted. His hand on my arm was still warm. That told me he was still alive.

'Narjes and the kids found it hard to push the cart into Sarya's yard. "Dayê," I heard one of Sarya's daughters call out. Keeping the cart handle supported in some place to keep it on an even keel, Bijar and his friends started to boast about their strength and speed. I could hear someone hurrying towards us.

'"We don't need hay," it was Sarya. My heart leapt with joy.

'"It doesn't matter, my child. Just show us the way to your barn. This cart holds some things that you like." I could sense she was laughing up her sleeve when she said that.

'The cart started to move again. I was surprised that she didn't ask more questions. Bijar and his friends were giggling, obviously thinking of the fun they would have when it was all revealed to Sarya. The presence of a group of strangers trooping in made the surprised cows low loudly.

'The weight of the hay was lifted off our chests. The sneezes I had been controlling started in full force.

'"Hozan!" Sarya started to cry loudly.

'"Shhh . . . don't make noise!" Narjes commanded in her peremptory tone. "There are spies everywhere."

'Sobbing, Sarya examined Hozan's damaged body. He was unconscious. Seeing his state, his children too had started to weep.

"Look here, you have to take them to the hospital. Instead wasting time crying, find ways to do that." Narjes, took a small piece of cloth and started dusting me to get rid of soil and specks of hay. I tried to get up. My leg had gone numb. Sarya noticed me only then. She broke down once more and folded her hands in worshipful gratitude.

'"This is not the time for all that, Sarya." I turned away my face in embarrassment. I was not accustomed to such show of gratitude.

'"What is to be done now?" Sarya wondered with a frown on her comely face.

"'Is there someone who can drive this car?" Narjes asked. Sarya gave a start and turned to her daughter. "Baby, go fetch bapîr Abdullah." Within seconds, her eldest two daughters crawled under the fence at the rear of the house and disappeared.

"'He's our neighbour. He can drive."

'Sarya turned her attention back to Hozan. She tried to drip water into his mouth in between his cracked lips. I took the clay pot and poured all the water in it into my mouth. The coolness embraced my mind and body, removing the trepidation and distress I had undergone till then.

'When some of that water fell on Hozan, he groaned slightly. Still weeping silently, Sarya wiped his face and neck with a damp cloth. Displaying her decayed teeth, her youngest daughter smiled at me, hanging onto her mother's dress.

'Moments later, the sounds of her eldest daughters could be heard. An old man followed them, lifting the fence's cables and walking underneath them. He was shocked by the sight before him.

"'What's this Sarya? Why didn't you let me know all this?" He sounded rather cross.

"Pîrê, we can discuss all that later. Can you drive that car?" Narjes intervened.

'He went to the car. I sent the key to him through Sarya's daughter. He started the car and drove it up close to the barn. It was not easy to get Hozan into the car. The women and children held various points of sheet he was lying on and managed to carry him like a bundle into the back seat. Although semi-conscious, the pain must have been excruciating; he screamed in protest. On hearing his cries, Sarya and her children started to wail again. I hopped and skipped and somehow managed to haul myself into the front seat.

"'If the police stop you, what will you do?" Narjes asked.

'"Ah, you didn't recognize me, did you? I am a Turk! No policeman is going to stop me." He sounded peeved.

'I looked back as the car slowly left the yard. Narjes, with blood clotted on her head wound, stood holding up Sarya who seemed to have fainted. The children stood around with sorrowful faces. From now on, Narjes would take care of them. You shouldn't think of or worry about anything! Anything at all. I cautioned my recalcitrant mind.

'Don't think about the explosions in the distance; about Berivan waiting for nightfall in that half-built house with only a rotting corpse for company; about Hakar and his wife waiting for their darling son who had been brutalized before their own eyes and hauled off. DO NOT THINK!

'I kept my eyes closed and didn't even try to find out where we were being taken.'

Abdullah

"That's my name, Abdullah Bölükbaşı!" The old man refused to drop his eyes as the policeman kept staring at him. "If you have any doubts, here's my *kimlik kartı*,"[1] he pulled it out from his pocket.

"'It's okay sir, you may go," the policeman took a step back as if allowing free passage. "There's an order from the top that all cars should be checked. That's why . . ." He was apologetic.

'When he returned to the driving seat, I looked at him suspiciously. "How do they know you?" I couldn't control my curiosity.

"He would have heard my name. I was in the police."

'I felt as if someone had taken my breath away. He was ex-policeman. And a Turk to boot! Could Sarya have been so stupid?

'As if he could read my mind, he said, "Don't worry. I'm not going to cause you any trouble. Sarya is like a daughter to me."

'Embarrassment didn't allow me to look at him; I kept looking out of the window. The car eventually entered a hospital premises. It was a small one with bare minimum facilities. It was full of patients. The sight of blood-drenched clothes, burnt torsos and dismembered bodies numbed me. Although everyone there was busy, after a little while, Hozan was carried off on a stretcher.

"'How about your leg?" the old man asked me, deeply concerned. He looked at the swollen limb and the dirty bandage with a troubled mind.

"'Don't worry. Let someone be free. I'll see the doctor." I consoled him.

'In reality, the pain was killing me. When I felt that I may not be able to bear it anymore, I joined the long queue of patients. Throwing away the cigarette he had been smoking, Abdullah stopped a nurse who was hurrying past. "Look at that leg. Allow him to meet the doctor."

"'Pîrê, everyone here's in the same boat. Hustling doesn't help!" She showed her anger.

"'He's been shot, child. Please help," Abdullah's voice turned meek.

'The nurse looked at me. My look, as if I'd collapse any moment, and the horrific state of the wounded leg seemed to have shaken her. She kept the tray in her hand on the stretcher next to her, held my shoulder and helped me walk. Abdullah quickly joined on the other side and propped me up. She made me lie down on the bench in the nurses' station and examined my wound.

"'Don't worry, I'll fetch the doctor soon," she said kindly.

'Abdullah waited at the door, watching me. He was around seventy years old. His hair was completely white, skin wrinkled and frame thin and lanky with a concave spine. What could he have done that even the present-generation policemen recall his name? I turned away so that he wouldn't notice that I was watching him.

'Nurses' uniforms were hanging in the room. There was a table with a pot of water and three or four other benches. Unable to suffer the worsening pain, I tried to keep my leg up on one of them. It was like a log. I was unable to lift it even with both my hands. Impotent, I started to curse through my clenched teeth.

'Abdullah came towards me. He sat down on one end of the bench and stroked my shoulder. There was no option but to suffer the pain till the doctor arrived. I leaned my head, damp with sweat, against the wall and bit down on my pain.

'The doctor took another half hour. Youth and the enthusiastic earnestness of a newly-passed out doctor were evident in him.

'"My apologies. We don't have enough doctors here," he said and started examining my leg.

'"There are chances of it getting infected. You should take the medicines on time. You should not move your leg. Can you do that?" He looked at me unconvinced.

'Abdullah interjected, "I'll take care, doctor. Please prescribe the medicines."

'The doctor cleaned the wound and dressed it. Gradually, an injection on my buttock made the pain bearable.

'"We have no place here. That's the only reason why we are letting you go. If there are no other complications, come back in a week," the doctor told us while prescribing the medicines.

'"Doctor, we had brought in another patient—Hozan. What's his condition?" Abdullah asked anxiously.

'"Hozan?" The doctor tried to place him.

'"A young man with broken bones all over his body. He may be around thirty or thirty-two years old."

'"Ah, yes! I got it. He can't be taken away now. He may have to be here for some days. He has three fractures. Contusions and wounds on top of that."

'"After dropping him home, I shall come back with things for Hozan."

'The doctor nodded sympathetically at Abdullah. We walked out slowly. "What were you in the police?" Abdullah looked at me keenly. Although I hesitated a little, I ploughed on. "I need your help."

'"This isn't enough? You need more?" His tone was mocking.

'"Yes," I said firmly.

'Abdullah looked quizzically at me. After helping me into the car, making me comfortable and getting into the driver's seat, he said, "First we need to find a medical store. Let me know what help you need. Don't forget that I am now old."

'I narrated the story of Hakar. After listening to it, he was lost in thought as we drove. We located a medical store. He left me in the car and went to buy the medicines. Each packet came with hand-written instructions on its carton.

'"Drink lots of water and take rest." He was driving towards Cizîr. "You stay in Sarya's house. She will look after as if you were a king."

'"I know that," I muttered, not very pleased. I had an impression that he would not help me.

'"I know Hakar. I've seen his son a few times. Never thought he'd get into trouble," he said, as if replying to the questions inside me. "I make no promises. Since I am not in service, there are limits on what I can do. I still know people in the force. Let me try."

'That was all that I needed.

'After dropping me off at Sarya's home, Abdullah went back to hospital with the essentials for Hozan.

'"Sarya, who's he?" I asked her.

'"Our neighbour. Lives alone; he's a widower."

'"Do you know what he was?" Sarya looked at me in surprise.

'"I don't know. He was already here before us. Once he fell sick and nearly died. I nursed him back to health."

'I realized it was no use probing her. I had no other choice than wait for Abdullah's return. Sarya informed me that Narjes and her kids had gone back. The pushcart that had saved our lives was standing in the yard. It had become Sarya's children's toy.

'Abdullah turned up again after two days. After giving Hozan's clothes for washing to Sarya, he turned to me. "I had enquired about what you had told me."

Anxious to hear the news, I sat up in my bed. "Lie down!" he smiled. "Hakar's son is in police custody. I've told the people concerned not to file charges against him."

"'He had suffered a lot of injuries. Possibly fractured bones too," I said with trepidation.

"'Don't worry. He has received medical attention," Abdullah said, trying to console me.

"'Let me go till Hakar's house. I must inform them." I found it hard to abide.

"'No. You should take rest. As soon as I had information on his son, I called on Hakar."

'I peered at him. "Who are you?" I asked him again.

"'An old policeman!" he whispered as if it was a secret. The mischievous laughter in his eyes rendered me speechless. After accepting washed clothes from Sarya, Abdullah left from there.

"'Do you know Hakar?" I asked Sarya who came in bearing a bowl of soup.

"'Hakar bapîr gives us raisins always." Sarya's daughter thrust her head out from behind her mother.

"'I know him; his house is not far from here. How do you know him?" Sarya was curious.

"'I met him once. Can you go till his house? Both of them are not keeping well."

'Sarya nodded agreeably. After serving me lunch, with a basket of eggs in hand and her youngest daughter clinging to her skirt, Sarya set out for Hakar's house. She instructed her three children playing in the yard to keep an eye on me. When they started to come every five minutes to me asking, "Uncle, do you need anything", I had to scold them and tell them to scram.

'I had been shifted inside the house. I lay in royal repose, using Hozan's blanket that had been promised to me earlier. In addition to three square meals a day, I was plied with boiled eggs, soups and savouries in between mealtimes. Her hospitality overwhelmed me so much so that I wanted to run away from there. I had only two days' medicines left. I decided that after a visit to the doctor, I would leave the place.

'I was woken from my reverie by voices talking in hushed tones.

'"Son!" Hakar entered the room and hugged me. His tears dampened my shirt.

"What has happened? Did you get any information about your son?" I was anxious.

'Hakar lifted his head from my shoulder and looked at me.

'"He's back home!"

'"What? He's home?" I was flabbergasted.

'"Yes, didn't you know?"

'"No!" My mouth hung open. I recalled the impish smile in Abdullah's eyes.

'"They left him at our door. He has fractures and contusions. They have beaten him brutally. They didn't kill him. Son, I know it was you who rescued him!" Hakar said with marked relief.

'"No, it wasn't me!" I protested vehemently.

'"Two boys who had shouted slogans along with him have been beaten to death. No one knows where the others are, in which jail or even alive. Mustafa, I know it's only your goodness that's making you deny your role in this. You did indeed save him."

'I was in a dilemma. For some reason I had the feeling that it wouldn't be prudent to reveal Abdullah's name. I had realized by then that he was staying in that place without revealing to others his true identity, whatever it was.

'"He's in the hospital. My wife is stuck to his side. Sarya reached just when I had come home to pick up some things. Son . . . It is you . . . It's because of you! God will bless you!"

'I had no option but endure a gushing Hakar who seemed to believe that I had waved some magic wand to spring his son from gaol.

'"Did you spring his son from the jail?" Sarya asked me when Hakar had left. I remained silent, unable to decide how to respond.

'"They have nobody. You have done a noble deed. Allah will keep you!" She raised her hands to the heavens in supplication for blessings to be showered on me. Her eyes were moist. I was bemused. Their deification was unbearable. My heart ached to return to Sur at the earliest, to unburden myself of all the fraught happenings of the last few days and to drink myself silly.

'It took me another week to return to Sur,' Mustafa was winding up his tale. 'Everyone believed that Arman was killed in action. Since I believed that was better for the safety of the family, I didn't tell even Dewran the truth.'

'We all insisted that Dewran accompany Gul to her place of study. He got a visa as a cook in a restaurant to prepare Turkish dishes. There was no other way. If he had stayed back, the police would have taken him way. His mother couldn't have survived another tragedy, devastated as she was by the first,' said Esat, who had been listening to everything all the while.

'What can be done now?' Timur asked desolately.

'We'll have to search for Seetha. Find her. Gul and Dewran should be with Arman. They will not let us get close,' Mustafa spoke, while carefully rolling a cigarette.

Outside, birds chirped and warbled non-stop. Timur imagined that, since it was winter, grains were hard to come by for the birds. Suddenly he recalled one loose end.

'Were you able to find out who Abdullah really was?'

Mustafa laughed sardonically. 'He was a member of the Millî İstihbarat Teşkilâtı.[2] Perhaps you know it better as MİT. One of the agents who had captured Öcalan on his way to Nairobi airport and exfiltrated him. A trusted one who, when ordered to capture someone, would turn up with his corpse.'

'What made him change?' Timur found it incredible.

'Age brings wisdom in people?' Akbar chortled from one corner of the room. 'Timur, what's your next step?' he asked.

Timur was staring out through the window with dead eyes. He had no idea what was to be done next.

'The inside information we have is that she's not in police custody. That's not entirely credible.' Akbar seemed to be lost in thought.

'Let's try to tap bus and taxi drivers as discussed yesterday,' Mustafa suggested.

'What if she has been picked by Arman or Dewran?' a suddenly sanguine Timur asked.

'We can't discount that possibility.' Akbar yawned. He shifted his position and snuggled up on the chair.

'You can't be so indolent. We can't take rest till we find out what's happened to her,' said Mustafa, angered by Akbar's lassitude.

He turned towards Timur, 'You should leave today. The police must know who accompanied Seetha. The name and address in the hotel register is yours, right? If you get into their hands, don't dream of being able to lead a healthy life for the rest of it.'

'How can I leave without getting some information about Seetha?' Timur looked at Mustafa. He fancied that if he requested enough, he may be allowed to continue there.

'Are you an imbecile, Timur, or is it because you really don't realize the severity of the situation? This is a country that sentences people to a minimum forty years' jail term for the "crime" of participating in a demonstration.'

'Ah, no! That's all misinformation. I have also heard such malicious propaganda.'

'Misinformation!!' The house resounded with laughter.

'You are an impossible cretin, aren't you?' someone shouted amidst the raucous laughter.

'You blockhead . . . this Akbar's brother, when he was twenty-one years old, he was jailed by your police for participating in a protest march. It's now been twenty years. It'll take another twenty years for him to be released.'

Timur looked at Akbar. He was stone-faced without even a hint of smile.

'How's that even possible?' Timur stammered.

'That's how a fascist government works. Sow the seeds of fear to nip in the bud voices that may be raised against them.'

The laughter had died down.

'Do you now believe that what happened in Sur is only malicious propaganda?' Mustafa asked.

'No!' Timur's head stayed bowed.

'Even though a citizen of this country, you had no idea of all this, did you? Our rulers have this special skill of keeping everything under wraps.'

Silence reigned in the room.

'Shall we take a look at the bus terminal?' Mustafa asked.

Some of them were to interview taxi drivers; others, bus drivers. They also accepted Timur's suggestion that refugees sleeping on the storefronts near the hotel should be asked if they had witnessed anything out of the ordinary.

Once the course of action was decided, things happened quickly. Akbar made another pot of tea and placed it on the table.

After the morning constitutionals, and a glass of tea each, they left one by one.

After shifting the wooden plank, Akbar managed to lock up the door, ran after the others and caught up with them. They split up in small groups and went in different directions.

Timur was with Akbar, and they headed to the bus terminal. Their hopes of getting some lead were not mislaid. The man they had met the previous night was talking to a group of workers in front of the parked buses. He hurried towards them upon seeing Timur.

'I was going to call you,' he said, looking flustered. 'Last night, a girl had taken a bus from here to Silvan. Although she was covered up completely, from her accent when she asked for the ticket, this guy here could figure out that she was a foreigner.'

A short-statured adolescent came forward. He was sweating even in that cold.

'She got down at the last stop. I don't know anything more than that.'

'Will you be able to recognize her, if you see her again?' Akbar asked in a rough tone.

'If you scare him like this, he will clam up,' Timur whispered in his ear.

He showed the boy Seetha's photo he had in his phone.

'Since she had wrapped her face with an orange shawl, I can't be sure,' the boy expressed his helplessness.

'Orange? Are you sure that the colour was orange?' Timur asked, excited.

'Yes, I remember. Such patterns are not seen on local clothes. A design with orange background and green and blue mangoes and flowers scattered on it.'

Timur looked at Akbar. 'Definitely it is Seetha. She had that shawl around her neck all of yesterday.'

They thanked the boy and the supervisor and started to walk back. 'I can't understand why she had to go to Silvan.' Timur started to ponder.

'Well, well . . . you didn't get it, did you? Silvan is the last bus terminal before Dewran's village, Çîçika.'

'Çîçika? Why should she go there?' Timur wondered aloud. 'For sure, he couldn't be there!'

'We can't predict how women think. But what I wonder is how she would have travelled from Silvan to Çîçika!' Akbar's surprise was apparent. 'Çîçika must be about twenty-five kilometres from Silvan. There's no bus service. There's only an unpaved road through the hills. Even a driver familiar with the terrain will take over an hour for the trip.'

'Oh! What could she have done alone in the night and that too with no knowledge of the local language? Could she have gotten into some problem?'

In despair, Timur sat down on a barrel he saw nearby.

'You shouldn't slump down so quickly. Either there was someone there to help her, or she could have engaged a taxi. Come, let's find out.'

'Do you have Dewran's parents' telephone number?' Timur asked, refusing to perk up.

'Mustafa should have. But after Arman's disappearance, it's as if they have cut all ties with the world.'

Holding his throbbing head in both hands, Timur wondered what the next move should be. He realized that he had not slept a wink the previous night.

He felt a hand on his shoulder. 'Are you Timur Kemal Özdemir?'

Timur turned and looked. Police! Armoured vehicles were parked by the side.

'Yes.'

The guns in the policemen's hands, till then held lazily, were now pointed at him threateningly. Timur felt fear would make him faint.

'We have some questions for you. Please come with us.'

Where was Akbar? Timur looked around. There was no sign of Akbar.

The street pedlars and their customers around them acted as if they had not noticed what was happening. Only the children with their golden bread bangles looked on sympathetically, too scared to approach.

With firm hands on his shoulders, the policemen led him to the armoured cars.

'Seetha, I could do nothing for you.' Timur broke into tears.

The stony-faced policemen around him betrayed no emotion. Instead of taking the turn for the Sur police station, the vehicles turned towards the highway and sped away.

Dewran

'This is the house,' the eldest among the urchins called out to Dadwar when they reached a curved door overhung by grapevines.

One of the children started to bang on the door and shout.

'These children will scare people,' Dadwar hurried out of the car as the noise level increased.

In the meanwhile, the door had been opened. An old man with greying hair and a calm look emerged from inside. His face showed surprise when he saw the gang of urchins led by a donkey foal.

Dadwar quickly went up to him. Seetha could see him talking nineteen to the dozen, pointing towards the car and its passenger. After listening, with no marked change of expression, the man called to someone inside the house, 'Aireen . . .'

Adjusting her scarf, an elderly woman came out. She was rubbing her eyes to be rid of her sleepiness.

He took her aside and spoke. While listening to him, she was also repeatedly looking at the car with apparent curiosity. Seetha could see that her face reflected happiness and she was smiling.

'They know about you,' Dadwar told Seetha.

Aireen came towards her. 'This is Dewran's mother whom you have come to meet,' Dadwar introduced her.

The woman held Seetha's face in her hands, kissed her cheeks, and taking her hand, led her inside. Though Seetha tried to pull out her purse to pay Dadwar, Dewran's father stopped her. He gestured to her that he would pay, and throwing a hand over Dadwar's shoulder he led him outside.

With Seetha's bag in one hand, Aireen led her into a room with light blue walls. She had firmly gripped Seetha's hand as if she was afraid Seetha would run away. Seetha assumed that Dewran would have told his mother about her in detail. They stood looking at each other, words failing them.

Dewran's father entered the room and said something to his wife, as if scolding her. With a smile, Aireen left the room. Before exiting, he switched on the heater and made sure the windows were firmly shut.

Seetha could hear them talking in the next room. The aroma of cooking also reached her. A little while later Aireen came in with a bowl of steaming soup, a plate of rice topped with boiled vegetables and meat cooked in tomato gravy. Seetha was famished. The woman watched with obvious relish as Seetha enjoyed the spiced meat strips and the thick soup.

Then she came in with clean linen and while making the bed, through sign language conveyed it was Gul's room. Seetha looked around. The family children's photos were hung haphazardly on the wall. She walked around the room, looking at each one of them.

Dewran's mother pointed out her children in the photos one by one. She touched each of them fondly. Seetha could sense the sob stuck in her throat. After failing to hide it, she left Seetha and went out of the room.

It was late morning when Seetha woke up. Looking through the window at the yellow leaves waiting to fall, she curled up, reluctant to leave the comfort of the bed. From outside, she could hear alarmed clucking of hens after they had laid eggs. The pleasant warmth from the heater lingered in the room.

A peaceful and blissful morning! She was getting some repose after many days of stress and precariousness. If only she could remain within the abode like a pupa in its cocoon!

Someone knocked on the door. Aireen opened the door and poked her head in. Along with her, a smorgasbord of food aromas rushed into the room, nauseating Seetha. As she contemplated running for the bathroom, Aireen came and sat on the edge of the bed. The bilious taste in her mouth made Seetha gag. When she was sure she would throw up, avoiding the startled eyes of Aireen, she leapt off the bed, threw down the sheet and ran into the bathroom.

The aftertaste of bile persisted even after she brushed her teeth. Although hungry, she was afraid that if she ate anything she may throw up again. It was bright outside. The uncharacteristic brilliance of the winter sun chased away Seetha's tiredness.

The house had large, unadorned rooms. Aireen was busy in the kitchen. Seetha watched her adroitly prepare stuffed vine leaves. After rolling one she showed it to Seetha and said, 'Dolma.' Seetha assumed it was the name of that dish.

Pointing to a covered plate on the table, Aireen continued to make dolmas. It had boiled eggs, powdery cheese, thinly sliced cucumbers, diced tomatoes and fruits, arranged artistically. A smaller plate filled with pomegranate arils and a glass of milk alongside aggravated her hunger.

Aireen had stopped rolling vine leaves and was watching Seetha eat. Seetha found the strong smell of the kargi tulum cheese disagreeable. Stealing glances at Aireen, she picked off bits of cheese and put them in another plate. She saw Aireen smiling to herself watching her antics. Seetha understood that her secret could not be hidden from this mother for long.

There was a sudden sound as if someone hefty was trying to ram the kitchen door down. Aireen continued as if nothing was happening. Seetha was afraid that the thin door would give way. When the scratching sounds on the door continued unabated, Aireen stood up wearily. She took a large vessel kept on the side and filled it with rice boiled along with bones.

When she opened the door, Seetha immediately recognized the dog that had been head-butting the door impatiently to get in—the mutt that had grudgingly moved out of the path of the car the previous night. How had he reached here?

A beaming Aireen re-entered the kitchen. She pointed to the dog, and said, 'Dewran . . . Roja . . .'

Ah! So, this is Dewran's Roja. He had never told her that he was so huge! An amused Seetha watched Roja slurp up the food greedily, sneezing and grunting.

After breakfast, she went out to look at the compound of the house. Compared to the arid land around it, their plot looked entirely different. Winter seemed to have stopped at this gate. Though the trees had shed leaves, the vegetable garden, including aubergine and beans plants looked healthy. Horn flies that feed on cattle blood buzzed around. Hens clucked and pecked in large pens fenced with barbed wire. Cows mooed from inside a long barn with grass roof. An orange lily looked dolefully at her from between the grass that had evaded the winter's clutch.

She kicked off her shoes and enjoyed the softness and chill of the dark, green grass. Roja, who was rolling on the grass to get rid of fleas, slowly approached and sniffed her. As if savouring an ethereal fragrance, the dog kept smelling her long tresses.

Was he searching for Dewran's smell? Seetha patted him cheerlessly.

Aireen came running out of the house. She scolded Roja loudly and pushed him away. Not pleased, he moved away and started to roll on the grass again.

A car arrived outside, trailing a cloud of dust behind it. The man who came in had light, hay-brown eyes and bore a remote resemblance to Dewran. When he saw Seetha, he smiled and greeted her.

'Aylan!' Aireen hugged him. After holding him to herself and probably inquiring after his well-being, she introduced Seetha to him, holding her close as well. Though she did not understand anything Aireen said, she was pleased that her voice and expressions were full of affection. Aylan then turned towards Seetha, 'Be cool, I am Dewran's cousin.' He spoke in unaccented English.

Aylan listened with misgivings as she recounted how Gul and Dewran had left without revealing anything clearly and how she and Timur had set out in search of them.

'You shouldn't have done things in haste,' Aylan said gravely. 'Dewran is here. But he cannot come home. If he turns up here, he will be arrested. Gul had stayed here for a few days, but once she realized she would be used as bait to catch her brothers, she also left.'

'Where are they now?' Seetha could not contain her curiosity.

'We don't know. Chances are all three of them are together.'

Aylan doubted if she really understood the gravity of the situation. 'I've to assume that the police now know who you are. They are likely to come here too searching for you. Why don't you go back?' He looked at her with concern.

'After I meet Dewran once, I am ready to go to any hell.' Her eyes were flooded with tears.

'That's not going to be easy. He's in hiding.'

He waved his hand in the direction of the mountains surrounding them. 'The militants are all over there. But I don't know if our boys are there. Since there aren't many trees and undergrowth, they live in caves and dugouts they have created amid the rocks. After the attacks on Cizîr and Sur, although the majority had moved to Syria, a few of them are still living in these mountains.'

Seetha looked up helplessly at the forbidding dark mountains, which stood like immovable sentinels.

'O God, what should I do now? Will I have to search for him in these mountains?'

'As per the last information we have, Arman is attached to one of the YPG regiments. Their units travel to various locations as ordered by the commander. A boy who had gone in search of a lost goat saw Arman in that mountain. Scared that it was Arman's ghost, he fled from there. At least, now we know he's alive. That's a consolation.'

'So, it's possible that Dewran too is in this area.' Seetha gave him a hopeful look.

'The chances are less. The place is crawling with spies. They'll give him away. Therefore, it's very unlikely that he'd do such a stupid thing as remaining here. He knows the police are looking for him. We don't know how he managed to return to Turkey. However, the police knew of it and landed up at this house. We heard from the police of his arrival here.'

'So, the police must know of my arrival here too. And they would be here any moment, eh?' Seetha asked disappointed. She realized that she may not get a chance to meet Dewran.

'That's quite possible.' His voice was filled with helplessness. 'Why don't you go from here? I'll help you to reach Silvan. It's better that you don't fall into the hands of the police.' Seetha did not miss the fear in his voice and on his face.

'Where can I go? I don't have a place.' Despondent, Seetha bowed her head. 'I've done nothing wrong. Let's wait and see. There'll be some way.'

Aylan nodded, unconvinced.

Roja was lying near their feet. Disturbed by the silence that had fallen, he licked Aylan's fingers and looked at him pleadingly to attract his attention. Aylan started to pet and cuddle him. Pleased, Roja lay still with his eyes closed.

'Dewran always mentioned Roja in his conversation. I never imagined he would be so huge. When I saw him first, I thought he was a calf.'

'This is a sheepdog. The breed is Boz Shepherd.'

As if he understood they were talking about him, Roja bared his teeth.

'He should be named Hound of Çîçika,' Seetha laughed. After watching her cheerful face for a minute with concern, Aylan rose and said, 'I'll have a word with my aunt.' He entered the house.

After he had lunch with them, Aylan left. He instructed Seetha strictly not to leave the house.

Deciding she would join Aireen, who had lain down on a mat for her siesta, Seetha picked up a pillow from her room and came out. Aireen was not asleep yet. With tired, black rings around her eyes, she had a fixed stare as if she had thoughts crowding her mind.

When Seetha lay down beside her, Aireen shot her a searching look. Unable to bear the scrutiny, Seetha turned her face. Aireen hugged her. When she felt sobs racking Aireen's body, Seetha could feel her own eyes welling up with unshed tears. The suppressed sobs of those two helpless women fell and shattered within the four walls of the room.

Dewran's father returned in the evening with a basketful of pomegranates. Seetha stuck to Aireen as she prepared cinnamon-laced tea. He handed over the hamper to Seetha. His knowing smile made her wonder if Aireen had told him that she was pregnant.

The aroma of the tea; the red pearls of pomegranate on the plate; their sweetness; the smile on Aireen's face as she hovered around her . . . it felt as if nothing had been lost in that moment. Seetha looked around in happiness. The house, a mother, nothing has been lost. If only this day, this happiness, would not end!

After they had dinner together and watched TV for a while, when Seetha lay down to sleep, Aireen came to her with a bottle of oil that had a piercing fragrance. She applied it liberally on Seetha's swollen legs. The pleasure and warmth of those calloused hands applying the oil softly made Seetha descend into sleep.

There was darkness everywhere. A light appeared at the distance; Seetha raced towards it. It was a lantern. A golden glow had spread. *Isn't that Dewran?* Yes, it was.

Seetha reached out. But he was receding from her.

Dewran! Please wait. For once, please wait. Listen to me, listen to what I have to tell you. After that you may go wherever you want to!

She was panting.

'Seetha . . . Seetha . . .' Someone was calling her softly.

She opened her eyes. In the dim light of the candle, she saw a face very close to hers; pistachio green eyes; where had she seen those green eyes before?

'Dewran . . .! When did you come?' she half-screamed and half-blurted out.

'Shhhhh! Don't make a noise.' He covered her mouth.

As if their bodies had melted, as if they had fused into each other, they went into an embrace.

'Why did you have to come here?' stroking her head Dewran asked, when her sobbing subsided. If an inch of life is left in me you know I'd come back to you.'

'That inch of life matters, right? That's why I came in search of you. You should stay alive. My child needs his father.' Seetha said with conviction.

'What did you say?' She sensed the jolt that passed through Dewran.

'What I said! That my child and I need you!'

Dewran reeled back as if stung. With his head held in his hands, he started to babble like a mad man.

'O my God, I never knew . . . I didn't know . . .'

He was crying. Seetha tried to console him desperately.

'Let's get back to Barcelona. I never imagined things were so bad in this place.'

'Go back? Don't think that would be so easy!' Embracing her again, he looked into her eyes. 'I had come to take you with me.' After a pause, he continued, 'We could have crossed the Syrian border. But that's not possible now. In this condition you will not be able to come with me.'

He covered his face.

'You should have never come! At least you and our child would have been safe. None of us will survive now. No one will be left alive,' Dewran lamented.

'I'll come with you,' Seetha said.

'Don't be silly,' Dewran hissed, losing his cool. 'We'll have to walk hundreds of kilometres through these mountains to reach the spot under our control in Syria. It's well-nigh impossible for a healthy woman. There isn't even a forest trail. There are other routes, but they are fraught with danger. It's possible that police will catch us.'

'I was only worried about you, Dewran. I had no knowledge of all these things,' she spoke softly, overwrought by guilt.

'The police know you are here. They are hunters waiting with a tethered lamb as bait.'

'How do you know?' Seetha looked at him inquisitively.

'Like they have their moles, we too have ours,' Dewran said solemnly.

'Aylan and the driver who brought you here are in their custody. The roads to the village have been blocked by the police.'

'Aiyyo, Aylan was here yesterday!'

'He was taken into custody on his way back from here.'

'Gul, where is she?' Seetha asked grimly.

'Gul and Arman are in Syria. Gul has already joined YPJ. Arman is in charge of one of the training centres of YPG.'

Seetha kept looking at him without batting an eye.

'Why can't you surrender? You've done nothing wrong. Do you have pay for Arman's sins? The police will let you off after questioning.'

A smile crossed Dewran's lips as he listened to her inanities.

'The crime of being Arman's brother is enough for me to be charged with every crime under the sun and to be thrown into a dark dungeon for life.'

He kept gazing at her helplessly.

'I don't have a choice. If I am caught by them, there are only two possibilities—one, I will die of torture; two, after a minimum of forty years or so I may get out of jail with a broken body and spirit. You tell me, which is better?'

'If Turkey is so dangerous for you, what are you doing here now?'

'My training is in Syria.'

'So, what brought you here?'

'The past one week I was in Diyarbakır. One of the guys in the group that had to come to Silvan for some work fell sick. As his replacement, they needed someone who knew the place well. My being here is therefore by pure chance.'

He stroked her hair as she lay with her head on his chest. 'I had information from the time you left Sur by hoodwinking Timur.'

'What can we do now?' Seetha looked at him in panic.

'There is no choice. I will leave before daybreak. The police will arrest you.'

Blood drained out of Seetha's face.

Wiping away her tears, he tried to console her. 'Don't be scared. You should tell them that you had come here with no knowledge about my family or the political situation here. That is the truth too. Some things are in our favour—you are an Indian studying in a European university; if anything happens to you, both Spanish and Indian governments will get involved equally. These people know that. So be bold.'

Seetha had nothing to say.

'We don't need this child. How will you bring him up all by yourself?' Dewran said suddenly.

Seetha's body quivered when she heard his dead voice.

She screamed, 'This is not your child. Go away! I'll bring up my child.' She tried to push him away. Dewran hugged her more tightly.

'It won't be easy for you. That's the only reason why I said it. Turkish spies will tail you all your life.'

'It doesn't matter.' Her tone was firm. Dewran buried his face in her hair. His hot tears wet her body.

Seetha tried to catch sounds from outside. The police may turn up any moment now. In desperation, she clutched the wearied form that leaned against her shoulder. Every passing moment was gruelling.

A bird chirped from outside the window. Dewran scrambled and rose to his feet. He looked at his watch. 'It's time. I've to go.'

Seetha stared at him. Dewran yanked her to her feet.

'Get up. It'll be dawn very soon. Before I leave, for once, I want to walk on these village paths holding your hand.'

Seetha changed clothes mechanically. He patted her hair into place and straightened the collar of her woollen sweater.

After opening the door quietly, Dewran stood still. His parents were seated on the sofa in the living room.

'I . . . I thought you all were asleep . . .' he stammered.

Aireen dissolved in a hail of tears. He held her like he would have held a baby.

'I've to leave now. The police will be arriving soon. I should go before that.' He kissed the tear-stained cheeks of his mother.

After giving his father a quick hug, Dewran stepped outside holding Seetha's hand. Aireen's suppressed sobs could be heard from behind them. Although it was close to dawn, it was still dark. The world ahead of Seetha was steeped in darkness.

Suddenly, there were sounds of scampering and thrashing about. Roja came out leaping out of the darkness. Unable to contain his happiness after seeing Dewran, he gambolled, jumping and chasing his own tail. The startled hens clucked in disapproval. Dewran was straining to bring the excited Roja, who was jumping all over him, under control.

Dewran's father emerged and scolded Roja. Although Roja quietened down, it was clear that he was raring to leap on to Dewran and play with him.

'His name is Rojava.[1] Everyone here shortened it to Roja,' Dewran grinned.

The dim street lights were a dull yellow. Seetha tried to work out the hour. 'It must be past 5 a.m.,' Dewran said as if he had read her mind. His hands around her gave her warmth.

'These moments are ending. Don't be sad,' Seetha told herself.

The village streets, with their dust dampened by the dew, were deserted. A light or two were on in some of the houses. In the diffused glow from the bulbs yellowed by age, she could see some movements in the barns of the houses.

'Everyone in this village is a relative. It's better if I don't run into any of them now. They'll buttonhole me and get the whole story out of me.'

Seetha remained silent. Noticing her silence, Dewran hugged her hard.

'It had always been my dream to hold my girl's hand and walk down these streets of my village. It's now been realized.'

Sounds of scampering and panting could be heard from behind them. Roja was racing after them.

'He must have given *bav* the slip,' said Dewran, laughing.

Seetha could see a fence at a distance. 'That is a boundary of the village. You don't come beyond that,' Dewran said.

Seetha nodded. Her eyes had run dry. Unaware of what was happening, wagging his tail, Roja scampered around them.

It was a tall and sturdy fence made up of tree trunks driven into the ground, their branches uncut and twigs woven into one another filled the interstices. Dewran stooped under it easily and got to the other side. Tarrying for a moment as if unsure how to bid her goodbye, he leaned over and, kissed her fully on her lips as if sucking the very life out of her.

'I'll be back! Wait for me!'

Seetha stood benumbed, watching him melt into the darkness. With his curly tail held stiffly, Roja ran after him.

She lost track of time. When the sky turned copper red and flies started to buzz around her, Seetha started to shuffle her way towards the house. Strength had seeped out of her. The early morning chill made her shiver like a leaf in the wind.

Milkmaids carrying vats brimming with milk looked at her curiously. Shepherds followed them with their flocks. Their shaggy-haired dogs bared their teeth and directed their deep-throated barks at her.

When she reached the house, a bellow from inside jolted her. A police Jeep was parked beyond the curve on the road. As she ran into the house, the sight that met her made her blood run cold. Dewran's father's face had turned red from being slapped. His nose was bleeding. Aireen lay curled on the floor, clutching the feet of a policeman.

'Why are you hurting them?' Seetha's voice quavered with anger and sadness.

The *yüzbaşı* turned to her, leering.

'Dewran's lover! Gather your stuff and get into the vehicle.' He was no longer bellowing.

She knew protesting was of no use. She shoved whatever she could lay hands on into her bag. Dewran's father was seated on the sofa. Aireen was still lying on the floor, sobbing. Seetha bent and touched her shoulder.

'Come with us, slut.' Someone caught hold of her jacket, pulled her up and shoved her roughly. The sight of her collapsing like a bundle of clothes made Aireen hurriedly scramble and get off the floor. Roaring like a nursing tigress, she leapt towards the policeman.

Seetha watched in horror the rifle butt being raised. She lay still on the floor, listening to the sounds of blows being rained on Aireen, and her cries. Kicking away the prone, bleeding body of Aireen, the policeman went out.

One of the policemen caught hold of Seetha's hand and pulled her. 'She's heavy,' he said as if weighing a piece of meat. There was a howl of laughter.

From the corner of her eye, Seetha could see Dewran's father crying, hugging Aireen's bleeding, motionless body. The sight of bright red blood from a head wound flowing down the floor towards the door made Seetha feel faint.

Seetha, who had fallen again after being pushed, was dragged the rest of the way to the police vehicle. Ignoring the heads that were popping up beyond the fences, they lifted her and dumped her into the vehicle. Her bag, which was flung in after her, fell on top of her.

Mouthing a string of obscenities, the policemen entered the vehicle in a triumphant mood. As they started the van, Seetha broke down completely.

'Terrorist's slut! And you're whining?'

As she lay curled up on the floor of the van, someone kicked her head viciously with a heavy boot. When the van gathered speed on the main road after leaving the bumpy roads of the village, someone shouted, 'Look . . . look there!'

Seetha lifted her throbbing head.

'Roja!'

The mutt was chasing the police van through the cloud of dust raised by it. He leaped towards the van like a war horse. Although he missed and fell head on, he scrambled up and continued the chase. It was a terrifying sight. The bared teeth and blazing eyes told Seetha that he would not back down. As he raced down, gathering enough momentum to leap onto the van, she could see indistinctly through the cloud of dust some people running after Roja.

'Faster . . . faster . . .' the policemen urged the driver.

'Damn! Kill him . . .'

Gun barrels poked out through the gun ports of the van with armour plates and bulletproof windows,

'Stop . . .!!!!' Seetha screamed.

Shots rang out. Roja, frozen mid-air in his leap towards the van, collapsed like a cut-down heavy sack on to the road, where he lay whining and writhing. The people in pursuit had reached him and stood around him wailing and screaming.

Seetha bawled. The policemen laughed raucously and cheered. 'Shoot it again . . .' someone said.

The gun barrel poked out again. Seetha leapt up like a demented person and before others could react, grabbed the gunman's arm. She shrieked as if she had lost her mind and bit down hard on the hand. Screaming with pain, he threw her off. As she collapsed to the floor like a weak kitten, the policemen kept kicking her till they could no more.

They kicked her unconscious form into one corner of the van. They started to boast in their coarse voices thickened by constant smoking. Churned by its wheels, the dark dust rose up like a black curtain behind the van. Leaving behind the check-posts, the watchtowers, and the sentinel-like mountains, the van slowly drove through the deserted roads and climbed down the sharp curves.

Blood

'How come your feet are like this?'

'Are like what?'

'How are they so soft?'

'How else should they be?'

'Have you walked on tender grass in the spring? Do you know how it feels to step into scorching hot sand set on fire by the sun?'

'What kind of nonsensical questions are you asking? You should've been a writer.'

'That's true . . . but first answer my question.'

'When I was a child, I would walk all over our family property. You have not seen my native land! Full of greenery, verdant fields, trees, rivers, mountain ranges . . .'

'But looking at these dainty, soft feet like that of a Turkish princess I can make out that you have not walked on the sands of a beach or over stones in the riverbed any time recently.'

'Don't tickle me. If you want to go out, why don't you say that. It's been a long time since I've been anywhere. Shall we go on a long trip like you suggested?'

A piercing shriek of a woman was heard. Seetha was startled into wakefulness.

There was no Dewran. There was no soft bed or his warmth. Her body was stuck to the dirt and dampness on the floor. Her limbs were stiff and frozen because of cold. She tried to get up from the filthy, stinking floor. Lightning pain shot up from her legs— as if she was being beaten brutally on her soles with truncheons. The pain was akin to skewers being driven into her legs.

She mumbled with her dry lips, 'Water . . .'

Not knowing if anyone was there to hear her, she kept repeating weakly, 'I need water . . .'

Someone caressed her hair. 'What are you saying? What language is this? I can't understand you.' Someone was speaking in broken English.

Seetha tried to open her bleary eyes. Where was she?

'I need some water . . .'

'Let someone come, I'll tell them,' the voice said kindly. The face was not visible in the darkness.

The scream was heard again. Although it got cut off mid-way as if someone had covered the woman's mouth, it echoed among the walls of that big, empty room before eventually dying off.

Seetha shivered with fear. 'Who's that? Who . . .?'

Without replying, the woman with a bucket and broom in hand made her exit. The door clanged shut, its ringing sound making it clear that it was a heavy steel door.

Although Seetha tried to move her body, which had become stiff like a piece of firewood from lying on the frozen floor, she failed.

The pain was excruciating. When the flesh in the soles— already beaten into a pulp—touched the floor, every nerve in her body screamed in pain. The truncheons rose and descended repeatedly.

'Where's Dewran?'

'Where's he? I too don't know. At least you can tell me if you can be so good . . .'

The copper leads glinted in the light. The shock of the electric current passed from tip to toe. Juddering convulsions of the trussed-up body strapped immovably. When the answers did not meet the expectations, the electric current shot through the body like a carving knife, followed by death-like blackout. She felt as if she was drowning, as only to be revived by the cascade of water poured on the face.

'I don't know . . .'

'. . . where Dewran is . . . where Arman is . . . I don't know . . . for the love of God, please put a stop to this . . . I'll die . . .'

An exhausted Seetha murmured, 'I don't know.'

She lifted a dead arm and softy touched her belly. 'Baby . . . are you still there? You must be hurting in there, no?'

Her throat was parched. It had been hours since she had had a drop of water. She tried to call out.

'Anyone there? Some water . . .'

A door closed somewhere. Was that someone running along the corridor?

Clanging sounds like metal pieces being dropped on the floor, followed by their reverberations, reached her. A sharp scream followed. O God, what was happening . . .

She could hear approaching footsteps.

'Water . . . water . . .' she pleaded as loud as her parched throat would allow her.

The footsteps stopped at the room's door. She fancied the woman may have returned with some water for her.

'Why are you bleating?' An emotion-less masculine voice demanded.

'A little water!'

Seetha broke down. Every fibre in her damaged body screamed out, 'Water . . .'

He approached her slowly.

'You want water, don't you?'

Something was unzipped. Before she realized what was happening a warm spray of water fell on her face, hair and chest.

Urine!

Seetha retched. She curled up like a millipede and begged with her hands joined in supplication. With great relish the man proceeded to complete what he had started and, before leaving, hawked and spat on Seetha's face.

She could feel convulsions and something rolling up in her belly. Rolling her head with her mouth open, she gasped for air as if in the throes of death. She retched as if her viscera were being pumped out. All that came out was some bile. As she continued to retch, her bruised body started to cramp. She screamed in pain.

Someone opened the door again. She joined her hands again.

'For mercy's sake, please, don't do anything to me.'

With the bile and urine dripping out of her mouth, she tried to slither her way through the slime.

'No, no, no . . . it's me, I won't do anything.'

It was the woman. Her kindly voice lessened Seetha's whimpering. As she sat sobbing, she tried to see the woman's face a clearly in the darkness of the room. After keeping the things in her hand in a corner of the room, the woman came to her. She tried to lift Seetha off the floor. Unable to place her feet on the floor, Seetha screamed in pain.

'Keç, try to stand up. We'll try to have a bath.'

Seetha sat up slowly. Unable to bear the pain and fatigue, she collapsed back on to the floor.

'Water . . .' she whimpered.

'If they come to know I have given you this, they will kill me.'

She extricated a bottle of water from inside her dress. When she opened the lid and applied the bottle to Seetha's parched lips, helping her drink, she was mouthing some imprecations in Turkish. Cool water! Seetha felt that her body, throbbing with pain and thirst, was healing because of the coolness she was ingesting.

'I have been ordered to give you a bath and get you ready in half an hour.'

She was terrified.

'Will they interrogate me again?'

'I don't know.' She spoke in an undertone.

The bathroom was close by. She felt her life was being wrenched out of her at every step she took. She was unsure if the wetness she felt between her legs was from urine or blood.

As she limped along hanging on to the woman's shoulder, she saw the mildewed walls of the bathroom and its nauseating, slippery, never-washed floor. The stench made her retch again. She threw up the water she had drunk only a few minutes before. Leaning her against the wall, the woman started to pour icy cold water over her. She sucked in her breath and started to shiver violently.

'Stop! Please stop . . .' she cried.

The woman picked up a piece of soap that had been stuck into the gap between the pipe and the wall.

'Your body is soiled and has urine all over. If I don't clean you up properly, they'll rebuke me.'

Ignoring Seetha's protests, the woman used soap and water generously, rubbed down and cleaned her body.

When the water hit those spots where her skin had been abraded by the ropes used to tie her legs and wrists, they burned.

Water, like icy needles, kept hitting her face. The soap lather that slipped down from her head and entered her nose and mouth when she least expected, suffocated her. The memory of being grabbed by her hair and her head being dunked under water made Seetha writhe in a breathless panic. The struggle for breath while trussed like a bird and unable to move an inch! Bursts of laughter erupted from nowhere as if from another world.

With water entering her nose and mouth, terrorized by the feeling that she was drowning, Seetha's eyes bulged, and she clutched the woman. Bewildered, the woman held her by her shoulders and shook her.

'Look here . . . it's me!'

Seetha stared at her, incredulous. The light that entered through the small ventilator loopholes on the bathroom walls enabled her to get a better look at the woman. Her face seemed to have been constructed out of melancholy. Avoiding Seetha's teary eyes, the woman held her close, shushed and comforted her by patting her back. And she towelled down Seetha's shivering body as she would have wiped a child. She made her wear an old but clean dress and walked her to another room.

'Where are you taking me?' Seetha asked, through her chattering teeth.

'I was asked to give you a bath and bring you to them. That's all I know.'

Her voice was dead.

She was not led to the room where she was interrogated after being brought in following her arrest in Çiçika. There was a wooden bed in the new room. She was relieved that she would be spared the bone-chilling cold that crept in while sleeping on the floor. After letting her in, the woman left after closing the door behind her.

She looked at her diffused image in the grimy windowpane. The old dress she was made to wear was an oversized tunic. She recalled her childhood when she would stumble around wearing her father's shirt. The dress made her acutely aware of the presence of a familiar fragrance. Did it have the aroma of the cigarette-smell laden kiss that her teary-eyed father had planted on her cheek at the airport when she left for Barcelona? Or did it carry the fragrance of Dewran's aftershave lotion? She lifted the dress up to her nostrils and inhaled deeply the scent that invoked some indistinct sweet memories.

The spare walls around her rudely intruded into that charming scene. She felt that the spider in one of the corners was growing by the second and trying to reach her with its long spindly legs. Seetha closed her eyes and shook her head to clear it. Memory of the interrogation room's blazing white lights burning into her eyes made her eyes water.

To move to the bed, she gingerly picked each foot off the floor and placed it down. Bolts of pain shoot up her legs with each effort.

Someone who had been banished from everyone's lives . . . Her parents who valued the reputation of their family over their daughter had forsaken her! Although compelled by his circumstances and innumerable bondages, even Dewran had found her dispensable. *My baby, do you need this mother of yours?* She patted her belly gently.

The room was warm. The bed was hard, but the clean smell of the sheet was comforting. Seetha noticed some brownish stains on the wall next to the bed as if someone had flung colours at it. They varied from faint ones which someone had attempted to wash off before abandoning it to deep burgundy ones which looked fresh. She moved closer to check.

Blood! A shocked Seetha flinched and reeled back.

Blood . . .! They were going to interrogate her again. Possibly using more heinous torture techniques than the one from the previous night! The memory of the lashing truncheons brought back the pain in her legs that had subsided a little. She broke down completely when she recalled how she had bawled holding her soles, begging them to not beat her any more. She felt all strength drain out of her. She was overcome by drowsiness and felt dizzy. Her last meal had been more than twenty-four hours ago. She keeled over onto the bed. Her eyes closed.

A noise came from the door. Someone had opened it and entered the room. An army officer in his uniform—dark olive-green peaked cap with golden trimmings on the peak and a chest covered in medals. His uniform and bearing were different from that of her interrogators of the previous day. He was also older. She desperately searched for some sign of compassion on his face. After entering, he latched the door behind him.

'Seetha!'

He leered, displaying his yellowed teeth. A scream that she was trying to suppress escaped from her throat. He poked her belly with the swagger stick in his hand asking, 'Are you keeping well?'

The mocking question made her shrink back into one corner of the bed. The swagger stick was being pushed deeper into her belly.

He knows! He knows that she is carrying a child! They have her phone! They would have read every mail and message!

'Please don't hurt me!' she begged. 'I know nothing; I was not aware of anything either.'

'I know that . . .' The swagger stick had snaked its way into her dress. 'I have flown down from Ankara only to meet you. I had instructed no one should lay their hands on you. Did they do anything to you?'

'They beat me . . . they electrocuted me . . . they water-boarded me . . .' Seetha sobbed.

'Aha . . .! Only that? Do you know Arman killed my brother?'

Seetha wept helplessly.

'I know nothing. I have got caught up in all this without any intention on my part. Please leave me out of this . . .'

'His revenge for his whore friend getting killed in some clashes in Cizîr. What should be done to traitors and anti-nationals? He set off a bomb killing my brother and other soldiers. Shouldn't I have my revenge? Shouldn't I?'

He brought his face close to hers and looked piercingly into her eyes.

'You tell me! Shouldn't I take revenge?'

Unable to respond, Seetha shrunk back.

'I had set my eyes on his sister, but she gave us the slip!' He took up Seetha's long tresses in his hand and smelt them.

'I'll make do with you. If you are hurt, he too will feel the hurt. Then let him come to avenge whatever's going to happen to you.'

His bad breath nauseated Seetha. With one yank, he tore her dress; he flung away the swagger stick and cap to one side and mounted her. Seetha screwed her eyes shut. Resistance would be of no use. She believed if she stayed still, at least she would be able to save her child. With a low growl, the man started to violate her debilitated body. The medals on his chest swung to and fro in front of her eyes.

'You bitch, are you playing dead?'

He spat on her face. The spittle joined her tears, and they flowed down together from the corner of her eyes. Every time she thought he would spend himself, he drove himself harder and harder into her, smashing into her damaged body. Wolf whistles could be heard from the outside. Hoots of laughter rose from beyond the door as if they were an echo of his beastly grunts and low growls, and her own screams from the insufferable pain.

It was over, eventually. After straightening his uniform, now damp with sweat, while picking up his cap he growled, 'Don't think you are being spared. Some of my friends are coming to meet you.'

Seetha was numb all over. As soon as he exited, four or five men who had been waiting at the door entered. Although she tried to cover her nakedness with the bedsheet, they yanked it off her.

The horny men started commenting on her body parts. They picked up the swagger stick left behind by the previous man and started to poke it into her private parts. Though the pain was excruciating and made her squirm, with her eyes closed, Seetha tried to lie still like a statue. That only seemed to provoke them more. With lecherous grins, two of them undressed, flung away their clothes, and approached her.

There was a sudden banging at the door. Some men could be seen standing beyond the door which was ajar. Their uniforms suggested they were high-ranking officers like the first visitor.

'Please save me,' she tried to get off the bed. The men who were inside the room dressed in a hurry and vanished.

The newcomers stood around Seetha, surveying her. With lustful eyes, they cracked lewd jokes and cackled. One of them stubbed a lit cigarette on her breast. Seetha shrieked in agony. That made them hoot with laughter and howl like wolves.

As she stood swathed in the bedsheet and begging for mercy with folded hands, one of the men pushed her frail body on to the bed.

The four men left the room only after a few hours. The barely breathing body of Seetha hung half out of the bed, like a broken doll. When they saw the officers leave, those waiting at the door rushed in. They jostled one another for the first chance to violate her. When they found that she was unconscious, in their frustration, they tried to slap her awake, yanked her urine-drenched hair and pulled her down to the floor.

Only then did they notice the blood on her body and on the bed. Some of the men stepped back. Others swore at her and spat on her body. And they left the room, repulsed by the blood.

Those not ready to give up yet lifted her and dropped her back on the bed. Some men stood at the door watching the spectacle. One of the men picked up the swagger stick that had faeces and blood at its tip and poked her breast with it. Her body lay still like a corpse. The bleeding and her gaunt body aroused some of the men more. At every given opportunity, the men who stood around the bed with the futile hope of reviving her, pinched the livid bite marks on her breasts and kept tweaking her swollen lips. Oblivious to the defilement happening to her body, Seetha lay unmoving.

One among those who stood by impatiently fondling their organs, which they had pulled out of their unzipped trousers, placed a finger under her nose to check if she was still breathing. He could feel no breath. Her swollen lips with blood clots had cracks as If she was at the last stage of dehydration. He felt that she should have been given some water at least. With a shake of the head towards his friends, who were still rooting for action, to indicate it was all over, he walked out. From the bunched-up sheet on the bed, blood had started to drip on to the floor. The body lay like a pale, inanimate doll soaked in blood.

Prison

'Timur Kemal Özdemir!'

'Yes! That's my name. But you have not told me yet what is my crime!'

He faced up bravely to the officer who stood in front of him with pursed lips and an accusing stare. He appeared to be a higher-up in the army. On his dark olive uniform, the medals attached to the rows of ribbons on his chest had a cold, dull shine.

'Do you know what the punishment is for those who help traitors and militants?' he asked ominously.

'I know, but where and how have I helped them?' asked an astonished Timur.

'What were you doing in Sur?'

'I went to Sur to help my friend. She's an Indian. She doesn't speak Turkish. She knows nothing about Turkey and its politics. She has come in search of her lover.'

'You didn't know of the terrorist connections of Dewran, whom she has come in search of?'

'I have told you enough times that I didn't know. He is a Turkish citizen. He has not spoken to me one word against the country.'

'What about his sister?'

158

'Gul is different. She reads international politics in University of Barcelona. She has differences of opinion with Turkey's foreign policies. Nothing wrong in that—we are a democracy. However, what I do know is that to brand those who dissent as anti-nationalists is a mark of fascism.'

The officer's face turned red.

'Shut up! Don't try to teach me! You are still alive only because your surname is Özdemir.'

Timur's whole aspect underwent a transformation.

'You may be able to silence me. I'm a coward. However, as a citizen of this country, I'm also responsible for all the atrocities that you, with the backing of the government, commit against the Kurds. There will be a time when the public will come to know of all this. You may not be able to stop it then.' He spoke fearlessly.

The officer was trembling with rage. He swung his leg viciously, enough to send Timur and the chair flying and land in a heap in a corner of the room. Bellowing, the man picked him and smashed him against the wall.

'Even your uncle, Kasim Özdemir, will not question me why I have done it. That's the kind of talk that's coming out of you now.'

Timur's nose was bleeding. He wiped it with the back of his hand. His face was plastered with blood and tears.

'You should understand one thing. My only interest was Seetha's safety. I had no idea what was happening in the Kurd-majority regions,' he said helplessly. The officer relaxed his grip on Timur's shirt. He sat wearily on the cold floor, leaning against the wall.

'But now I know!' Timur lifted his head and looked at him with apparent loathing. 'All that's happening in Kurdistan is your doing. You are killing people like vermin. They too are Turkish citizens like you and me, yes? How come there are different laws for Kurds and us in this country?' Timur was panting with emotion.

'Go and pose these doubts to that minister uncle of yours. Apologists like you are more dangerous than traitors like Kurds.'

He hawked and spat on Timur in disgust and left the room. The sound of the heavy metal door being slammed shut after him reverberated through the place. Timur continued to sit listlessly leaning against the wall. He was famished.

He calculated that two days would have passed since he was brought there. In that small, windowless room, which let in neither sunlight nor sounds from the outside world, such as bird songs, the passage of time was unmeasured. Only sounds from within the building could be heard through a narrow gap on top of the door.

Except for a rickety wooden chair, the room was bare. The chairs legs were wobbly. Timur used it only when he was being interrogated. The rest of the time, he was curled up on the cold floor or pacing around the room. He was drained by the stress and strain caused by the search for Seetha and the interrogation and physical and mental torture that he underwent thereafter. Every nerve and fibre in his body yearned to crawl under a heavy, warm blanket and sleep, dead to the world. However, a blindingly bright light overhead denied him sleep.

Using the sounds and smells that reached him, Timur tried repeatedly to guess the hour and place. However, the blood-curdling sounds, enough to drive an ordinary man mad, broke long periods of congealed silence at irregular intervals—occasional sounds of boots stomping past the door; the slamming of steel doors; piteous screams; episodic sobbing; splintered pleas.

Timur tried to cock his ears to make out if the cries came from a man or woman. However, those agonized cries caused by excruciating pain, after bouncing off walls and doors reached him as indistinguishable wails from someone of indeterminate gender. When a wail was heard, the dread that it was Seetha's gnawed his insides.

There was a sudden knock on the door. Even the prison worker who came in to throw in a piece of bread—around the time Timur would be feeling death from starvation was imminent—never sought permission to enter. Timur laughed sardonically, thinking this as ridiculous as seeking permission from the sacrificial lamb.

The person who entered was someone whom he had least expected. His uncle! Although he was not in his official dress, there was no diminution of majesty and nobility in how he carried himself. Timur failed to hide his sheepish smile. The incongruity of Timur's embarrassed smile paired with his soiled clothes and his bloodied face saddened his uncle. Timur tried to get up from the floor where he lay curled up. His uncle stood in silence, gazing at his pale and emaciated face.

'What should I tell your father and mother?' The gentle question disarmed Timur. He remained silent.

'You may tell that I have been jailed for the crime of trying to aid a helpless woman.' Timur said, looking into his eyes.

'That could be true in the beginning. But after that you became a party to the anti-national activities of Kurds and spoke in defence of them.'

'*Genç amca*,[2] I have done nothing treasonous. I've not helped traitors either. Kurds are citizens of this country. Isn't exterminating them treasonous? I'm not doing that!'

'It's better that you keep your mouth shut. I've come to take you home. Go home and stay with your mother for some time. Forget all this; eat well and get your health back.'

When he turned to leave, without looking back, he said, 'Get up and come!'

Timur tried to stand up. He had pain all over his body, the result of the interrogators forgetting occasionally that the man in front of them was a minister's nephew. As he shuffled out of the room into the corridor, Timur was stunned by the cold darkness of the place. After his arrest, since the police had placed a hood on his head, he had no idea where he had been brought to.

The corridor looked endless. On either side, there were rooms that were locked up. He assumed that it was a jail where pre-trial accused were housed.

Timur found it hard to catch up with Kasim and the jail officials who were striding ahead deep in conversation. During the past few days, he had received little food and water. The small of his back was hurting terribly from one of the vicious kicks he had received. He felt he would collapse if he did not get some water to drink in this condition. As he made his way ahead gingerly, holding on to the wall for support, a shriek from behind the nearest door shocked him. It sounded as if a knife was being turned in someone's wound. The sound from an animal that was being slaughtered.

Did that sound like Seetha? A shiver ran up Timur's spine. Things were tumbling down behind that door. The shriek rose again. It seemed to create ripples in that corridor. With surprising manic strength, he leapt at the door and started to bang and kick it.

His attempts to break down the unforgiving door failed. Unwilling to give up, he continued to kick at the door, but the pain in his back made its presence felt. As he collapsed, convulsed with pain, the sounds behind the door ceased, providing him some relief. The shriek died halfway as if the person had been gagged suddenly.

'Open the door . . . please open the door . . . she is innocent,' still banging the door, Timur cried out plaintively.

Hearing the commotion, his uncle and his retinue came running. Although they stood stunned for a few moments, one of the senior officers recovered and with a slap sent Timur to the floor. Kasim Özdemir came forward. He looked on helplessly at his nephew squirming on the floor in pain. He ordered the officials with him to lift Timur and place him in his car. As if in a delirium, Timur was blurting out things without any filtering. His face flushed from mortification, Kasim hurried towards the car. He was worried about his own reputation getting hit if the recent events became public knowledge.

Only after cleaning him up and getting him dressed in ill-fitting clothes bought off the street, did Kasim present Timur before his elder brother. Kasim gave Timur's parents—shocked at the sight of wounds and bruises on his body—an elaborate and embellished version of the events and left with a warning that Timur should not be allowed to go outside.

Timur was resting on the sofa after soaking himself in a long, hot bath. He was incensed by his mother's tear-filled eyes and his father's melancholic silence. He asked Kasim, who was leaving with the smug satisfaction of having done his duty, to wait.

'Genç amca, you are a minister in the government that rules this country. Can you tell me what Article 17 of our Constitution says?'

Kasim looked rattled.

Timur's mother went to him and gripped his shoulder. 'In our culture we don't challenge elders.'

'The Constitution is the essence of our culture. He is a minister. Let him tell us.'

Kasim stood for some time staring at him in silence.

'You don't know, do you? Let me tell you! It says that no sonofabitch has the right to question the right to life of our citizens or to assault them physically or mentally.'

Timur was trembling with uncontrolled emotion. Without waiting for further edification, Kasim, with a nod at his brother, left in a hurry. The driver and his security detail entered their vehicles.

Timur screamed after him, 'Legally, neither you nor your army nor your godfather has the right to impinge on the dignity of the Turkish people or torture them!'

'Damn your torture chambers,' picking up a shoe lying close by, he threw it at Kasim.

'Timur!!' his mother, Zehra, exclaimed in astonishment. Ignoring her, Timur limped towards his room. Zehra sat down in a corner and wept. To see her smart son—who had gone to Barcelona to study—come home with his health and mind destroyed was beyond her sufferance.

Letting out a long sigh, her husband hugged her and tried to explain the gravity of the situation. He warned her not to behave in a way that might provoke Timur. The famous lawyer that he was, he could understand the reasons for his son's ire.

Timur was calm when sat for dinner after a long sleep. As if to apologize for his rude behaviour, he kept hugging his mother, planting kisses on her cheeks and tickling her.

'Baba . . . I need your help,' Timur whispered in his father's ear, making use of his mother's absence when she returned to the kitchen.

'Only if it's to accompany you to the hospital,' a smiling Bahadir replied. 'We'll do it tomorrow?'

'No . . . it has to be now.'

'Okay.'

Zehra's reappearance, who came in bearing the dishes made specially for her son, cut short the brief and confidential conversation. It had been a long time since they had dined as a family. After cracking jokes, making his mother laugh and eating a hearty meal, the son and father left saying they were going for a drive. The well-lit, wide roads of Istanbul, now deserted, stretched before them. As they drove towards the hospital, Timur filled his father in with the details of what had passed with him. Bahadir, accustomed to listening to such cases daily, was not surprised by what he heard from his son.

'I shall go to the Indian consulate tomorrow. The ambassador is a friend. He's now in Istanbul for some meetings,' he said in a pensive mood.

'You should take rest. I'll handle this.'

'I shall,' Timur assured him.

Bahadir was relieved after the doctor assured him that Timur had no serious wounds or fractures, and only contusions. They left after Timur was advised rest and prescribed painkillers. Zehra was asleep by the time they reached home. After watching his sleeping mother's serene face for some time, Timur went to his room.

The next day morning, when Zehra arrived in his room with a cup of tea, she was met by the sight of a bed unslept in. With no wrinkles, the soft bedsheet with floral motifs looked as smooth as when she made the bed the previous night. The window facing the garden lay open. A lark singing welcomed the cool morning. After keeping the cup on the table, she sat down on the bed, defeated.

The sound of sobs made Bahadir peep into Timur's room. He was missing; Zehra sat on the bed, sobbing with her face in her hands. A glance was enough for him to understand that Timur had decamped the previous night. He took the cup and drank the cold tea in one gulp.

'My son is not a terrorist as claimed by Kasim,' he said in a fury. 'He landed in all these problems because he was trying to help his friends. It won't happen again.'

Zehra lifted her head and looked at him expectantly with eyes brimming with tears.

'Why, because he's no longer alone. I'll use my money, experience, knowledge and contacts made over all these years for it. I'll search for and find that girl, come what may.'

Bahadir left the room.

Zehra started to weep again. After listening to her sobs for a little while, the lark started to sing again in the exhilaration of witnessing a new morning embracing the world in all its glory.

Rojava

Dewran focussed on the bird circling high above him. He was unsure if it was a vulture or an eagle. From the way it wheeled, circled and glided, he decided it was an eagle searching for leverets or chameleons on the ground.

Dewran was waiting for Arman in front of a training camp for YPG recruits. Yoga and *Jineolojî*[1] classes were being held in some of the rooms of the scattered buildings. Since he knew everyone would break for lunch soon, he was not hassled by the need to wait.

Soon, the trainees started to emerge from the buildings. He could figure they were not newbies from their darkened skins, muscular bodies and bright eyes. He was surprised by the proportion of foreigners in their midst. The news that the international brigade was attracting new recruits was, therefore, not a lie.

He listened to snatches of conversations as they passed by him. Droll, sing-song, foreign accented Kurmanji. For reasons unknown, he felt his eyes burn. This world is not so bad! There are at least some people in this world who believe that no one is beneath others, and everyone has the same rights, he thought with a sigh. He rubbed his face vigorously to hide the tears that were spurting in the corner of his eyes.

Dewran had recognized that the passers-by were members of the Anti-Terror Units being trained to hunt down and exterminate the sleeper cells of Islamic State in various corners of the world. They were the elite, hand-picked from SDF[2] and YPG. When he thought back on the days he had aspired to be one of them, a self-deprecating smile spread on his face.

Now there is only one picture in his mind—Seetha's ashen, swollen face; her tear-filled eyes; her growing belly; his mother's cries. He cursed himself again.

For the last two days, he had survived on a piece of bread and an apple that remained in his backpack. The smell of food from the kitchen inflamed his hunger. He could recognize it was the standard fare—whatever vegetables came to hand were diced and boiled along with rice and salt. He wished someone would fry a chicken—that was a rarity and as good as being granted a boon. The thought made him salivate. Immediately he felt mortified. He had no knowledge of Seetha's state. And here he was, worried about his own hunger!

The trainees hurried towards the dining hall. He could see Arman walking slowly after them. He was deep in conversation with a tall American who was with him discussing some paper in his hand and missed the waiting Dewran. The American was carrying a shiny M-249 light machine gun on his shoulder effortlessly. On the arm of his camouflage uniform, green, yellow and red stripes were visible—a symbol of the alliance with YPG.

After the conversation was over, he warmly shook hands with Arman and marched towards his vehicle.

'For how many days?' Dewran asked, walking up to Arman, who noticed his brother only then. A sad smile broke through the scraggly beard growing on his face.

'I don't know. Perhaps till they are with us.' They watched the Jeep disappear in the distance, driving along the single dirt track that cut through the vast wasteland around them.

'Do you know why I have been asked to join the training on immediate basis?' Dewran asked anxiously.

'I don't know.' Arman turned away his face uncomfortably. 'Your training was incomplete. You were sent to Silvan only as an aide because of your familiarity with the territory. In between, to attend to your personal affairs, you took leave. Trainees are not given leave. The training should be completed with full responsibility.'

'But I needed a few more days!' Dewran muttered.

'You are a troublemaker! Mother is in the hospital. Your lover is in police custody. What can you do for them now?' Arman sounded censorious.

Although he was expecting the news, it still shook him. During his journey back into Syria, he was starved of news. He looked up at the heavens helplessly as if beseeching help. The merciless sun stared into his eyes, challenging him. A tear rolled down his cheek. An upset Arman tried to console him.

'Mother has twelve stitches on her head. She had lost blood by the time she was taken to the hospital. But she is out of danger. She is tired. No other issues.'

'Seetha . . .?' Dewran stammered.

'We only know that she's still in police custody. Our people are trying to find out.'

'She is pregnant,' Dewran said, hesitantly. He was not in the habit of discussing such matters with his brother. He nervously looked at him from the corner of his eye. He saw his face getting clouded with concern.

'Don't worry. We shall see.' Arman looked preoccupied. That his mind was thinking furiously was manifest.

'Didn't you see what happened in my life? My love for Dilva ended up in Gul having to quit her studies and exile herself, leaving behind our parents. Now you too! I wonder what more is in store.'

A sorrowful Arman bowed his head. Dewran could see a tear glinting in the corner of his eyes.

'We Kurds are unlucky people. Good education, good jobs, enduring love . . . we are not destined to have any of these. Accursed lives!'

Dewran could not bear the guilt he felt when he heard the quaver in Arman's voice. He wished to inform his brother than none of it was intentional.

'*Biraye mezin*,[3] I did nothing intentionally. I met Seetha for the first time when I visited Gul. They were housemates in Barcelona.' He was using the opportunity to apprise his elder brother of what had happened and how.

*　*　*

When Gul had called in that morning, she informed him that she had found a cheap place to stay with a Spanish family. Since his uncle's restaurant, where he was employed, was always busy, he asked for a two-hour break with great reluctance. It was easy to locate her address. The locality, with good connectivity, parks and plenty of shopping places, was a residential area of rich Spaniards.

People who become lonely when they age, often offered accommodation to students to try and bring some colour, noise and excitement in their lives. Dewran guessed Gul may have found such a place.

Dark crimson bougainvillea climbed artistically on the white wall of the house. Gul, who was waiting anxiously for him, waved gleefully from the first floor. She seemed to be liking the place.

She ran down the stairs built on the side of the building to avoid disturbance to the residents on the ground floor.

'Come up, don't you want to see my house?' Happiness and enthusiasm danced on her face.

Since he knew she had another girl staying with her, Dewran hesitated.

'Isn't your friend there?'

'So what? Come . . .'

Gul pulled him by his arm.

Possibly because she had heard their voices, a girl appeared at the window above them. She was wearing a bright yellow dress, the colour of sunflowers. Dewran felt breathless. Such bright, shiny eyes. He sighed.

'Is she a Kurd?'

'Ah no! Indian. She has Kurdish features, doesn't she?'

Dewran did not register whatever Gul said after that. He kept nodding to whatever she said. She kept prattling while she made tea. She felt happy upon seeing him enjoy the coconut-filled biscuits.

'They're made by Seetha. I also ate a lot. Very tasty.' She picked up the crumbs on the plate and dropped them into her mouth.

'Why are you not introducing her?' he asked casually, when he got an opening. His sister was sharp and could detect the slightest change of expression.

Seetha emerged from the room in response to the shouted invitation by Gul. There was one more thing on her face that entranced Dewran—a glittering diamond nose stud that shone as brightly as her eyes.

'I was under the impression that only Kurdish women wore nose studs and rings. Our cultures may be related,' Dewran said shyly after they were introduced.

Gul looked at him amazed, 'Biraγê mezin, you have started to notice women's jewellery?'

She's going to spoil everything! Hurriedly, he tried to correct himself.

'I've seen our women wear them back home. I didn't know Indian women did too. It was an innocent question!'

Watching him being shy and squirming in embarrassment, the girls laughed till they had tears in their eyes and their sides ached.

That had been the beginning.

Later, Dewran met Timur in that house. Along with Seetha, he was doing research under Prof. Arnau. On Sundays, all four of them wandered along Barcelona's beaches and, by turn, tried paella in various restaurants.

Dewran started to notice with alarm the shiny diamantine eyes stealing glances at him. Beyond jamming with his friends, playing football, and drinking some beer out of sight of his elder brother, he had done nothing adventurous in his life. A belief that friendship with girls would diminish their masculinity had kept Dewran and his friends from cosying up with women.

Seetha spoke about her native land incessantly. Her words hid her desire to return to her land. When Timur and Gul described the beauty of sunset at the Kadıköy coast and the errant seagulls that woke one up before sunrise or the fascinating depths of the Sea of Marmara or the bewitching hills of Kurdistan and tried to bring Seetha to her knees, she always had something to counter them with from Kerala.

On some days, Timur had exhibited the traits of a typical bourgeois Turk. He would hold forth on his president's administrative reforms, new roads, mosques or the history of the Ottoman Empire. When unable to bear with much longer, Gul would attack him like a wounded tigress. She abused his president who stole money meant for refugees' food and blankets. She narrated how the coffers were being filled from sales of oil commandeered by ISIS. She ranted till Timur bowed his head in mortification and guilt for having extolled a president who caused his citizens to starve, let their children beg on the streets, and promoted racial hatred and genocide in his country.

Those evenings were so fulfilling, so luminous. Two people, tied up in their stolen glances, and yet tongue-tied. Two others, who were at each other's throats like fighting cocks. For that limbo to end, Dewran had to wait for Gul to take a trip to Madrid. How could she have given up on an opportunity to gallivant about in Madrid using the ostensible reason of attending a seminar arranged by the university? As soon as he gave the permission, she emptied his purse and expropriated everything in there. Dewran smiled when he thought about it.

He had taken Seetha's mobile number. However, he spent two days wondering how to open the conversation and what should be the follow-up. When he considered that Gul would be back in less than two weeks, he picked up courage and called Seetha. He had called with the plan that he would open with the intimation that he was still in town and if she needed any help, she could call him.

As soon as she answered, he understood that she was neither in the university nor at home. There was a lot of noise in the background. She spoke sotto voce between slogans being shouted and police announcements through loud hailers. She cut the call saying she was participating in a demonstration, and she would call back.

Dewran lost focus at his workplace. The TV had been telecasting live these demonstrations since the morning. They were processions for Catalonian independence. Police was using water cannons and shooting at the demonstrators with rubber bullets.

When he thought about Seetha taking part in this agitation, he felt he would go mad.

The restaurant was buzzing with people. The chef was working like an automaton. Dewran found it hard to concentrate. He was making repeated mistakes. When his uncle saw him arrange marinated meat—still on the skewers which hadn't yet been placed in the oven—in plates for serving, he gave him a mouthful, and pushed him out of the eatery. At least some of the customers, while drinking wine and munching on spicy kebabs, tried to listen in on his uncle's frank opinion on the degenerate new generation and his imprecations on them.

A Kurd was no stranger to demonstrations, baton-charges and police firing. Yet an unnamed fear gnawed him from the inside. *Why was she getting involved in things that did not concern her?* He was becoming angry. *If Catalonians needed independence, they would fight and win it. How was this girl concerned?*

When he went out, it was clear that large-scale rioting had happened on the streets. Abandoned footwear and a broken bicycle, as if someone had flung them around, were lying scattered. When he saw a burning vehicle at a distance, he decided to call her again. She answered immediately; she was panting and her voice was breaking.

'Where are you?' Dewran asked anxiously.

'I don't know. I'm hiding.' He had difficulty in understanding her whispered reply.

'Why did you go out at this time?'

'I was bored sitting alone.' She sounded embarrassed.

'Send me your location through WhatsApp. I'll come.'

The message notification arrived. The place was around two kilometres from where he was. No vehicles were available. If he were to run, it would take him ten minutes.

It was a small, isolated lane in a locality with small shops and large villas. The place looked deserted. Darkness was falling.

A panting Dewran looked in all directions. Her phone had stopped ringing. Where would he go in search of her? He walked around, a nervous wreck.

'Zzzhhhh,' someone hissed. Startled, Dewran turned around. A head slowly appeared out of a garbage bin. 'I am here.'

Seetha! Dewran reached her in one bound. 'Why didn't you stay home? Why get beaten up on the streets?' He gave her an angry stare.

'I was bored stiff being alone for two days. Prof. Arnau had said he would come to the library. I had come out to meet him.' She looked sheepish.

'You could have called me. How did you reach *here*?'

'When he said that he was joining the demonstration, I accompanied him.' Dewran's anger made her bow her head.

'Arrgh! That was incredibly stupid!'

The dirt and grime on her clothes worried him.

'Did you fall down somewhere?'

'When the police started their baton-charge, we started to run. I fell while running,' she spoke hesitantly.

Seetha was limping.

When she started to walk back home, supporting herself by clutching his arm, she wondered where her shyness had disappeared.

There were no vehicles on the roads other than police cars with their sirens that zipped past. Bus services had been cancelled. The wail of ambulance sirens could be heard occasionally cutting through the heavy silence.

Seetha's house was around 8 km away. They walked unhurriedly, often resting on the roadside benches. A cup of tea and some almond biscuits from a bakery kept open by an intrepid old man took care of Seetha's fatigue. Her eyes sparkled with love when she looked at Dewran.

The look muted Dewran, who had been profusely sermonizing her till then. He lost his voice to her dark eyes that seemed to have sunk harpoons into him. He mumbled in Kurdish, 'Looks as if she is hidden an entire ocean in her eyes.'

'What did you say?' Seetha asked curiously. He shook his head in negation. But the smile that was playing hide-and-seek on his face made her blush.

The amused bakery owner, discretion slowly triumphing his bravado, and wanting to down his shutters fearing a fresh round of stone-pelting, watched the pair of lovebirds in front of him. Usually, his young customers kissed and smooched with gay abandon.

'These two are seriously lacking in passion,' he told himself. He placed a bottle of Crema Catalana that he had preserved for special occasions in front of them and said, 'Don't pay me, kids. But you two enjoy.'

A surprised Dewran thanked him.

'What is this?' Seetha asked.

'This is Catalonian liqueur. Are you not familiar with it?'

Seetha picked up the bottle and examined it.

'It's a woman's drink. Take a sip . . .'

'I've never drunk before,' she said timidly.

'It's made with milk, eggs and sugar and some cinnamon, lemon, vanilla and caramel. And a bit of alcohol for namesake. It's very tasty. But if you are not accustomed to drinking, don't!'

Seetha snatched the glass he had filled for himself.

'Let me try.'

'I was joking. If you are not accustomed to drinking, don't!'

Dewran tried to repossess the glass her hand. Seetha evaded him, turned to the side and chugged it down fully.

'It's so tasty! Feels like I'm having vanilla ice cream. Just that there's a bit of bitter tanginess.' She looked greedily at the bottle.

Dewran moved the bottle away. 'You don't drink this. The bitter taste is from the alcohol.'

'Absolutely no problem. I liked it. Pour it again!'

She insisted; he complied hesitantly. He watched with trepidation as she quaffed it thirstily. Dewran could perceive a flush and lassitude spreading on her face.

'Let's go. It's getting dark.' He tried to pull her up.

'Wait! What's the hurry? We'll leave after sometime,' she requested.

'Are you coming?' Dewran was losing his temper. If Gul came to know of this, he would never hear the end of it.

Leaving the half-empty bottle and money on the table, Dewran and Seetha left the bakery. He held her close, feeling the softness of her body. He could smell the special fragrance from her untied hair that he had never experienced before.

'What have you used on your hair? Such a beautiful scent!'

In spite of himself, he buried his nose in her tresses.

'Did you like it?' She raised her head and looked into his eyes.

'Hmmm . . .' Dewran whispered.

He controlled the temptation to kiss her moist lips.

'It's hair oil infused with herbs and camphor. My mother's gift as a hair growth tonic.'

Her words had started to slur. Dewran smiled and hugged her closer indulgently.

They did not realise how long they had been walking. Dewran found it difficult to take her up the stairs. After helping her onto the sofa and instructing her to lock the door securely, when he turned to leave, she called him from behind.

'What happened? Do you need something?' He took the blanket that had slipped down and covered her properly.

'You had asked me to call if I am lonely. I am lonely.'

'I should go. It's getting late.'

'Don't go.'

Seetha squeezed herself against the back of the sofa, making space for him to sit beside her. He could not have sat down without touching her body. The warmth that spread from her body to his own made him tremble. When he saw the suggestion of sweat above her upper lips, although nervous, he could not stop himself from caressing her face. His fingers ran over her half-closed eyes, proud nose and unpainted rosy lips. Seetha kissed lightly on the fingers that caressed her.

'I like you,' she whispered.

His burning lips covered hers with a passionate kiss.

* * *

'Dewran, come out of your reverie.'

Arman's words brought him back from the dream world.

'Inform her university. University of Barcelona is one of the premier institutions in Spain. They won't keep quiet,' Arman spoke thoughtfully.

'That's true. Her guide is a significant presence in the Catalan independence movement.'

'Send him an e-mail. Copies should go to Indian embassies in Spain and Turkey, the Indian foreign minister, prime minister and president. All media houses in India should be tipped off. We've no time to waste.'

'We've no proof that she's in the Turkish Army's custody.'

'No need. Our parents will testify. We are anyway in the deep end. What more can happen to us? You should not lose Seetha the way I lost Dilva!'

Arman was searching for something on his mobile. He showed it to Dewran. 'This piece of cloth. Do you recognize it? The design has some Indianness about it.'

It was a Facebook profile that shared vignettes of the Turkish Army's exploits and heroism. One that spread toxic racist content against minorities. The picture on Arman's phone showed four or five drunk young men. Most of them had only their underwear on. However, their close-cropped hair and muscled bodies screamed that they were soldiers.

While the picture with the caption 'Enjoying Indian meat' may have, prima facie, looked harmless to others, Dewran's eyes were glued to the piece of cloth that one of the men had tied around his head. It was the dupatta that Seetha had worn around her neck on the night when they last met, and which had gotten soaked with her tears. A light pink one with colourful elephant, peacock, flower and vine motifs.

A searing flame rose from his belly and set him trembling. He leaned on Arman's shoulder for support.

'This is hers.' His voice broke.

Throwing his sinewy arm around him, Arman held him close like he would a child.

'Don't be sad. This means that things are not good. Yet, we shall try.'

Dewran burst into tears.

Stroking his head and shoulders, as he kept trying to comfort his brother, Arman looked up at the circling eagle with unconcealed fury. A body engulfed in fire was dancing in front of those eyes. His hands closed into fists. His body throbbed like that of an adrenaline-fired, battle-ready soldier. Suddenly there was a volley of shots from the nearby firing range. Arman watched vengefully as the peacefully gliding eagle got startled and flew away, frantically flapping its wings.

'Enough of crying. We've no time to waste. We've things to do.'

Holding Dewran's hand, he walked towards his room.

The Baby

She felt as if she was being swamped by puffy clouds—white downy cotton balls that blocked her vision.

Close, but not close enough to touch. Unable to anchor the feet, yet able to keep moving. As if swimming in air; gliding without touching anything. It is fun. No one was around. Not even a fly. Deafening silence. Unbearable. Ah . . . mother! No voice came out. Gathering all strength, once more . . . Ammae!

Sounds of running feet.

Open your eyes . . .

Someone was stroking the cheek . . . excruciating pain!

No . . . No . . .

Thank god! She's regained consciousness! Call the doctor!

Move aside . . . bring that stand here . . .

Open your eyes . . .

Such a gentle voice . . .

Is it her father?

Soft fingers searching for the vein. This is a hospital!

Pain again. A needle was being inserted.

It's nothing. Please open your eyes . . .

It's her father! The same voice. But her father doesn't converse in English! No, it can't be. This is someone else.

Someone was wiping her face with a wet cotton swab. Was it her father?

Maybe she should open the eyes and peek?

A man with grey hair and grey beard. Fluffy, white cotton dresses. Is this heaven? Wherever you reach after death, does it look like this?

He was smiling and checking the speed of the infusion that ran into the cannula. It's a doctor. She must have fallen somewhere. But where is amma? She's going to get smacked for this by amma.

Lucky! Amma isn't around. Only forms in fluffy white dresses floating around. Amma doesn't wear such white frocks. Her colourful cotton sarees are well starched and stay stiff like flapping boards. She looked so good in them. Maybe she's gone out. Will pretend to be asleep when she returns.

Plop . . . plop . . . plop . . . the fluid was falling in drops.

Plop . . . plop . . .

. . .

'Are you sleeping?'

A cool, slim, soft hand on the forehead. The distinct smell of disinfectant. How white is his hair? Thin, like silver strands. Never dyed!

'It's okay. Take rest.'

Sounds of papers being flipped through.

'Seetha—is this a Persian name?'

'It sounds like an Indian name, doctor.'

'Possible. India women have such long hair and dark eyes.'

'How did she land up in this hell?' The man was looking at her with concern.

If her grandmother—who named her Seetha so that her own son's first-born would be like King Janaka's daughter—were to see her, how would she react? Would she ostracise her?

Surely, her mother would have informed her by now. Her granddaughter, who had gone to study abroad, was carrying a non-Hindu, foreigner's child in her womb.

Her grandmother would have indulged in breast-beating and cursed her mother for sending her grown-up daughter to study abroad.

She would have locked up the portals of the *tharavad*, banning her entry forever.

My baby . . . are you aware of all this hue and cry?

A still womb. *He is biding his time, lying low.*

'Seetha, don't move your hand. We have had terrible difficulty in finding a vein to set the cannula.'

A young woman's voice. There were many people in the room.

When she shifted her head, shooting pain! Every cell screamed in pain as if daggers were being twisted in them.

Groan.

'Lie still!'

The tone was peremptory.

Why's the room so white? Not even a speck of dust on the ceiling. No pregnant geckos, their eggs seen through their diaphanous bellies, as they pretended to hold up the ceiling.

This side room looks more beautiful. It was so nice to see the light streaming through the thin, white curtains. Aren't those white oleander flowers in the vase on the bedside table?

'Are you thirsty?'

It is that martinet lady! I am not going to talk to her. Let the doctor come.

Her lips burnt terribly when they were being swabbed with damp cotton. When she moved them, she tasted blood—as if bruised skin and clotted blood had been fused together.

It's not water! It's blood!

'No . . . no . . .'

The woman was feeding her blood, not water!

Blood!

'Seetha . . . Seetha . . . don't try to get up.'

'Doctor . . .!'

Bells were ringing . . . one . . . two . . . ten . . . hundred . . . thousand . . .

Darkness!

. . .

The whole body is wet.

Lather. The smell of the green soap that amma loves.

Back again to that bathroom!

The same damp, slippery, dark bathroom.

She is being bathed. She is being bathed and readied!

'Don't bathe me! No . . . no . . . Stop it!'

'Child I'm only wet-sponging your body!'

'Don't do it. Don't . . .'

'Hey! Don't move your body!'

'Someone help. Hold her! I'm not able to!'

She had to escape. If she can trick this woman, it will be easy. Arrrggghhh . . . the pain!

Everywhere inside her, knives were being thrust in and turned.

'She's bleeding!'

'Call the doctor.'

'Seetha what are you trying to do?'

'Take that tray.'

Pain . . . pain . . . pain . . .

She was sinking. Deep into a slumber . . . into darkness.

. . .

Today, the oleanders are red.

They looked like splotches of blood against the white lace-trimmed curtains.

What is the doctor sitting and doing there?

He sat unmoving. A white statue that looked out through the window, seated on the chair placed next to it.

He was looking at the thin white smoke emitted by a chimney outside the window.

Someone pushed the door open.

There is no knocking. There are no manners! There is no comforting smell of disinfectant.

The sound of boots!

No clinking of cutlery and crockery. No sound of the vacuum cleaner. No swish of the wet mop.

The old sound!

She should scream.

The tongue seems to have descended into her throat.

She was choking.

A heavy weight had descended on her chest.

The white statue came to life.

It turns its head like an inanimate thing showing signs of life.

'Doctor, I heard she has regained consciousness.'

'That's not correct. Opening eyes doesn't mean she has regained consciousness.'

'When can we take her away?'

'She's not in a good condition. She opens her eyes sometimes. The other day she haemorrhaged. If you take her now, things will become worse.'

The statue stood up.

'She's in no condition to be moved. I can't be answerable for her death.'

'We have our own doctors too.'

'Yes, I know that. That's why you had to bring her here with the embryo hanging out of her.'

'Embryo?' Yes, that was the word used. 'Embryo!'

'Whatever you say, we'll take her!'

'Not possible. Leave this room right now. Playing military and police and all that can be done outside this room.'

'You'll suffer for this.'

'Yes. I shall be ready. But get out now!'

The sound of door being slammed shut.

Sounds of approaching footsteps.

Hands tearing you apart.

Pain . . . pain . . .

'NO! Don't come near me . . .'

The hand is stroking my forehead.

'Have no fear. I won't let them take you.'

Tears. A hail of tears. A torrent of tears.

I am unable to stop them.

I am unable to stop anything.

'My baby . . . my baby . . .'

'Since you have overheard it, I can't hide it any longer.'

'My baby . . .'

'Open your eyes for once please. I can only tell this while looking into your eyes. Slowly, gradually. Here, I shall wipe your face. There's only dim light in the room. You can open your eyes without any fear. Exactly like that, and now look at my face.'

'My baby . . .'

'You are a brave girl. A real fighter.'

Silence!

'My child, I couldn't save your baby. Your heart was failing when you were brought here.'

'My baby . . .'

'Your baby was not in a condition that we could save it. We lost it. You should not cry like this. You were brought in with a completely broken body. You have internal wounds. You may bleed again.'

'My baby . . .'

'I'm going to sedate you.'

'Would my baby have felt the pain?'

'Why are you not saying anything? Whatever you are saying, I am unable to understand. You are talking in a language unknown to me.'

Some things should be understood by people speaking any language. For example:

- Tears
- Rape
- Baby . . . yes, baby . . . are you not able to understand this?

You are correct. Whichever language I tell you this in, you will not understand. Even in your own language.

His wails when you would have torn him out of me.

Who would have heard that? Could anyone have heard that shriek?

Why did you save me? Why did you let me survive?

The mother of Dewran's child!

That is a mortal sin!

This grand empire of yours will be burnt down to ashes.

Shoot me with all the drugs in that tray. End it for me. Once and for all.

'Ammae . . .!'

Is that me crying?

No, it's my baby crying.

Darkness was descending.

It is all dark now.

Mibang

'They have left no loopholes. They covered every possible angle when she was taken in.'

Bahadir's frown lines had deepened. Agitated, he kept doodling on the paper lying in front of him.

Emine gazed at him with concern. After the heated debate he had had with his friends in the morning, Bahadir had not left his cabin. It was only a little while ago that he had summoned Emine and asked if she could help him in a case. She could not believe it. The only exchange between them till then were the congratulatory, if mildly surprised, smiles that he had given her at times when she had offered her diffident comments when legal points were being discussed.

'A girl—she's suspected to be under police custody. She's missing. There are witnesses to her arrest by the police. What would you do?'

'If it's a crime committed by a single person, the police can keep the person in custody for forty-eight hours without charging the person with the crime; if it's by a group, that'd be ninety-six hours,' Emine said timidly, unsure if she was saying the right thing. In order to get rid of the dryness in her mouth, she greedily drank the glass of water on the table and ended up coughing.

'With permission from a judge, this can be extended up to twelve days.' Bahadir sounded perturbed. 'Which means that we can do nothing to bring her out for another nine days.'

He pushed a piece of paper towards Emine.

'Call this number and ask for a meeting. Tamo Mibang, the Indian ambassador. It's urgent. It would be great if I could meet him today.'

'Sir, he may ask what the meeting is for?' Emine said diffidently.

'A girl, an Indian citizen, is locked up in a Turkish prison. Illegally. The meeting is about getting her freed.'

Bahadir left the room. The arguments with his senior colleagues in the morning had drained him. Although he stood for a long time on the balcony taking in the cool sea breeze, the embers within were consuming him from inside. He dearly wanted a chilled beer.

Although they were Turkey's leading attorney firm, Bahadir and his associates never took up the briefs of those accused of being militants and terrorists by the government. Occasionally, Bahadir, in his personal interest, would appear for human rights violation cases. However, his associates were adamant that they would not get involved in cases where government policies or its stand were questioned.

'Haven't we made enough money? At least now we should take up public interest cases,' pleaded Bahadir in their regular morning meeting, after presenting the background.

'How can this be a public interest case, Bahadir? This abets extremists. A case that could shake the very foundations of our law firm. We don't need this.' Bairam, who had been listening intently and taking notes, put down his pencil with an air of someone who has had enough.

'What's the connection between the extremism and terrorism that you talk of and this case? Wouldn't our reputation gain from rendering legal services to rescue a foreign girl who has been kept in illegal custody?'

Bahadir felt an acute helplessness.

'We aren't going be famous in this country by helping an Indian girl. If it was a white-skinned European or American, maybe we could have tried,' opined Zahran.

Bairam seconded Zahran, 'That's correct. Even if she was a Pakistani, we would have gained via other benefits. An Indian? No, Bahadir. Not only that no good will come out of it, but it could actually harm us.'

'Bahadir, I'll back you up. But don't forget one thing. We have twenty-five juniors working under us. Including other staff, forty-two people draw their salaries from us. Do you want all of them to end up jobless?' Kadir, who had been listening silently till then, asked irascibly.

'I can't believe that this organization will be destroyed if we came to the aid of a helpless girl.' Bahadir too was losing his temper.

'Your approach in this case is overly emotional. What should be concern is the abetting of terrorism that she could be charged with,' Bairam stuck to his guns.

'Don't we know that she has no connection to all that you claim? As a worst case, they may be able to produce some love-letters or mushy text messages that she may have sent. Through our intervention, we may save the life of an innocent person.' Bahadir was back to pleading.

'If the government is able to capture the targeted extremists by leveraging this girl, that will be an achievement for the government.'

Bahadir lost it when he heard Bairam's words. Flinging down the notepad and pen in his hand, he railed, 'What according to you is militancy and extremism? Let's define that first!'

Kadir and Bairam looked at each other.

'Some of the Kurds took up arms to defend themselves against the pogrom and violent attacks that have been unleashed against them. If they hadn't done it, this country would have wiped out every Kurd by now. Not even a baby would have been left behind. They too are citizens of this country. They are being annihilated by those who should be protecting them. Don't treat them as equals; at least start treating them as human beings! Then members of all these organizations will lay down their arms.'

The silence of his colleagues only added fuel to the fire.

'You are cowards. When I wore this black coat and robe for the first time, I had taken an oath upon my integrity and conscience that I shall help enforce justice. Our Constitution lays down that all citizens are equal and that it is the duty of those who govern to ensure that this equality is guaranteed. To protect the innocent is our duty.'

'Bahadir, when it's a question of survival, who remembers such oaths?' Kadir responded smiling upon seeing how overwrought Bahadir was.

'Keep that mocking smile to yourself. I don't need your permission to prosecute this case.' Kicking the chair away, Bahadir bustled out of the room. The junior lawyers who congregated near the conference room, on hearing the kerfuffle, dispersed quickly, pretending to be busy with their tasks.

Bahadir paced in his cabin like a caged lion. He was aware that the girl's life was in extreme danger. Each moment they delayed action reduced the chances of saving her unharmed. When he considered that getting Timur back to lead a normal life was well-nigh impossible if something were to happen to Seetha, he felt a dread. The noose was tightening. He searched in his mobile phone frantically as if looking for an invisible contact. Who was there? Who had the courage to stand with him at this hour?

The mobile suddenly rang in his hand. Zehra had been calling from the morning. There was no word from Timur. The livid bruises and wounds on his body . . . his sudden disappearance in the night . . . he could imagine Zehra's panic. What could he tell her? He answered the call with a resigned look.

'Do you have information about him?'

'No, but he'll surely call. Please tell him that there's progress in what he asked me to do.'

Someone coughed politely behind him to attract his attention. Emine was waiting by the door leading to the balcony for him hang up the phone.

'He said that if you would go to the consulate, he can meet you in half an hour. If not, then at 6 p.m., at the Balon Café at Kadiköy.'

'So, Mibang realises the gravity of the situation.'

Bahadir lit a cigarette.

'I'm going home. I'll meet him at Kadiköy. Please inform him. If I have any meetings today, please reschedule them.'

Emine left.

With his eyes fixed on a few seagulls wheeling in search of prey far out in the sea, Bahadir blew smoke rings into the air.

On his way home, his mind was occupied with a concern— what to tell Zehra. He knew that she held a grouse that he was supporting Timur in all his shenanigans. He would have to explain things patiently to Zehra. She should be proud that her son had grown into a decent man who could not bear to see and remain unmoved by the sorrows of his fellow men.

As the car took the curve towards his house, he could see the bright red-and-white bougainvillea flowers that hung above the gate, challenging the cold of the winter. However, when he saw Kasim's shiny black Mercedes in the driveway, Bahadir's face fell. He had left the previous day after listening to Timur's tirade and insults. If he had turned up today also, without his entourage, there should be sufficient reasons.

Kasim rose from his seat when he saw Bahadir. His face was gloomy. Zehra was leaning against the door post. Her unhappy face made Bahadir furious. Had this guy come here to make things worse? 'Serve the food!' Sensing the vexation in his tone, Zehra quickly went inside.

'Kadir called me. He told me that you are starting the legal process for that girl. All of them are very disturbed.' Kasim wasted no time in broaching the subject.

Bahadir's persistent silence emboldened him. 'Birayê mezin, what are you doing? Timur is indulging in unlawful activities. Should you be encouraging him?'

'Are you trying to teach me law?' Bahadir said impassively. He took off his shoes and leaned back against the sofa.

'Birayê mezin, you'll destroy the good name earned over these years,' Kasim said crossly.

'All these years I worked for myself. Only to make money and earn fame. At least for the rest of my life, I should do something for others.'

His calm reply infuriated Kasim. He flared up.

'Do you think about me at all? If the higher-ups come to know that my brother is helping militants, I won't remain a minister for long.'

'So, your ministership is the issue.' Bahadir laughed. 'Have your food and go.'

'Yes, my ministership is the issue. I need to preserve it. I shall myself inform those who matter about your activities.' Kasim was trembling with anger.

'You do whatever you have to do. Remember only one thing—you have reached an age when you should stop running after power and pelf; it's time you outgrew such impulses.'

'Why don't you give all these advices to that fathead? I'll teach both of you a lesson.'

Kasim stomped out.

Bahadir looked at a startled Zehra and winked mischievously.

'You don't get worried about all this drama. You should feel proud that our son's noble-hearted.'

Bahadir reached Balon Café exactly at 6 p.m. Toying with a half-empty cup of coffee, Mibang, who had arrived earlier, was seated in a corner from where he had an unimpeded view of the sea.

'The most exquisite sunset in the world. Do you have any doubt, Mibang?'

'And the tastiest coffee in the world too . . .' Mibang laughed and replied, standing up to receive Bahadir.

A seagull was perched on the side rail eyeing the biscuits on the table and expecting to be fed.

'Doubtlessly so! Only the fortunate can sit on this chair and enjoy both at the same time!' said Mibang, keeping his eyes on the old railway station behind the Haydarpaşa ferry post on the opposite shore, that shone in the coppery light of the setting sun.

'What happened to the plan of selling that building to that hotel group?' Mibang asked casually.

'There have been massive public protests, as you know. It would appear that the government has shelved the idea, at least for the time being.'

For some time, Bahadir watched quietly the acrobatic seagull swooping and catching the biscuit pieces that Mibang was throwing in its direction.

'I assume that Emine had indicated the reason why I wanted to meet you.'

'Yeah, she had told me. It's not something pleasant to talk about or listen to.'

Flinging the last bits of biscuits at the greedy seagull who was waiting expectantly, Mibang turned to face Bahadir. The smile on his face had vanished.

'We had received some emails yesterday on this matter.'

'So you are aware of this!'

'Yes, we know. But it's scarcely believable!'

'Don't disbelieve it! If my guess is correct, not a word in those mails would be falsehood.'

Mibang gave Bahadir a searching look.

'How do you know that?'

'Don't worry, I didn't send them.' Bahadir laughed.

'I shall narrate some other time how I came across the information. We don't have the luxury of time. My experience is speaking here. That girl's life is in mortal danger.'

'Bahadir what can I do to help someone who the Turkish government alleges has terrorist connections? You also know that your jails hold many foreigners involved in such cases. I don't have to tell you that as per international laws, countries where terrorist acts are committed, have the last word on the fate of the perpetrators.'

'Mibang, haven't you understood that she landed up in this mess without any intention and involvement? To top it all, she is pregnant too.'

Bahadir was getting furious at the non-committal attitude of Mibang.

'Isn't it your responsibility to ensure that she's safe and exits with her life? Do you have any idea where this will end up if the press gets scent of this? It can result in wrecking our bilateral relations.'

'Bahadir don't think I haven't taken any action. Emails to Turkish authorities have been sent in the morning itself. We have information that an Indian girl is in your custody. We have demanded that we should be given the opportunity to ensure that she is safe, and we need permission to ensure that she receives legal representation. They cannot avoid replying to those messages.'

The waiter who had come to collect the empty coffee cups asked if they wanted to order anything more.

'Would you like to have some raki?'

'Why not?' Mibang agreed. The tension was giving him a headache. From the time he received the mails, he had been worried about whom all he would have to give explanations. His taut nerves eased as he recalled raki imbued with fragrance of star anise and a light sweet taste.

Balon Café was famous for its seafood fare. Bahadir ordered dishes after dishes as if he had decided to give Mibang the treat of his life. Bahadir was exhausted from his day's stress and confrontations. Chewing on crisp fried squid rings, he was knocking back glass after glass of raki without adding water or turnip juice, as if he wanted to get drunk quickly.

Mibang was nursing his milky white raki—that the otherwise colourless liquid turns into on addition of water—gazing indulgently at the myriad criss-crossing boats as they sliced through the golden blanket that the sun had spread over the Sea of Marmara. On the table, the crystal-cut glasses, ice pail and ice cubes refracted the red light of the setting sun brilliantly, making the space incandescent. He mused that if the new headaches that the day had brought were not there, how much more enjoyable that evening would have been.

His phone rang. It was an unsaved local number. After some hesitation he picked up the call. When Mibang's face went pale as he listened to the caller, Bahadir understood that a major problem was rolling in.

'I'm busy. Call me tomorrow.'

After he cut the call, he drank the remaining raki in a single gulp.

'The local correspondent of *Euro Times*. They too have received emails. She wants to talk about Seetha, the Indian girl in police custody!'

Mibang looked helplessly at Bahadir.

'There are people working behind the scene. Our Ministry of External Affairs has already enquired about this today. The mails have reached the Indian president, prime minister, and reporters of leading newspapers. This can't be wished away.'

'India and Turkey are signatories in the Council of Europe's international agreements on prisoner extradition. However, you are aware that in case of extremism and national security, these agreements do not come into play,' said Bahadir, while refilling his glass.

'But what proof do they have of her indulging in terrorist activities?' Mibang's face was flushed from anger and alcohol. The coolness of the evening notwithstanding, his forehead showed beads of perspiration.

'Which is what I was trying to tell you a little while ago. You've been here for some time now. Do you think arranging proof is a difficult thing to do here?' Bahadur laughed bitterly.

'I hope we get her back alive and in one piece.' Mibang did not sound hopeful in the least.

'That's the thing, Mibang. She's a girl! And moreover, pregnant. They will torture her.' Bahadir spoke thoughtfully.

'Those who should know would have come to know by now that the search for Seetha has started. That might just about keep her alive. You should receive a reply tomorrow from the Turkish authorities. Whatever it is, please inform me.'

Bahadir rose to his feet after draining the glass. It had been years since he had drunk so much. After he paid the bill and walked on unsteady legs towards the exit, Mibang followed him.

'It won't be a good idea to drive now.' While Bahadir was trying to find a taxi, Mibang took his hand in his own.

'They'll try their damnedest to not release her.'

Sensing his helplessness, Bahadir gripped Mibang's hand firmly to give him courage.

'And we'll do our damnedest to save her.'

He flagged down a taxi.

'Don't worry, Mibang. This is a battle we'll win.'

Ignoring the look of disbelief on Mibang's face, Bahadir opened the door of the taxi for him. When the tail lights of the car disappeared in the distance, Bahadir walked slowly towards the seashore. On the opposite shore, surrounded by an ethereal luminescence, the Blue Mosque stood proudly reaching up to the starlit sky.

'Will have to win the battle . . .'

Closing his eyes, he breathed in the smell of the Sea of Marmara that encircled him.

The waves that had turned saline from the tears and blood spilled into them for centuries, were smashing their heads against the rocky shoreline, lamenting.

Mustafa

'I can't recognize these roads,' he said while turning the car carefully on to the street. 'But then, those days, what was here that was worth retaining in mind? The smell of rotting flesh. Firing. What could have remained in my memory but burnt corpses, raped bodies, and screams of people? What was Cizîr more than a graveyard?' He sighed.

'Is the basement where Dilva died here?' Timur asked, groaning inside.

'Died?' Mustafa gave him an angry stare. 'After she was gang-raped, the place where she lay was set on fire after petrol was poured over her. That's how it should be phrased.'

Timur bowed his head as if he was guilty of some crime. He could not understand why he had to feel guilty.

'It's somewhere close. We're going there. Having come this far, how can we leave Cizîr without paying homage to Dilva?' Mustafa spoke softly.

Although Timur was conscious that every minute of delay was worsening the risk of something bad happening to Seetha, he was unable to object to the detour. Every time Mustafa said Dilva's name, a girl resembling Seetha, standing inside a bonfire with flames leaping all around her, called out to Timur to save her. Try as he might, he could not touch the form as the image of it getting incinerated into a handful of ashes played in his mind in the loop.

Mustafa could sense his anxiety. Only when he promised that they would not spend more than half-an-hour in Cizîr did Timur calm down a little.

That morning, when Timur had reached in front of the broken door of Mustafa and Akbar's house, it did not look like an inhabited place. Dawn was breaking; the front yard was covered with fallen leaves. Some wooden pieces to be used as firewood were kept leaning against the wall. There was no other sound in the front of the house, other than the chatter of birds from the leafy trees that belied the aridity of the land. Timur was vigilant, worried that someone may be watching him as he headed towards the house. He glanced around anxiously.

Since it was night-time, during his previous visit he had not noticed the pathetic state of the street. It was squalid and reeking; all the garbage of the town seemed to have ended up there. The suspicious driver of the car that brought him from the airport hung around for some time—possibly aching to know what a decently-attired young man was like him doing in this seedy part of the town—before he decided to drive back. To mislead him, Timur walked towards an old mosque ahead of him. Only after the taxi had gone around the corner and disappeared, did he turn back towards his destination.

The building looked as if it would collapse on itself any time. They had occupied a house that had been abandoned by its original occupants. He could easily identify the crumbling building from his previous visit. A bird that flew in holding dried grass in its beak, hopped from branch to branch observing the stranger who had suddenly appeared out of the blue. When he knocked, a sleepy-eyed Mustafa peeped through the cracks in the door.

'Oh, it's you! I'd thought it was the police.'

He stepped out cheerfully. Timur observed that the chill in the air had given him goose pimples on his exposed hairy, sinewy forearms.

'Didn't the police beat you to death?' Mustafa chuckled. However, his demeanour revealed his happiness in meeting Timur again.

Inside, the house was warm. Timur had failed to notice in his previous visit that there was a coal brazier in one corner of the room. The clothes that were heaped on the chair on that day were now folded and hung from the clothesline. It appeared as if considerable time had been spent on tidying up the house. Timur gratefully sat down on a chair, waiting for Mustafa to return with the teapot.

'Where's Akbar?' asked Timur, after failing to find any sign of his presence.

'I don't know. He's not turned up for the last three or four days. He also went missing the day you were taken away by the police. He has not called even once. Who knows what's happened!' Mustafa said, busily making tea. Although he spoke with his usual gruffness, Timur could recognise the fear and concern in his voice.

After listening to the whole story as he sipped the hot tea, Mustafa gave Timur a measured look.

'Kasim Özdemir's nephew! How ironical! That apart, how is it that you didn't tell us this?'

'From the beginning you've all been treating me like an enemy.' Timur's tone reflected his pique.

Mustafa laughed. 'Unintended, Timur. Life has turned us into what we are.'

'It doesn't matter. I need your help to find Seetha. I have no friends in Istanbul whom I can trust in this matter.'

'Does your father know that you have come here? Will the police come in search of you?'

'No. My father is aware of what has happened. He will help us.'

Mustafa mulled over things. The tea in his hand was turning cold.

'I don't think they'll even show her the consideration even if she's carrying!' Timur's eyes brimmed over.

'Don't go on and on about her pregnancy! And to top it, spill your tears too. You're driving me crazy with this.'

Mustafa ruffled his own hair with his usual tetchiness. He had been thinking hard for some time on how to resolve the matter.

'Abdullah! Let's go meet Abdullah. He's the only one who can help us at this point.'

Excited, he jumped up from his seat.

'That secret police guy? He's been retired for a long time now.' Timur scowled, believing Mustafa would only end up wasting his time.

Mustafa laughed.

'You don't know his reach and influence. No policeman can pass out of their training academy without having heard of the legendary exploits of Abdullah Bölükbaşı. For them, he's the great hero who has saved the country from separatists.'

Donning an old jacket, Mustafa stepped out and placed the planks to block the doorway.

'Shall we go by car? Do you have money with you to fill petrol?'

'Yes, but where's the car?'

With an impish smile, Mustafa showed him the old Mercedes parked behind some bushes beside the house.

'My God, in this jalopy?' Timur's jaw dropped. He recalled his father's friends who would make a great deal about antique cars such as this one. Although Timur had misgivings, when Mustafa turned on the ignition, the engine started without much protest.

'Arman's father has asked me to keep the car till Arman comes back. I had offered to drive it up to Çîçika. But who listens to me? He believes that Arman will return some day and drive this car to their place,' Mustafa said with a sigh. 'I run the engine once in a while, dust and keep it clean. I feel like taking it for a spin sometimes but can't afford this gas guzzler.'

On their way, they took in a full tank of petrol at the first fuel station they found.

Mustafa had a happy grin. 'After this car came into my hands, it's the first time that it has had a full tank of petrol.'

The car had turned into the highway to Batman. The distance to Cizîr was around 250 km. Timur calculated the travel time in his mind.

'Will it take four hours to Cizîr?'

'In normal times, no. But there are check-posts all along the way. We'll be delayed,' Mustafa said, steering the car carefully to avoid potholes.

One more day will end soon without any news of Seetha, Timur thought fretfully.

What Mustafa said was true. Once they passed Mardin, check-posts started appearing one after the other. The massive concrete check-posts of Nusaybin had huge Turkish flags painted on them. The once fantastical red now appeared minatory to Timur.

'Look at that—that's the third biggest wall in the world. What if the citizens have to beg? What if they have to starve? Your president has built a wall!'

Mustafa's mocking words pointing at the wall separating Syria and Turkey made Timur screw up his face in humiliation.

'Have you started again? I have told you many times that I'm against such activities of the government,' Timur muttered through his clenched teeth.

'The world talks about the walls at the Mexican and Palestinian borders. They are criticised. No one has anything to say about this 764 km-long one built on our chests!'

Timur sat silently gazing at the soldier inside the watchtower built atop the wall. Facing the Syrian territory, the man stood still like a statue, gun in hand. The border area between Syria and Turkey was occupied by Kurds. *What did the government achieve by building the wall which the world assumed was to stop the influx of refugees into Turkey? How do these men and women who flee for their lives when they are attacked from all sides become refugees? The uncles, aunts, grandmothers and cousins of Turkish Kurds were living in Syria, across the border. How do the lines drawn on the maps and border walls erected by power-hungry political overlords for their convenience and interests deny humans their rights on this earth?*

Unable to find answers to the questions that in his mind, he sat with his head bowed.

The car left Nusaybin behind and sped towards Cizîr.

'Many changes are said to have happened in the Cizîr after the assaults started. That day I had escaped from there like a wounded dog, crawling out with the help of Narjes. Shall we go there? I'd like to meet her. After that we'll call on Sarya and Abdullah.'

Timur nodded mechanically.

When they entered the town, the first sight that met their eyes was smashed and broken buildings.

'Nothing much seems to have changed here,' Mustafa said, dejected. The destroyed town lay on apathetically on either side of the road. The road, pitted from explosions and the slip-shod attempts to repair them, posed a challenge to both Mustafa and the tired old car's suspension.

'Why the hell did I decide to come here?' he yelled as he tried to manoeuvre the car out of a deep pothole.

'Don't we have to see Dilva?'

Mustafa pretended to not hear Timur's question. However, after that, he negotiated the ruts and potholes with more self-control.

He started to mutter again when he saw a group of policemen in front of a school. 'Even now schools are their police stations. So many years have passed since the annihilation of this place. Yet!'

Timur watched everything in disbelief. He found it hard to convince himself this too was a part of Turkey.

In many places, ancient granite slabs that had once paved the roads had been dug up and heaped on the roadside. 'Why are you destroying the heritage of this town?' Timur asked silently, gazing at the face of every soldier who stood with guns along the road.

Mustafa seemed to be oblivious to all that. However, the deepening frown on his already clouded face made Timur nervous.

'This is the Bostancı Caddesi,' Mustafa parked the car on the side.

'The Mazlumder[1] report states that close to three hundred perished in three basements. As per their figures, to be exact, two hundred and sixty-six people. It's only a guestimate based on the charred remnants found in the basement. The first massacre took place here,' said Mustafa as they walked ahead. He was searching for some landmarks or recognizable buildings.

'Building number twenty-three.' He kept muttering while walking. 'Where the hell is it?'

He searched for it with a manic energy. He was sweating despite the coolness in the air.

'Mustafa, I remember what you said that day. Berivan had pointed out this place to you in the night. How do you expect to recognize it now?'

In his frenzied search, Mustafa did not hear whatever Timur said.

'Twenty-three ... twenty-three ...' a mumbling Mustafa stopped in front of every building and read out the number plate like a lunatic.

Timur ran to him and stopped him. 'What are you *doing*? The police are all around us.'

Mustafa had a blank look on face. Suddenly, he sat down on the pavement and started to sob.

Timur was worried that someone may notice them. Compared to Sur, the air in Cizîr was menacing. Timur felt that the government wanted to keep the devastated town that way to set an example. They had done no repairs. With bullet holes and shell pockmarks, the fire-licked, destroyed buildings stood there like ghost houses or a dystopian movie set. The Turkish flag painted in blood red on every pillar on the way were like needles poking and hurting his eyes.

All the walls had the picture of a smug, smiling Turkish president.

'You did all this!' said Timur, gnashing his teeth.

Armoured cars were passing by them. Although Timur stood in front and tried to cover Mustafa, he did not succeed. He felt that soldiers near a tank parked a little away from them were looking in their direction. Deciding that they should leave before attracting any more attention to themselves, he pulled Mustafa to his feet and led him to the car.

'Dilva will understand.'

Struggling to hold the weight of a lurching Mustafa, as they made slow progress, Timur murmured, 'She must be watching you, don't weep like this.'

Timur was in a hurry to get away from the buildings—with large hollows made by shells for walls and missing roofs—that looked on the verge of collapse. After pushing a sobbing Mustafa into the passenger seat, he quickly started the car and drove away.

Timur did not stop the car till they reached the banks of the gently flowing Tigris. He did not know the way to Sarya's house. Hoping that the cool breeze from the river would help Mustafa regain his composure, he lowered the window glasses, stepped out of the car and walked down to the riverbank. Enjoying the coolness travelling up his body, with his eyes closed, he stood in the ankle-deep icy water.

'Timur, we must leave.'

After a little while, he heard Mustafa hollering. The voice echoed from the brown soil on the other bank of the river, on the Syrian side. Timur turned back to see Mustafa had gotten out of the car. He stood against the backdrop of burnt and broken buildings that stood like a warning to voices that may be raised against the regime.

'Come here,' Timur beckoned him. He came down readily. His face was gloomy.

'Really icy water; get in and see.'

Mustafa rolled up the legs of his jeans in silence and stepped into the river. The chilly wavelets lapped gently against their feet.

'It's getting late. Shall we leave?' asked Mustafa, cupping his hands and splashing water copiously on his face.

'Are you hungry?' asked Timur. He himself had had only a toast and tea on the 1 hour 50 minute-long flight from Istanbul. Mustafa had not eaten anything.

'Sarya's kitchen will always have something to offer,' he said, laughing.

'Only now have I got the full picture of what has happened here. On my flight I was reading the UN report.'

Mustafa's face flushed when he heard that.

'UN report! What do those buggers know? Some two thousand have died they say? A statistic created by counting the bits and bones of corpses they could find.'

Timur was at a loss how to respond. He cursed his own lack of forethought in broaching this subject again.

'What about people incinerated without leaving even a piece of bone or hair? People who were buried alive by the soldiers? Those who were "disappeared"? In which statistics will your UN include all of these? Women who have been raped or raped and killed? Young men who have been beaten to within an inch of their life and now live as cripples? Our babies who did not get medical attention and died from infections from the shit they mixed in our water tanks? In which of your statistics have they been accounted for?'

Mustafa was hyperventilating. Although Timur tried to find words to comfort him, he failed. He felt he had no right to even console him. Within a few minutes, Mustafa regained his equanimity. He got into the car and started to drive, pouting like a child.

Considering the difficulty in entering the grounds, they parked the car by the roadside. Sarya and the children were shocked and thrilled to see their unexpected visitors.

'We are famished, Sarya. Do you have anything for us?'

Timur observed that Mustafa was behaving as if she was a close relative of his. Sarya, who was still standing with her mouth agape at Mustafa's unannounced arrival, ran into the kitchen cheerfully as soon as she heard the request.

The aroma of mutton being heated wafted from the kitchen. Within a short time, she appeared with platters laden with food. Steam rose from the boiled eggs sprinkled with salt and pepper. Along with the mutton, they ate the soft ekmek liberally garnished with grated almonds after applying olive oil and salt.

After they had their fill, and they lay down on the carpet spread on the patio, when Timur considered what they were doing, he felt a self-loathing. A good-for-nothing idiot who, after having a royal meal, was now lying in comfortable repose on a soft pillow, when he had no information whatsoever about Seetha. He sat up in a panic.

He could blame only himself for trusting this impulsive fellow and setting out on the wild goose chase. He would do well to leave the same evening. He looked resentfully at Mustafa resting peacefully with his head on a bolster.

Sarya's children were peeping in and chuckling. Timur felt they wanted Mustafa to play with them. The youngest daughter brought out her toys and arrayed them on the carpet. She was looking at Mustafa expectantly.

'You said Hozan will be late, right? We'll return after meeting Abdullah.'

Mustafa rose to his feet.

'Bapîr is in hospital,' Sarya's daughter said, without taking her attention off her toys.

'In hospital?' Mustafa was shocked.

Sarya, who had come in with our tea, replied, 'Old age complaints. In the morning, Hozan takes food to the hospital and then goes for work. He drops in at the hospital on his way back too. You know we don't have anyone else!'

Her voice was melancholic.

'Why didn't you tell us as soon as we arrived? Where is he admitted?'

Mustafa went into the yard after ascertaining the address. Timur bid Sarya and her kids goodbye and followed him, finding it hard to keep up with him.

'The man is old. I hope nothing happens to him,' Mustafa sounded worried. Timur could feel desperation creeping in his voice. This was their last hope. Before they started for Cizîr, he should have prevailed on Mustafa to call Abdullah and check on things. Concentrating on his driving, Mustafa did not seem to be in a mood to converse. His gimlet eyes were focused only the road, with his mind in turmoil.

It was a spartan hospital. Abdullah bore a great resemblance to the mental image Timur had created from the descriptions that Mustafa had given now and then in his narration.

The piercing look from his emaciated form as he lay alone on the hospital bed sent shivers through Timur.

'Mustafa!'

Mustafa hugged him as Abdullah, on recognizing his visitor, tried to sit on the bed.

'You had my telephone number. Why didn't you call till now?' Mustafa was cross.

'Oh, it's nothing serious. Besides, Hozan and Sarya are there to help me.' He gave a wan smile.

'Even then, you all alone here, in this state . . .' Mustafa looked on the verge of tears.

'Will you stop it? I'll be discharged this evening. Next time, for sure, I shall call you.'

A wearied Abdullah had to raise his voice to stop Mustafa's protestations.

After inspecting the food containers kept on the table and being satisfied, Mustafa peeled an orange and started to feed Abdullah its carpels. While doing it, he described in detail the purpose of their visit.

Abdullah's piercing stare was fixed on Mustafa's face all through the narration.

'I had told you not to get into trouble,' he muttered irascibly as Mustafa's narration wound to a conclusion. He slapped away the hand offering him orange carpels.

'What am I supposed to do? In this old age, I can't afford to be beaten up by the police!'

'You don't have to do anything. Just find out for us where she is kept . . .'

'. . . provided she is alive,' Abdullah said, looking at both of them.

'If things are as you have stated, she will not be alive. Since they don't have enough evidence to charge her with any crime, her arrest won't be recorded. What remains is the vengeance part. That would be over and done with by now.'

Timur, who was seated on a chair in the corner, leapt to his feet. Abdullah's stark words had made his skin crawl and unnerved him.

'Please help us . . .' he grabbed Abdullah's hands and pleaded abjectly. 'You have to save her. She is being punished for the crime of falling in love with a Turkish citizen, unaware of the problems we have in this country.'

Abdullah pulled his hands away in unease.

'Do both of you smoke? Go out and have a smoke or drink a tea or something. I need to be alone for a little while.'

His unemotional and peremptory tone made Timur look at Mustafa despondently. He thought Abdullah was dismissing them.

'What kind of a man is he? We wasted this day!' Timur said savagely as he followed Mustafa out of the hospital ward.

'Not at all! This means by the time we return after having some tea, he would have the information!'

Mustafa appeared cheerful. They drank tea and smoked a cigarette each before returning to the room. They could hear someone talking inside. They assumed that Hozan had reached there.

When he saw Mustafa, with a sound indistinguishable between a cry and a laugh, Hozan dropped the bag in his hand and hugged him tightly. Mustafa's eyes also brimmed with tears.

Timur stood aside smiling in the knowledge of how the rescue and the risk-filled journey from Cizîr had bound them for life.

To get back Mustafa's attention, from his lamentations of not being able to meet Narjes and her grandchildren, Abdullah coughed lightly. He placed a scrap of paper in his hand on the edge of the bed within Mustafa's reach.

'She isn't dead,' Abdullah whispered. A suggestion of a smile appeared on the thin pursed lips.

Timur felt a wave of relief-filled happiness.

'Beykoz State Hospital, Istanbul.'

Mustafa read the words on the scrap of paper and looked at Abdullah with disbelieving eyes. Nodding his head imperceptibly, he lay with his eyes closed, a beatific, if smug, smile on his face.

'What is to be done now?' Timur asked as they drove back.

'Will your father help?' Mustafa asked doubtfully.

'Certainly.'

Mustafa was lost in thought.

'Now you drive. I've some work.' After handing over the wheel, Mustafa picked up his mobile phone.

'Book a ticket for me too. We've to reach Beykoz hospital tomorrow by 10 a.m.' The tone was the usual commanding one.

Without waiting for Timur's reply, Mustafa pulled up his legs on to the seat, curled up into a ball and drifted into sleep.

Beykoz

'The flight is going to be late.' Timur said to no one in particular.

'They're not small kids. They'll take a taxi and come.' Mustafa scowled and turned to the youngster he had been chatting with. His plan was to meet up in front of the hospital with some students from Diyarbakır. However, unsettled by the police cars that were zooming past and the suspicious looks of people around them, he instructed the waiting students to meet them in a nearby park.

Although he had not briefed them fully, he had dropped some hints. His plan was that if a demonstration had to be held in front of the hospital, he could take the help of Kurd students of Istanbul University. However, the information that the students gave him was not heartening. Mustafa realized that the paucity in numbers and the fear generated by repression would prevent his plan of protest from succeeding. Timur, drinking tea a little away from where Mustafa sat in despair on a bench in the park, looked on sympathetically.

Placing a cup of steaming tea in front of Mustafa, Timur said, 'You drink this first. Then we'll think of other things.'

'I am hungry.' Mustafa was exhausted and drank the tea in gulps. Timur looked at his watch; it was close to noon. He helped Mustafa, who sat slouched on the bench, to his feet.

'The professor and his retinue would have their lunch and come. There's food truck right across; let's have something.'

They took in the aroma from the marinated meat sizzling over coals. Mustafa licked his chapped lips, desiccated by the merciless dry and salty cool breeze.

'I'll have a sheesh kebab.' Mustafa ordered as soon as they reached the food truck. They sat down on the chairs placed below the trees, away from the smoke rising from the barbecue grill.

'You didn't order anything! Aren't you hungry?' Mustafa asked.

'I must go home. It's been two days now since I left without a word to my parents.' Timur kept looking at the watch anxiously.

'What are you waiting for? Why don't you leave before it's late?' a surprised Mustafa asked.

'Have you forgotten about the professor? They'll reach the hotel in half an hour. I've reserved a room for you too there.'

Mustafa laughed. 'Did you see the students who've coming running when I called? Their hostel rooms have enough space. I'm not accustomed to sleeping in luxurious hotel rooms.'

'Please don't say that. The atmosphere at home isn't the best right now. Otherwise, I'd have surely taken you home.' Timur said apologetically as he picked roasted chilli pieces of Mustafa's plate and popped into his own mouth.

'More than that, the professor may have things to talk over with you. I shall introduce you to each other.'

They walked towards the hotel, enjoying the pleasant sunshine.

'Abdullah had called,' Mustafa said.

Timur had noticed him talking over the phone and Seetha's name was mentioned. Although he assumed it was Abdullah at the other end, he was afraid to ask what he had conveyed.

'What's the point in hiding it from you? She's fighting for her life.'

The coldness with which the words were delivered sent a chill through Timur. He grabbed Mustafa's arm as if seeking support.

'Seetha's baby . . .' Mustafa stopped talking. Timur pulled up. Mustafa watched nervously as his eyes turned bloodshot.

'Her baby . . .?' Timur grabbed him and shook him like lunatic.

'Tell me!' The blood drained from his face, and it turned into a shade of deathly pale.

'Her baby couldn't be saved. They are fighting to keep her alive. Chances are very poor.'

Mustafa said this as if there was nothing to be held back. He had been worried how Timur would react when he heard the news. He exhaled loudly as if he had offloaded a crushing burden that was upon him. Timur sat down on a bench next to them. Unable to process what he had heard, he started to pull the hairs on his heard manically.

'Why didn't you tell me about the baby as soon as you had the information?' he screamed, uncaring that people around them could hear him.

'For this very reason. Instead of doing what you have to do, you'll start hollering!' Mustafa was angry.

'At this moment, the baby doesn't matter. She's alive! Are you not able to comprehend that? Seetha *is* alive. NOT DEAD! She's hanging on.'

Leaving Timur to wallow in his grief and indignation, an irate Mustafa strode ahead.

'Scream and shout, whatever happens!'

As if to get even with everything in this world, Mustafa kicked viciously the garbage bin in front of him. Timur sat on the bench like a defeated man. When he saw Mustafa disappearing from his sight, he got up wearily and followed him. They walked the remaining one kilometre to the hotel like strangers, one walking behind the other.

The hotel was in the city centre. After checking at the reception with its backdrop of colourful pictures sold near the Blue Mosque, Timur came to Mustafa.

'They are not here yet. We can go to the room and wait.' His tone was conciliatory. Still scowling, Mustafa did not respond. Not talking to each other, they waited on either side of the lamp post in front of the hotel.

Before long a taxi stopped in front. His drawn face, unkempt hair and beard had rendered Timur unrecognizable. As he went past, not paying any attention to the two scruffy young men, Timur stopped him.

'Good afternoon, Prof. Arnau.'

He stopped and turned around.

'Timur . . .! Why do you look like a scarecrow?' He looked stunned.

'My friend Mustafa will tell you all that's happened so far,' Timur said, pushing Mustafa to the front. 'I need to rush home. I'll have a word with my father and hurry back. He is a lawyer.'

Prof. Arnau watched as Timur hurried towards a taxi waiting some distance away. The doe-eyed woman with Prof. Arnau regarded Mustafa with an amused eye. Only then did Mustafa become conscious of his attire—he was dressed in an old T-shirt and a stained pair of jeans. He had no jacket to protect himself from the cold. To hide his embarrassment, Mustafa stroked and patted down his unruly beard and walked ahead of them into the warm hotel reception.

'You are Timur's friend, eh?' Prof. Arnau asked, following him.

'Yes,' he responded, gripping the hand that had been extended to him warmly.

'What is happening here? The other day, the head of the Philology Department received an email claiming that Seetha was

in mortal danger. It contained a scarcely believable story. Timur's
call came when we were all in a tizzy.'

Prof. Arnau looked at Mustafa anxiously.

'Who was the sender of that mail?' Mustafa asked. His
voice was tremulous with emotion. Someone unknown too was
pulling the strings for Seetha. Mustafa could imagine who that
would be.

Prof. Arnau pulled out a sheet of a paper from his bag. The
familiar yellow, red and green logo of the YPG militia could be
seen on top of the letterhead. Mustafa took it from Prof. Arnau's
hand and read it.

'Everything written in this is true. Seetha is held by the
Turkish government. They'll not let her live.' Mustafa wiped his
face to hide his agitation.

'Come, let's go to the room.'

Prof. Arnau wondered if the receptionist, who appeared
busy checking the registers, was actually listening into their
conversation. After receiving the keys for their rooms, he walked
along with Mustafa towards the lift. Prof. Arnau's companions
followed them.

'This is Montse, the representative from the Women's Studies
Department of the University.'

She was middle-aged with crow's feet and a drowsy look on
her face. After she was introduced, she stood on tip-toe to kiss
Mustafa's bearded cheek.

'I am the president of the student's federation, Marc Herrero.'
A bespectacled young man in the group cheerfully shook hands
with Mustafa.

Mustafa gave them a look of gratitude.

'It is so good of you all to come. Especially Montse.' He could
not continue as he was choking.

Mustafa wondered if his association with Timur had caused
him to indulge in uncontrolled display of emotion.

'What did you mean by that?' Montse's droopy eyes widened and brightened up.

'Timur may have informed you during his call that Seetha is here, in Beykoz hospital. Her baby . . . perhaps he may not have mentioned it.' He had difficulty in completing the sentence. All three of them threw worried glances at one another trying to make out what he was saying.

'Come to my room, we'll talk there,' Prof. Arnau said.

Mustafa hesitated. His shabby clothes and body odour made him uncomfortable. He followed Prof. Arnau with the thought that with no change of clothes at hand, there wasn't much that he could do about his appearance.

'I have no clothes with me. Bring some when you come,' he messaged Timur while walking to the room.

When Timur received the message, he was in front of his mother. Zehra had never raised her voice on him. Since he was born after she had lost two babies at childbirth, she considered him a God's gift. However, that day she went ballistic. He found it hard to look at her face, now flushed with anger.

He acknowledged that he had acted without considering the pain he was causing his parents. He tried his best to explain matters to her. However, she was cross with him since he had left home without telling her anything.

'Your father said whatever you're doing is not wrong. And I trust him.'

'*Anne*, then what is the problem?' he asked wearily. Zehra had already informed Bahadir that their son had returned. Timur's interrogation was taking place in between his mother's cooking, because Bahadir had said he would return in time for lunch with their son.

Timur wanted to have a shower and get cleaned up before his father arrived. He feared that his father would be furious to see him in a dishevelled state.

'Wherever you'll go now, you have to first inform me,' Zehra said, not ready to brook any nonsense. Planting a kiss on her cheeks, Timur agreed.

'I promise. I'll inform you and only then go anywhere.'

When he heard the car entering the driveway, he ran to the bathroom.

Bahadir observed his wife's expression as she served the food. When he saw a pleased look on her face instead of the storm clouds he had been expecting, he inferred that Timur had succeeded in placating her with his explanations.

Since Timur's face looked gloomy and he did not want to spoil the mood at the table, Bahadir secretly signalled to his son to meet him at his office after lunch.

The office was full of bookcases, stacked from top to bottom. The heady smell of books that could be enjoyed only in a library, lingered inside the room. After listening to the events till then, Bahadir lay in an armchair, smoking a cigarette and mulling things over.

'What's your plan?'

'Baba, I need your help,' Timur said in a pleading voice. 'There's no doubt that the girl is in the hospital, fighting for life. She's lost the baby too. However, before we take the next step, we need to ensure that the girl is indeed Seetha.'

'How can that be done? Even if it's a hospital that she's in, she will be under guard. And under police observation.' Bahadir looked at his son quizzically.

'Only I can identify her. Find a way to somehow get me into the hospital.'

'I hope you know how dangerous this thing that you are proposing is?' Bahadir asked, looking into his son's eyes.

'I know. This morning I was in front of the hospital. The place is crawling with policemen.'

Timur avoided his father's gaze. Bahadir remained silent for a short while. He was aware that his son was not going to back down.

'All right. I am acquainted with a doctor who works there. He can't refuse if I request. However, be aware that if you fall into their hands, even Kasim won't be there to get you out.'

'I don't have an option, baba. Maybe my future won't be in jeopardy even if I abandon her now. But how can I ever sleep peacefully after that? Or dream? Or laugh?'

When Bahadir saw his son's face, like the sky on the verge of a cloudburst, he realized that trying to dissuade him would be futile and foolish.

'All right, you get ready to leave. I have a few people to call.'

After seeing Timur out, he shut the door.

Timur filled a bag with some clothes. He guessed that his clothes would fit Mustafa. After changing into fresh clothes, he surveyed his room—the dusty guitar in the corner; a childhood photo hugging his mother; the abandoned bird's nest visible through the open window. He let out a sigh.

Bahadir was waiting in front of his room.

'I have shared a contact in your phone. Dr Adil. He'll help you. The doctor who's treating the girl is his friend.'

Timur was relieved. He looked at his father gratefully. However, Bahadir's face was clouded with worry and care.

'Adil said it's not easy to get into the room and meet her. There are guards. There are police patrols all around the hospital too.'

Although he could sense the dread in his father's words, Timur did not respond. Bidding goodbye with only a nod, he put on his backpack and went out.

'Timur . . .!'

Bahadir called from behind him.

'Your anne and I have only you. Don't forget that.'

His eyes were moist. He had never seen his father look so vulnerable. Forgetting that he was an adult, he hugged his father like a child would.

'That's enough. Your mother may be watching. Call me whatever it is.'

Bahadir gently extricated his son from himself.

Timur left after saying goodbye to Zehra. He had told her that since he would be with his friends, he may not be able to come home for the next few days. Only after he promised to call every day did she ease up a little.

On his way to the hotel, he called Dr Adil who said upfront that only because Bahadir had requested him, was he abetting something so dangerous. A woman in police custody was being treated in the hospital. The senior doctor Ömer Armağan was in charge of such cases. Dr Adil agreed that if Timur managed to reach in the evening, he would arrange a secret audience with Dr Armağan.

Timur left his bag with Mustafa and headed to the professor's room. The three of them were discussing the news Mustafa had filled them in with. Prof. Arnau, who was sprawled on the sofa, sat up straight when he saw Timur walk in.

'You, Timur and Seetha, have me as your research guide. I was till now under the impression that we three were very close. And yet, despite landing in such a fraught situation, I'm surprised and disappointed that you didn't think it appropriate to let me know.'

Timur knew there was more than a grain of truth in those words. He tried to justify his actions like a child caught lying.

'There was no time. I came to know only the day Seetha decided to leave for Turkey. All I could was at least tag along with her. Mustafa would've told you about the developments after we landed here.'

Prof. Arnau remained silent. The thought that this disaster could have been prevented even if he had an inkling, haunted him. Everyone was busy planning the next course of action. The incredible story that Mustafa had told them had shaken them.

'I'll be sneaking into the hospital this evening to check on Seetha. We need to confirm if the girl is indeed her.'

Prof. Arnau appeared cheered by the news. He sought more details. All of them agreed on the need to ensure it was Seetha.

'Why delay any more. It's already evening. Call the doctor. I'll ask Mustafa to join us.'

Marc called Mustafa on his mobile and invited him to the professor's room. Timur dialled Dr Adil's number. His hand was shivering due to mental tension.

'Timur, there is a small restaurant called Timboo close to the hospital. At 6 p.m. a girl will come and drop some garbage in the bin next to it. Wait around that in a group. As if out of negligence, she'll drop a small packet behind the garbage bin. It'll contain the uniform of an hospital attendant. Take it when no one is looking. Go into the restaurant toilet and change into that.'

'But how will I get into the hospital?' Timur asked.

'There's a photo badge of someone who is of your age and resembles you. If challenged, you can flash that. Use the small door on the north side of the hospital, by the side of the X-ray room. In fifteen minutes, a girl will be waiting for you there. She will take you to Dr Ömer.'

Timur looked at the watch; it was past 5 p.m. There was no time to lose; he had to leave immediately. He thanked Dr Adil.

'Timur, Dr Ömer may help you. Don't feel bad, but don't call me after this. To be honest, I'm scared.'

There was a quaver in Dr Adil's voice. Timur felt guilty. He conveyed his sincere apologies for putting Dr Adil in a tough spot and disconnected the call.

The others were waiting anxiously for the news. When he described the plan to get into the hospital, they looked relieved. Prof. Arnau instructed Timur to change into nondescript clothes. In ten minutes, they emerged out of the hotel.

'We should look as if we are getting into Timboo for a coffee.' Prof. Arnau said when they were in the car. He had misgivings if Timur, being a gentle soul, could carry out such escapades. Prof. Arnau consulted with Montse if he should go in Timur's place. She, however, reminded him that only a local, Turkish-speaking person could do the impersonation.

They reached Timboo before 5.30 p.m. It was an inexpensive restaurant frequented by patients' bystanders and other visitors to the hospital. No one had the demeanour of fine-dining restaurant patrons. It catered to gloomy-faced people who had no time for others around them and were trying gobble down mechanically whatever was placed before them and vacate the place as quickly as possible.

Marring the atmosphere of a hospital, three or four armoured cars were parked in front. Black-uniformed, sharp-eyed soldiers with sub-machine guns were patrolling the area. They observed every passer-by with practised eyes. One of them stopped Timur's group and asked what they were doing there. He accepted Timur's innocent reply that they were headed for a coffee.

Eating out of two packets of potato chips, they stood in front of the restaurant as if waiting for someone. They could see the garbage bin kept near the side of the restaurant. They moved next to it before 6 p.m. pretending to be engaged in an amusing conversation.

Around 6 p.m. they saw a girl headed towards them with two or three plastic garbage bags. She strolled lazily towards the bin, paying no attention to anyone, threw the bags into it, and started to walk back in the hospital's direction.

Timur saw the package lying on the ground near the bin. He moved towards it pretending to discard his empty bag of chips. He ensured that as he did it, the bag on his shoulder slipped down and when he bent down to retrieve it, the package too came along with it.

When they were sure no one had noticed the transaction, they entered the restaurant. Everyone except Timur sat around a table and ordered snacks and coffee. Timur walked unhurriedly towards the toilet.

He was trembling all over. After shoving his own clothes into the bag, changing into the white hospital staff uniform and pinning the ID card on his left chest, he glanced at his reflection in mirror on the back of the door before exiting the toilet. No one would suspect him. His nervousness dissipated.

He placed his bag besides the table where others were seated ostensibly enjoying their coffee, and walked out without waiting for their reaction, with the confidence of someone who had donned that uniform for years.

The girl stood chatting with the security guard in front of the X-ray room. When Timur approached, she smiled, bid goodbye to the guard and walked ahead. The guard did not seem to have noticed Timur.

She walked quickly and entered the elevator. Timur followed her. People got in and out of the elevator whenever it stopped. Unnoticed by others who were lost in their own worries, Timur and the girl stood gazing at each other.

No one got off or on at the fifth floor except the two of them. The silence and ominous atmosphere made Timur uneasy. It reminded him of his own cell in the jail and the endless dark corridor in front of it. He avoided looking at the guards at the elevator doors. One of them patrolling the corridor gave the girl, who accompanied Timur, a friendly smile.

She walked towards room no. 11. Timur's body trembled with stress as he stood in front of its huge door. When the door opened, he was enveloped by a coolness and the smell of disinfectants. There was another door ahead. Two pairs of slippers were placed neatly by its side.

'Wait here. Let me talk to the doctor.'

The second door closed behind her. It was an intensive care unit, possibly used only in such hush-hush cases. Timur looked around him. The room was bare except for two cabinets. The thin uniform was not good enough to protect against the chill in the room.

She came in a little while.

'You can go inside.'

She helped him into a sterilized dress and soft shoes. The room was dim-lit. A man with a halo of white hair on his head welcomed him.

'Hello, Timur. Adil had spoken about you.'

He pointed at an inert form on the bed on the other end of the room with a host of tubes and monitor leads connected to it.

'That is the girl you have come to see. Check out if she is the one.'

There was no one else in the room. The buzz, and metronomic clicks and dings of the machines were the only sounds. After hesitating for a moment, when he started to move, the man stopped him.

'Do you realize that the girl is dying?' he mumbled. Timur stood helpless and unable to respond.

'She has internal injuries. They are severely infected. From the moment she realized that she had lost her baby, she appears to have chosen death. Like someone who has given up on life, her body is not responding to medicines.'

Timur's throat felt parched. The doctor recognized the dread in his eyes. Holding him by his shoulder the doctor gently led him towards the bed.

'Adil told me that you are her bosom friend. I only agreed for this in the hope that your proximity may bring some change in her. You shouldn't cause her any distress.'

He nodded like mechanically and walked slowly towards the bed.

A stranger's face! Was this really Seetha? Tubes were connected to a mask covering her nose and mouth. The face was covered in livid bruises. Her lips were misshapen and had blood clots as if they had been chewed up by wild animals. Her bloodless skin looked like that of a wax doll. An IV was connected to a cannula on left wrist. Her black hair was tied up; some strands were slipping down the pillow on to the bed.

'Seetha . . .' Timur called softly.

He was afraid that the stress would make him fall faint. With whimpering lips, he called again, 'Seetha . . .'

Her eyes showed rapid movement. He fancied she was looking through her dark, lush eyelashes.

Like someone who had lost his mental balance, he turned towards the doctor waiting behind him and with folded hands pleaded, 'Please save her . . . please somehow save her.'

The doctor placed his hand around his shoulders and led him to the door.

'Is this the girl you were looking for?' he asked anxiously.

Overwrought, since he was not able to vocalize, he merely nodded his assent. The doctor stood thoughtfully regarding his teary face.

'I thought there was a movement in her eyes when she heard your voice. Something like a reaction when an unexpected person appears before you. Did you notice it? Or is it only my fancy?'

'I did see it doctor. I thought she was looking at me.' Excitement made his voice quaver.

'We shall watch what happens hereafter. Now you may go.'

He handed over a bundle of soiled bedsheets to Timur. A nurse with a tray full of vials and syringes was waiting outside.

'I shall call. If needed, you may have to come again.'

The door closed against his noble face. Timur felt the bundle on his shoulder weigh more than a sackfuls of iron. With leaden steps he followed the girl who walked ahead smiling pleasantly at all the policemen till the elevator.

Barcelona

Marc ate the gozleme in his plate and looked at Montse's plate. She had not touched it.

'If you want have it,' she said, pushing the plate towards him.

'Forgive me, Montse. I'm starving. Moreover, this is very tasty.' He spoke in an apologetic tone and lifted the thin bread flap to inspect the meat balls and mushrooms inside it.

'Eat, this is an age when you must eat a horse.'

She sighed.

Since they were consuming as if they had starved the whole day and kept ordering different dishes, no one found it strange that they were there for a long time. Montse kept refilling her cup and encouraging the others to eat.

When the hour they were expecting Timur to return passed, Prof. Arnau, seated on the opposite side of table, gave Montse a meaningful glance. He could see beads of perspiration on her forehead from the tension she was undergoing. He winked at her as if requesting her to calm down.

He too was growing nervous. Timur should have returned long ago. To check on how things were outside, he picked up a cigarette and stepped out.

The armoured vehicles were still parked outside. Two policemen were smoking in front of the restaurant. He could see Timur walking down from the distance, weaving his way between others coming from the hospital. His hunched back and wavering steps made him look old. Watching him diffidently for a short while, he pocketed the unsmoked cigarette and re-entered the restaurant.

'Timur will reach now. You all go in together to the men's room. After he changes his clothes, all of you should come out together. I will pay the bill and come to the door.'

He pulled out his wallet from his faded jeans' pocket and went to the cash counter. Picking up the crumbs on their plates and putting them into their mouths, Mustafa and Marc rose to their feet. Without showing any hurry, Montse sat at the table, toying with her coffee cup. She took deep breaths to calm her trembling body and regain control over herself. When she saw Timur walk in, she rose slowly from the table and walked towards the restroom.

When he saw Timur, Mustafa chortled and handed over the bag he was carrying for him. Timur took the bag and entered one of the stalls. Having seen how stony Timur's face looked, the three of them looked at one another. From behind the door came a wail of helpless, deep anguish.

All of them felt that if anyone came into the men's room it could lead to problems. Montse, who was ostensibly washing her hands, hurried and knocked on the stall door. 'Timur change your clothes quickly and come out. Or we're all going to be in trouble.'

The crying stopped. Mustafa and Marc waited at the restroom door, listening to the snatches of sobs that escaped from Timur despite himself. Timur emerged in a couple of minutes. His eyes were bloodshot, and face flushed. To get rid of the signs of crying, he washed his face with lukewarm water for a long time.

'Prof. Arnau must be waiting outside after paying the bill. He can't wait for long like that!' Montse tried to chivvy them. Mumbling an apology, Timur walked out of the restroom. Timur and Mustafa walked ahead of him talking and laughing loudly drawing attention away from Timur. Montse brought up the rear, busily searching for something in her bag.

Together with Prof. Arnau who stood smoking a cigarette outside, they walked to their hotel.

They split into two groups to avoid drawing undue attention. Marc and Mustafa played the part of two jovial young men, Prof. Arnau and Montse followed them looking like a careworn middle-aged couple. From Timur's frozen look, all of them could make out something grievous had happened to Seetha.

As soon as they entered the hotel room, Timur collapsed onto the bed.

'Tell us something!'

'Her face looks like a ghost's. She's more a corpse than a living being. I was terrified by the sight.'

He covered his face as if her form had appeared before him again.

'What do you mean? Wasn't she moving?' Montse asked solicitously. With feminine indulgence, she tousled the unruly shock of hair on his head.

'No, she wasn't moving at all.'

Everyone looked at one another. Prof. Arnau plonked down on a chair by his side.

Suddenly Timur's sobbing stopped. 'I don't know if I imagined it, for I was distraught at that time. When I she heard my voice, I felt she looked at me through her eyelashes. There was a movement in her eyes.'

'I will kill this bugger.' An enraged Mustafa let out a string of expletives. 'From the way he was acting I had thought she was dead.'

He looked at others, his eyes blazing. A smile of relief appeared on Prof. Arnau's face who till then was seated with his head cradled in his hands.

'Can you all leave him be for some time?' Montse said with affectionate admonition.

'You sleep for a while.'

Montse got off the bed after pulling the duvet over Timur. Everyone moved to Mustafa's room leaving Timur to sleep in peace.

'It has to be her,' Prof. Arnau said.

'What's more, she's alive too. From what I gathered, she recognized his voice.' Montse added.

She turned to Mustafa. 'Why are you losing your temper so quickly? Can't you show some patience?'

'I apologize. I am fed up with his wailing. I lost it because of that.'

'Not everyone can have the same mental strength. He is a type who wears his heart on his sleeve. Despite that, does he shy away from carrying out his responsibilities to his friend?'

Prof. Arnau also tried to counsel Mustafa. 'After we leave you must treat him with patience.'

'Are you leaving?'

Mustafa blinked. A dread of being left alone in the battlefield consumed him.

'If possible, today itself,' Prof. Arnau said, while using Marc's mobile phone to look for flight tickets.

'We won't be able to do anything in Turkey. Your people will nip it in the bud. We have to start there—in Barcelona,' said Marc. 'Since Seetha is a student at University of Barcelona, the protests should start there. We need the undivided attention of the press and various administrations' support in this matter.'

Prof. Arnau and Montse smiled, watching his interpretation of things and his confidence.

'The very first wallop must be a resounding one. The city should tremble! No one should be able to ignore this matter thereafter. We can start tomorrow. My friends are ready and committed.'

Marc was raring to go; his blood was boiling.

'Let's think it over,' Prof. Arnau said. 'We have enough time before our flight to have a short meeting with Timur's father.'

After they got ready, they tried to wake up Timur. He was fast asleep, oblivious to all the sounds around him. Mustafa and Marc tried to shake him awake; they tried to pull his leg. The knowledge that Seetha was alive had lent a new vigour to all their actions.

It took some effort to wake him up. He was sleeping like a baby, dead to the world. He sat up with bulging, unfocused eyes for some time as if he had been physically lifted out of a deep dark well. Although he had been shaken to the core by the sight at the hospital, the knowledge that Seetha was alive had freed him from a great dread that had been troubling him recently.

'Can we meet your father?' Prof. Arnau asked, after shaking him by the shoulder as he sat there, still not sentient and like a statue.

'To meet my father? Yes, we can go. He too will be happy,' Timur replied, rubbing his eyes indicating his sleep deficit.

'When did you sleep last?' a concerned Montse asked.

'It's true, I have not been able to sleep for the last many days. I was afraid that she was dead.' Timur looked sheepish.

Prof. Arnau patted his shoulder affectionately.

When Timur called his father to inform him that he and his friends were coming to meet him, Bahadir felt that the meeting would help clear up a few things. He said that he was still in the office, and they could meet there. Most of his colleagues had already left. Claiming that he was expecting some clients, Bahadir took upon himself the responsibility of locking up the office.

'Things look hopeful. At least we have come this far,' Bahadir said, after being briefed. His relief and happiness in Timur getting in and out of the hospital without trouble was apparent on his face. He agreed with the plan that protests should start in Barcelona.

'Seetha, a student at University of Barcelona, is on a visit to Turkey. She goes missing there. There are witnesses to her being taken away by the police. It is understood that she is now in Beykoz hospital after being brutally gang-raped and losing the child she was carrying. Isn't it enough that the media is told only this much?'

Bahadir looked at everyone's face, seeking their endorsement. No one had a different opinion. The moment the news got published, he gave them assurance that he would start legal proceedings against Seetha being kept in illegal custody.

Montse chipped in. 'I guarantee support from and participation by human rights groups and feminist organisations.'

The bright faces around him gave even Bahadir hope, jaded as he was from watching what was happening in Turkish politics over the years. Suddenly he jumped up from the seat, as he had remembered something.

'I know that a journalist here has been making enquiries about this matter. Let me find out how to contact her.' He went out his mobile phone in hand.

'Why are you taking on this headache?' Mibang's words were slurring. Bahadir could make out he was drinking. 'I shall message you the number she called me from; she said her name was Pinar or something.'

'Many thanks, Mibang. Just one more thing. You had sent a mail to the Turkish authorities asking if an Indian citizen called Seetha is being held in a Turkish prison. Did you get a reply?'

'This morning we received a reply that such a person has not been arrested. Till that mail was received, I was on pins and needles. Let's have a drink and relax.'

Bahadir laughed. 'Mibang, the mail says she has not been arrested. It doesn't say she is not in their custody, does it?'

There was silence from the other end. Bahadir could infer that the man was stunned by the question and its possibilities.

'You helped me. I will reciprocate it with some useful information. Seetha is being held by the police. She's fighting death in Beykoz hospital.'

'Where did you get this information from?' Mibang asked breathlessly. Bahadir could imagine that Mibang had not believed his words fully.

'Am I not from this country, Mibang? Moreover, what would I gain by misleading you?' Bahadir laughed.

'Arrrgh! What all problems are in store, God knows!' Mibang sounded worried.

'You should relax now. You have already done what you were required to do. Now wait for the ball to land in your court.'

When he returned to his room, the others were getting ready to leave. After providing Pinar's name and contact details to Prof. Arnau, he turned towards Timur and Mustafa.

'You two wait here. They will find their way to the airport by themselves.'

Prof. Arnau gave Bahadir a questioning look.

'When the protests start tomorrow, they will take in Timur for sure. He is the primary witness of Seetha's arrival in Turkey and all the subsequent developments.'

Bahadir turned towards Mustafa. 'Tell me, have you had any interactions with the police so far in your life? Tell me only the truth.'

Mustafa gave him a bitter smile. 'I don't have to tell you that taking birth as a Kurd in itself is a confrontation with the system. Other than that, I've committed no crime. I've done nothing against our Constitution. There are no legal cases against me.'

'If that be the case, it's advisable that you return to Sur,' Bahadir was categorical. 'What you have stated is very true—your Kurdish origin is the start of your problems. For helping Seetha, Timur is going to get into more difficulties. He is already in their cross hairs. You, however, have had no direct connection to Seetha. You have not seen her even. If the police get you, you will be in a far worse situation than Timur. Go back home. That is best for you.'

Bahadir looked at Timur as if to ask if he concurred in his view. With pursed lips, he was staring into the distance.

Mustafa met Bahadir's eyes. 'I was not an orphan. Yet, I have lived on the streets from a time I can remember. Ours was a large family with many children. I was the seventh child of my penniless parents who could not feed their children even one square meal. When I was hungry, along with my friends, I begged on the streets; grew up sharing whatever we cadged. We all stuck together amidst the riots, butchery, repression and pogroms. This was the reason why the might of the Turkish state could not subjugate the Kurds. We are not that people who abandon those who are with us in times of danger. Your son is my friend. Whatever might happen to me, I shall not abandon him in this condition.'

His voice trembled with emotion. Bahadir remained silent, unable to find adequate words to respond to the outburst. Surrounded by grim-looking faces, he tried to lighten the mood through a disarming smile.

'Let both of them go underground from tomorrow. It can be arranged, nothing to worry.'

He walked all of them to the gate, to see if he could help them get a taxi. The goodbyes were short or merely conveyed with nods of their heads. They watched the yellow cab disappear into the distance.

'You both go in. There's a coffee machine in the meeting room. And biscuits. I'll be with you in a minute.'

Bahadir went to his room. He returned after a few minutes. Timur and Mustafa were waiting for him after having had their coffees.

'A car will arrive within a few minutes. A friend needs workers at his factory. They provide accommodation too.'

'What about the protests . . .' Timur stopped mid-sentence. He gave Mustafa a chagrined look.

'What protests? Here, in Turkey, it will take a few days more for anything to start. You need to hide. Once the demonstrations start in Barcelona, they will do everything they can to destroy the evidence, which means catching you. If you get caught, that'll be your end. And Seetha's too.'

He kept his gaze steady on them to check if they understood the gravity of the situation. He took out two small phones out of his pocket and handed them over.

'For the next few days only use these. They have new SIM cards. Save only the essential numbers and hand over the phones you are using now.'

Timur and Mustafa complied with his orders. Even the normally talkative Mustafa had fallen silent. Bahadir could sense fear simmering inside both of them. While they waited for the car to arrive, he went and sat beside them with a cup of coffee in hand.

Marc had been busy on his phone from the time they had reached the airport. Although they had divided responsibilities between the three of them, he was clear in his mind taking it forward eventually was his own. From the time they had left Bahadir's office, he had been planning what tasks to allot to each of his friends.

Prof. Arnau, who had started out as a journalist, had many friends in the press. He called and informed all of them that he had an important news to give them the next morning. Montse was left with the task of getting together the teachers and various organisations.

The news about Seetha spread among the students like wildfire. Everyone was familiar with the Indian beauty who used to be seen on campus dressed in colourful clothes with long tresses flowing in the wind. After the initial bewilderment, Marc's friends dispersed to design and print the posters for the next day. He showed Prof. Arnau and Montse pictures of students spread throughout the campus, exhorting the community to go on strike, which was being spread on social media.

'It will take nearly four hours for us to reach Barcelona. It would do us well if we all could sleep on the flight. Once we land, sleep may become a luxury,' said Marc, pulling up the blanket to cover his head. Montse and Prof. Arnau agreed with him.

Marc shifted to another empty seat to let both of them sleep in peace. He requested the stewardess for a beer to calm his nerves. Revolutionary zeal more than blood coursed through his veins—he was someone who had beaten back and had been beaten up while conducting street protests. Usually, he and his cohorts would have the land reverberating with their slogans and flags while espousing political causes. This time it was going to be for a girl. When he recalled her attractive, sweet smile whenever they ran across each other in corridors or in the library, he felt a heaviness in his heart. He used the time to plan the next few days' actions and note them down.

A group of excitable students waited for them at the airport. Deciding to meet up next morning at the university, Prof. Arnau and Montse left for their homes and Marc to the hostel along with his friends.

Unable to sleep, Marc reached the campus in the wee hours of the morning. He was surprised to see a few others had beaten him to it. Most of them were carrying colourful hand-written posters.

They informed him that the WhatsApp messages had gone viral. Since he had to await the arrival of Montse and Prof. Arnau, Marc joined the students to stick the posters.

By the time Prof. Arnau arrived in his office, Marc was already there. Montse arrived within few minutes. When Prof. Arnau said lightly that he had mentioned the protests to be held at the university gate in his conversation with his journalist friends, Marc was irritated. When, with a scowl on his face, Marc got up to leave without uttering a word, Prof. Arnau instructed him to sit down.

'Wait, do you have anything concrete in your hands to prove this allegation?'

'Seetha's air-ticket; her photos taken at Sur by Timur.'

'Where is the proof in there that she was abducted by the police? If the media has to take this up, they will need solid evidence.'

'What is to be done for that?' Marc asked belligerently.

'We don't have the time to run after the press proffering evidence. If this has to become news, the students here must get out on to the streets. If you throw the traffic into chaos and bring the city to a grinding halt for the cause of Seetha, no journalist will be able to ignore it. I don't have to tell you that the level of coverage will depend on the intensity of the protests.'

An impish smile appeared on Marc's lips.

'God wills that she stays alive all this time,' Montse chimed in. She left promising to meet them at the protest venue after she had met all the other teachers.

Prof. Arnau, rushing after finishing his classes, and Montse after meeting the teachers, found it hard to reach the protest venue at the gate. Students were streaming in groups from all the departments. As she was getting crushed in the throng, Prof. Arnau clasped her hand and squeezed through the students and made way for her.

Marc was visible to everyone, standing on a chair with a megaphone in his hand. His deep voice and measured delivery attracted even the passers-by and the crowd kept growing around him. Prof. Arnau and Montse witnessed once more Marc enchanting the people around him with his eloquence, like a magician turning everything around him into motionless forms with a wave of his wand.

Unlike on the previous occasions, he was using the language of emotion than of reason. One among them was fighting for life in a Turkish hospital. He laid on thick the tortures she had undergone, the inhuman gang-rape she suffered, and the loss of her baby as a consequence.

The students watched in disbelief as his voice broke uncharacteristically when he talked of equal rights that allows every human to inhabit this earth, irrespective of his or her race, colour, creed or gender. His question—which government in the world had the right to deny Seetha's child's right to born—seared their hearts and minds.

When he concluded, an uneasy silence prevailed for a little while. Tearing it to shreds, a shrill female voice rent the air, 'Down with fascism . . .'

The crowd enthusiastically took up the chant. Students who were listening spellbound to the speech from the various floors of the university buildings started to shout slogans at the top of their voices. The university, an island of greenery in the middle of the city, throbbed and pulsated with the energy of the agitating students.

Prof. Arnau saw that Marc was searching for someone in the milling crowds. Along with Montse he approached Marc.

'I was looking for you. Did you hear my speech?' he asked expectantly. Prof. Arnau clasped both his hands in silent congratulations.

'Brilliant.' Montse hugged him.

'Forget this, wait and see what is going to happen tomorrow,' shouted Marc as he was being dragged away by his friends.

Although Prof. Arnau had called and informed everyone, none of his journalist friends turned up to witness the protests. He could see that Montse was sad that the media was ignoring them. Prof. Arnau consoled her with a suggestion that the media may have thought it was a storm in a teacup about an eccentric girl with a wanderlust.

Despite being preoccupied with arrangements for the next day, in the evening Marc found time to come to Prof. Arnau.

'Good that you have come. I was about to call you.'

Marc looked at him quizzically.

'Did you notice that despite informing them in person, no media person turned up?' Prof. Arnau lit a cigarette and sat down on a bench. 'Sit here!'

He offered Marc a cigarette when he sat down beside him.

'Did you get police permission for today's demonstration?'

'We had not planned for such a big protest. We never imagined this would attract so many people. Normally, for a crowd of this size, we should have taken permission.'

'It's not easy to get media support in this matter. We should look at other options.'

Marc was listening carefully to understand what he was driving at.

'A protest filled with violence. The city should come to an absolute standstill! Blood should be spilt on the streets! The police will be forced to bring out everything in their armoury. Then the media will not have the option to ignore the protests; and they shall have to explain to the public what led to such violent protests. I don't see any other way to drive Seetha's case into the public conscience.'

'So, tomorrow's protests? I was leaving for the police station to take the permit.'

'Don't go,' Prof. Arnau said peremptorily.

Marc kept his gaze on Prof. Arnau. Only now he understood what Prof. Arnau was driving at. Suppressing the laugh that rose in him, he stood up.

'Tomorrow Barcelona will come to standstill.'

'You're breaking the law. There will be a legal case against you. Don't forget that!'

'I may not be able to come to class every day. There are no impediments to earning a degree from inside a prison cell. None of this is more important than Seetha's life!'

Raising his hand, Marc hailed his friends and walked towards them.

Prof. Arnau noticed that even though it was late evening, Montse was everywhere checking on the preparations for the next day. Although he reassured her that Marc and his gang would be taking care of the next day's protests, she refused to leave for home.

Students sat around in small groups writing posters and making placards with Seetha's picture on them. Marc and his team were by a small pond in the quadrangle of the main building, finessing the plans for the next day. Occasionally, angry shouts and clapping could be heard from the group. Without a soul outside being aware of it, a silent mobilization for a battle was happening in the BU.

'Arnau . . .' Montse shook him awake. 'I had called Bahadir. He has information from the hospital—Seetha is improving; her body is responding to the medicines.'

Enrique mused whether this lady, who always had a dolorous look on her face, could smile so brightly. To celebrate the good news, they had some red wine from the nearby bar before they split up.

Uncharacteristically, Prof. Arnau woke up in the middle of his sleep. Dawn was still far away. He got dressed and went out. He walked through the city watching it wake up gradually and get into the stride for the day. The early birds gave a quick, curious glance at the picture of a foreign girl on the new posters that had appeared on walls and lampposts and went about their ways. Filled with their worries, as they hurried to their workplaces, none of them noticed the students stealthily occupying vantage points in city.

Suddenly, Marc and his group roared on to the main road in front of Universitat de Barcelona with banners and placards, blocking traffic in both directions. Hundreds of students backed them up. Marc's plan was to stop traffic at the various nubs in the city simultaneously and without warning. They blocked tram station entrances by tying large banners across them. Although they were caught off guard for a little while, the police, enraged at the lack of advance notification, went on to the streets armed with their truncheons, water cannons and rubber bullets.

A continuous hail of stones descended on the Turkish Consulate. The sight of a huge effigy of their president burning in front of the consulate sent the employees scurrying for cover. Tourists got scattered in the mêlée. Street vendors, cursing loudly and questioning the parentage of the students, bundled their wares and sought refuge in the buildings around them. The angry police and ambulance sirens echoed ominously off the walls of the historical buildings. Within minutes the great city of Barcelona ground to a standstill.

Factory

Mustafa and Timur were taken by Emir to a factory that produced women's garments. Their accommodation was in the workers' dormitory. For Timur and Mustafa, it came as a relief when Emir told them they were assigned to the packing section and with minimal training they could learn on the job.

Emir was the owner of four or five factories in Istanbul's suburbs. He tried to cheer them up by regaling them with stories of his childhood escapades in the company of Bahadir. Emir also reminded them that under no circumstances should they reveal who they were and if that should happen, it would be the end of his factories and even himself, and that would also mean all his workers would lose their livelihood.

They entered the decrepit flat when the exhausted employees were having their dinner. They were assigned one room to themselves. The honest, good-natured men welcomed them, sharing the last piece of hardened bread and two cold bitters.

Mustafa was careful in following the instructions given by Emir on the way. Since they were afraid that Timur may blurt out something, he had been instructed to keep quiet and not talk. The workers were keener to hit the sack after being dead tired from the day's labour than make small talk with the newcomers.

One thick sheet each was kept to spread on the hard planks
of the bed and to cover themselves with. The sight of the stained
patchwork pillows nauseated Timur. The sheets and pillows
were being used by the previous occupants of the room. Galip
and Osmanek, the other occupants of the flat, stood at the door,
guiltily watching them arrange their stuff. Galip said apologetically
that if they had known about Timur and Mustafa's arrival, they
would have at least washed the sheets.

None of this seemingly affected Mustafa. He ate what was
offered with great relish. After thanking them for the sleeping
arrangements, happy that he had had his fill, throwing a disdainful
glance at Timur who sat forlorn on his bed without changing,
Mustafa stretched out on his bed. Within a few minutes, he was
snoring away. Keeping the foul-smelling, soiled pillow away,
Timur covered himself with the sheet and tried to find sleep.

Unaccustomed to such spare life, Timur's back was hurting
from the hard planks of the bed. Since the room had no heaters,
the soiled sheet was the only protection against the cold. If at
least he could fall asleep he would be spared the reek of the sheet.
When he recalled the soft mattress and the fresh-smelling sheets at
home that his mother used, Timur's eyes welled up.

Blinding lightning flashed through the skies, lighting up the
room. The clouds that were threatening to unload fulfilled their
promise. Propelled by the wind, curtains of water were smashing
against the glass panes of the window and cascading down.
Listening to the stormy lullaby that only rain can sing, his eyes
gradually closed, and he drifted off to sleep.

Knocks on the door woke them up the next morning.
Bewildered on waking up in a strange place, they sat for some
time staring at each other uncomprehendingly. Galip, looking
fresh, was at the door. Informing them that the vehicle to
take them to the factory would arrive at 8.30 p.m., and they

should get ready and have their breakfast before that, he went to prepare food.

Using the cold water kept in a metal bucket for his bath made Timur's teeth chatter. His whole body was aching from sleeping on the hard planks. He washed the sheets and pillow covers using the soap kept in the bathroom. When, shivering in the cold, he emerged from the bathroom with the wet clothes stacked on his shoulder, Mustafa, his toothbrush sticking out of his mouth, was at the door. His jaw dropped at the sight.

'Why did you wash these now? When will they dry in this cold?'

'I'm unable to stand the smell.' Mustafa could not control his laughter upon seeing Timur's helplessness.

'There's no hot water.' Timur whispered between his chattering teeth when he was close to Mustafa.

'Hot water . . .?' Mustafa stood agape. He stopped Timur as he passed him.

'Once I had some infection and fever when I was a child. Everyone thought I would die. My mother sponging my body with the water she had heated in a small pail kept on the embers in the stove is the last time I remember having a hot bath. Even at the height of winter I haven't bathed in hot water. I guess you know that to heat water we need firewood or gas or electricity? Money has to change hands to get hold of these. Have you even seen any money in my pocket? For that, one needs to be employed. You are a fool to think that these poor men will have enough money to enjoy hot baths!'

The sarcasm in those words was not lost on Timur.

'Why are you not working?'

'I completed my schooling. The trouble started when I joined college, which I did using the money saved by scrounging and scrimping. I'm a Kurd. Who'll give me a job? I'm ready to work as a labourer. But then, in our place, there are tens of thousands of young men who are as qualified or even better qualified than me who are waiting for such jobs.'

'Let's see this through. We'll try.' Timur tried to console him.

'I don't need your job,' said Mustafa in his usual scornful tone, pouting, as he went into the bathroom. Galip, arranging the breakfast items to the table, was observing them.

'What was the discussion about?' he asked with a friendly smile.

'We were talking about food.' The sight of the plates in Galip's hands made Timur reply thus.

'Pardon us, we serve very simple food here. If you want, you can eat from outside. Or you can join us.'

The mortification of having to talk about one's privation was pronounced in his voice.

'Of course, we shall share and eat whatever is available,' Timur responded with alacrity.

He decided that he should give the men some money at the soonest possible. After wearing his clothes, he extracted some notes and went to the dining table. Galip offered him a plate filled with sliced cucumber, tomato and carrot.

'Have this. Meanwhile, I'll peel these boiled eggs.'

Timur shoved the currency notes into the hands of Osmanek, who was seated at the table. From the previous day's conversation, he had gathered that the stooping, grey-haired Osmanek was a supervisor in the factory.

He looked at the money in his hand and at Timur in utter bewilderment.

'What's all this money for?'

Timur realized he had dropped a clanger.

'That's money for our monthly expenses.'

'Son, the rent is deducted from our wages every month. We shall settle the water and electricity when the bill is received. The money for your food for this month . . .' he pulled out a few notes from the bunch '. . . for that this will be enough. If more is needed, I shall ask you. Take the rest and keep it safe.'

Timur returned the money to his wallet. He had to be careful, he reminded himself.

'Instead of pottering around, go and eat something. We'll leave by 8.30,' said an annoyed Mustafa, who had emerged with only a towel around his waist.

Their spare breakfast consisted of boiled eggs sprinkled with pepper, green salad and bread. The bread, baked that morning, was soft. Mustafa nodded in gratification at the sight of Timur eating it with obvious relish.

The car arrived exactly as 8.30 a.m. It had a passenger in addition to the driver. He frowned when he heard the new workers were going into the packing section.

'We have more than enough there.'

'The patron asked us to join there. If you have any complaint, talk to him,' said Mustafa, reverting to his cantankerous self. Timur rolled his eyes at him. Mustafa angrily turned his head away and kept looking at the sights through the window. The man in the passenger seat remained silent. Mustafa's grumpiness had its uses, Timur mused. He also watched the passing sights.

It was a medium-size factory, running five hundred sewing machines. They passed the halls with humming machines and stores which held heaps of satin fabrics and laces. Osmanek stopped when they reached a room stacked with cartons.

'You both wait here. Let me have word with the supervisor.' He left. Timur and Mustafa looked at each other. They started to feel that they may have found a safe lair to lie low.

'What is the latest on Seetha? Did you get any news?' Mustafa asked.

'I should call Dr Armağan after a little while. It would have been good to meet her once more!'

Timur pulled at his beard distractedly.

'If you expose yourself now, you'll never see daylight again. Don't tell me you were not warned. Forget the idea of meeting her again.'

Silence descended on them. Not wanting Timur to be imagining things and fretting about them, Mustafa tried to change the subject.

'I wonder if the protests have started in Barcelona.'

Timur lifted his bowed head.

'I too was thinking about it. However, don't make any calls. If needed, baba will get in touch with us.'

A slim old man walked in. Osmanek was with him.

'Patron had called and told about you yesterday.' He had a friendly smile. After the introductions were done, Osmanek left the room. The old man too left after instructing them to stick labels on the cartons as per the list he handed over and stack the cartons according to the list.

After a little while Timur nudged Mustafa and asked, 'Should we call that doctor?'

'Try.'

Putting down the labels and glue stick, Mustafa sat down amidst the labels that lay on the floor. Timur extracted the phone from his pocket. However, as if he had an afterthought, Mustafa grabbed his hand.

'Don't do it. His phone may be under observation. It's dangerous.'

'But who told you that I'm calling the doctor?' Looking at the mischievous smile on his face, Mustafa smacked his forehead in disbelief.

'Does it mean you managed to get that girl's number?'

'Shhhhh . . .' With a finger on his lips, Timur gestured to Mustafa to keep quiet.

'There are notices everywhere that phone calls are banned during work hours,' Mustafa warned him.

'Please relax. I'm calling no one. I've sent her a message. She'll call back. Now, go and work.'

Timur resumed his work after shoving the phone into his pocket. Mustafa, with a sullen face, picked up the labels and started to paste them.

The phone rang after half an hour. Mustafa could not make out if it was good or bad news from Timur's expression as he only grunted in reply. Till Timur ended the call after telling her to call on that number and inform him if there was any news, Mustafa was on pins and needles.

'How's she?' he asked expectantly. Without replying, Timur merely hugged him tightly.

'Are you going to tell me anything?' An irate Mustafa pushed him away.

'She is showing improvement. The doctor says it has happened after my visit. Her body is responding to the drugs.'

Mustafa got his breath back. Unable to contain himself, Timur laughed uproariously and shook Mustafa by his shoulders.

'That's enough. Let that old man not see us. Let's finish this work before he returns.'

Mustafa returned to his work. Hearing approaching footsteps, Timur dropped the phone into his shirt.

'Come sons, it's coffee time . . .'

Osmanek peeped in from the door. They followed him after stacking everything in order. The canteen was in a small building in the same compound. The aroma of coffee hung in the air. The workers who stood with coffee cups and plates of savouries looked with curiosity at the newcomers.

'This place is crawling with girls,' Mustafa whispered, conscious of the flirtatious glances thrown in their direction.

'Will you shut up?' Timur hissed at Mustafa, taking care to hand over the coffee cup to Osmanek without spilling.

'They are not rich or educated. But smart enough to give birth to four or five children and rear them and earn money by rearing an equal number of cows,' Osmanek said, suppressing a smile. He had taken a shining to the new recruits. From the time he saw Timur, a hope of getting him as a son-in-law had raised its head in him.

'We haven't come here to get married,' Timur said, without taking his eyes off his coffee.

'I know who's captured your heart.' Mustafa said, when they were walking back to the factory.

'Who?' Timur tried to act nonchalant.

'Gul.'

Timur stared at Mustafa with an alarmed look. His face was drained of blood when he saw the smile lurking on Mustafa's face.

'Why are you blanching like this?'

As if he had not heard the question, Timur removed Mustafa's arm off his shoulder and hurried away from the scene.

When they were back in the room, he broached the subject again.

'I knew it from the first time we met.'

'Look here, there's nothing going on between us. I don't understand where you get such fancy ideas from!' Timur sounded grave.

'May be nothing is going on right now, but you love her.'

Mustafa caught him by the shoulder and turned his face towards himself. When he saw Timur struggling to meet his eyes, he felt sympathetic.

'It doesn't matter. Do you remember my getting cross with you when you showed extra interest in Gul? I knew it from that moment on.'

'I admit it, I like her.'

Timur looked up, screwing up his courage. When he saw the soft look on Mustafa's face, he lost some of his shyness.

'At that time, I didn't know what kind of a man you really are. Which was why I had reacted that way. Please forgive me.'

Timur did not respond to Mustafa and sat with his head bowed. He was trying to recollect when was the last time he had thought of Gul. During the blind flight of the past few days as if running over coals, there was nothing but the piteous face of Seetha in front of him.

'You should forget her. I guess you know that without me having to tell you. Right?'

Timur looked up.

'Those who take up arms for a cause, leave everything behind them. Even their own mothers. It is a journey with no return. Her memories will only weigh you down.'

'I know.'

Timur sat down and resumed the labelling work. He was gloomy. Unable to suffer the deafening silence, Mustafa tried to focus on the work on hand.

By evening, the tedium of the job gripped them. When Timur saw the other workers leaving, chatting gaily and laughing loudly, he wished to return to those times when, in the company of friends, chewing on crispy barbecued squid rings and imbibing copious quantities of raki, nights were turned into days of celebration at the beach-front restaurants of Sea of Marmara.

Osmanek was waiting at the gate. As they walked towards him, the sight of an approaching police Jeep halted them in their tracks. The vehicle stopped in front of Osmanek. Mustafa caught hold of Timur's hand and they slipped inside a group of workers, who were still streaming out.

Osmanek was talking to the policeman who had come out of the Jeep. In between, when pointed towards the factory, Mustafa's grip on Timur's hand tightened. He could not see an escape route. If they attempted to get back into the factory, the security guard may challenge them. Mustafa winked at Timur to reassure him. He did not let go off Timur's sweaty hand. They passed Osmanek who was busy conversing and walked till the bus stop, a small distance away, where people were waiting.

Suddenly, there was a shout from Osmanek, 'Hey, Tabib, come here . . .'

Tabib was the name Mustafa had given for Timur. He was also happy that he had the opportunity to christen himself. After toying with many names, he had chosen Sohab which meant gold. So, when the call came from behind them, Timur did not realize they were being summoned.

'Tabib . . . Sohab . . . here, look here . . .'

Mustafa stopped. 'Timur stop. We have been spotted.'

Timur stopped. Everything is coming to end, he said to himself. Osmanek waved his hand and beckoned them. The policeman watched them. Timur broke into sweat despite a chill in the air. His eyes were fixed on the gun in the policeman's hands.

'They are newcomers. They are staying with me,' Osmanek introduced them.

'You are the new workers? And when did you start work?' His eyes were boring into theirs.

'They started today. Emir has selected them.'

'Have you come to the factory for the first time today?'

Timur's mouth had run dry. No sound came out of his mouth even as he tried to speak.

'Yes.' Mustafa spoke up, aware that Timur was incapable of vocalizing.

'Before coming here, where did you work?' he asked Timur, pinning him with his stare.

When Osmanek was surprised when he saw how drained Timur's face was.

'We were in Ankara. In a butcher's shop. We got fed up. That was when a friend told us that there was an opening here.'

Mustafa sounded convincing to the policeman. He bid goodbye to Osmanek and drove away.

'Why did you go there? Didn't you see me standing here?' a surprised Osmanek asked. His old eyes seemed to be gauging them and with suspicion.

'We didn't want to disturb you as you were in a conversation. Also wanted to see if we could have a cup of coffee somewhere close.'

Osmanek's doubts lingered. He had the distinct feeling that the young men had tried to avoid the policeman. The old man's sixth sense told him that something was not right when he recalled Timur's silence and his pale face.

'You had coffee from the canteen. If we are not at the gate on time, that blockhead driver will leave us behind. Then we'll have to change buses twice to reach the flat,' Osmanek muttered, not trying to hide his irritation.

He had a stormy face and spoke to no one till they reached their dormitory. Mustafa, in order to erase Osmanek's suspicions, first tried to lighten the mood by cracking a few jokes. Galip, unaware of his intentions, joined him in the jollity. Even Baris, who occupied the front seat as he had done in the morning, forgot the morning's spat and joined in the laughter.

Osmanek had eased up by the time they entered the dormitory. He accused himself of being unduly critical of everything. Possibly what the young men had said was the truth. Also, who is not afraid of the police these days? After his bath and prayers, his feelings of guilt increased. When Galip returned with the meat he had been sent to buy, Osmanek asked Timur and Mustafa to do the cooking.

To make it evident he was holding nothing against them, he sat in the kitchen sipping a beer, flashing his tobacco-stained teeth in open-mouthed smiles, and joined in their conversation. Two more contributors to their victualling corpus had cheered him up. The newcomers were young, strong and had an appetite. They needed good food. He decided to include meat in their daily dinner fare.

While overseeing the cooking, Osmanek narrated an incident of theft that had taken place in the factory the previous week. The policeman had come to enquire about that. He stopped at the gate when he found the supervisor himself waiting there.

When he narrated the conversation between him and the policeman, Mustafa and Timur tried to act as natural as possible without making eye contact. Someone had broken the lock on the gates and taken away some expensive machines which had been kept outside so that they could be sent for maintenance. Osmanek was showering the choicest of abuses on the thieves for depriving them of the machines during their peak orders season. While dicing the meat and roasting it with onions, Mustafa and Timur tried to keep the conversation going by asking the right questions and making suggestions to find the thieves.

Osmanek and Galip agreed to do the washing up after the dinner. Timur's sheets were still damp. He was very tired since he had slept fitfully the previous night. As soon as he reached his plank bed, he collapsed on to it.

After a few minutes, his breathing became rhythmic. Mustafa took one of his sheets and covered Timur with it. It was late. He was experiencing an ordered life for the first time. He thought it was not a bad thing to work the whole day and then return home and go to bed with the stomach full. Deciding that he should wake up before Galip called them, Mustafa also lay down to sleep.

Timur was woken by the sounds of things being knocked down. It was pitch dark. There were ear-splitting sounds of metal vessels being flung around. He switched the torch on his phone and sat up on his bed.

'Don't switch on the light,' hissed Mustafa. He was kneeling and looking through the keyhole of the door.

'What's all that noise?'

'Policemen. Don't show any fear. Their way of looking for the missing machines. Take all your money and shove it into your underwear.'

'What's that for?' Timur was agape.

'Do it fast,' Mustafa gnashed his teeth. Timur obeyed immediately.

'I am going to open the door. Or they will be suspicious.'

Rubbing his eyes, he walked out of the room. Timur followed him.

'They are the newcomers. They are innocent,' Osmanek said in a pleading voice. When he heard sounds of things being broken, he ran towards the kitchen. They could hear Galip pleading with the policemen not to destroy things as they tried to find the stolen machines.

A fat policeman tipped up Mustafa's face using his truncheon and asked, 'Where were you working before this?'

Timur repeated faithfully whatever Mustafa had told the other policeman in the evening. His stomach felt hollow; he was afraid. He was trying to act like Mustafa would do on such occasions.

Although it sounded plausible, the policeman's suspicious eyes were scrutizing them from tip to toe.

'Show me your kimlik kartı!'

'For making the employment papers, we had handed them over to the patron at the time of joining. They've not been sent back,' Mustafa said in grovelling tone. The policeman seemed to have believed him. He ordered the policemen, who had finished with kitchen, to check Timur's and Mustafa's room. Although he had handed over every document to his father before leaving Istanbul, the thought that something may have remained in his bag that could identify him made Timur's knees go weak.

'There are only some clothes inside,' the disappointed policemen declared as they emerged from the room.

One of them was holding up Timur's wallet made in shiny, high-quality leather. It shone in the torchlight held by him.

'See this? This was found in one of the bags.'

The fat policeman took it off him. He looked at it carefully, turning it in his hands.

'Whose is this?' he asked.

Timur mouth was parched.

'It's mine, sir,' Mustafa said quickly.

'Something as expensive this? Your one month's wages won't be enough to buy one like this.' The policeman sneered.

'Someone gifted it to me, sir,' Mustafa looked shy. A smile appeared on the policeman's face when he caught on the insinuation.

'Let this stay with me. You'll get more such gifts.'

He shoved it into his pocket. The policemen who had wound up their search and were ready to leave, grinned. When the sound of their boots receded, Timur gave Mustafa a guilty look.

'If you want to parade your fancy stuff here, we'll end up in prison. Don't tell me I didn't warn you.' Mustafa hissed through his clenched teeth. Aware that if Mustafa had not stepped in, the game would have been over for them, Timur bowed his head in admission of his guilt.

The room was in a shambles after the policemen had searched it. Osmanek instructed them to go to bed only after putting everything back in order. While picking up and replacing things strewn around—all the time mouthing cuss words—Osmanek suddenly perked up.

'Guys, you said your kimlik kartıs are with Emir. But usually, they are handed over to that sleepyhead accountant Yavuz!'

Mustafa realized that the old man was still harbouring suspicions.

'The patron may have taken it only to check. He may have forgotten to hand it over,' Mustafa said glibly and got busy with the picking and stacking. Osmanek did not pursue that line further. However, Mustafa felt his suspicious eyes on him all the time.

It would not be easy to win his confidence. Mustafa could feel his instincts getting sharper as they did whenever he had to face danger.

Bahadir

'Will he get food and all that in time there?' Zehra asked Bahadir when he was heading for a siesta after lunch.

Three days had passed since Timur's departure from home. Although he had promised to call every day, she assumed that he was in a place or situation which did not allow him to make the calls. She attributed the same reason for her husband's uncharacteristic taciturnity and vowed not to trouble him with questions. However, a fretful mother's mind did not allow her to keep the vow.

The question did not register with Bahadir who was lost in his thoughts.

'Did you ask something?'

He stopped and turned around. When he saw the cascade waiting to tumble down from her eyes, he kept down the portfolio bag. He felt guilty that due to his own mental tensions, he had forgotten to update Zehra about Timur's status. He held her close and kissed her forehead.

'Instead of worrying yourself sick over such things, you could have asked me. He's safe and sound.'

'Are the police looking for him?'

Bahadir scanned her face. He thought it would be best to be honest with her.

'Not right now, but they soon will be on his heels. It's better that he remains out of their clutches right now.'

'Is my son in the company of good people?'

Zehra burst into tears. Bahadir did not know how to console her.

'He's with a friend who'll even sacrifice his own life for him. He's being fed and has a place to stay. If you start crying like this, I will lose my courage. Now's the time when we need to be strong for his sake and to support him.'

The phone rang. When Marc's face showed up in the caller ID, Bahadir quickly bade his wife goodbye and walked towards his car.

'Our plan succeeded. All Spanish channels are full of Seetha's face.' Marc's voice was bubbling with excitement.

'I had watched too. It will spread to the rest of Europe. Turkish media will not be able to remain a silent spectator. After all the disruptions you have caused, hasn't your police done anything?'

'We only caused a gridlock in the city. We were beaten up. Since there hasn't been destruction of public property, I can only hope that police will not lay serious charges against us,' Marc was laughing when he said that. 'We'll be out on the streets tomorrow too. We'll continue the agitation till there's a solution.'

'Be careful. Don't get injured and end up in hospital. All our plans will come to nought,' Bahadir said laughing. Suddenly, his voice turned grave. 'I need to tell you something important. Don't call me on this number again. I shall send you another number. Pass that on to Arnau and Montse too. Please convey my regards to them. Tell them it's all good here.'

Since he was on the phone, Bahadir was not conscious of the traffic around him and the commute time. A couple of clients were waiting for him. The day's meetings stretched into late evening. Since it had become a practice for Bahadir to work late, all the others exited without waiting for him to leave.

'Coffee.'

Emine placed a cup on his table. It was already dark. She stole a glance at her watch.

'Come and sit here.' He turned his computer monitor and pulled a chair to the table from where she could see it. Bahadir had already explained to her in the evening what they were going to do and the events that led to it. The offer that if she was scared, he would take someone's else help, scared her more, but she did not show it. How could she say no when the country's leading lawyer was asking her to assist in a legal case that was going to end up as controversial and therefore high profile?

Bahadir's gaze was fixed on the photo that filled the monitor— Marc pressing his hand against the wound on his head. Blood was streaming down his face. Bahadir turned his face away. After showing Emine a few more similar pictures, he turned the monitor towards him.

'We have to prepare a letter.' He leaned back in his chair and closed his tired eyes.

They had to prepare petitions for the various UN committees.

Bahadir explained to her the crimes of abduction and forced disappearance of people by the government authorities, illegal detention, human rights violation and denial of a woman's and her unborn child's rights.

After taking notes with alacrity, she moved to her computer to type the letters. The sounds of the rhythmic clacking of keys could be heard. Suddenly Bahadir saw a shadow pass by the window.

'Who's there?' he shouted and leapt up from his chair. Through the white, thin curtains he saw another two or three forms slink past the window.

'There are people outside!' he whispered.

Emine was petrified; her face became pale. After telling her to calm down, he went to the window and looked on either side. The place was deserted except for the black trunks of winter's leafless trees.

'Maybe I was imagining things,' he said to reassure the trembling Emine. The calling bell sounded suddenly shocking them.

'You wait here; I'll take a look.'

Bahadir walked to the door. Before he could open the door fully, those outside barged in impatiently.

A group of armed policemen. Although he was taken aback for a moment, Bahadir recovered quickly.

'What's the matter?'

An officer sporting a handlebar moustache stepped forward. The dull shine of the array of medals on the man's chest and his starched uniform with sharp creases gave rise to an unknown dread in Bahadir's mind.

'We've information that people with terrorist connections are visiting this office.'

'As per my knowledge, none who meets that description comes here. Moreover, we don't handle such cases.'

'We've received information from this office that legal aid is being extended to people incarcerated for terrorist connections.'

Bahadir fell silent. He was aware that his colleagues opposed his help to Seetha. More than being mere colleagues for long years, they were part of his life too. He wondered in agony how they had developed so much animus towards him that they should rat on him.

'Move aside,' the officer shoved him roughly to the side. Some ten or twelve policemen rushed in. Bahadir could see Emine trembling inside the room. He gestured to her to come to him.

'Who is this?' the officer asked in an intimidating tone.

'My assistant.'

'Do you both live here?' the man asked with a lascivious smile.

'Move this side.' The tip of his swagger stick brushed her trembling pink lips, and her curly hair that fell on her shoulders.

'Did his son come here today?'

An indistinct sound emerged from Emine's parched throat.

'Say it loud, you bitch . . .' The scream stunned her. Bahadir thought she may faint any moment. He helped her to sit down on the sofa.

'Why are you intimidating her? Am I not his father? Ask me!'

'Then tell me, where is Timur?'

'I don't know where he is. He may have returned to Barcelona.'

'Do you now handle cases which have a bearing on national security?'

'Currently none.'

The man laughed when he heard the reply.

'When you say currently none, it means it may happen in future, doesn't it?'

Bahadir remained silent.

'I know you are smart. However, don't think you being Kasim Özdemir's brother will save you all the time.'

Kasim! A doubt cropped up in Bahadir's mind. Could this be a charade set up by Kasim along with his minions to scare him away from Seetha's case? Bairam and Kasim were good friends.

One by one, the policemen came out of the rooms after their search.

'No one, right?' the officer asked. When they did not try to read the notes being prepared by Emine, his suspicion that this was a stage-managed raid to frighten him strengthened.

All the policemen had eyes only for Emine, who was curled up on the sofa. The sight of their lecherous eyes wandering all over her body made her flinch and shrink into herself more.

'Be careful while trying to defend militant anti-nationalists. I have the power to arrest you and her for undermining national security.'

A terrified and pale Emine looked at him beseechingly. Bahadir's heart was pumping with fear. He ignored it and said, 'Don't try to teach me the law. I haven't wiggled even my little finger to challenge the Turkish Constitution. However, you will be answerable to the courts for the transgressions you have committed now. Let's not forget that.'

A few of the policemen sniggered. With a grunt, the officer and his troops left the office.

'I had warned you of the dangers,' Bahadir said, sitting down beside Emine. He stroked her hair gently. As if unburdening herself of the tension and terror she had undergone till then, she burst into tears. He sat there for a long time, hugging her body wracked by sobs.

'It's very late. You go home now. From now on, I shall handle everything myself.'

Emine stood up slowly when she heard it. Her face was puffed up from the crying.

In his attempt to save Seetha, what if this girl too ends up in prison . . .! The very thought shook him. After handing over the file with the notes prepared for him, she walked towards her scooter parked by the side of the office. Bahadir called her back, 'Don't go alone. I'll come with you.'

Emine did not protest. Bahadir felt guilty when he watched her walk towards his car, after fetching her bag from the scooter. She looked like a college student, possibly only as old as Seetha. The thought that pushing her into such dangerous situation was an unforgivable act troubled him.

Unable to bear the overwhelming silence inside the car, Bahadir switched on the radio. The roll of military drums came through. He ground his teeth and hurriedly pressed the buttons. After skipping some loud, cacophonous stations, he hit one from which the slow, soothing clarinet music of Mustafa Kandıralı flowed out. Bahadir glanced at Emine who was leaning back on the passenger seat with her eyes closed. He could see unshed tears in the corners of her eyes. The uneasiness made him accelerate more.

Emine's apartment was near the Kadiköy coast. After getting down from the car, she crossed over to the driver side and stood by his window and smiled to console him. He felt a coolness in his heart.

'Don't worry. I can handle this case alone.'

'I felt afraid. This was my first experience. If I lose my nerve and step back, how will I ever work in Turkey as a lawyer?' Emine said.

Bahadir kept gazing her for a short while.

'Whatever it is, kiz,[1] let's not do it. If you are working with me on this, I won't be able to sleep in peace. We'll find some other way. Go and try to sleep peacefully.'

He reversed the car. Although he thought of going home, he changed his mind quickly. He scrolled his contact list and stopped at Pinar, the journalist whose contacts Mibang had provided him. *Euro Times* correspondent. Despite his misgivings on whether contact with journalists at this point would lead to more fraught situations, he dialled her number.

Pinar was busy filing her story for the day. After Bahadir identified himself and the purpose of the call, she left what she was doing and stepped out.

'A minute please. Let me go out. There are people around me. One can't be too careful while discussing such matters.' Pinar's words put him in two minds.

'Do you have a problem talking on the phone? If it's not inconvenient, I'd rather meet you in person.'

'Shall I come to your office?' Pinar asked.

'No. If it's not inconvenient for you, please come to the Balon Café at Kadiköy.'

She hung up promising to reach there in thirty minutes.

'Fear. In this land of snitches and stool pigeons, the strongest emotion is that—fear!' murmured Bahadir.

Rain was in the air, threatening to come down any time. Watching people hurrying to their homes, Bahadir sat in the car in Balon Café's parking. He used the time to read through the forms to be submitted to the various UN committees and the file that Enime had handed over. Now, he had to do all the work. Throwing back the files on the back seat, he sat in the car and smoked. More dark clouds rolled in. The smell of the sea and cool spray that the wind carried freshened him up a little.

After a while, a car drove in through the gates. When a tall, slim lady stepped out of it, he assumed it would be Pinar. She smiled and waved as she saw him watching her, with his head sticking out of the car window.

'My apologies. I had some work which I needed to complete today. I am sorry that I had to drag you all this way in this weather.' Bahadir apologized with utmost sincerity as they climbed the stairs to the restaurant.

'Not a problem! If you had come to my office, we wouldn't have had as much privacy.'

Bahadir had decided that he would confine himself to only telling that the girl who had disappeared was the one who had accompanied his son on a visit to Turkey and would not reveal the back story of her love affair. He could see her sharp, perceptive eyes watching his every movement. Bahadir noticed her high cheekbones, set jaw and her pursed lips that spoke of her determination. It would be difficult to keep things away from her. He felt uneasy.

'We're meeting for the first time. Shall we have something sweet?' he asked to reduce the tension in the air.

She nodded. 'Since what we are going to discuss is anything but sweet, let us,' Pinar said, her gaze boring into his eyes.

Bahadir sat down across her. He described the attacks on Seetha while in custody and the human rights violations she has continually faced.

'I was aware of you speaking to Mibang about this.'

'Yeah, I had called him. I have some contacts in the police. I had called based on information I had received. It didn't get me much.'

'We're friends.'

'I guessed as much when you called.' Pinar put her notepad back in her bag. 'What's your interest in this case?'

Her questioning look was making him uncomfortable. He was accustomed only to asking questions. Now the time had come when he needed to answer them. It was better to get into the practice, someone whispered from within.

'Seetha is my son's friend. They're both research students in Barcelona.'

To divert her interrogative mood, he asked her how the Turkish media was responding to the students' protests happening in Barcelona.

'The TV channels are carrying footages of the protests. The slant given is that protests are against the disappearance of a University of Barcelona student in Turkey.'

Pinar gave Bahadir a searching look. 'No one has started saying yet that she had come to meet terrorists who have a bounty on their heads.'

Watching the blood draining out of Bahadir's face, she smiled and took a cigarette from the packet lying on the table.

'How do you know this?' Bahadir tried his best to keep a straight face.

'I did tell you that I've some friends in the police.'

She pushed the empty plate in front of her and lit the cigarette.

'Shall we move to the balcony?' Bahadir too picked up a cigarette.

The terrace, the usual smoking zone of the café, was deserted, in deference, perhaps, to the cloudburst in the offing.

'Don't you want to help her?' Bahadir asked, enjoying the cool air and the cigarette. He wanted to know where her loyalties lay before revealing anything more.

'I know for sure that most of the people branded by the police as anti-nationals and traitors are wholly innocent. Whoever has picked up a gun has been compelled to retaliate or have had enough of the injustice. I don't know what made Arman and his younger brother choose this path. According to the police, she is a part of their gang.'

They pulled chairs and sat facing the sea.

'Do you believe what the police have told you?'

Bahadir watched for any change in her expression.

'I don't think so. An Indian girl studying in Barcelona. She would have managed to land a scholarship somehow and come to study. It sounds so implausible! I'd love to know how she got caught up in all this. If she deserves help, help her we must!'

Bahadir felt he could trust Pinar. Her words carried the ring of truth. He explained succinctly what compelled the brothers to take up arms and how Seetha ended up in Turkey.

'She was pregnant! And they never mentioned it!' Pinar exhaled showing her exasperation.

'We can now only use the past tense. The brutal torture and gang-rape took her child's life. She lost it.'

Pinar lit the next cigarette. Even in the falling darkness, Bahadir could see her face was taut and bore the look of rage mixed with horror.

'Bahadir, I would like to help you. What must I do?'

He smiled.

'Please keep this alive in the news. What else can you do?'

'I trust you know that I have my limits. Many of my colleagues are behind bars.'

'Hmm . . . I know that.' Bahadir said pensively.

'The government won't brook the slightest voice of dissent or criticism. How many brilliant journalists have been locked up, charged with treason?'

To hide her eyes turning bloodshot, Pinar turned her face away and looked up at the darkening sky. 'I chose this profession to tell truth to the power. Now I live by writing stories favourable to the government in a manner that sucks up to them!'

An uneasy silence prevailed.

'Let me get in touch with my colleagues in India and Spain. What we need now is to keep the pot simmering. The news should be prevented from dying out.'

While leaving, she turned around as if she had forgotten something and asked, 'When will you submit the petitions to the UN?'

'Tomorrow itself. There's no time to waste.'

'I hope you know of the plethora of such petitions that they receive?' She sounded despondent. 'I'm not sure how much I can really help you in this case.'

He smiled seeing her helplessness. 'Kardeş,[1] the media is present not only in Turkey.'

Pinar smiled back and waved her hand. He watched her tail lights recede and looked up at the sky as thunder rolled in the heavens.

His life was now going to be divided in two parts—before he sent the mails and after he sent the mails to the UN.

Fame, career, friendships and relationships! Everything would be sacrificed. It did not matter. *Timur, you opened my eyes.*

The dark clouds that had been threatening for a long time sent down pelting rain. The giant drops hit his body like small rubber bullets.

Where would Timur be now? He had been gone for two days now. Emir had said that he and Mustafa were put up comfortably in the workers' dormitory. Timur was a complaint box if the food was not tasty and the sheets not clean. It was unlikely that the amenities there would be to his standard. Timur would have to reconcile with many things he was unaccustomed to till then!

Slapping the water off his body, Bahadir entered the car. Two people seated in a black van at one corner of the parking looked at each other. One of them started the vehicle in a hurry as Bahadir eased the car out of the parking. He was immersed in his thoughts while driving, there was heavy rain and the van kept a safe distance behind other vehicles. Bahadir never noticed it on his tail.

Pinar

From the cabin across hers, Halil was watching Pinar seated at her table, distractedly playing with a small globe. He felt that she was oblivious to whatever was happening around her. Ayran waving goodbye and walking out with his camera or the office boy bringing the usual 6 p.m. tea for her did not seem to have registered with her. Only the cries of Yezda reverberated in her ears and she was deaf to all other sounds.

Unable to stand the sight of her seated like a statue, Halil entered her room with his cup of tea.

'Come, let's have a smoke.'

Pinar followed him after picking up the cigarette packet and lighter. Having a cup of hot tea and a smoke and chatting with colleagues, standing below their office, usually helped in amelioration of the accumulated work pressure.

This time they chose to sit on one of the concrete street-side benches and discuss the latest crop of unexpected news. Halil noticed that the otherwise boisterous Pinar—voluble in critiquing and ridiculing political personalities—was uncharacteristically silent. Since experience had taught him that asking her for the reasons would leave him no wiser, he did not bother to dig into it.

As they were going back in, a girl approached them with a bunch of freshly cut corn on the cob. Her dark face and shaggy hair spoke eloquently of her privations. Held in thrall by her tired, piteous eyes and shabby clothes, Pinar was unable to move forward.

'For all the goodness that is in you, buy at least one cob. It's only six liras.'

Scared by Pinar's stare, she turned towards Halil. 'Will you buy? It is very sweet.'

Halil paid her and bought two cobs. He offered Pinar a few kernels, as she stood watching the girl run towards a few students seated on an adjacent bench.

'What she said is true. It's very sweet.'

Pushing aside his hand that held the kernels, instead of entering their office building, Pinar started to walk towards the seashore.

'What happened? You've been behaving like this for some time now,' Halil asked. He felt something was seriously amiss.

'Yezda had called,' Pinar said after sitting down on one of the benches. 'She had seen one of the stories I had done on Seetha yesterday.'

'So what?' Halil raised his eyebrows.

'She says I will also be dumped into prison. She can't be blamed. She may be scared because of Tujela. Despite all my efforts to keep it under wraps, someone has told her about the two raids at my home.'

'She is forgetting that you had helped her. For the last three years, you have been bringing up her child.'

'I don't deny that. Tujela is like a daughter to me. But the fact remains that Yezda is her mother. She has the right to be worried about what will happen to Tujela if I also end up in prison.'

'Does that mean you should stop doing your work?'

'Halil, for the crime of doing my work, I too will have to flee like she had to. Else, they will lock me up. Like that girl selling corn on the cob, my Tujela too will end up on the streets.'

Watching tears flowing down Pinar's cheeks, Halil stood motionless.

'If you are so worried, give up Seetha's story. If you agree, I shall do it. I have no family, no kids, no encumbrances.'

'There's no escape. The legal trammels of this country lead one into a bottomless quagmire. I am already neck deep in it.'

They turned and started to walk back.

'Tomorrow Abid leaves for Belgium. He's found a small job there.'

Halil stopped. 'What will you and Tujela do then?'

'They have cancelled my passport. Since Tujela is Yezda's daughter, we might as well forget about a passport for her.'

Halil ground his cigarette under his heel and followed Pinar quietly as she walked into the office building. Everyone in the office tried their best to avoid references to Yezda. For them it was a name that reminded them of their brand of the Damocles sword.

Yezda was the most brilliant journalist among them. Her life was upended from the time three trucks sent by the Turkish intelligence agency—full of armaments meant for Syria-based militants—were stopped at the southern Turkey border, following orders from a public prosecutor of Adana. She reported in detail the legal action that followed this incident. Hundreds of journalists were jailed for reporting and publicising that incident. On top of a jail term, the government imposed on Yezda a punishment that no mother could bear—they removed all the legal rights she had as a parent over her two children.

Aware of what awaited her in the jail, Yezda fled to a refugee camp in Greece. From there she was able move to Canada. Although with the help of a friend she was able to get her eldest child to Canada, the one-year-old Tujela remained stuck in Turkey. Unable to withstand the harassment by the police, when her husband filed for and won a divorce from her, the little Tujela was truly orphaned. To escape from the responsibility of bringing up his daughter, Yezda's husband handed over the child to Pinar, his wife's best friend, and vanished from their lives.

Pinar was certain that she too would be flung into jail one day or the other, by the government using trumped charges of conspiring against the state. When she assumed Tuleja's responsibility, the entanglements around her became more complicated. She decided to exile herself after things reached that stage, from where it appeared as if she would have to spend the rest of her life in dehumanizing torture in some dark dungeon. However, whenever she thought of the ignominy of having to flee her country—conceding defeat to the evil forces and hanging her head in shame—the fighter in her militated against it. The news of Seetha reached her when she was going around with the thought that, before fleeing, as a last hurrah, she should set the country roiling with an exposé of her own.

Although Halil soon got busy with his work, Pinar could not concentrate on the things she had to do. She felt comforted by the thought that after Abid leaves the next day, she had to only fend for Tujela and herself and let out a sigh of relief.

The phone rang. 'Pinar?'

A flat, unemotional voice. 'I'm calling from Pandora Bookshop. The book you have ordered has come.'

Pinar was surprised. She was certain that she had not ordered any books from Pandora. She quickly understood someone was trying to get in touch with her.

'Ah, the book. Right. I'll come straightaway.'

'When'll you reach? You know that this book is in high demand. If you're delayed, there will be other takers.'

'I'll be there in thirty minutes.' The call was disconnected.

Pinar quickly collected her bags and other stuff. Something told her this was someone connected to Seetha.

After parking her car, she walked towards Pandora. She looked around to check if she was being watched. Everyone seemed to be hurrying along, preoccupied with their own business. The bookshop was crowded since it was evening. Students looking for their textbooks and people who thought they would pick up something to read on the way, were nosing around the bookshelves.

As soon as she reached, she started to slowly make her way through the aisles as if browsing through the neatly stacked books, secretly studying the faces of everyone around. She was disappointed. There was no one who stood out; they all seemed to be busy rifling through the pages of the books or trying to find the books of their favourite authors.

'Madam, the book you had ordered is here.'

It was a young man who at first glance looked like a government official with his pressed clothes, clean-shaven face, and neatly cropped hair. An attractive man. Like an office-goer, he carried a laptop bag and a lunch bag. He lifted the book in his hand and showed Pinar. She walked up to him.

'Did you call me?'

'Yes.'

Pinar looked suspiciously at his gentle face. As if searching for a book on the shelf, she asked softly, 'Who are you, what do you want?'

'I read your story on the protests in Barcelona and about the girl who disappeared here in Turkey. That's all good. But it had very little flesh. If your management agrees, would you be able to publish Seetha's story?'

'I need rock-solid, incontrovertible proof and witnesses. There are already too many legal restraints on me and my paper.'

'The residents of a whole village will bear witness. She was abducted from the village of Çîçika, close to Silvan.'

Although she was still harbouring suspicions, she heard him out.

'Dewran's mother who tried to stop them is still in the hospital. You can also use the statement given by Timur, who was accompanying her. I may be able to even get a picture from Seetha's hospital room.'

'I don't doubt these are all truths. But if I write this story as narrated by you, I won't be able to survive. You may know the circumstances under which my colleague Yezda had to exile herself. Even the dog squad that had smelled and discovered that convoy was deported from this country.'

'Even if you don't write Seetha's story, Pinar, I know you won't be allowed to remain here.'

Pinar stared at him. 'Who are you?'

'My name is Arman.'

The books fell from Pinar's hands. 'Of Cizîr . . .?'

He nodded slowly.

Pinar stood stunned looking at his impassive face. Words got stuck in her throat.

'Just the crime of meeting you is enough to land me in some godforsaken dungeon for life.'

After recovering from the initial shock, she started to walk out of the shop.

'Pinar, I'll be able to help you. I can get you and your child out of Turkey.'

As if she had not heard what he had said sotto voce, presenting the girl at the counter with a forced smile, Pinar almost ran to her car. The sudden shock and fear made her tremble all over.

Arman! What a transformation!

She tried to imagine—minus the lush moustache and beard and thick-framed glasses—if it was the same person seen in the photos that had appeared so many times in the newspapers.

Although she wanted to put as much space between him and her as possible, Arman's words kept coming back to her. An exposé enough to shake the administration to its rotten core. A safe passage for her and Tujela from Turkey. Possibly this man could help her.

She sat in the car, swayed by the dilemma. Her heart told her that she should not let go of the opportunity. She could see the slim form watching her from the door of Pandora. After debating for some more time within herself, she gestured to Arman to come to her.

Arman, who hurried to her, made sure no one was watching and slipped into the passenger seat.

'The photo your promised. The names, addresses and telephone numbers of those who will bear witness to the police abducting Seetha.'

'You'll get all this tomorrow.'

'You have promised to get me and Tujela out of the country?' Pinar looked at him expectantly.

'Any European nation would be ready to give you political asylum. For that you have to leave Turkey. Those arrangements I shall do.'

'How will I get in touch with you?'

Despite wanting to ask many more questions, she could not frame them. She seemed to be having a brain-fade.

'Don't worry. I'll be there whenever you want me.'

He took her hands in his own as if making a pact. After Arman disappeared into the red-tinged gloaming, like a shadow dissolving into the darkness, Pinar kept sitting in the car reliving the warmth of his hands and solace that his words had brought. She felt disappointed for not watching out to see if Dewran was with him. She ran through the faces of everyone she had seen in Pandora over and over again in her mind. She could not recollect anyone's face except the gentle looking Arman's with its sunken cheeks and soft eyes. He had all the aspects of a young college teacher.

Even if he walked into a police station, no one would recognize him. The people's claim that, like a ghoul, he was haunting every policeman who had had his fun raping Kurd girls in the basement and burning them and small children alive at Cizîr was no old wives' tale. Pinar sighed and started her car.

The next morning, after seeing off Abid, she reached the office later than usual. He had lingered at the airport door, unable to take his eyes off her . . . he struggled to extricate his fingers that he had intertwined with Tujela's. Although it was moot if they would meet each other again, both were careful to not betray in front of Tujela any of the feelings burning up their insides.

He was already late for the check-in. Without bothering to wipe the tears welling up in his eyes, he covered the child with kisses. Carrying his small valise, when Abid walked away without looking back, Pinar stood rooted to the spot, clutching Tujela's hand and with a heavy heart.

After returning from the airport, in the absence of Abid, the house frightened Pinar like a lifeless body would. She did not feel like going to the office. She shuffled around the house listlessly, her body and mind felt exhausted. Although she dearly wanted to empty the bottle of vodka that was inside the fridge and curl up in her bed, since she knew that Arman would be sending the information that she had demanded, she left Tujela with her mother and left for the office.

She went to her cabin only after checking with the receptionist if anyone had come to meet her. No one had. The day's mail only had her bank statement and an invitation to a painting exhibition by one of her acquaintances. After a cursory glance, she chucked them into the waste bin. She had had little sleep the previous night. Trying hard to keep her drooping eyelids open in the cool air from the air-conditioning, she tried to focus on the tasks on hand.

'Don't you want to eat?' When Halil asked her this, in spite of not being hungry, she stood up from her desk. Although she feared that Arman may turn up when she was away, the need to have some fresh air prevailed.

When the receptionist girl saw Pinar, the former lifted up a McDonald's bag and hailed for the latter. 'I was going to bring this to your cabin. The boy delivered it just a minute ago. It's still warm.'

Halil looked at Pinar in surprise. Pinar, who never passed up on opportunity to get out of the office for some relaxation, was ordering in food? Pinar too had to struggle to hide her own surprise.

'I was tired. I had ordered thinking I won't go out. And then forgot all about it.'

An astonished Halil stared after the departing form of Pinar, who had grabbed the bag from the receptionist and was hurrying towards her cabin. She always shared whatever she was having. Assuming Abid's departure had upset and distracted her, he headed for their regular eatery, the Kebab House.

Once she reached her cabin, Pinar tore into the packets. Salad, chicken wings, burger, and a small cake. The usual fare from McDonald's. Nothing more. Unable to stand the suspense, she took the bag she had torn, straightened out the wrinkles and looked through. Everything was blank. She kept staring at the paper cartons. Was this a trap? She decided not to have that food.

Dropping all the packets into the waste bin, a tired Pinar rested her head on her desk. She felt a coffee may revive her. As she reached down to pick her bag, her eyes fell on the salad carton. Among the lettuce, tomato and olives was something that did not belong there. She picked up the carton. A small packet anointed with olive oil and black vinegar lay concealed inside. It was well wrapped in plastic and taped tightly. She opened it carefully. It contained a flash drive. Her thirst, hunger and tiredness now seemed like a distant memory. She let a smile appear on her face.

After a little while, *Euro Times* Investigative Editor Oscar Anderson received a message from his Istanbul bureau chief, Pinar Güneri, on his phone—she had an explosive story in her hand, something that could shake up the diplomatic relations between countries. Before she filed the story, she wanted to have a word with him. Anticipating the importance of the story, he set a video conference call in thirty minutes.

Pinar dove straight into the story without even exchanging pleasantries. She started with Arman's story. Anderson was no stranger to stories of young men taking up arms and joining militant organizations to avenge the death of their dear ones. He listened about Dewran and his sister having to leave Turkey, his falling in love with Seetha, and the next developments with mild interest. However, when the story moved to the circumstances under which Seetha had to come to Turkey and the torture she had to undergo there, with the sixth sense of a seasoned newshound, he leaned forward in anticipation. He could smell the makings of a news that would kick up an international furore.

Pinar showed him the photo sent by Arman. It looked like a photo taken in a hurry from the door of a hospital room. When zoomed in, an IV stand, a hospital bed and the gaunt face of girl lying on it were visible. Her black hair tumbled down the side of the bed like a black serpent. The sad eyes in the middle of livid bruises on her face seemed to be looking helplessly at the photographer.

'What is to be done now?' Pinar asked, as he kept staring at the photo.

'Did you check the authenticity of this photo and other details?' Anderson asked, his eyes still fixed on the photo.

'It's certain that the photo was taken at Beykoz hospital.'

'How do you know?'

'I have other photos of hers with me. It is Seetha, for sure. Look at the floor tiles. Photos of Beykoz hospital rooms are available on the Internet. The Iznik tiles are the same. If you zoom in further, you can see the initial "BSH" embroidered at the corner of the sheet covering her.'

'That's very good.' A rare smile flashed on Anderson's face and quickly disappeared.

'There are some addresses in the pen drive. Details of people who witnessed Seetha being taken away by the police. They are residents of Çîçika. And ready to give witness. We have stringers in Diyarbakır and Nusaybin. They can interview these persons. It's a day's work,' said Pinar.

'Pinar, aren't you scared? Already there are legal cases that you are party to.'

She replied after a moment of reflection. 'I'm scared. However, I would like us to publish this news.'

'This will compromise your security. They will try to harass you, hurt you. We can publish this in England under another reporter's by-line.'

'No, Mr Anderson. This should be published under my by-line.' Pinar was adamant.

Although he wanted to warn her again, aware that the quick-witted woman at the other end of line would be more aware of it, he kept his counsel.

'Then let's not waste time. Since we have decided to go forward, let's not lose the element of surprise. The news should come out presenting every damning evidence that there is and with unexpected swiftness denying them any opportunity to counter. Whoever is covering those villages should not forget to shoot enough visuals. The news should hit simultaneously through our channel.'

Pinar nodded.

'Mr Anderson, one more thing. You know there are a stack of cases against me. Yezda's child staying with me has provoked them very much. I plan to leave the country along with the kid before this news breaks.'

Pinar paused and looked at Anderson who was watching her anxiously. She continued with some hesitation.

'Will our headquarters extend me any help?'

'Do you know how many of our journalists are in prison in various parts of the world?' Anderson said helplessly, looking up at the heavens.

'Yes.' Pinar bowed her head in guilt.

'Your immediate concern should be not to land in a prison. Anyway, you said you plan to leave Turkey. Let me know as soon as you cross the border. Let's see what can be done.'

Pinar nodded again in agreement. She could feel, fraught with misery, the weight of the helpless loneliness that she would have to face during the next few days, slowly descending onto her shoulders.

'Good luck. If you run into any problems, I'm always available on my mobile.'

Anderson's face disappeared from the screen. Pinar sat back in the chair with her eyes closed. She was happy to have received the permission to move ahead with the story. She could also feel the chill of fear that was enveloping her at the same time. She was not aware what caused the chill—whether it was the precariousness of the coming days or the dread of the consequences that lay in wait for her because she dared to publish the story.

She closed all the windows on her screen and opened a new one on Word. A pair of fearful eyes in a terrified, exhausted face full of bruises stared back at her from it.

'You won't have to remain like this for long,' she murmured at the screen.

Her fingers started to race over the keyboard.

Escape

When she heard the soft ding from her laptop, Pinar looked up from the keyboard.

Email from Naif, the stringer from Diyarbakır. She read through his mails. He had been given the task two days ago. There were many mails with video attachments. Pinar quickly glanced through each. The youngster seemed to have done a professional job. Dewran's mother speaking from her hospital bed, her head in bandages, and her voice weak; Aylan fulminating in rage and anguish; villagers who witnessed the incident—Naif had interviewed them all.

One of the videos caught her attention. It was clear the person who had taken the video was running while recording it. The video started with the rear shot of a police vehicle bumping over a dirt road raising and trailing dust in its wake. In the background, voices could be heard yelling and cursing. All of a sudden, a huge dog leapt into the frame out of nowhere. It surged ahead of the videographer and presumably others running behind the vehicle shouting imprecations. With a deep, booming bark, the dog tried to leap onto the back of the police vehicle. Screams and bellows could be heard, followed by the sharp reports of guns being fired. Pinar cut the volume and watched the video again.

Although the dog had failed in its attempt to land on the vehicle, it scrambled up and tried another running leap at the vehicle. It was shot mid-air and crashed to the ground. Crying children could be seen rushing towards the inert form of the dog. The video ended with a close-up shot of a five- or six-year-old boy hugging the bloodied neck of the dog and wailing.

Pinar dialled Naif. 'Was the video of the dog sent by oversight? What's the story?' Naif understood the confusion in her voice.

'Did you notice the police vehicle? Seetha was taken away in that vehicle. The dog running after the vehicle and getting shot is Dewran's. One of the men who was there had shot this video.'

Pinar watched the video on loop.

'Many of the villagers are witnesses to what happened. The man who shot the video and the kid who's hugging the dog and weeping have narrated everything to my camera.'

'Aren't they afraid?'

'Even fear has its limits. They have suffered a lot. The villagers hold Dewran's father in great respect. The police went into his home and did all these atrocities. You should see what they have done to the old lady's head! The people there realize tomorrow it could be their turn.'

'When will she be discharged?'

'I can't say. Her skull is fractured. She has lost a lot of blood too. She's lucky to be alive.'

Pinar thought of her own mother. The thought whether they would take out on her mother their frustration and anger of not getting Pinar herself terrified her.

Naif was silent at the other end. He had the blues.

'Pinar.'

'Yeah, what?'

'How's the girl now?'

'She's alive, but still in custody.'

'How long will we have to keep suffering like this, Pinar?'
Naif's voice was breaking. She felt he may even burst into tears.

'Aren't we all trying to change the present dispensation? We
have to publish this tomorrow.'

Next, she called Bahadir, but his phone was engaged. She
returned to the videos. There was a tearful narration by the child
about Roja being shot and killed by the police; Dewran's mother
testifying how she was hit on the head and sent crashing to the
floor; and how her son's pregnant lover was dragged over the
ground and taken away. Pinar's mind went numb.

By evening, she would have to send her copy and visuals to
Anderson. Once they were published, she would find it hard
to stay in the country. There was no sign of Arman, who had
promised to do everything to facilitate her escape. She was a fool
to be led by the confident look on his face when he made the offer.
She should have had a plan B in case he failed to turn up. Pinar
went out of the building for a smoke.

It was imperative that she and Tujela stay away from Istanbul
for a few days. She tried hard to think of someone who could give
her refuge. Who would open their doors for someone branded as
a traitor? They would be aware that they would get dragged into
needless litigation and troubles with the police.

She stubbed out the cigarette and walked back to her cabin.
Notwithstanding her palpitating heart, she completed the stories
by evening and sent them to Anderson. She also attached Timur's
and Seetha's itineraries, air tickets and details of the hotel where
they stayed in Sur.

She left the office late in the evening only after ensuring she
had left behind no important or incriminating document. She had
informed their London head office that she would not be attending
office from the next day. The chief editor agreed to her suggestion
that Halil could be given the temporary charge of the bureau. He,

like Anderson, was of the opinion that the piece could be published under the name of another correspondent, but Pinar did not agree. A kind of obdurate death wish had taken root in her.

She walked towards the garage in the basement of the building without stopping to say goodbye to anyone. How many years had she spent in this office! And yet she had to steal away from the bureau chief's chair, fleeing like a felon. She suddenly remembered her mother and Tujela and after wiping her face, slipped into the driver's seat.

'Pinar . . .'

Someone said her name softly from the back-seat. She was shocked out of her wits. Shivering, she turned back slowly. In the darkness of the garage, she could see an indistinct form slowly rise up from the back seat. Before she could scream, his hand had covered her mouth.

'Don't make any noise. It's me, Arman!'

When he saw signs of recognition appear in her bulging eyes, he eased his grip on her mouth.

'You scared me to death!' Pinar said when she recovered enough to speak. Her body trembled uncontrollably, like a lone leaf fighting the wintry breeze.

'I could find no other way to talk to you alone. Please forgive me.' In his guilt, Arman took her hand which was lying limp in between the seats. That comforting touch opened the floodgate of her tears. He kept stroking her hand till she calmed down and stopped crying.

'I had promised to help you, hadn't I? Now stop crying!'

When her sobbing stopped, he spoke.

'I have heard about your people visiting our village. What are you planning to do, can you tell me please?'

'Tomorrow the full story will be published, leaving out nothing. It's not merely Seetha's story. It will be your story too, of Dewran and Gul too.'

'I never thought it would get done so quickly,' Arman said in a congratulatory tone.

'There was no other way. This Friday, the court will be ruling on some of the cases that have been dogging me. Would you be able to take me and my child away from here?' Her dead voice and its pleading tone tore up his insides.

'Of course. We'll do it tonight. Go home and get ready to leave. Carry only your documents and minimum clothes. Take only enough to fill a backpack. We'll have to travel a long way.'

'Where shall we meet?'

'By 9 p.m. get into Medipol Mega University Hospital. Take a taxi. Don't forget to explain in detail how your child has suddenly fallen sick.'

'After I reach there?'

'After registration, go inside on the pretext of meeting the doctor. There is a small exit by the side of the hospital canteen. Leave through that. Outside, you'll see a brown Renault Duster. Get into it.'

Pinar nodded mechanically. Arman got out of the car without bidding goodbye. However, he turned around as if he had forgotten something and knocked on the window glass.

'Do you have a burqa?'

Pinar shook her head to indicate she had none.

'Would you be able to organize one?'

Shops would be closing soon. However, Pinar recalled a small garment shop on her way home that closed late.

'After you are inside the hospital, you should wear the burqa without anyone seeing you. No one should recognize you and your child boarding the Duster.'

Pinar agreed to follow his instructions. She watched him in the rear-view mirror as she drove off.

'What a man!' Pinar sighed.

Saying goodbye to her mother was not easy. She had given Tujela a bath as usual and dressed her up. After collecting her, Pinar could not find the courage to take the next step.

'Why, kiz evlat,[1] are you overworked? You look very tired.'

'Yes, anne, these days, things are hectic,' Pinar said, taking care to keep her voice even.

When I will you see again, anne? Her eyes asked her mother wordlessly.

Her daughter's unusual behaviour and unwavering gaze made her suspicious that everything was not all right. When she wanted to ask her about it, without giving her an opportunity, Pinar walked ahead. She imprinted in her mind the image of her mother in a blue dress standing beside the lush wisteria flowers in her garden. Don't look back! she admonished herself. If you look back, you'll never leave this place! After she found a sanctuary somewhere, she would take her mother too, Pinar decided.

There were only a few things to pack—certificates; title deed of the house; documents pertaining to the legal cases; Tujela's two frocks; medicines; undergarments for both. After putting them in a cloth bag, when she took up the newly bought burqa, she sighed deeply. She looked at the clock. It was time to leave. She took the mobile phone and searched for taxi company numbers.

By the time she locked up and reached the gate after one last check, the taxi had arrived. For someone who usually avoided striking up a conversation with chatty drivers, that day she answered all the questions the driver had for her. She was able to convince him that Tujela, who was asleep on her shoulder, was running a temperature. Concerned that a single woman had to take her child to the hospital at that hour, the sympathetic driver showed readiness to accompany her to the doctor. However, she politely thanked him and refused the offer.

After she completed the registration, she was asked to wait. The kind receptionist tried to calm her down when she saw the alarmed look on her pale face. She assured her that the delay was only because the paediatrician on duty had been summoned to the operation theatre.

The hospital corridor was not crowded. Only a few grouchy bystanders and patients were present. Pinar looked around to see if she was being watched. None looked suspicious to her. The gloom and silence of the hospital, the grave-looking nurses who were hurrying up and down, and thoughts about the car waiting for her by the side of the canteen made her nervous.

The toilets were deserted. Dressed in a raiment which she had never wanted to wear in her life, for a second Pinar stood staring at her own unfamiliar reflection in the dim mirror. She exited the toilet after changing what was worn by Tuleja, who was curiously watching her mother's transformation.

She had to locate the canteen. When her efforts failed, she approached an attendant who was pushing a wheelchair. Glancing at his watch he said coldly that the canteen would be closed. When he saw her pleading eyes and the child she was carrying, he seemed to reconsider and pointed to a corridor.

'That will take you to the canteen. The door may be closed. But there'll be someone inside. If you tell them Khalid sent you, if there is any food left, they will give you. Don't be late . . .'

Ignoring Pinar's bowed head in gratitude, lost in his thoughts, he started to push the wheelchair along. Suddenly Pinar noticed two men coming from across her. As she watched them walk down slowly and deliberately looking all around them, her heart went into overdrive. Turning the child's face so that it would not be visible to the men, she slowly sat down on a chair.

They were looking at the faces of patients waiting to see the doctor. Possibly because she was in a burqa, they did not look at her and walked ahead. Pinar rose to her feet and hurried towards the corridor leading to the canteen. It was narrow and poorly lit. On either side were examination rooms, now deserted. The strong smell of disinfectant made her sneeze. She was afraid that in her rush, in a long, impeding and unaccustomed dress, and carrying the weight of the child, she may trip and fall. She kept looking behind to see if she was being followed. The sound of her heavy breathing echoing off the walls made her more nervous.

Kantin, written in large letters, could be seen from some distance away. The doors were closed. The canteen was in an annexe to the main building. Shifting the child from one hip to the other, Pinar tried to find if there was an exit nearby. She saw a gate through which presumably groceries and gas cylinders were brought in. *This should be the exit that Arman had mentioned.* She sighed in relief.

It was dark. The workers seemed to have switched off all the lights before they left. In the dim moonlight, she approached the gate. She was shocked to see a padlock on the latch. She shook the gate and tried to move the latch. Nothing gave; the gate was strong and tall. It loomed above her like Mount Suphan. Carrying Tujela, there was no way she could have climbed over the gate. Defeated, Pinar stood resting her head against the cold metal bars of the gate. She was at a loss.

She tried to stretch out and see if there was any car outside. Her view was blocked by the wall of the adjacent building. Nothing was clearly visible in the darkness.

The weight of the child fatigued her arms and shoulder. The men in the corridor would have realized that their targets had given them the slip and must be searching every nook and corner by now. She would not be able to get out through this gate. She thought walking out of the hospital through the main entrance and trying to find the car on the other side would be too

dangerous. However, if she delayed too much, Arman may decide
to leave.

Suddenly, the headlights of a car switched on beyond the
wall. A scream got stuck in her throat. They were leaving! She
gave one desperate tug at the padlock. There was a click and the
lock twisted in her hand. It was not locked! She pulled open the
gate and ran out sobbing. There was a car on the other side of the
wall. The sight of a woman dashing across must have made the
driver switch on the lights again. She collapsed into the arms of
the person who emerged from the car.

After receiving the child from her tiring arms, he supported
the weight of her body and patiently waited for the sobs racking
her body to subside.

Tujela had woken up and started to sniffle. Pinar took her
back, trying to become calmer. Only then did she notice that the
man was not Arman. Recoiling back from him, she peered closely
at the man. No! It wasn't Arman. The man seemed to understand
her perplexity.

'Pinar, don't be afraid. I have been sent by Arman. He will
join us soon. Please get into the car.'

Of course, they needed to get away from there quickly! She
got into the car. The man started to drive. Holding the sniffling
Tujela close to her chest, she tried to rock her to sleep, and sat
staring through the window.

The car stuck to the small lanes and side streets. Although the
question of when Arman would join them was trying to break
through her, she kept the impulse under control.

The sweet smell of tobacco hung in the air. The man was close
to fifty years and kept his eyes peeled on the road and offered no
conversation. She kept the bag to the side, laid Tujela on her lap
and stretched out her legs.

After about fifteen minutes of driving through unknown roads, the car stopped in front of an old mosque. The crowd in the big granite-paved courtyard was thinning. Pedlars were getting ready to leave for their homes along with their carts.

The driver got out of the car and lit a cigarette leisurely. After a while, Pinar saw a tall man emerge from the mosque and walk towards the car.

'He's coming,' the man said in his grating voice, threw away the cigarette and got into the car. Pinar screwed up her courage and watched the approaching man. She decided to escape through the other door if it turned out to be someone other than Arman.

There was some resemblance to Arman. A long white tunic worn over a pair of loose *şalvar* and long beard with silvery grey hairs reaching up to the chest gave him the look of an austere *molla* coming out of the mosque after prayers.

'Quick,' he said, opening the door and sitting down beside her.

'Arman!' Pinar covered her face with her hands. She found the change unbelievable. 'I didn't recognize you!'

Without paying attention to her, Arman turned to the driver. 'Is everything okay? Was anyone following you?'

'No concerns. I did take a roundabout route. When you reach a suitable place, you should change these number plates.'

Arman glanced at Pinar. He gave a grunt of satisfaction at her attire.

'Sorry, we are going to travel as husband and wife.'

After putting the rucksack which lay on the seat to the side, he checked if her daughter was comfortable.

'Were you scared?' The solicitous question made Pinar tear up again. He patted her shoulder and said, 'Don't worry. I can well understand.'

To distract her mind, he took out kimlik kartıs from his bag and showed her. With their stained, tattered edges no one would believe they were newly made ones. She looked with amusement at her blurred photo—uncharacteristically wearing a scarf.

'Should anyone ask, we are returning to our home in Van after visiting relatives here. I'm Ahmet Ağa and you are Esmeray. Your daughter's name remains the same.'

'Where are we going?'

'We are headed to Reyhanli. We'll rest for a day and then go across the border.'

'Syria!'

'Yes, there's no other route to take you out.'

Pinar looked at her own hands bitterly. How many stories have these hands filed about the conflagration on the streets of Syria and refugees fleeing for their lives! And ironically, fearing for her own life, she seemed to be destined to seek refuge in the same land!

'We have to travel 1100 kilometres. It'll be a good idea for you to get some rest.'

'What's that proverb—a good companion shortens the longest road?' Pinar gave him a grateful look.

The car had reached the highway. Pinar hugged the sleeping Tujela. The tall sodium vapour lamp posts bathed in their own yellow light kept flashing past. As did tall minarets with their multi-colour lighting. *My dear Istanbul, when will we see each other again?* Not bothering to wipe the tears that appeared at the corners of her eyes, Pinar stared out of the window.

Istanbul

'Hello, since morning I've been trying to contact Pinar, your chief of bureau. Her mobile is switched off. Is she now in office?'

'I'm sorry, she's on leave. Halil Bozkurt is holding charge in her place.'

'All right.' Bahadir hung up with his mind in turmoil. While reading the morning news he suddenly remembered that Pinar had called him the previous morning. Something was wrong. As he sat staring at Seetha's picture that filled his screen on *Euro Times*'s website, he felt the mystery behind Pinar's sudden disappearance was deepening. Bahadir picked up his mobile again.

'Hello, I need to talk to Halil Bozkurt.'

'I'm sorry, he's busy. If you leave your name and number, Halil will call you back.'

He hung up after giving his details. A storm was brewing somewhere—the howl of the wind as it rushed through window; the moist, organic smell of the sea; the cawing of a colony of seagulls as they wheeled and swooped over the sea, looking for refuge . . .

Although the curtains fluttered around manically like white foamy waves, Bahadir did not close the windows. He lay back in his large chair, savouring the taste and smell of his cigarette's strong tobacco.

Bahadir was tipped off by Mibang in the morning. Things were moving at breakneck speed. *Euro Times* had brought international attention on Seetha's case. Their channel and website had launched a coordinated campaign. It was not merely Seetha's story; there was a stream of stories on everyone connected to her— what compelled Arman to join the militants; the circumstances in which Dewran and Gul had to leave the country; the villagers' witness accounts of Seetha being abducted after being brutalized. It was comprehensive, watertight reporting.

When Zehra came to the door of his room, although he tried to change the channel in a hurry, he gave up when he saw that the news in every channel had the same story. The previous day, when he was discussing Marc and his friends' arrest with Prof. Arnau, Zehra was by his side. When she understood that those arrested were Timur's friends, she became agitated. It did not take her much time to accuse him of encouraging children when they strayed, instead of correcting them. This was the prelude to dissolving in a hail of tears.

Unable to countenance more questions and lamentations, Bahadir had reached office early. He was, however, unable to focus on the work in hand. Zehra's angry, teary eyes did not leave him in peace.

Feeling miserable, he kept staring at the carvings on the ceiling. She could not be faulted. Timur was her only son. Her raison d'être. She had great expectations for his success, him being a topper all through the years. She had no dreams beyond his studies, job, marriage and children. Her son, whom she wanted to be by her side all the time, was now staying at some unknown place at the mercy of strangers. Contact with him was confined to rare snatches of whispered conversations from wayside public phones he managed to access out of sight of others. He may be arrested any time and put in prison. Her distress was not unwarranted.

To shut out unpleasant thoughts, he went back to watching the news. The news had gone beyond mainstream media. Social media was blazing with Seetha's story. TV channels in Europe and India had picked it up as well and were running with it. The student demonstrations in Barcelona gained a lot of international attention. #Seetha was trending at the top on Twitter. Facebook, YouTube and Instagram were filled with youngsters' posts in support of Seetha.

With Marc and his friends languishing in police custody, other university campuses had taken up the baton of protest and it was spreading fast. Bahadir laughed when he watched a truncheon-wielding, black-uniformed member of the National Police rushing towards the students. The youth are the same everywhere. The thought that they could be beaten into submission was a pipe dream.

The curtains were flapping hard in the wind. He watched dark clouds roll in over the sea. Bahadir tried to focus his mind as if trying to second-guess the timing of the *coup de grâce* the sinister enemy was aiming to deliver. The birds who lose their nest and nestlings will lament. Large fish will perish and float on the angry, roiling waters of the sea. Before long all of that would be forgotten. None of this will stop the bells of Hagia Sophia from ringing.

Unexpectedly the mobile rang. An unknown number. He answered the call after an initial hesitation.

'Baba . . .'

Bahadir's eyes became moist. The voice was like a cool, soothing balm on his inflamed heart.

'Baba, can you hear me?'

'Yes my *sevgili oğlum*,'[1] Bahadir responded quickly.

'Saw the news. Looks like trouble. What's the situation?'

'You're not in the picture any longer. The villagers say that she had gone to the village all by herself. Travelling together with a fellow student for some distance is no crime. Moreover, the staff in Diyarbakır hotel attest to how she had given you the slip.'

'Does it mean I can return?' Timur's voice had a mixture of happiness and thrill.

'I shall tell you. Not before that. And once back, you'll stay at home. Since the world has now taken ownership of the issue, you are no longer needed.'

'Okay. Both of you should remain calm. I'll call tomorrow.' The line was disconnected.

The energy that Bahadir received from a voice that had always delighted him was not a little. For the first time a hope rose in him that he would be able to extricate Timur out of the present troubles.

The sounds of someone sounding off a car horn in apparent rage woke him from his reverie. He could see Kasim, who had leapt out of his car, railing at his watchman. Smiling because Kasim had changed his car again, Bahadir went down to the reception area on the ground floor.

Kasim was apoplectic in his rage, his face flushed and steam coming out of his ears.

'You'll get me thrown out on my ear!' he bellowed.

'What did I do?' a serene Bahadir asked, settling into the comfort of the sofa. He wished he could get a cup of hot coffee.

'All the channels claim that you have submitted appeals for that terrorist in the UN. Everyone is asking me for an explanation.'

'Kasim, you go do your work. I'm a lawyer. Have I done anything illegal?'

'Yeah, from today I'll be doing only my work. Let father and son not think that they can keep escaping using my name. Lawyer, I believe! You are a traitor. The charge against you is that you have colluded with the bureau chief and conspired against the government!'

Bahadir felt a chill run through him. Pinar would be in deep trouble. He wondered if she had already been taken into custody.

'What are you rambling on about?' he asked as if he was aware of nothing.

'Are you trying to act innocent after hiding her?' Kasim shrieked.

Relief flooded Bahadir. Pinar had escaped! He realized that she had foreseen the danger and made good her escape.

The smile on Bahadir's face infuriated Kasim even more.

'When the inquiry starts, I shall state that I have no relationship with you. Don't tell me I didn't warn you.'

Bahadir watched impassively as Kasim stomped out of the building.

'Sir,' Emine called softly from behind.

Watching Kasim's tantrums, she had been standing there, scared.

'Your phone has been ringing all this while.'

She handed over the mobile and hurriedly went inside. Bahadir had noticed that after that night's incident, Emine always ensured to keep the maximum distance between them. Kadir and others had already begun to isolate him. He thought ruefully that if he did not hold a substantial share in the firm, they would have kicked him out the moment he had decided to take Seetha's case.

The missed calls were from the *Euro Times* office. He immediately called back. Halil seemed to be waiting for his call. After mutual introductions there was an interlude when both were unsure what to say next. Halil confessed that apart from the fact that Pinar was busy with the Seetha story over the past few days, he had little information.

Pinar's sudden, unannounced disappearance and the subsequent developments had shaken Halil. Even before the phone calls from the head office conveying his new responsibilities could be completed, he had to give explanations to the police who barged in without any ceremony. Halil told him they had asked if Bahadir used to visit Pinar in their office.

Bahadir understood that he was cautioning him.

Kadir entered his room unannounced. 'The police are outside.' He did not hide his animosity. 'Never in the history of this firm have we had to go through such indignities.'

He slammed the door shut as he went out.

'Halil, we'll talk later. The police are here.'

'Wait,' Halil said. 'They have come to take you away. Can you delay things by about fifteen minutes?'

'Why?' Bahadir was surprised.

'My reporter will be there within that time. The world should know you have been arrested.'

That struck Bahadir as a good idea. After promising to do his best, Bahadir shut himself up in the toilet. When he did not come out for a long time, Kadir came in search of him.

'What are you doing here? Before the police tear down this place, will you please come out?' Kadir shouted, banging on the toilet door.

'I have an upset stomach. Ask them to wait a little.'

Kadir went out grumbling. The *baskomiser* of the police was an acquaintance. However, Kadir found his brusque manner humiliating.

'Please wait for a little while. He has an upset stomach,' he spoke in an apologetic tone.

'Okay, but we need to search his office.'

Kadir led them in. Bahadir was still inside the toilet. The baskomiser picked up the mobile and laptop and handed them over to one of the constables. The files and documents revealed nothing connecting him to Seetha.

One of the constables knocked on the door impatiently. The sound of running water could be heard from the toilet.

'I'm coming . . .' Bahadir said. It took some more time for him to emerge from the toilet.

Wiping his wet hands, Bahadir said, 'My apologies for making you wait.' He calculated that Halil's reporter would be reaching any time now.

'What's the matter, baskomiser?' he asked innocently.

'We've come to arrest you for the crime of conspiring with *Euro Times* chief of bureau Pinar Güneri to carry out treasonous acts.'

Bahadir laughter.

'Where's the evidence?'

The baskomiser brought his mobile out. He showed Bahadir the picture of him standing with Pinar outside Balon Café.

'Suspicious of your actions, the police have been following you for the past few days. It's only because you are a senior minister's brother that we're taking the trouble of explaining this to you. We've no time to lose. Let's go.'

Making no protest, Bahadir accompanied them. Bairam and Zahran were at the door, berating someone. When they saw Bahadir and the policemen approaching, they made way. Two young men were waiting in the yard with cameras. The baskomiser lost his cool since he knew that the visuals would go live as the men carried wireless transmission gadgets in their backpacks.

'I'll throw all of you into jail!' Forgetting that the camera was transmitting live, he barked and leapt towards the young men. One of the constables restrained him and whispered something in his ear. He brought himself under control.

'We'll meet again,' he said with marked rancour, staring at Ayran, who was shooting the scene.

'You asked for evidence. What more evidence do you need? We've not been here for ten minutes and already these guys know of it.'

He pushed Bahadir roughly into the police van. When he entered the barred vehicle, Bahadir could feel the ruthless and unemotional coldness of the steel enveloping him.

Watching the scenes of the arrest unfold before him on the TV screen, a disturbed Mibang got up from his chair and paced the room. The report said that while efforts were on to get Seetha released, the senior lawyer who had outed the story and started legal proceedings had been arrested. The scenes of him being bundled into the police vehicle were carried by all channels as their main news. The Indian channels too had taken up the news with enthusiasm and vigour. Mibang had been receiving innumerable calls from senior bureaucrats in the Ministry of External Affairs and journalists since morning. He looked in fury at the phone as it had started to ring again.

'Discussions are on at government level. Senior officers in the external affairs are handling this at their level. A delegation from the ministry will be coming here, that's the information. That's all I have for you!'

He flung the mobile in disgust onto the sofa. He looked into the mirror and checked his clothes. Already his driver had come twice to remind him that the Turkish foreign minister had summoned him to his office to discuss Seetha's case. Mibang straightened his tie and walked out of his room.

Minister Shahnaz Gülizar showed none of the cordiality that she had shown when they met during official dinners and tea parties. After the formal greetings, she touched upon the subject without any preamble.

'You do know that the government has the right to imprison anyone who is a threat to the nation's security?'

'Madam minister, there's no evidence whatsoever that Seetha has done anything against this country. She came in search of her lover because there was no news about him. What's the need to read anything more into this?'

'The girl came trying to meet terrorists. There are witnesses. She was arrested from the house of Arman—a terrorist.'

'At least now you have admitted that she has been taken into custody. This act of honesty is heartening and gives hope. Please look at the reply I received when I had asked for information on this matter.' Mibang pushed towards her the message that stated that Seetha had not been arrested. The minister took a cursory glance at it and pushed it back towards him.

'Mr Mibang would be aware that when terrorists are taken, the arrest may not be recorded immediately.' Her tone had softened.

'I shall not claim that such provisions are unwarranted in the present political climate in the country. However, what was the unholy hurry to brand the girl as a terrorist? The Turkish Police also have the responsibility for stating how her health has deteriorated so badly. You are also aware that she was pregnant when she arrived here.'

'The police report states that she was in a bad state when she was arrested. She was staying with extremists. We are not responsible for whatever happened during that time.'

How is this woman capable of lying so glibly without even a muscle twitching on her face? Mibang kept his gaze on her face. When he thought rather than prove points, his primary aim should be to have Seetha released, he tamped down on the rising fury inside him.

'She is a mother who's lost her child. Under these extenuating circumstances it is my prayer that she should be shown special consideration as a woman.'

Gülizar frowned.

'How, Mr Mibang, is that possible? That she is a woman or that she has lost a child does not constitute grounds for special treatment. She has relationships with terrorists. In your country, would someone like this be released on a simple request?'

'In that case, please have her arraigned in the court. As per our bilateral agreement, if she is indicted and sentenced, she can undergo the imprisonment in India.'

'The police are still gathering evidence. The rest of the process will follow in due course.'

Mibang realized that Gülizar was not in a mood to make any concessions. It was only a show put on to claim that the Turkish government was in touch with the Indian ambassador.

'If that is the case, madam minister may please make arrangements for me to meet Seetha.'

'That too doesn't look possible currently. Since her health is poor, she is under treatment.'

Mibang's face reddened.

'Mr Mibang, this is how it is. Anyone visiting this country is bounden to obey its rules. There is no doubt that this girl has been in touch with terrorists. As per anti-terrorist laws, her actions have been inimical to state security. There are witnesses for this; evidence for this.' Gülizar was categorical.

'Witnesses! What's the saying, "Whenever man commits a crime, heaven finds witnesses?" May you too be able to find such a witness! Or else you shall have to hand over Seetha to the Indian state.'

It took him a great effort to hide the bitterness in his tone.

His hopes were low while walking out of the meeting. He thought this unpleasant meeting presaged larger problems to come. Mibang knew that winning Seetha's freedom was going to be difficult and the meeting in the name of discussion was only for a unilateral declaration of the government's policy. He wished he could have at least met her once.

The wretched state of foreign prisoners in Turkish jails featured constantly in discussions among the diplomats. The majority of them were journalists. But they were the ones who chose to play with fire, fully conscious of the repercussions. Mibang was despondent wondering what the fate of this ingenuous girl would be.

The piercing colour of the country's national emblem emblazoned on either side of the president's larger-than-life photograph on the wall of that huge building hurt his eyes. Mibang was compelled to withdraw his gaze, unable to bear the effulgence from the graphic.

His mobile buzzed. The foreign secretary, Neeraj Shukla from New Delhi. To escape from the howling sea breeze, Mibang got into his car before accepting the call.

'Good afternoon, sir, I was just about to call you.' Mibang examined himself in the mirror to check if the dust and leaves blown up by the wind were sticking to his jacket and gelled hair.

'What's Gülizar's response?'

'Not ready for any compromise. They are planning to move ahead and charge her with terrorism,' Mibang did not mince his words. 'From my conversation, I understand that they have a strong case against her. The minister said there are witness statements incriminating her. The police report claims that she had suffered all the trauma before she was arrested. Unless we hit them with everything we have, they are not going to budge from their position.' His words reflected his sense of helplessness and despair.

'If she's been charged with terrorism, Turkey will not be amenable for any diplomatic overtures. Your guess is correct— this is a problem that's not going to get solved easily,' Shukla said, thoughtfully.

'Citizens of countries more powerful than ours are incarcerated here for alleged, unproven crimes. We can only try our best to get

Seetha released. Don't keep much hope. What's the scene there? On TV I did see the protests happening,' Mibang enquired.

'We have issues here. Protests are taking place in university campuses. You know of the campuses where she had studied in Kerala. They are waiting for an opportunity to go on strike. The mainstream and social media are lending their support. In Kerala, this has become a Centre versus state issue, with the Union government being painted in poor light.' Shukla sounded worried.

'Sir, we have to rescue her somehow. Turkish jails are no place for a girl like her. She won't be able to take it.' Shukla could sense the genuine concern in Mibang's voice.

'We must keep the pressure on. There's no other way. The Spanish government may join in. The students there have taken to the streets. We must also ask the UN to intervene.'

'Is the delegation from Delhi reaching tomorrow?'

'Assuredly. They reach by 6 p.m. Turkish time. Another person is also coming. May work in our favour.'

'Who's that?'

'The girl's uncle. He's a national-level leader in the ruling party. He reaches tomorrow morning.'

Mibang's uneasiness continued to linger even after the conversation ended. It had started to pour. Raindrops fell on the car like pelted stones. The wind had picked up strength and speed. A small branch with leaves landed on the windscreen blocking his view. Mibang took the car to the hard shoulder.

'What time will you reach, sir?' A message from the attaché.

'The meeting's over. Any emergency?'

'Sir, things are looking bad here. There are demonstrations taking place in campuses. Students have gathered in front of police stations. Thousands are present in front of Beykoz hospital shouting slogans.'

He disconnected and placed the mobile on the seat. The water was flowing over the road like a black river. All the garbage in the city was getting carried into the Sea of Marmara. Mibang pushed the recline button of his seat and leaned back comfortably.

He would wait till the rain stopped. The city needed a lot of cleansing.

Hospital

The sea!
One after the other, waves were smashed on the rocks and splattered . . . screaming in rage, the sounds of pounding waves that bore a hurricane within.

With her eyes closed, Seetha tried to channel the fury of the sea into herself. The impulse to smash everything that appears in front of it. The lust to pound everything into submission, drag them down and drown them in its depths.

'Are you listening?'

The doctor!

Is sea erosion eating up your country? Shouldn't the indelible blood stains of all the blood that has spilled on this land for centuries be erased? Maybe these waves will do the work.

'Why are you staring at me like this?'

Seetha shook her head to convey she did not mean to.

The statue-like sleepless vigil near the window had ended. However, he called on her at least five or six times a day. Even if she offered no response, he would ask after her welfare, and examine her wounds. For a little while, he would sit by her side silently on a stool, pressing his cool hand against her forehead.

'Did you hear it?' He pulled the stool close to the bed. 'Are you able to hear the uproar?'

Why is this man smiling?

'The sea!' Seetha moved her scab-covered lips slowly.

'Did you say the sea?' He lifted his eyebrows in surprise. 'Listen carefully . . .'

He ordered the nurse who was filling a syringe near the medicine cabinet to open the window. She pulled the snow-white curtains to the sides and opened the windows with considerable effort. Along with sounds of the raging sea, the warm rays from the sun playing hide-and-seek with the dark clouds, birds' chatter, and fresh air bearing the fragrance of the oleander flowers of the bouquet kept on the windowsill came rushing into the room.

Not waves but sounds from a thousand screaming throats!

'What's that noise?' The quivering words came hesitatingly out of a throat that had congealed from long disuse.

'You have a lot of friends, don't you?' She saw him laugh for the first time.

'I've no one.'

'Well, can't you hear slogans being shouted? That is for you!'

The numb look on Seetha's face made his own face fall.

'You don't believe it, do you? For the past few days, groups of students have been lurking outside the hospital. Now, by the moment, their numbers are growing. I feel we are no longer alone.'

Seetha closed her eyes.

'I want to sleep.'

'Okay, you can sleep after this injection.'

Pain. She moaned.

'I know, even the lightest touch will pain you. But this injection will help you. There, that's done!'

How much love do those fingers carry! Humans can touch one another this way too.

She could feel sleep taking over her.

The sounds from outside were reaching her in waves. Someone closed the windows. It did not matter; the sound was still sneaking through. Rising and ebbing; with a measured cadence; like the distant lullaby of the waves.

Seetha opened her eyes painfully to the sound of someone shouting angrily from the corridor. The sudden arousal from her sleep gave her a splitting headache. Damn the man!

Bright light was assailing her still drowsy eyes. If only someone would pull the curtains close! The argument continued outside the room indistinctly. The nurse stood with her ear against the door, listening in on the fracas.

Suddenly the decibels shot up from outside. Orders were being shouted. Things were being knocked down. The nurse leapt back in fear when something seemed to ram against the door with great force. When she approached the bed to check on Seetha, whether she was awake, Seetha closed her eyes and pretended to be asleep.

The sounds died down eventually. After a while, someone pushed the door open and entered. Soft sounds of the rubber sandals. It was the doctor. He spoke in whispers to the nurse.

Curiosity made Seetha peek from the corner of her eyes. The doctor was seated on a chair in front of the light pink oleander flowers. The nurse was applying something on his forehead. Even though she spoke in undertones, her words came out in hisses as if under extreme provocation. He was speaking softly as if to calm her down. She tried to catch their words and failed. Anxious, she tried to call the nurse.

'Aha! We thought you were asleep!' He sounded cheerful.

Seetha's eyes gained focus and were arrested by the sight of his bruised face.

'It's nothing. There was some water on the floor outside. I slipped and fell.'

I don't want to see anything.

'Seetha please open your eyes.'

Stopping the nurse from doing more ministrations on his head, he came towards the bed.

I don't want to see anything.

From the corners of her eyes squeezed shut, despite herself, tears continued to flow down.

He took up her hand that was lying listlessly to the side and held it gently.

'Do you know how many students have gathered here to force them to set you free?'

On one side of his forehead, with his white hair strands lying carelessly over it, clinical dressing covered what looked like a small wound. She was shocked at the sight of his livid, swollen right cheek that seemed to have been hit hard with a blunt instrument.

'Why have you got beaten up like this?' Seetha screamed. The doctor was shaken by the distorted shrieking from a throat which, till then, had produced only whispered sounds.

'They will take me away under any circumstances. If not today, then tomorrow. You don't have to get yourself killed for my sake.'

She broke down completely.

'Look here, you should not get emotional like this. Your wounds have started to heal slowly.'

With compassion he stroked her hand that lay shivering in his own.

'Forget all this. I had come to show you this.' He held up his mobile to her face.

'I don't want to see!' She turned her face away from him.

'Don't say that! Day and night they are keeping a vigil only for your sake.'

With affection, the doctor swabbed her eyes that she had screwed shut adamantly but were still leaking tears.

'Look at this picture once. Just this one picture.'

Seetha opened her eyes. She looked impassively at the crowd in the picture on the mobile's screen.

Truly that was a really sizeable crowd. Students. *How many of them are you going to kill? You will tear how many of them out of their mothers' wombs and laps and burn them alive?*

Like you did to my baby?

A knife was being twisted inside her.

'Look at this; that boy is carrying your picture.'

That is true: It is me.

Who is this? I know this person. I've seen this face somewhere.

'Why are you staring at the photo?' the doctor asked anxiously. 'Do you know this person? Do you remember him coming here to meet you a few days ago?'

'Timur!'

'So, you know him!'

'Timur . . .!'

'Don't cry, I'd like to help you.'

'This is Timur.'

'Talk to me. Would you like to meet him?'

'Umm . . . yes.'

'Shall I call him here?'

'Umm . . . yes.'

'But you have to promise you won't cry. Your body should not get agitated.'

'I won't cry.'

'All right, but it's not going to be easy. There are as many policemen out there as there are students. Let me try.'

Are you leaving? Don't go! I'm scared! They'll be waiting for you outside.

'Why are you clutching onto my gown?'

A sob convulsed her body.

'Why are you crying? Don't you want Timur to be brought here?' He looked at the fingers still holding tightly the edge of his gown. 'All right, I won't leave. Don't cry.'

Someone was banging on the door loudly. The doctor's look changed. He let go of Seetha's hand and leapt to his feet.

'Hey! Stop it! Who's kicking the door?'

The nurse opened the door quickly. A blast of warm air rushed into the temperature-controlled room.

'Why do you need to batter the door down? I would open it for you anyway. Don't you know this is an ICU?'

The sounds of boots!

Not again . . .! Seetha shut her eyes tight again.

'Why does this whore need intensive care?'

'Didn't I tell you some time ago that her injuries have all become septic? We have kept her alive with great difficulty. Her body has started to respond to drugs only recently. I am begging you. Give us a few days more.'

'So, you've been ravishing her inside this room?'

Lecherous sniggers could be heard.

'You can't be blamed. She's a first-rate piece of ass. The boys here have all had their fun.'

Enraged, the doctor's voice rose above all of them.

'I was trying to remain dignified till now. Get out of the room!'

Something fell in a clatter.

'We're taking away this whore. Get out of our way.'

'If you're brave enough to do that, give it a try. This is no longer your private issue. The whole world is now looking at what's happening here. She is no longer an orphaned Indian with no one in her corner. Can you see the students waiting outside? No one can take her away when they are there. Try if you can!'

From a pleading tone, his voice had taken on a menacing edge. Seetha lifted her head in fear and tried to see what was happening. She was afraid that the police may hurt him again.

'Are you a Turk? Traitor!'

She watched the frail form in the white gown stand like an impregnable wall in front of a row of dark olive uniforms.

'Shoot, you coward, instead of merely pointing the gun at me. Women you have raped into shreds, men whose bones your boots have shattered into fragments, bodies you have slashed into ribbons for fun, children you have burnt alive—for the last many years they have been my patients. Eating a few bullets is better than that. Why don't you kill me?'

The voice had turned stone cold. The nerveless, emotionless frigidity of death. Believing that the gun aimed at his head would go off at any moment, her body trembled uncontrollably.

Everything went silent suddenly.

Then there were receding sounds of boots on the floor. Had they left?

Seetha tried to lift her body slightly. The nurse put pillows behind her back and head to prop her up.

'They've left. Were you scared?' The doctor came towards her. His flushed face was bathed in sweat.

'No, you are there. I have no fear.'

Taking her hands again in his own, he sat by her side, head bowed and deep in thought.

A slim girl arrived with a tray of food for Seetha. As the aroma of food predominated the ever-present smell of medicines and disinfectants in the room, after a long time, Seetha experienced hunger.

'Keep the tray there and come here for a moment.' The girl lifted her head to check if she was being summoned. Although her hair had been put up in the fashion of nurses, youthfulness shone on her face, as if she had just stepped out of a school uniform. 'Seetha, she will help you. She's a friend of ours.'

Seetha was amused by the child-like smile.

'After you have had your food, sleep for a while. I'm not going anywhere. You see that chair by the window? I'll wait there.'

'Timur . . .?'

'Timur will come. Don't worry.'

After bowing down to listen to his instructions, the girl left the room quickly. Shifting into a more comfortable position, the doctor closed his eyes. Soon his breathing became rhythmic. Watching him curled up in that fashion, soon Seetha could feel drowsiness overcome her too.

'Who's Timur to you?'

Seetha did not know when the doctor had come and sat down near her. It was dark. Stars were shining in a sky that had been overcast for the last so many days. She seemed to have been asleep for a long time.

'Seetha answer me, who's Timur?' He repeated the question. She did not respond immediately.

'My friend.' Her voice quavered. 'A friend who'd never forsake me. A friend who'd never betray me even in exchange for his life.' The doctor who had to strain to catch her faint, husky words, smiled sadly.

'I've lost everyone—my child's father, my mother, my country. I've lost everything. Timur is the only one left. He knew his life was in danger. Yet he was by my side . . .!'

'It's never that everything is lost for anyone. Even in the driest desert there'll be at least one green stalk. It's left to us to convert it into a garden.'

Seetha did not respond.

'What are you thinking?'

'About my mother.'

'Shall I inform your mother?'

'No.'

'Why?'

'She'd be ashamed of me.'

'How can a mother be ashamed of her own daughter?'

'In our country it's like this. A family's reputation and prestige reside between the girl's legs.'

Someone was knocking on the door.

'I'll check; it can't be the police. They don't knock, they only kick.' He was laughing when he said it.

A young attendant entered diffidently. His tired-looking face was hidden behind a generous beard and moustache. Where had I seen him before?

'Timur!'

Shocked by her voice, he bounded towards her bed.

'Seetha!'

'Why is your face so dark and drawn?'

Timur burst into tears when he heard her feeble, indistinct voice.

'Why are you crying?' Seetha extended her arms towards him. 'Come here. I'm not able to get up.'

Timur hugged her greedily as if she were his own life that was ebbing away.

'Oh! Don't hug me hard. I hurt everywhere.' Seetha spoke in a tired voice that bore both tears and laughter. Overwhelmed by his bubbling enthusiasm and joy, she started to cough.

The doctor who was watching the scene, smiled and came forward.

'Young man, her body is broken. Even a caress from you can be painful.'

Timur bowed his head at him in gratitude. He kept laughing and blabbering as if he could still not believe that Seetha was alive.

'Seetha, you're still alive!'

'Yes, I'm.'

Seetha reached out, pulled his head and held it against her body.

I am not sure if this body can still be described as alive. I don't know what all still remain inside. My baby. My love. My soul. All are lost. Something resembling a cracked eggshell remains.

Timur pressed his face against her palms. The tears on his still moist cheeks caused her disquiet. His eyes ran over the blood clots on her face and scabs formed over the wounds on her lips.

'Why are you crying?'

'I wasn't able to help you, protect you. Please forgive me.'

'You shouldn't weep like this. Turkish men are the same as men from my place. You shouldn't cry. Doesn't go well with your masculinity.'

'All of this is my fault.'

'Timur, I had given you the slip and run away, have you forgotten?'

'I should have taken more care. I should have deduced what was in your mind,' Timur said, choking on his sorrow.

'Stop it there! I don't want to see anyone crying.' Seetha turned her face away in disgust.

'Okay, but then neither should you cry. Nor run away anywhere.'

'Where can I go? I've nowhere to go now. They sent me to this hospital. I now lie here. They'll take me back to prison. I'll go with them. Do you want to take me with you? Take me. I can come with you too.'

Timur gave the doctor a disbelieving look.

'Don't worry, Timur. All this'll go away. The trauma of everything she has gone through; the medicines. It'll take some time for you to have the old Seetha back.'

The doctor's assurance that such a reaction was natural was comforting.

'May I talk to her in private?'

'I can't leave this room. She has taken a lot of time to respond to the medicines. I'm afraid that the tiniest of provocations may be enough for her to have a relapse. Which I can't risk.'

The doctor returned to his usual seat by the window.

'I shall sit here. If you talk in whispers, your voices won't reach me.'

'That's fine, doctor. Thank you very much.'

'Seetha, are you asleep?'

'No, sit by my side for a little while.'

She caught his shirt and pulled him towards her bed.

'Don't talk too much. The cuts on your lips are bleeding already from under the scabs. Are you in pain, Seetha?'

'Pain! No pain can hurt me anymore!'

'Haven't you stopped spouting nonsense even now? I can't be here for long. Should the police turn up suddenly, there'll be serious problems. Now listen carefully to what I am going to tell you. My father has sent a petition to the UN that you have been abducted illegally by the police. They will have to produce you before a judge immediately.'

With a blank look in her eyes, Seetha tried to listen to him carefully.

'The students are highly agitated. Not only here; in Barcelona too. We are no longer alone. The Indian missions too are apprised of the matter.'

'So?'

'So, you won't have to return to prison anymore.'

The look of disbelief on her face made Timur tighten his grip on her hands to reassure her.

'I'm certain of it. You must believe me.'

'The Constitution does not run this country. Guns do.'

'It's not that simple. It's now a problem of Spain and India too. They'll not let it happen. Are you laughing?' Timur demanded angrily.

'Who are they to let or not let anything happen?'

'What you say may be true. But in the present international climate, the guys here will not really enjoy international media banging on about a helpless foreign girl being tortured and tormented in this country.'

'Forget all this. Leave immediately. The police may come here anytime. I don't know how they let you in with all this fuzz on your face.'

'I'm not alone here. Our friends are with me.'

'Friends? Which friends?'

'The ones we met in Sur. Akbar, Mustafa and others.'

'Mustafa? Who is that?'

'You don't know him. I'll introduce him one of these days.'

'This uniform fits you well. Don't throw it away.'

'No, I'll come again wearing it.'

'You're hurting me with your kisses.' Seetha tried to smile, pushing him away. Although she looked tired, her face had brightened.

'No one will take you away now.' Timur said the words as if taking an oath.

As a mark of his gratitude, he kissed the hand of the doctor who got up from his seat to bid him goodbye.

'Goodbye. I'll be back.'

'A sweet young man,' the doctor said as he watched Timur exit from the room. He pulled back the window curtains.

'You look very tired. Sleep for a while. Does the noise from outside bother you?'

'No.'

Seetha wished she could tell him that it sounded more like a lullaby.

Home

Emerging from the comfort of the centrally heated airport into a blast of cold wind, Somasekharan shivered, his teeth chattering, like a man with ague. Dark clouds and humid air had shrouded Istanbul like a wet blanket since the morning. The murky, overcast conditions deepened his anxiety and sapped his mental strength.

He had to call home. He had left a home that resounded with wails as if mourning the dead. Somasekharan searched his pockets for his mobile phone.

'*Ammava,*[1] OB vans of TV channels have surrounded the house since the morning. They stopped *cheriachan*[2] who was headed here and asked him many questions.' Without responding to Seema's breathless plaint, he asked her to hand over the phone to her father.

'Soma . . .' A lump rose in the normally voluble Somasekharan's throat when he heard Seetha's father's gloomy voice.

'*Etta,*[3] please don't worry. I've landed in Istanbul. Some negotiations are going on here. Let's see how things shape up,' he tried to sound convincing.

'Soma, you know how things are here. Our tharavad's fair name has been besmirched forever . . .' his voice broke.

'Etta, you don't worry. Once the next thing comes along, the people will forget this.'

'Which one do you think the people will forget . . .? Her carrying a bastard child? Or the soldiers taking her and . . .?' The words ended with a racking sob.

Somasekharan was nonplussed. He had always looked up to his sister's husband—an admiration mixed with respect tinged by fear. And that man was sobbing like a child now!

'Etta, you shouldn't forget one thing. Our party is in power now. I am a national executive member of that party. It won't take us a lot of time to prove that all this has been fabricated.'

There was only a helpless whimper from the other end.

Somasekharan dropped the mobile into the pocket of his jacket. He did not find the need to wait for the delegation from India. He decided to go directly to the consulate and find out the latest position.

The sight of an Indian phoning from under the neon sign of İstanbul Sabiha Gökçen Uluslararası Havalimanı had the taxi drivers hover around in anticipation. He beckoned one of the youngsters who was watching him expectantly.

'Indian Consulate,' instructed Somasekharan, settling down on the cold seat.

'Demonstrations are taking place in the city centre. We'll have to take a longer route.' The taxi driver was careful not to upset a customer whom he had found after a long wait.

Somasekharan grunted Illustrator. He was preoccupied with the situation at home. He also did not see the small groups of students carrying placards and posters with Seetha's photos as the car passed by them.

'Aren't you Indian?' When the driver spoke again, he replied in the affirmative, not hiding his irritation.

'These protests are for the sake of an Indian girl,' the driver said, as he manoeuvred the car expertly through the dense traffic of the inner lane to avoid the blocked main roads.

Somasekharan was startled. He tried hard to remain nonchalant.

'For an Indian girl? What's the reason?'

'She was in love with some militant. He left her after living together for a while. When she came here looking for him, she was caught by the police. Now she's trying to escape alleging that she had been gang-raped and consequently she had a miscarriage, et cetera.'

Finding no takers for his story, the youngster stopped his prattle and started to concentrate on his driving. Although the wind and rain had ceased, preoccupied with fighting the traffic on the muddy, water-filled roads, he failed to notice his passenger's moist eyes and his efforts to hide it.

Somasekharan reached the consulate when Mibang was getting ready to leave. Though Mibang resented him barging in without an appointment or intimation, he did not betray it. Somasekharan introduced himself, taking special care to emphasize his position in the party and to bare his fangs, without actually baring them.

'Sir, we're doing everything possible to have her released,' Mibang tried to reassure him. 'Nothing happens here as per protocol. As soon as I'd come to know there was an Indian girl in police custody, I'd taken the initiative to make enquiries. Leaving behind all the work in Ankara, I'm camping here to resolve this matter. However, at first, they flatly denied that such a person was in custody.'

'What's the status now?'

'I met the minister today. I was summoned to the ministry to discuss this issue. The meeting didn't give much hope. However, she did admit that Seetha was in police custody. Moreover, this has been confirmed in an official e-mail sent to the Indian Embassy after the meeting.'

Unable to decide what to make of it, Somasekharan rubbed his forehead.

'Please do not worry. Normally, in such cases, the embassy appoints a lawyer on behalf of the prisoner. As our luck has it, a lawyer has been already doing certain things to help Seetha. Unfortunately, he has run into some problems now. Not to worry, we can appoint someone else. The Indian diplomatic delegation has reached already. We can take the next steps tomorrow after consultations with them.'

Reluctantly, Somasekharan got to his feet. He found their pas de deux and diplomatic rigmarole tiresome. After reaching the hotel, instead of trying to sleep off the tiredness of his long journey, he sat on the balcony worriedly mulling over things.

The next morning, Somasekharan arrived at the consulate early. Mibang, upon seeing him at the reception flipping through a Turkish newspaper, wished him politely.

'What's the programme today? When is the meeting?' Somasekharan asked without any preface.

Mibang understood that he was angling to join the delegation.

'It would be better for you to go to your room and rest there. I shall inform you as soon as the meeting is over.'

'I shouldn't come?' Somasekharan felt insulted. His overweening pride about his wealth of experience in being part of innumerable political discussions and mediating disputes between big guns came crashing around his ears. 'It won't be a bad thing if I come. After all, she's my niece. Are any of the people involved experienced in such negotiations?' Anger was rising inside him.

'It's precisely because it is your niece that you shouldn't be there. If this has to be handled dispassionately and diplomatically, the persons involved should not be related to Seetha.'

'All of you together will send her to hell.' Somasekharan stood up.

'Sir, I do understand your concern. Piyush Mitra, who was Indian ambassador to Turkey for four years, is in the team. He knows all the Turkish politicians and bureaucrats well. All the others in the delegation have rich and varied experience. You should remain calm and wait patiently.'

Mibang asked his office assistant to fetch a taxi for him.

'As soon as I have any information, I shall apprise you,' he bent down to tell Somasekharan, who was seated in the car, and hurried back into the consulate. Somasekharan leaned back on the seat. A sudden feeling of helplessness overcame him.

He spent the next four hours like a caged tiger, pacing the room, switching on the TV and surfing the channels. He did not touch the food he ordered on the room service. He controlled the impulse to return to the consulate. He decided that Mibang, who had not shown him enough deference, should be taught a lesson.

Finally, the phone rang.

'Mibang, tell me!'

'There's happy news. You have the permission to meet her. Today at 5 p.m. be at the Beykoz hospital. Your pass is with me. Can you come by the consulate in the afternoon?'

'Permission to meet her? When are they releasing her?' Somasekharan was losing his temper.

'Sir, perhaps you have not understood the gravity of this case. We should consider ourselves extremely lucky to have received the permission to meet her. Please go and happily meet your niece. The rest you may leave to us.'

Somasekharan hung up grumbling. He believed that his exclusion from the delegation had led to this delay. He left for the consulate after having his lunch. Mibang could not help but notice the peeved look on his face.

'You are distressed because you don't know the nature of these negotiations. It's pure haggling. The tug of war happens using the commercial pacts between the two nations. You have nothing to contribute to that. Your presence may aggravate and indeed weaken our position. Please have trust in us. You have no other option.'

Although Somasekharan believed that there was some truth in Mibang's statement, he did not get off his high horse and maintained his grumpy look even while accepting the envelope from Mibang.

A large group of students was thronging in front of the hospital. Instead of dropping him inside the hospital, the driver dropped him outside, and left in a rush.

Somasekharan kept staring at the tall pale building besides the tree-lined avenue.

She is somewhere inside. He smothered a wail that rose inside him and swirled around, fighting for release. He remembered the day when he had gone to Seetha's home after her birth and how his brother-in-law had, with a mischievous smile on his lips, placed the infant on his lap unexpectedly and how he, afraid the baby may slip out of his hands, held her close to his chest and had sat still till his sister came in with a cup of tea. The warmth . . . the smell of breast milk . . . today, with her body and psyche destroyed and chewed out, that baby is held in captivity in conditions worse than in a penal institution. His hands were clenched into fists. An urge to smash everything in sight surged through his veins.

He was brought back from his reverie by the prattle of a group of children that passed by him. After watching them merge with the crowd in front of the hospital, he read the name on the envelope in his hand. Ayaz Aydin! Vexed at his efforts to read the designation in front of the name coming a cropper, he dropped it into his pocket.

Police vans were parked in a ring around the hospital. Rifle barrels poked out menacingly through the small holes in the wire mesh protecting the glass windows. Defying the armed police patrolling the place, students stood in small groups talking loudly. Somasekharan had difficulty breathing as he squeezed his way through the throng, in which, irrespective of their gender, everyone seemed to be puffing on cigarettes. He approached the nearest available policeman and showed him the envelope.

After subjecting Somasekharan to scrutiny, the policeman gestured to him to follow, which he did with a fluttering heart. He saw some officials behind the glass doors, deep in conversation. The insignias on their caps, epaulettes and medals on their uniforms gave the impression they ranked high in the army. The policeman turned back after pointing out one among them.

Somasekharan had to wait a bit to catch Ayaz's attention. At the start of the conversation itself it was apparent that the man did not have an iota of friendliness in him. Somasekharan did not pass up the opportunity to impress upon him his standing in the ruling party, more than his relationship to Seetha. Not a muscle moved in the man's stony face. After perusing the contents of the envelope, he glowered at Somasekharan as if he were an enemy. After rattling off some instructions to a soldier he had called to his side, the man turned back to his group.

The soldier was possibly a low-ranking officer. He held his gun close to his torso with such felicity as if it was an extension of his body. He asked Somasekharan to follow him. Somasekharan followed him meekly. The coldness of the gun's steel barrel seemed to have spread on to his face too. Somasekharan could see that the man was carefully avoiding his eyes as they rode the lift.

They reached a dark corridor that had soldiers patrolling. Except for the intimidating sound of boots on the floor, there was silence all around. The soldier accompanying Somasekharan asked for directions from one of the soldiers there. After giving Somasekharan a protracted stare, the man pointed to a door. Somasekharan walked behind his companion, dodging the piercing looks of the soldiers.

The loud knock on the door elicited a response from a feminine voice. A young nurse poked her head out of the door that she had opened partially. Having listened to what the soldier had to say, she smiled amiably at Somasekharan. Her smile acted like a soothing balm on his heart that had been on tenterhooks all the while.

'I can't confirm if you can meet her. I'll have to follow the doctor's orders.' With a friendly pat on Somasekharan's hand, she drew back into the room. When he looked at the closed door, fear and agony made his heart flutter uncontrollably.

After a little while, a man emerged from the room. A halo like snow-white hair framing his head was his most noticeable feature. He hurried forward and grasped Somasekharan's hands solicitously.

'Are you Seetha's father?' The compassion and benevolence in his voice made Somasekharan's eyes moist.

'I'm her uncle.' His voice shook.

'I had information that a relative of hers was on the way. I'm Dr Ömer Armağan. Seetha is under my care. Let's sit in the next room and talk.'

The room was meant for nurses to rest. A couple of nurses' uniforms hung from hooks on the wall. A clay pot of water and a glass on top reminded Somasekharan of his thirst. A girl who stood in a corner leafing through prescriptions looked up in surprise. With a nod of his head, the doctor indicated that she could leave.

'You may be aware of what's happened to Seetha?' the doctor spoke after a minute's silence.

'Yes.' Somasekharan spoke with difficulty. He was afraid that he would break down completely.

'Don't be upset. What's important is that she's alive. Your niece has fought bravely.'

The doctor was disconcerted by the tears streaming down Somasekharan's face.

'How's she now?' Somasekharan asked when he calmed down.

'She's improved a lot. Her internal organs had suffered grievous damage. She had lost a lot of blood too. Her pregnancy was terminated, as you know. The mental trauma on top of everything! She survived only because of her grit.'

'Can I meet her?' Anxiety made his voice quaver.

'When I heard of your imminent arrival, I had indicated about it to her. I was apprehensive that meeting a relative suddenly may discomfit her. She did not respond to the news.' He continued after a small break, 'It didn't appear as if she had heard it.' He exhaled and rose to his feet. 'Please don't feel bad. Let me ask her once more. I won't be party to anything that may cause her distress.'

The door closed behind him.

Somasekharan fidgeted and rubbed his hands, signalling his impatience as he waited. He was aware the meeting would decide the future of their whole family and that of Seetha. When the wait seemed to be interminable, Somasekharan started to pace the room.

'Mr Somasekharan,' the doctor pronounced the name with a thick, droll accent. 'Are you adamant that you should meet her?'

'Why, what's happened?'

'After lying silent for a little while, she started to cry. She cannot have any emotional trauma in this state. It took me a long time to calm her down.'

'I can't leave without meeting her. If today's not a good day, I can return tomorrow or day after tomorrow.'

The doctor thought for a while.

'Let's try. Come with me.'

Somasekharan's legs felt leaden as he trudged after the doctor. Ignoring the soldiers who looked on suspiciously, the doctor opened the door of the adjacent room and let him in.

The room was very cool. A mild smell of fresh linen and medicines enveloped Somasekharan. Nodding politely at them, a nurse bearing a tray of medicines left the room.

Standing at the door, Somasekharan could see someone lying on the bed by the side of a cloth-covered stand.

'Come . . .' the doctor invited him in as if it the most natural thing to do.

Somasekharan stood stunned watching the form on the bed. A soft, cotton sheet covered it up to its neck. The face was full of livid bruises; lips that had been bitten viciously were unrecognizable, covered as they were in dark scabs. Since her hair had been snipped off haphazardly, they stood up like spikes on her head. Her eyes, swollen from her constant crying, appeared bulbous in her emaciated face. They stared unflinchingly at Somasekharan.

'Mr Somasekharan, I shall be sitting by the side of the window. Unfortunately, I can't leave this room.'

The doctor walked towards the window. Gently caressing the oleander flowers in the vase, he focused his attention on the hubbub that could be heard from the outside.

After standing motionless for some minutes, Somasekharan extended his hand and touched Seetha's pale toes peeping out from under the sheet.

'*Molae* . . .'

There was a sudden sign of recognition in her wooden face. She turned her face towards the window and started to mewl in an unnaturally splintered falsetto voice, her body racked by sobs. The irritation caused in her wounds—that were healing—from being stretched, compelled her try to scratch out the scabs on her lips.

Somasekharan eased himself into the chair placed near the bed. He could feel himself going weak in the knees. He nestled her leg in his palms as if it was a fledgling squirming to break free.

Disturbed by Seetha's sobs, the doctor rose from his seat.

'Seetha, if you are finding it hard, he can come tomorrow.'

She shook her head to indicate that was not needed. In between her sobs, she extended her hand towards Somasekharan, as if inviting him to move closer.

'All right, but stop scratching your wounds,' admonishing her, the doctor returned to his seat.

Somasekharan pulled the chair so that he was seated in line with her face. He presumed she would not be able to talk loudly.

'Molae, why didn't you inform me?' asked Somasekharan plaintively when her sobbing decreased. He felt as if her icy hands that he was now grasping were burning his own. She lay there gazing at him without saying a word. The same kind of look that, twenty-four years ago, she had given him, flicking open her tiny eyelids. A shudder ran through him.

'Why hadn't you informed us?' He was angry at no one in particular.

'I had told amma.' Although her voice was weak, he heard her well. 'One can't tell everything to everyone. I can tell my mother. But, uncle, she disowned me. I had no other option but to come here.'

Watching her drawn face, Somasekharan was unsure what he could say to comfort her.

'Why did you come here now, uncle?' The question stumped Somasekharan.

'I had to make sure you were safe,' he stammered.

'It's not for taking me home, is it?' The chill in the words that tumbled out through her broken lips was beyond his sufferance.

'Molae, how can I take you home at this stage?' He spoke diffidently. He realized that he was not doing justice to her.

'That's so true, uncle. The good name of the family, eh?' He could see a sardonic smile flitting over her disfigured lips.

'Once we're through all this, I'll get you an apartment in Delhi. Or you can return and complete your PhD. Then we'll find you a job. Don't think this is the end of everything.'

'Why can't I return to Puthuruthy and stay with my mother?'

Somasekharan remained silent.

'Tell me, why am I not being taken to my mother?'

'The public there will tear into you. You'll end up feeling whatever you suffered here was a mere inconvenience. They will ridicule and humiliate you. They'll openly point fingers at you. The men will prey on you. It won't be you alone, the whole family will become their victims. Do you want me to explain about our people back in our place?'

'If my father and mother can't face all this for my sake, there is no sense in them claiming to be my parents. Let that also come to an end along with many other things that have ended for me.'

'I'm there for you. Isn't that enough?'

'When my mother has disowned me, what am I to you? Please go away. Don't ever return here looking for me.' Seetha's voice had gone up several notches. The doctor, watching the protests outside, turned back to look at them.

Slogans and loud bellows could be heard from the yard. Someone's scream came through indistinctly. Pulling the window shut, the doctor moved towards them.

'Seetha, why are you raising your voice?' he asked her, stroking her forehead gently and looking quizzically at Somasekharan who sat with his head bowed.

'Uncle, look at me. I am safe here. You can hear the ruckus outside? That is for my sake. I've friends who love me. I've this doctor who takes care of me. They won't let anyone take me away from here. My life is now more valuable for them than their own. But for my mother, apparently the reputation of the family is more important!'

Seetha was panting. She was short of breath and found breathing difficult. One of the half-healed wounds on her lips opened again and started to bleed.

Somasekharan rose to his feet. Her bloodshot eyes and bleeding lips sent a chill through his spine and turned his legs into jelly.

'Don't ever come here again!' gathering all the strength in her debilitated body, Seetha screamed at the man who was leaving the room with his head bowed. Her body was convulsing like that of an epileptic.

'Seetha, what are you doing?' the doctor exclaimed, distraught. The nurse, realizing her services were needed, rushed in.

As if fleeing from the rising tide of the alarmed voices behind him, Somasekharan hurried out of the building. He ignored the soldier near the lift and his questions, and staggered out as if the fire in her eyes was chasing to consume him.

Outside the hospital, the police were brutally attacking the protesters. The police smashed their truncheons on the heads and raised hands of the protesters who were seated on the ground. They dragged the students to the police vehicles. The protesters scattered and then reassembled again away from the police, shouting slogans at the top of their voices. Rotten tomatoes and placards were flung at the police.

Somasekharan tried to flatten himself against the building and inch his way forward. The policemen looked at him with surprise as he inched ahead with a blank, apathetic look on his face when all hell had broken loose around him. Slogans were being shouted in wave after wave. The students who were being thrashed were running past him.

Suddenly, a shot rang out without a warning and startled Somasekharan. Wide-eyed, he looked around him. A young man had fallen to the ground. The others who had run away to escape the beating, ran back yelling and wailing. Although the police tried to chase them away again, their hearts did not seem to be in it. The sight of blood oozing out of the young man's body onto the bituminized ground made Somasekharan close his eyes.

One of the students who had come running back, flung himself on the ground near the body and started to wail, 'Timur . . . Timur . . .'

The body had gone still after a brief convulsion; the student mercilessly shook it by its shoulders trying to revive him and then stood up in his bloodied clothes and started to scream for help, trying to pull out his hair by their roots.

After the initial inaction caused by numbness, the students gathered up the body and tried to enter the hospital. Somasekharan leaned against the wall for support as the sight of blood drops falling on the ground had made him dizzy.

There was more commotion. Somasekharan looked around for the source. The students carrying the body were pushing and shoving the policemen blocking their way. The students bawled, beseeched and shrieked in turn. The stone-faced policemen were unmoved and stood like a wall, stopping them from entering the hospital.

The students seemed to have realized that pleading to the merciless policemen was a waste of time. They spun around and ran holding their wounded comrade. They were talking loudly and shouting instructions to those following them. As the group passed him, Somasekharan looked into the peaceful face of a wounded young man who was being borne on a stretcher made of many intertwined arms. Blood was gushing out of the wound on his chest. On the ground, an unbroken trail of blood drops marked the group's progress. Screaming maniacally and at times babbling, one of his friends was also running behind the group.

The protesters in front of the hospital had dispersed. The footwear, placards and flags that were scattered around were being swept to the side by the hospital sweeper using a blue broom. The man brought a bucket of water and poured it over the pool of blood.

The policemen were chatting and laughing loudly. Somasekharan realized that they were congratulating themselves. Dragging his unsteady feet, he walked towards the gate. He saw an ambulance speed away from the hospital gate, its sirens blaring. After waiting for the wailing sirens to die down, stepping around the still fresh blood on his path, he slowly went out of the gate.

Distance

'Which hospital should I go to?' the ambulance driver shouted his question. 'If Paşabahçe, I'll have to turn left; if Medistate, I've to go right . . .'

The bewildered students looked at one another.

'Decide quickly, the roads are full of policemen,' the driver shouted again.

'His wound is serious. Medistate has better facilities. Let's go there,' someone spoke up.

The ambulance turned right and picked up speed. People, startled by the siren, gave it a cursory glance and went back to whatever they were doing. The impersonal, apathetic city continued to throb at a slow beat amidst all the violence, gunshots, sirens and screams.

'How long will it take?' Mustafa asked in a trembling voice, trying to warm Timur's cold palms by rubbing them constantly.

'Car takes ten minutes,' said one of the students, whose eyes were fixed on the road.

'Ten minutes? He'll die. I had given his father my word that I'll take care of him.'

Mustafa broke down completely. As he looked at the blood-soaked body, he felt he may faint. He placed his trembling hands gently over the wound to staunch the bleeding.

'Other vehicles are giving us way, don't worry. We won't even take ten minutes to reach there.'

'Do you know his blood group?' one of the students asked.

'I've no idea,' said a flustered Mustafa.

'Medistate has a blood bank. However, we had better be prepared.'

'I'll have to call his father and check with him,' said Mustafa. He remembered only then that Bahadir was in prison. 'His father is in jail.'

'In jail?' the students looked at Mustafa anxiously.

'Yes, you would have seen the recent news about a lawyer named Bahadir being arrested. This is his son.'

'Bahadir's son?'

All of them stared at Timur's still gaunt face, deathly pale from loss of blood. His body was swaying gently from the ambulance's motion. One of the students who had regained his presence of mind after the initial shock, started to make calls from his mobile phone.

'All of you should reach Medistate immediately. We will need blood donors. I'm not sure of the blood group.'

'In another minute we'll reach,' the driver shouted from his cabin. 'Someone call and inform the hospital.' One of the students called the hospital's emergency department.

'We're coming in with a man who's been shot in his chest. We should be there in less than a minute. Please keep everything ready to receive him . . .'

Medistate Kavacık Hastanesi!

The bold lettering on the building rising up to the sky was visible from a distance.

When the ambulance stopped at the main door, attendants and two young doctors came running to meet it. Mustafa and others leapt out of the ambulance to make way for them.

The doctors entered the vehicle and checked Timur's condition. Although Mustafa tried to catch their conversation, he failed. He broke down upon watching the gurney, on which Timur lay, being wheeled away by the attendants. The sight of Timur's blood on his clothes sent him over the edge. The other students watched helplessly as he stood teary-eyed with his hands raised to the heavens, begging for some mercy. Their eyes too were getting moist.

The doctor who stepped out of the ambulance spoke to them, 'None of you should leave. He's being moved to the operation theatre. He's in a critical condition. One of you should come and sign the consent documents.'

Flinging his stethoscope around his neck, he bounded up the steps of the hospital.

'I'll go.' Gönül, a bearded and long-haired young man with calm eyes followed the doctor.

'We've to inform his family. Do you know anyone other than Bahadir?' A student who seemed to be in charge, squatted next to Mustafa who was sitting on the floor.

'I don't know. I've heard that the minister Kasim Özdemir is his father's brother.'

The students' eyes widened in surprise.

Someone said, 'I remember reading this at the time of Bahadir's arrest.'

'Let's inform him.' Two students moved to the side holding their mobiles. The student sitting beside Mustafa helped him up and both headed into the hospital.

'We'll be near the operation theatre,' he called out to the others.

They found only a few people in front of the operation theatre. An old lady was seated on a chair. Two young men who appeared to be her sons were pacing in the waiting area.

After making Mustafa sit in a chair, the young man waited at the door of the operation theatre. He stopped a nurse who was about enter the OT.

'We are the friends of the young man who has been brought in with a bullet in him. If you need blood or anything else . . .'

'We've a blood bank. However, if we need blood we'll let you know. Please relax now,' she said kindly.

The student sat down beside Mustafa. Although Mustafa's head was bowed, he could see tears streaming down his cheeks into his thick beard.

'My name is Zeki,' the youngster introduced himself. 'We are students of Marmara University.'

Mustafa remained silent. When he saw there was no response, deciding not to trouble him further, Zeki became engrossed in replying to messages on his mobile. Gönül joined them after a little while, walking down the corridor in silence.

'Timur's blood group is AB negative. In our college, only three have that group. One of them is a girl. I have asked all three to reach here immediately. They've started from there,' he whispered in Zeki's ear.

'Did they say anything about his condition?' asked Gönül, throwing Mustafa a sidelong glance.

'It's not very good. The bullet is lodged within him. He has lost a lot of blood too.'

Suddenly, a group of policemen appeared at the end of the corridor.

'They're headed here!' Zeki rose to his feet in alarm.

The policemen reached them, their eyes scanning every inch of the way.

'Why are you here?'

'We've come with a patient,' Gönül replied in a serene voice.

'Leave this place, now!'

'Why should we leave?' Zeki asked.

'The minister is coming here. We are getting everyone to vacate this place.'

'We shall leave after we meet the doctor,' Gönül said politely.

'What's wrong with him?' the police officer asked, pointing to Mustafa who was sitting curled up on the chair. His dishevelled hair, bloodied clothes and manic looking eyes were enough to alert anyone.

'The blood is from the patient who met with an accident. He doesn't look too good himself.'

'Take him away. When the minister comes, we don't want scarecrows like him around.'

As if to show he meant business, he swished his truncheon. 'You heard me . . .'

He also shouted at the old woman seated a little away. Terrified, she jumped up from her chair, with her body trembling. Her sons hurried towards her.

'We'll leave . . .' one of them spoke deferentially.

Vain about his commanding power and overbearing persona, he preened himself and looked around to ensure that everything was secure before turning around and walking back. One of the policemen, as he tailed the officer, gestured to them to leave.

'Let's move to some other place,' Zeki said, tapping Mustafa's shoulder.

'What if he needs help . . .?' Mustafa started to weep.

'If we sit on the other side of that window, we can watch the OT door. If we sit here any longer, they will come back and drive us out.' Gönül put a friendly arm around Mustafa's shoulder and led him to the adjacent hall.

'Hey . . .!' Someone hailed from behind them.

It was the doctor.

All three ran back towards him.

'You had brought Timur in, right?'

'Yes, what happened?' a worried Zeki asked.

'The bullet has grazed his heart. We're doing an open-heart surgery. I came out only to inform you.'

Zeki's mouth went dry. The doctor turned on his heel and walked back to the OT with as much speed as he had come.

'I had promised his father,' Mustafa yelled. 'I had given him my word that nothing will happen to Timur.'

He looked at the tall doors that had swung shut once again and implored to them repeatedly.

'I made the mistake of promising him no harm will come . . .'

Gönül propped him up when it looked like he was swooning. They tried to take him away from there. Grabbing Gönül's hand and pushing it away, Mustafa started to bawl again.

'Take every organ from my body, my heart, my blood, whatever . . . but return him alive . . .' His scream made the stock-still woman sitting at the far end of hall give a start and look at him.

Zeki stroked his damp cheeks. 'If you shout like this, they will drive us out of the hospital. Don't cry!' Mustafa started to scratch his own face like a lunatic. Gönül hugged him and caressed his back.

'The surgeons here are brilliant. And highly trustworthy. We need to be patient. Come, let's go and sit there.'

It was a struggle to get him away from there as he stood rooted to the spot, staring at the OT doors with his bloodshot, tearful eyes.

Time passed like a crawling old woman. After an hour, a group youngsters arrived, among them was a slim girl. Zeki tried to recall where he had seen her grave-looking face and its spectacles. One of the youngsters handed over a packet to Zeki. He pulled out a T-shirt from it and offered it to Mustafa.

'The place will be crawling with police very soon. Didn't they say that the minister is expected to come? If they see the blood-soaked shirt, they won't let us be. Here . . . change your shirt.'

'Police? Why what happened?' asked one of the newly arrived students.

'The guy inside is Kasim Özdemir's nephew,' Gönül said. The new group looked at one another.

'If that is the case, if we are all found here, there could be problems.'

'I shall sit here with them. All of you wait outside somewhere,' the girl, who had been silent till then, spoke.

They could see two policemen enter the hall. The students quickly exited.

'Here, change your shirt.' Zeki threw the T-shirt into Mustafa's lap. He did not appear to have noticed it. The girl looked at him wide-eyed.

'Quick! Or else all of us will be in trouble.' Zeki whispered sharply into his ear. Mustafa looked around him uncomprehendingly as if he had just woken up from his sleep. Zeki lifted the T-shirt and held it in front of his eyes. 'Change now!'

When he saw Mustafa change into the T-shirt like an automaton, Zeki felt they should consult a doctor.

The wail of police car sirens outside reached them. They could see people bustle about and many enter the building. Surrounded by a group of men who seemed to be in control, Kasim Özdemir entered. In contrast to his usual elegant and polished style, he seemed to be dishevelled and shaken. After handshakes, the group took him to one of the rooms inside.

'He may come here,' Zeki said.

'What's it to us? So many people come and go in this hospital!' Gönül spoke nonchalantly.

'It's not as you think. He's a politician. He'll surely come to thank the people who had saved his nephew and brought him to the hospital. It'd be better if he doesn't meet Mustafa in this state. We also should be mum about going there to protest.'

Zeki turned towards the girl. 'Should anyone among them come here, please ensure that he doesn't attract their attention.'

She nodded in affirmation.

'My son . . .' a woman's cry rang out as if her heart was being wrenched out of her body. A distraught woman dashed in through the main door.

'Son . . .' she shrieked again. She dashed around in the reception area and its adjacent hall as if searching for someone. Unable to understand what was happening, the sleepy-eyed patients and bystanders who were seated around there leapt to their feet.

'What's the problem?' the girl asked Zeki, frightened by the piercing scream.

'I don't know. Possibly someone has died,' Zeki said.

Breathless from her crying, the woman lost her bearings and stumbled over the visitor's chairs and crashed to the ground and hit her head on the floor. The attendants and people standing around the reception rushed towards her.

'She may have come after hearing of someone's accident,' Gönül said with a sigh as they watched her limp body being taken away on a stretcher. Zeki gave him a meaningful look.

'Could she be related to Timur?' Gönül asked in consternation.

'Come, sit here,' Zeki took him by his arm and made him sit near Mustafa. The shriek had seemingly scared him. Zeki took pity on him as he seemed to want to shrink into himself, pulling up his legs on to the chair and curling himself into a ball, all the while darting furtive glances in all directions. His whimpering lips were moving non-stop as if he was chanting an endless prayer.

'I have some sandwiches and water. My mother had given them when she heard I was coming to the hospital.'

'Thank you, but I am not hungry,' Gönül said, looking at Zeki. He had had a frugal breakfast in the morning. Although all the excitement and clashes of the morning had exhausted him, he was still not hungry.

Zeki looked at his watch, it showed 8 p.m.

'It's getting late. Don't you have to go home?' Zeki was aware that in some families, girls were subject to curfew.

'It's not a problem. My people know I have come to the hospital.' She gave them a reassuring smile. 'My name is Yara. I'm Prof. Bahoz Çiçek's daughter.'

She took her father's name to remove any misgivings they may have. Both Gönül and Zeki knew Prof. Çiçek.

They introduced themselves. 'I'm Gönül, he's Zeki and that's Mustafa.'

'I've seen you in the college,' Yara said. She took out a bottle of cold water from her deep leather bag and offered them.

Zeki ran his tongue over his dry lips to wet them. He realized only then that he was very thirsty. After taking a mouthful of water, he passed the bottle to Gönül. He pressed his palms, cooled by the bottle and its dampness, against his burning face. Gönül approached Mustafa with the bottle.

'Drink some.'

Mustafa shook his head refusing the offer.

'You'll fall ill. At least drink some water,' he implored.

Mustafa pursed his lips. The dogged look on his face made Gönül step back in dismay. He gave Yara a grateful glance and took a sip from the bottle.

They saw a group of people coming towards them along the corridor—Kasim, accompanied by policemen and hospital administrators. The old woman who had created an uproar earlier was also among them. Kasim was holding the woman close to him affectionately and was walking slowly.

They stopped in front of the OT. The woman had started to weep again. With some hesitation Zeki and Gönül went up to them.

'What do you want?' an officer growled.

'We brought Timur here.'

Kasim looked up at them and said, 'Let them come to me.' He seated the lady in a nearby chair and walked towards them.

'What really happened? I heard he was shot in front of Beykoz hospital. Then why was he brought here?' Kasim asked anxiously.

'The police prevented us from entering. It took us some time to bring him here, ten to fifteen minutes.'

Kasim shook his head in exasperation. 'What is his condition?' he asked after some reflection.

'He was shot in the chest. The doctor said the bullet had grazed the heart. There is severe blood loss.' Gönül said softly. He was throwing sidelong glances at the woman. Kasim noticed it.

'She's Timur's mother.' He nodded at them and went towards the woman.

'Come . . . the surgery is going on. Let's go to the room and wait there. There's no need to wait here.'

He helped her up. He held up her body that had been enervated by mental anguish and the powerful tranquillizers that doctors had given her and slowly walked her towards the ward.

'I'll be here. I'm not leaving,' Kasim said after helping her lie on the bed.

'Don't we have to inform his father?' her words were slurring. Kasim could feel anger rising in him. He suppressed it and said helplessly, 'I'll try to do that. Please try to rest for a while . . .'

When he was leaving the room he spoke to his secretary by his side, 'Do you know how many times I had told the father and son they were playing with fire? Whatever it may be, make arrangements to inform him in the prison.'

'Shall we try to bring him here for a couple of hours?'

'He's charged with treason. Let's make an attempt. If news leaks that there was such an attempt, I shall have to answer to all the allegations. Check with our solicitor all the same.'

Along with the hospital manager, Kasim went to the senior doctor's room.

Yara took out a packet from her bag. The aroma of freshly baked bread spread wafted out of it. Zeki and Gönül realized they were famished, whereas till then they were not conscious of their hunger.

'Eat . . .' Yara offered slices of bread.

Another police squad stomped into the hospital. Zeki and Gönül did not stir from their places, assuming that they were part of the minister's retinue. The officer and his constables, after consulting the reception, came into the hall where they were seated.

'Did you bring in the young man who had been shot?' one of them asked Zeki.

'Yes.' Zeki and Gönül stood up.

'And this girl?' he pointed at Yara.

'She is a member of the blood donors' group of our college. She has come assuming blood will be needed.'

'Who's that?' he gestured towards Mustafa, still in his curled-up position.

'He's a patient. He was here when we arrived,' Yara said, sensing danger.

'All right, you must come to the police station.'

'Sir, why? The person we brought in is being operated on. How can we leave now?'

'Relatives are here to take care of his needs. Come with us and don't create any trouble. We know you were the ones who started the violence in front of Beykoz.'

Zeki and Gönül started to walk without protest. They were hoping that Yara and Mustafa would be spared.

'You too,' the officer shouted at Yara. She had been silent till then, but now her expression changed.

'Officer, I came here because I was told that the patient needs blood. I have not participated in the protest that you are talking of. I was in the Marmara University library till 5.30 p.m. You can check if you want.'

The officer who started to say something decided not to after seeing the determined look on her face. Wagging his finger at her menacingly, he shoved Zeki and Gönül to make them walk faster.

'I'll handle things here,' she signalled to Zeki who turned back and gave her a look of helplessness.

Yara could not decide her next move. After thinking for some time, she took out her phone.

'Hello . . .' the calm voice at the other end made her break down. 'Baba, my friends have been taken away by the police.'

'What happened?' Her crying made her father nervous. She narrated the incidents. Realising the gravity of the situation, he promised to do the needful.

'Don't worry. You wait there. The police will not come again. You have other friends who are around, that's what you said. Call and inform them. I'm coming to you.'

Yara wiped her face and looked towards Mustafa. Whatever had happened there did not seem to have registered with him. He had shifted his position and sat staring through the window at the darkness outside. Yara sighed and took the seat next to him.

What was she doing here of all places? Who was Timur? Should she just leave? The next moment she felt guilty for having such thoughts.

The OT door opened.

'Who is with Timur?'

Yara leapt to her feet. Mustafa, who was now staring at the wall, did not seem to have heared the question. Although she started to call him, she thought better of it.

'I'm the doctor.' An elderly man was at the OT door. She approached him slowly as if she was under an unbearable weight.

'What's your relationship with him?' The doctor looked at the young girl with concern.

'He's my relative,' Yara whispered. She could not anticipate what was coming next and the prospect frightened her.

'No one else is with you?'

'No.'

'Please sit here.' He joined her after she sat down on a bench by the side of the OT door.

'By the time he was brought here he had suffered massive loss of blood. Moreover, the bullet had grazed his heart.'

An irrepressible sob escaped her. The doctor held her close and sat looking at the darkness outside showing little emotion.

A chill enveloped them like the cold hands of the hapless Timur who lay under sedation in the OT with an impaired heart.

Syria

'What are you doing?'
Amira who was arranging stuffed vine leaves on the salver, poked her head out of the kitchen and asked, 'Do you need something?'

'Your mobile. Let me check if there is any breaking news.'

'It's there on top of the cabinet. If the children lay their hands on it, they'll take it apart. It's not of much use though. The internet connection is very patchy.'

'Let me try. It's been days since I've watched the news.'

Wiping her wet hands on her skirt, Amira emerged out of the kitchen. Moving Pinar out of her way, she stretched up and grabbed the mobile from the top of the cabinet.

'It's an old one,' Amira said shamefacedly and returned to the kitchen.

Pinar checked the phone; it was a very old model with scratches and oily fingerprints on the dim display. However, she felt a thrill holding it. After having lived an immersive life among news and breaking stories for many years, with all connections to the outside world snapped now, she was like a fish out of water.

'Don't check your mail. The Turkish intelligence will track you down if you do,' Pinar heard Amira call out to her amidst the clanging of pots.

'Will they reach here too?' she laughed, widening her eyes. 'I'll be careful.'

Although worried that bullets may pierce them any moment, as they sped through the night like wounded animals scared for their lives, and completed the last part running and crawling on their stomach in the darkness thanks to the reassuring role of Arman in the whole process, Pinar's flight from Turkey to Syria was relatively easy.

Arman had arranged their stay in a large house in the suburbs of Al-Malikiyah. The peaceful town under the control of Syrian Democratic Forces, was close to the Turkey-Syria border.

Sounds of Tujela playing with Amira's children outside could be heard. They had pulled out twigs from the fence and were building a playhouse. Children from their neighbourhood were also in the group. Tujela's dress was covered in brown dust. Pinar had never seen Tujela enjoy herself so much.

After watching the children for a little while, Pinar turned her attention to the mobile. The signal was weak, and websites were not opening. She looked around. There was a steep flight of stairs on the side of the house, leading to the terrace of the house. Maybe if she stood on the higher floor, the signal would be better. Instead of a handrail, the stairs had only an old, frayed rope stretched out on its side, which did not look capable of taking the weight of a child, let alone of an adult. She climbed the stairs, gingerly holding on to the rope.

From the terrace, the sight of golden-brown fields stretching from the border of the house till as far as her eyes could see was uplifting. Like small clouds, flocks of sparrows were wheeling, rising and descending on the fields. Pinar took a deep breath. She had not fancied that she could live like this, free and breathing in clean air. The Turkish border was about 6 km away on foot, through the fields that stretched out before her, looking like a watercolour painting.

To divert her mind from unpleasant thoughts, she turned away and tried to open the home page of *Euro Times*.

The signal seemed to be better than what it was inside the house. The graphics still would not load, but the text did. She read the updates from Turkey. Everything looked great. Halil was doing brilliant work, perhaps even better than she had done.

Her eyes were arrested by a news link. 'Student dies in firing in front of Beykoz hospital'. Clicking it open and reading it made the world around her go black. 'Following the police firing on the protestors in front of Beykoz hospital, Timur, a student, has been killed. He is the son of Bahadir, a lawyer.' There was reference to Bahadir's arrest too in the news.

When she had recovered from the shock, she checked quickly for other news on Bahadir in the recent days. The news about his arrest and slow-loading visuals came on the screen as she looked on in disbelief. Arrested for helping Pinar, a journalist charged with treason! When she felt her legs would no longer support her, she sat down on the hot terrace. They were taking their frustration out on him for not being able to catch her!

Suddenly, a doubt struck her. For the police to investigate and find out that Bahadir had nothing to do with her disappearance should be the easiest of things to do. This arrest had to have another reason behind it.

She read through the news items on Timur's death. Nowhere did it have any reference to his connection with Seetha's case. Her experience of many years kept prodding her mind—this was no ordinary death! She started to dial Halil's number but gave up upon reconsideration. Then, Pinar called out, 'Amira . . .'

She was busy in the kitchen, and it was unlikely that she would have heard Pinar's shout. Pinar, therefore, called one of the children playing in the yard. The children were speaking in Kurmanji, one of the Kurdish dialects. Although she could understand Kurmanji, she was not a fluent speaker. She managed to convey to the children that they were to fetch Amira.

'What happened?' Amira asked Pinar, who was seated by the side of tomato slices kept for sun drying and was still checking news sites. Since she was busy in the kitchen, she took some time to come to her. The sight of dried tear marks on Pinar's cheeks unnerved her.

'What's the problem?'

Pinar grabbed her as if seeking an anchor.

'I need to call Turkey.'

'Hasn't Arman told you categorically not to call Turkey?'

Amira stroked Pinar's shoulders to calm her down.

'Just once. If I don't do it, there'll be a lot of problem,' Pinar begged.

'Don't do it without informing Arman,' Amira said strictly. 'Let me try him.'

Amira took the phone from Pinar. The call did not go through. Then she called someone and left a message that Arman should get in touch with her the soonest possible.

'Now don't sit here and moan. Come down!'

'Amira, may I sit here for some more time . . . alone . . .?' Pinar gave her a hangdog look.

'Whatever the problems are, don't worry about them. I'm going down. After they are tired of rolling in the dust, the children will come for their lunch. Nothing's ready yet. I'm taking the phone with me. Arman may call.'

Amira went down the stairs briskly. Pinar's thoughts were full of the tragedy that had struck Bahadir. During a protest that had thousands of students, only Timur had been singled out and shot. Why was the press not joining the dots, not connecting the arrest of the father with his son's killing? As she tried to undo the knots, they were getting more and more tangled, increasing her anxiety.

Suddenly, she noticed a vehicle driving up on the narrow path between the harvest-ready wheat fields. She squinted against the bright sunlight. However, the cloud of dust raised by the vehicle made it difficult for her to distinguish if it was a jeep or a tractor. She fell back to her reverie, chewing on a salted tomato slice.

'Pinar . . .'

Someone was hailing her. She scrambled up in confusion, peeling open her eyes that had closed involuntarily. She was not dreaming. Amira was calling her from the ground.

'I'm coming.'

Pinar went to the stairs and looked down. A jeep was parked in the yard. The children were climbing all over it. Tujela alone stood to the side, looking scared. When she saw her mother, she ran to the bottom of the stairs and started to sniffle. Pinar came down the stairs slowly, holding onto the rope.

Two young men were inside the house. Refusing to sit down, they were pacing up and down. The guns slung on their shoulders could have scared Tujela. After freeing her skirt from Tujela's clutches, Pinar entered the house.

'This is Pinar,' Amira introduced her. The young men stared at her piercingly.

'Did you request to speak to Arman?' one of them asked. His brusque manner was disquieting to Pinar.

'Yes,' she nodded.

'He's not here. If it's very essential, we can connect you to him.'

'Yes, it's very essential.'

Seeing the grim look on Pinar's face, without further questions, he extricated a satellite phone from a leather pouch on a belt strung across his chest and went out. His companion was making friendly conversation with Amira in Kurmanji. He even tried to mimic baby talk with Tujela who was now hanging onto Amira, after having lost her grip on Pinar's skirt.

'Arman is on the line,' the young man entered offering her the phone. Pinar almost grabbed it from his hand.

'Arman . . .'

She started to talk only after she had walked beyond the grapevines in the yard, out of everyone's earshot.

'Where are you?'

'That's not important.' Pinar had a feeling that he was laughing when he said it.

'Tell me, what's the latest?'

'I could see the news of the past few days only today. Did you know of Bahadir's arrest and his son being shot dead?'

'Yes.'

'For one thing, the real reason behind Bahadir's arrest is not aiding my flight from Turkey. The intelligence must have known the truth that he was not even aware that I had flown the coop. Second, how is that where there were a thousand other protestors, only his son got shot?'

'What according to you is behind all this?' Arman had her attention.

'There's only one thing behind all this— -Scetha! She came to Turkey along with Timur. He had provided her with all the help. They were afraid that his father would start legal proceedings to liberate her. Which was why he was sent to prison. They shot and killed his only son to silence him.'

She could sense Arman's breath quickening on the other end of the line.

'What do you want me to do?'

'*Euro Times* should do follow-up stories on my reportage on Seetha. The world should know that Bahadir was thrown into prison and Timur was killed because of all this.'

'Whom should I talk to?'

'Halil Bozkurt. Their bureau chief. My laptop in the office will have photos of Timur and Seetha taken in Sur. They can be found in the folder named "Seetha".'

'All right. Anything more to be told to them?'

'No.' Pinar was relieved.

'Your passage out of Syria will be ready shortly. These days I'm rather busy. We'll meet again soon.'

'Take your time, I'm comfortable here.'

'Okay, be seeing you.'

The line was cut. Handing over the phone to the young man who was watching from the veranda, Pinar went inside.

She watched Amira load a basket full of vegetables grown in her kitchen garden in the back of the Jeep. The children ran after the Jeep for a short distance before turning back. Pinar was watching Tujela, who was raising hell in the company of other children. Did she ever have such peaceful days in her life? Pinar tried to recall.

Thumping sounds emerged from the kitchen. She walked in to help Amira.

At 4 p.m. an envelope landed on Halil's desk.

'A boy delivered it, asking it to be given to you in person.'

Without taking his eyes off the monitor, Halil picked up the thick envelope that had been lazily dropped on his desk by the receptionist. As he cursorily scanned the neatly typed text on the sheet of paper, he suddenly became alert. At the top of the sheet were the words 'Message from Pinar'. After reading through, he leaned back into his chair. The story was taking a different turn, the plot a new twist. He reflected for a minute on whether he should take it forward. The next moment, he wiped the doubt off his mind and pulled out Pinar's laptop from the table drawer and switched it on.

The folder named Seetha contained the photos that Pinar had mentioned.

As he looked at Seetha's and Timur's smiling faces that shone in the setting sun's light, Halil felt a stabbing pain in his heart. Their smiles, so full of life and energy, have been snuffed out once and for all. The body of one of them was lying in the frigid mortuary. The other one lay on a hospital bed, as good as dead. After gazing at the picture steadily for a short while, Halil printed a copy and tacked it on the pin board in front of him. Sending out a message to his colleagues to assemble in the meeting room in twenty minutes, he went back to what he was doing.

The next day, Yara woke up to the sound of her mobile alarm. Forcing her sleepy eyes open, she groped for her mobile in the bed. She switched off the alarm and scanned the headlines.

'Baba . . .' She ran out with the mobile. 'Did you see this?'

The professor, who watering his plants, turned and looked at her.

'Baba, the news says that it's possible that Timur's killing was a murder . . .'

'Don't shout like this and wake him up. Last night too he slept very late. He was whimpering even after he had switched off the light.' Wiping his hands on his pyjamas the professor took the mobile off her and read the news.

'If this is true, this will lead to bigger problems. His uncle is a minister. Not merely that, members of this family also run a number of big firms of this country. They will be out for revenge. The news also says Bahadir was framed.'

He went to the living room and switched on the TV. Yara was shocked by the visual of a bloodied man begging to be left alone with folded hands. As the camera panned out, she saw he was wearing a security guard's uniform. People were rushing into a building with crowbars and iron rods. They were smashing the glass façade and walls.

The news ticker at the bottom read, 'Young man who was shot denied treatment. Timur's death ascribed to Beykoz hospital's negligence. Violence continues'.

Father and daughter looked at each other.

'Till now Seetha's case affected only the Kurds in this country. It's now going to be a civil strife.' He switched off the TV.

'We should ensure that Mustafa doesn't hear of this.'

Yara peeped into her father's bedroom. Mustafa was sleeping like a baby on the bed.

There was a big commotion at the hospital the day Timur died. Yara's father had reached the hospital to fetch her. As he was climbing the steps of the hospital, a large group of policemen overtook him.

'Old man, move out of the way,' one of the policemen snapped at him. All the wide corridors had been overrun by ministers, policemen and Bahadir's relatives who had arrived on receiving the news. The professor had tried to call Yara many times; but her mobile was not reachable. Although he had asked one of the overwhelmed attendants who was cowering in one of corner whether he had seen a slim, bespectacled girl with long hair, he had gotten no answer.

He had passed the OT a couple of times in search of Yara. 'Where's this girl gone!' His anxiety had shot up. Finally, when he had seen a hall next to the OT, he had decided to search there too. He had found a despondent, heart-broken Yara hugging a catatonic Mustafa, oblivious to everything happening around him.

When he tried to help her up, she held his hand and pointed to Mustafa and said, 'He too goes with us.'

Although her voice had been quaking, the tone was firm. She had never been a stubborn girl. When he hesitated, she hissed, 'He goes with us or I'm not coming.'

Looking at her eyes glinting with tears and indignation, the professor had smiled genially.

'I don't know who he is. But have I not fulfilled all of your wishes so far?'

Dissolving in a hail of tears, Yara had hugged her father.

'Baba, you must understand why I'm adamant. If I leave him here today, tomorrow we'll have to see him on the streets as a raving lunatic. I'll never have peace of mind if that happens.'

He understood that the incidents of the past few hours had left a deep scar on her.

'My daughter, you don't have to explain so much. We're taking him with us.'

Initially, Yara's mother had been unnerved by the strange-looking man her husband and daughter had hauled to their home. The constant stream of tears falling from his docile eyes had disturbed her. For anyone meeting him for the first time, his unshorn and unkempt hair and beard, careless dressing and blank stare were unsettling. Within a few minutes, Yara's mother had realized he was harmless. She had taken over his welfare by ensuring his comfort and feeding him food to his taste.

'What is it, kız? Has he woken up?' Yara's mother called from the kitchen and asked after hearing the father-daughter conversation. Yara shushed her by placing a finger on her own lips and went to her room. Today is going to be a long day, she thought when she was getting ready for college.

'Do you need to go today? All the students are out in the streets. Violent attacks are happening in many places. It will only get worse,' the professor asked Yara when she started her scooter. She placed her helmet on the seat and walked up to him.

'You know that till now I've had no interest in politics. I've never believed such things affect me. I've never been part of a strike or a protest. However, that night, when I waited in front of the OT for a man who had sacrificed his own life for the sake of a friend, realization dawned on me that the apathy— which I believed was my smarts—that I had shown till then was a grave error.'

'That is true. But do you need to go to the protests? There will be violence and police will baton-charge. Don't forget that the boy was shot during such a protest,' her father spoke with concern.

'Baba, that death happened when I was there. Today's protests are for a life that was snuffed out and for a girl who, a near vegetable, lies fighting death on a hospital bed. If I don't take part, what's the point in calling myself a human being?'

Planting a kiss on her father's cheek who stood unblinking, she ran towards her scooter.

Before she had ridden far, she could see burnt vehicles by the roadside. Police vehicles were whizzing past, their sirens blaring. She stopped her scooter by the side and took out her mobile.

'Noor, where are you?'

'I'm at the campus. A massive protest is planned in front of the Ministry of the Interior.'

'Is everyone going to be there?'

'What else do you think?' Noor was cross.

'This time I'll also be there,' she said diffidently. There was a disbelieving, happy cackle from the other end. Even if it were a mocking laughter, it did not matter. She deserved it, thought a guilt-ridden Yara. In the distance, she could see a pillar of smoke rising into the sky.

The air was suffused with the choking smell of burning rubber. She had to reach the campus at the earliest. She dropped the mobile into her bag and started the scooter.

At the same instant, the *Euro Times* Istanbul bureau office was being laid waste by the police. When their cameraman Ayran rushed in on hearing the sounds, he was sent flying with a kick to his stomach and then bundled up and thrown into the police van. His camera came flying and landed on the floor of the van, shattering into pieces. Doubled up in pain, Aryan did not even have the strength to pick up the pieces.

Where is Halil? That was the police refrain.

'He left only early this morning. He usually comes in the afternoon,' a trembling Darya, in charge of the reception, managed to say.

'The police have gone to his house. If they don't find him there, we'll be back here. You all will be taught a lesson that you won't forget in a hurry,' the officer in charge screamed.

Halil entered from the other side just as the last of the police vehicles departed.

He froze watching the wreckage of scattered papers, broken chairs, smashed tables and destroyed cabins.

'Aryan has been taken away by them,' Darya was inconsolable.

'Did they hurt any one of you?'

'Look at me,' said Eldar, the elderly security officer. His lower lip was broken and bleeding from a blow. 'Not only this, but this girl was also pushed down by them. Look at her forehead.'

Halil lowered his eyes in guilt when he saw the red bump on Darya's forehead and her tear-stained cheeks.

'I'm old now. You should employ young, strong men as security here. At least they should have the youth and strength to stand the beating,' Eldar said despondently.

Halil looked at the wall- and ceiling-mounted CCTV cameras. All of them had been smashed and brought down. He turned around with a wicked smile and looked at the others. The uncharacteristic expression on his face frightened Darya.

'Do you all see this?' He pulled out a wall clock from its fixture. Eldar and Darya stared at the small device he had pulled out of a floral decoration that was kept on top of the clock.

'Not those,' he said, pointing to the cameras on the floor, 'those are fake; this is the camera,' and held up a bud-like device in his hand.

Both Darya and Eldar had no knowledge of this hidden device. Eldar broke into a cackling laughter, forgetting the pain of the blow and the trauma they went through.

'This is not the only one. There are other such cameras within and without the office. Since matters have reached this stage, let the world know the rest of the story.'

Halil walked to his cabin. His desktop system and its monitor had been smashed up. Instead of sitting down and toting up the losses, he extricated his laptop from a bag lying on a nearby chair with its arms broken. When he started it, many mail notifications popped up. One of them was a mail from Montse on a press meet being conducted at the University of Barcelona. After calling up the Barcelona bureau and ensuring that they were covering it, he started to check the footages of the attack on their office from the hidden cameras.

Within a few minutes, *Euro Times* started to telecast visuals of the attack on the Istanbul bureau along with that of Timur's death. The story caught fire slowly. Soon other channels also took up the story. These visuals were played by the Indian media too, along with the stories of protest in support of Seetha. The visuals of the attack went viral on social media. Twitter went berserk.

New agencies released the family's allegations that Timur was murdered and not shot accidentally, adding to the inflammatory news coming out of Turkey. The news stories hung above the country, like banks of clouds waiting to rain, capable of inundating the whole country.

That day, contrary to the normal practice of holding it in its large hall, the press meet at University of Barcelona was held in the quadrangle full of orange trees. Seated by the side of ponds with goldfish looking on curiously, the students listened to the speakers with restraint. Prof. Arnau and Montse spoke at length about their Istanbul visit and the information they had gathered. Their words reinforced the news that Timur's killing was a murder.

'Timur sacrificed his life for Seetha. He knew the dangers he was exposed to and yet, he set out to help this girl and met his tragic end. This young man should get justice.' Prof. Arnau's voice broke as he concluded his speech.

Marc took over the microphone from Prof. Arnau. He had been released by the police only that morning. When he heard of the press meet, instead of going home, he had headed to the campus. His unshaven beard, dishevelled hair and dark circles around his eyes gave him a drained look.

'Two among us students have been eliminated. One is dead already. The other is as good as dead. This cruelty has been unleashed on two innocent souls. I have this to ask the Spanish government—do our lives have no value? Why are you not intervening in this? You are scared of that man. That despot, that tin-pot dictator!' he shrieked.

Prof. Arnau tapped on his shoulder to calm him down. He took the mic from Marc's hands.

'Our demand is what Marc has stated. We need at least Seetha back alive! It's not the Spanish government alone but the European Union too that is continuing its culpable silence over Timur's death and Seetha's torture. What's happening in that country is the basest, the worst kind of human rights violations. The justice system is shackled and more or less completely immured in the hollow of the hands of the president. The rare criticism that comes his way is countered by the president with the threat that he would let out the inmates—kept in conditions worse than that of cattle—of his refugee camps into Europe. Why do we fear this? When will we acknowledge that this world belongs to all of us? Irrespective of the Spanish government's and the European Union's stand in this matter, till Seetha and Timur get their merited justice, we will continue this struggle.'

The students who had been silent till that point started to shout slogans. The demonstration was about to start. Placards went up. Roaring like a river in spate, the students streamed on to the main road, overtaking the media persons who were walking in silence, heaving their paraphernalia on their shoulders.

The detailed news from the press meet at the University of Barcelona was conflated with that of Timur's death and the attack on the *Euro Times* Istanbul bureau and widely flashed on all networks. When the teachers too entered the fray, declaring a strike with the demand that the Spanish government, the European Union and the United Nations intervene to get Seetha released, the protests in other universities in Spain gained strength. The fire spread to universities in other EU countries.

That evening, Mibang was called by the Indian foreign minister from Delhi.

'What's the status? At least tomorrow can we expect some resolution to this problem?'

'Talks are on, sir. I can't say with any certainty that there is progress. They are not ready to release her. Their stance is that they can't have a soft approach towards extremists.'

'I trust you are aware of what's happening here. With that boy's death, the protests are taking on a violent nature.'

'The negotiations for her release are down now to low-level haggling sir. The latest threat is that they'll stop all imports from India.'

The minister wondered if there was a twinge of exasperation and disappointment in Mibang's voice.

'What are you talking about? Don't be scared by such threats. More than 150 registered Indian companies operate there. Even their main airport, Sabiha Gökçen, till recently was run using an Indian company's investment.' The minister was angry.

'I know that sir. Piyush and others have done their homework well. He knows how to handle these people. Everyone is feeling confident.'

'I've something to tell you. A list of Turkish companies operating in India has gone viral on social media. There are calls to boycott and attack them. There's an intelligence report on my table, which warns of such things in the coming days.'

Mibang was in a dilemma.

'Do you know who is behind this? This should be stopped. If it happens, it will badly affect our chances of success in the negotiations here.'

'We don't know yet. But this danger is there.'

Mibang was lost in thought. If anyone in India wanted to get even, the only option before them was to finger these companies. He recalled the political connections that Somasekharan had. Mibang felt he was astride a time bomb.

'I have given this information to speed up things,' the minister continued. 'If we delay, this will get out of hand. If Turkish companies in India are attacked, the relationship between the two countries would be dented. Before these guys here burn down everything, find a solution to this problem.' He hung up.

Mibang rose from his desk. He needed to talk to Piyush. This problem that was worsening by the minute needed immediate reining in. His career depended on the resolution.

He was stunned by an explosion as he ventured out holding his car key. He could see flames going up at a distance. There was a convoy of fire trucks flashing past with their sirens hooting. Sounds of police cars and ambulance sirens, and screams reached him soon after that. The vivid coral-orange of the flames that refused to succumb to the gushing water from the fire hoses spread everywhere. In their fervour to turn everything into ashes, the flames rose to the skies.

At the same time, as if reflecting them, far away in Delhi's Jantar Mantar, thousands of candles lit for Seetha were shining peacefully.

Zehra

'There's no use of you sitting here. Please go home.'

Zehra lifted her eyes and looked at the petulant Kadir standing in front of her. She was sitting on the ground in front of the court building.

'Why did you bring her here?' he barked at Emine who was by her side.

'Because I thought that was the right thing to do,' Emine replied evenly.

'What are you doing here? It's been days since we've seen you at the office!' Kadir hissed.

'So? I was unable to help him because of your threats. Find someone else to do your slaving.'

Emine turned her face away. She had gone to meet Zehra at her home on the day the police had arrested Bahadir. Her presence was a big help to Zehra, torn as she was between her many relatives who were counselling and admonishing her in turns. Emine described to her what had happened in the office.

'How will I give them this case?' Zehra sobbed, curled up on the bed and listening to Emine. She was unable to stomach the betrayal from the people who were like family for so many years.

'Don't ever give them Bahadir's case! I have told you all this in detail to ensure that!' Emine said emphatically. Zehra nodded.

'What's your opinion about Osman?' Zehra asked her.

'Which Osman?' Emine, lost in her own thoughts, asked casually.

'Osman Kemal. Bahadir's friend. I've heard that he had appeared for the workers who died in a mine blast.'

'Ah! He is famous. And brilliant. His clients are the common people,' Emine enthused. However, the next moment she realized the possible danger in engaging him.

'He is also a human rights campaigner. And therefore, in the cross hairs of the government. Do we need such a guy?' She looked at Zehra nervously.

'Absolutely. At this point, I need men with a conscience.' Zehra shut the doors on any debate.

Even before Zehra had recovered from the trauma of her husband's arrest, the tragic news of Timur's death was sufficient to push Zehra over the edge. The visitors and relatives who came to condole with her made things worse. Realizing the seriousness of the situation, Emine left all her other work and started to look after Zehra.

Emine had heard only in the evening that Bahadir's bail application was coming up for hearing the next day. She thought it would do Zehra good if she could meet him once. Since he was charged with treason, only his lawyers were permitted to meet him. After she had the permission of the doctor who checked Zehra daily, Emine decided seek help from Kasim's wife, Tuba, to take Zehra to the court.

'I'll have to ask him,' Tuba hedged, when she heard the request. She had no doubts that if the news got out, her own relatives would pillory her. However, she did want to help Zehra.

Kasim was in the midst of giving guidelines for a press meet that some of their powerful relatives were planning to hold. Since he was haunted by the guilt of not protecting his elder brother, when Tuba asked for the permission, he granted it immediately and, without demur allowed her to accompany Zehra.

The media was present in full force at the court. Even Osman had no information on when Bahadir would be produced in court. Zehra, who had been waiting since the morning, along with Tuba and Emine, grew exhausted and slipped on to the ground. Emine's friends who were by their side tried to make her drink some water.

'Don't sit on the ground! Come, let's go sit in the car.' Tuba tried to help her up. Shaking her head in refusal, she continued to sit on the ground. Tuba started to look around, embarrassed by the spectacle they were making.

'Emine, can I go and sit in the car? You've all these people here,' Tuba asked after some time.

Emine empathized with how mortified Tuba felt. She knew that people would recognize her as Kasim's wife. She too thought it would be better if Tuba moved away from there.

'We've plenty of people here. Don't worry. Please go and sit in the car,' Emine reassured her. In the meanwhile, the media— waiting for Bahadir to turn up—focused its attention on Zehra, who was seated on the plain ground. Although they tried to ask her questions, she answered none, and continued to stare at something on the ground. It appeared that she was oblivious of what was going on around her.

Emine took a placard with only 'Justice' written on it from one of her friends and placed it front of Zehra. She had no courage to ask Zehra if she would hold it up. It was a plain placard written in black paint. Although a look of scorn passed over her face when she saw the word, Zehra held it up close to her for everyone to see.

The camera lens covers came off. They started to shoot and live stream. With the caption 'Bahadir's wife's sit-in protest at grounds of Istanbul Justice Palace' the visuals went live on all the channels. This drew a stream of spectators to the area.

Hours passed; there was no sign of Bahadir. Armoured vehicles arrived and departed with prisoners. Emine and her friends surrounded Zehra to provide her shade. Zehra's condition was worsening. When it looked as if she may collapse any time, Emine toyed with the idea of taking her back home.

'He's here . . . he's here . . .' Finally, when Bahadir descended from the police van, the media persons left Zehra alone and ran towards him. The scattered small groups of protesters, who were lost in conversation, became alert and ran after them shouting slogans.

Zehra, who had started to doze with her head resting on the shoulder of a girl seated beside her, woke up on hearing the uproar and looked around in bewilderment. Emine helped her up.

'He's here.' A rising sob convulsed Zehra's body. The girls around her helped her to walk forward.

'If we don't hurry we may miss him.' Emine tried to hasten their progress, holding her and moving as swiftly as possible through the crowds.

'Please give way . . .' she kept imploring.

Seeing the crowd growing, more policemen rushed forward.

'Run . . .' they swung their truncheons and tried to drive everyone away.

'Equal Justice!' the slogans were raised.

Emine stopped after watching a young man ahead of her getting beaten on the head and falling. Meanwhile, Bahadir had already been dragged out and taken into the court building.

'Let's not remain here.' Holding onto Zehra, Emine tried to dodge the people running helter-skelter and headed for the court building. The enraged protesters, despite being beaten up, congregated again. She heard the police asking for reinforcements on their wireless sets.

'Quick . . .'

And the next instant both Zehra and Emine were sent sprawling by the powerful blast of water from the water cannon. Screams and wails filled the space. When Emine tried to stand up, the next volley of water sent her tumbling on to Zehra's prone form. People were shouting to stop the water cannon. Zehra lay motionless. Kneeling down beside her, Emine tried to shake her drenched body into consciousness. The sight of blood oozing from her forehead onto the bituminized ground frightened her.

'Help . . .' she screamed.

People were running to them. They helped to turn Zehra's body into a supine position.

'Don't worry. She has only lost consciousness,' a young man tried to console the still wailing Emine.

The blood from the head wound that Zehra had suffered from her fall, mixed with the water and spread all over her face. The cameras around them kept clicking and flashes popped as Emine sat wailing on the ground with Zehra's head on her lap.

'This is a small surface wound. The impact of the fall may have caused the loss of consciousness. Let us take her to the hospital,' the young man who had examined Zehra stated.

When he was trying to lift her from Emine's lap, two men came running to help him. Zehra's eyelids started to flutter.

'She's regaining consciousness. Careful . . .' They lowered her back onto the sodden lap of Emine. Zehra opened her eyes with difficulty. When she found Emine's familiar face looking down at her, she hugged her with her both hands.

'Let's go to the hospital,' Emine said.

'No . . . no . . .'

'You've injured your forehead. We've to go!' Emine said firmly. She looked around for help.

'I've to meet him,' Zehra cried. With folded hands, she begged Emine, 'My child, I just want to see him. Please . . .'

Emine felt completely helpless. The bleeding had stopped. Still Zehra needed medical attention.

'They may be bringing Bahadir out now,' one of the men around them said. They could see the policemen driving out people through the door. Young men were running with cameras bearing logos of TV channels, searching for vantage points from where they could get the best angles.

'Let's try.' Emine tried to push her up from her lap. The young man beside her helped. Zehra sat up. The huge court building, the police vans and worried faces around her seemed to be swaying from side to side.

'The bleeding's stopped,' Emine said after inspecting her face.

'I've a car. I can take you to the hospital.'

Emine looked up. It was the same young man who had helped her move Zehra and check her wound. He was gazing at Zehra and pushed back his spectacles which had slipped down his nose. She could see the worry lines on his face. She felt he was trustworthy.

'We have come by car. But if you can accompany us to the hospital, it will be a great help.'

'I have to meet him. I won't come anywhere without seeing him,' Zehra wailed. Emine looked at the man helplessly.

'Let me give it a try.' He ran briskly towards the court building.

Emine continued to sit on the now-muddied ground holding Zehra close. Everyone's attention was focused on the court building's door. Emine felt that considering the volatile situation around the courthouse, it was not likely that Bahadir would be kept there for a long time. Another group of students was waiting beyond the boundary wall. She assumed their plan was to block the police vehicle carrying Bahadir and mark their protest.

'Can you get up?' Emine asked. Zehra nodded. She slowly rose to her feet, holding onto Emine's shoulder.

They saw the young man running back.

'It's over. He'll be brought out now.'

'Son, has he got bail?' Zehra asked in a slurred voice.

'No.' Avoiding her eyes, he shook his head. Though it was expected, Zehra broke into sobs. Realizing that Emine may not be able to bear the weight of an unsteady Zehra alone, he held her by the shoulder and helped walk forward.

Policemen were running; from somewhere slogan shouting had resumed. The young man tried to squirm his way through the crowd, pleading, 'Please make some way . . . this is his wife.' Those who looked back and saw Zehra's weary face, gracefully made way for her.

Bahadir was being brought from inside the courtroom. In the past few days, he had aged beyond belief. The sight of dark circles around his eyes and the stubble on his face made Emine inhale sharply; a sob was caught in her throat. To attract Bahadir's attention as his desperate eyes kept scanning everywhere, she raised her hands and waved.

When she saw the eyes that had passed her retrace their track and return, she held Zehra close and showed her Bahadir. Seeing his tragic look, with a shout she lunged forward. She slipped through Emine's powerless hands. For a moment, Bahadir stood still at the sight of her bloodied face, wet, shabby, sodden dress and dishevelled hair. And then he pushed the policemen around him and leapt towards his wife with a cry.

Although the policemen were caught flat-footed by his unexpected manoeuvre, they recovered quickly, grabbed him and hauled him along the floor towards their vehicle. Bahadir bellowed like a wounded animal and kept thumping the side panels of the vehicle. The enraged policemen pummelled him viciously, restrained and pinned him to the seat. Zehra bawled as she watched the vehicle leave with Bahadir.

'Let's go.' With tear-dimmed eyes, Emine walked to her car, still propping up Zehra. The students waiting on the road swarmed the vehicle carrying Bahadir and blocked its passage. Emine was forced to hug Zehra close to herself to prevent her from being knocked down by the hordes of policemen who were dashing towards the gates.

The police were mercilessly beating up the students who were preventing the police van from entering the road. Cries and screams filled the air. The students who were running fearing for their lives even ran into the court building.

Tuba, who could see Emine and Zehra approaching from a rows of students running helter-skelter and pursued by truncheon-wielding policemen, hurried up to them.

'*Eyvah*! What happened?' The wound on Zehra's forehead alarmed her.

The young man who had offered to take them to the hospital came running from somewhere.

'After offering to accompany us to the hospital, where did you vanish?' Emine asked severely.

'I was here.'

He opened the door and got into the passenger seat.

'We won't be able to leave through the main gate. Let's leave through the rear gate,' he instructed Emine who was driving.

After a glance at the exhausted Zehra lying in the back seat with her head on Tuba's lap, Emine started the car.

That evening, Bahadir's lawyer reached Zehra's residence to meet her. Emine brought the resting Zehra, her head bandaged, to the living room.

'Please forgive me Osman, I'm not keeping well,' Zehra said, while lowering herself onto the sofa tiredly. Her face had become pale.

'I needed your signature on a couple of documents.'

Unable to find words, Osman coughed. To see Zehra in such a condition was heart-rending for him.

'Bahadir had met the absconding journalist a couple of times. They have produced some photographs in court as evidence.'

'Isn't he a lawyer? He would be meeting so many people every day!'

'That is undeniable, Zehra. But if they want to frame someone, they will go to any length, use any dirty trick.'

'What do you mean?' Zehra frowned. She sat up slowly and looked at Osman intently.

'Producing witnesses in court is not difficult at all. Although the court knows well that the prosecution's professional witnesses are tutored, merely parroting what they have been taught, and bear false witness, it chooses to wink at these things.'

With her tired eyes, Zehra looked at Emine. 'Kız, can you take me to my room?' she requested. While taking Zehra away, Emine turned around, looked at Osman and said, 'Sir, can you please wait till I return?'

After keeping down the documents to be signed, Osman rose to his feet and nodded.

The inquisitive looks on the faces that showed up every now and then from inside the house irritated him.

'The bail has been denied. What do we do next?' Emine asked, while she accompanied Osman to the gate.

'We have to wait for the trial, what else can we do?'

Osman stopped. 'Till now the hope was that he'll get bail. That's over. When's his son's burial?'

'Tomorrow.'

'Zehra?'

'The doctor comes and gives her tranquillizers. Otherwise, it's difficult to control her.'

'Do you have people to help you?'

'Yes, the relatives take care of everything.'

'All right. After the documents are signed, you can send them through someone to my office.'

Osman saw a vehicle come up the driveway.

'That's the police!' He exchanged a look of concern with Emine.

'Sir, please don't leave now.' Emine tried to screw up her courage.

Two policemen alighted from the Jeep. Osman guessed who they were from their uniform and the medals on their chest.

'Is Zehra, Bahadir's wife, here?'

'Yes, but she is not keeping well,' Osman said.

'Who are you?' the officer turned to him.

'I'm their lawyer. Osman Kemal.' The man nodded as if to say the name was familiar.

'I need to see Zehra.'

'Sir, her condition is very poor. Tomorrow is her son's burial.'

'I must talk to her. I won't trouble her.'

Osman, seeing the politeness in the officer's words and his respectful behaviour, turned to Emine, 'Please check if she can come out.'

'Officer, what is the matter?' Osman asked in a friendly manner.

'That's to be told only to her.' His face grew dark.

Emine invited them in from the door.

'Sir, she has asked you not to leave,' Emine told Osman as he stood hesitating.

She followed the police officers into the house.

Zehra's condition had worsened. She was curled up on one side of the sofa like a bundle of old clothes.

'Both of you may leave,' the officer instructed Emine and Osman. Emine immediately went into the next room. From there she could easily listen to any conversation conducted in the living room.

'He's my lawyer. He stays here,' Zehra said pointing to Osman who was caught in two minds. Her tone brooked no opposition. The policemen looked at each other.

'We have to discuss something confidential.'

'I've no secrets now.' Zehra turned away her face in loathing. When they saw she was not willing to cooperate, unwillingly one of the policemen asked Osman to sit down.

'You'd have come to know of your husband's relatives holding a press meet?'

'Yes.'

'They allege that Timur's killing was a murder.'

'Wasn't it?' she said, her eyes blazing, as she sat up on the sofa.

'It was an accident.' The officer managed to stutter, finding it difficult to countenance the wrath of a present-day Lyssa.

'Amidst a throng of over thousand people, the bullet that pierced my son's heart was a mere accident, is that so?'

Zehra looked daggers at them.

'Tell me what have you come for really?'

'It's no secret that Bahadir's family controls the construction industry of this country. In the press conference, they have declared that they are withdrawing their support for the ruling party.'

Zehra tried her best to work out why they were telling her this.

'I've nothing to do with such matters. Tomorrow's my son's funeral. Finish what you have to say and leave me alone.'

'We'll make arrangements to have Bahadir's bail plea re-examined. You should talk to his uncle. Neither he nor the others are not ready to talk to the members of the ruling party.'

'So, my husband can get bail! However, will you be accountable for my son's corpse lying in the cold mortuary?' Zehra asked.

'Zehra, if we want, we can arrest you too,' the officer had his back up now. His patience had run out. 'I can arrest you now for trying to cause a riot in the court complex.'

'Keep your threats to yourself. Have your say and please leave. She will let you know her decision in due course,' Osman interjected.

'Who had taken you to the hospital today?' the man raised his voice, ignoring Osman.

'My husband's colleague. And some stranger . . .' Try as she might, she could not recall the face of the young man who had carried her up the hospital steps. The medicines she was taking seemed to have drawn a smokescreen on her memory.

'A stranger . . .?' he laughed derisively. 'Osman, since you are a witness to this conversation, we might as well tell you what is to be told. If I want, I can arrest her now. There is evidence that she tried to set off a riot and that she has connections to extremists.'

The officer stood up.

'Talk to their relatives who are raising a stink. If they behave, Bahadir's bail application will be reconsidered by the court next week. If not, this woman here is not going to attend her son's funeral tomorrow. Husband and wife will spend the rest of their lives in prison.'

With that, they left. Osman could see that the threat had had no effect on Zehra who sat there impassively.

'What is to be done now?' asked an anxious Emine, who appeared at the door.

'Who was with you at the hospital?' Osman looked be pondering over something.

'We don't know. It was a young man. We couldn't even ask his name at that time.'

'And then where did he go?'

'He was there till the doctor finished examining her. After that we didn't see him.'

'Be careful. Don't talk to strangers.' Osman was concerned. He was worried that they would have no compunction in arresting Zehra. He took Bahadir's uncle's telephone number and arranged a meeting.

'Call me whatever it is. I am going to meet Yadgar Özdemir now.' He said goodbye to Emine and left in a hurry.

Bahadir's uncle's palatial house was not far from there. He was pacing on the patio waiting for Osman's arrival.

'Who had come looking for Zehra?' He asked as soon as Osman reached.

'Yunus Erdoğan. The head of Foreign Operations of MİT.'

'Hmm . . . As soon as the press conference was over, many people tried to talk to me. I chased all of them away. That's why they are trying this roundabout route—via Zehra.'

'I don't know if you know the latest gambit. They threaten that they will jail Zehra too. In her present condition, she will not survive that. She's already half-dead.'

Yadgar stroked his white handlebar moustache and pondered.

'If I had been informed when the trouble started, Timur would've been alive today. Bahadir has started a hunger strike claiming he has been illegally detained. All that doesn't help. These sons-of-bitches need to be dealt with properly.' He turned up his moustache. Osman wondered how to placate him.

'Now's not the time to seek revenge. They said that if your companies and the trade bodies under your control continue to extend support, they'll give Bahadir bail.'

'So, we shouldn't take revenge, eh? I have Ottoman blood in my veins. One of my family members has been cut down. Are you suggesting I should abide with folded arms?'

'I didn't say that. I only meant that this is not the time for retribution.'

Yadgar thought for some time. 'It's not a decision that I alone should take.'

'At this point, it is advisable to not be confrontational and follow a path of conciliation. We've already lost Timur. We need to ensure we suffer no more losses.'

Osman could see Yadgar mellowing.

'The whole family is up in arms. I can't decide for all of us. Is it enough if I let you know? I can't talk to these bastards.'

'That's enough. As soon as you inform me, I shall convey the message to Yunus Erdoğan. If possible, please decide today. They've threatened that Zehra won't attend the funeral tomorrow.'

Yadgar nodded and leaned back in his armchair. Every cell in his body yearned for revenge. Osman departed after bidding him adieu, leaving him to his thoughts.

Darkness had fallen. Seated on the balcony of his apartment, Mibang was having a drink with Piyush Mitra. They had been informed in the morning that meetings were unlikely as the ministers and bureaucrats were busy because of the protests and rioting. Piyush had been enervated by the protracted negotiations spread over the last few days, replete with veiled threats, brazen dares and rare offers of concessions.

'Why are you so silent?' Mibang asked, pulling up his chair.

'I was thinking about the Kurds. What kind of a life do they have? Seetha also got caught because of the tussle between them and the government,' Piyush said, savouring on-the-rocks strawberry-flavoured vodka.

Mibang laughed. The bitterness in that laughter was not lost on Piyush.

'What's your opinion?' he asked Mibang.

'Before that, look at my face. What do you think of this flat nose and narrow-slit eyes? Do you feel like laughing?'

Unable to understand what Mibang was driving at, Piyush was bemused.

'Be honest, Piyush. Don't you feel like calling me *chinky*? I have seen a certain laugh in people's eyes which even the three letters, IFS, tacked behind Tamo Mibang, have been unable to wipe out. That laughter reflects a goofy image that the rest of India have created for people from the North East!'

Piyush was stumped. Avoiding Mibang's eyes, he poured himself another drink.

'Our lives are not different from Kurds' or vice versa. People alienated based on religion, looks, society and culture. Eternal victims. In some places, these are Kurds. In others, Muslims. In yet others, Adivasis. Elsewhere, Dalits. You too know this. To survive, every government needs people they can "other".'

Piyush remained silent. The edge to the conversation was hurting him.

'Kurds actually give life to the other Turks. They need Kurds to feel better, to feel they are not lesser. They need to convince themselves that there are others beneath them. A way to rise above their own debasement, to outgrow their feeling of inferiority. Every country has such peoples. They will continue to be second- and third-class citizens. They can be driven out by anyone. They can be beaten to death. They can be raped and buggered to death. Aren't things the same in our country, Piyush?'

'Do you really need to look at things this way?' Piyush said in a conciliatory tone.

'Absolutely, Piyush. Only then can you get an answer to your question. What happens is dehumanization. But, *you* won't be able to understand it. Because privilege blinds your vision,' Mibang exploded.

Piyush, bereft of words, kept staring at the bottle. He knew it was not the alcohol inside Mibang that was talking. When he looked at Mibang, he felt all the jeering laughter of his childhood and youth directed at his classmates from North-East turn around and spit at him.

'You've had one too many. Stop now.' Piyush also wanted to change the topic in any manner possible. 'Where's Somasekharan?' he asked.

'He's in his hotel room. He's a wreck after he visited the girl. He's very affectionate towards her.'

'He's a past master. A Machiavelli in Indian politics.'

Before Mibang could respond, his mobile rang.

'Secretary of the Turkish minister of foreign affairs . . . now what does he want . . .?' Mibang answered the call.

Piyush could see Mibang's expression change as the conversation progressed. He leapt up from his chair with a joyful look on his face and showered his interlocutor with fulsome words of gratitude.

'What's the cheering news?' Piyush asked as soon as he disconnected.

'They're releasing Seetha. Tomorrow, after producing her in the court, she will be released.' Mibang, unable to contain himself, drained his glass in a single gulp.

Piyush exhaled as if a heavy burden had been lifted off him. In their exuberance, they congratulated and hugged each other.

'You should leave for home tomorrow itself along with her. It's essential for things to cool down everywhere.' Piyush agreed with his suggestion.

'Let me inform Somasekharan. At least tonight he'll get a good sleep.'

As the two friends continued celebrating their victory by filling and draining glasses, a horde of people in Istanbul was preparing a send-off—the likes of which the land had never witnessed—for Timur who had come from dust, and was returning to it.

The Return

A small square of the blue sky seen beyond the brilliant white curtains; lumps of fluffy, cottony white clouds that scud across it. A smoke stack on which seagulls had made built their nests. Their constant squawking. The always fresh oleander flowers on the vase near the window. The colourful quilted cushion on the doctor's chair.

Seetha found it difficult to take her eyes off these sights that she could see anytime with a slight turn of her head. In all those moments when something inside her was whispering that she was falling into death's dark arms, the sound a tiny wing flapping, or a soft trill of bird, or the appetizing aroma of food would steal in through the window, reminding her of the colours of life.

A place that offered more protection than her mother's lap—she had to leave from there today. Whom could she ask where to? The doctor? He did not seem to know. The nurse had only informed her that the police would come at 9 a.m. to fetch her. She was being freed, apparently! What is freedom? What is she being freed from?

'You can walk slowly, can't you?' the nurse asked. For the past two days, with her help, Seetha had been trying to walk. Her legs—that with tottering, unsteady steps like a toddler's had taken her to the door, to the window, and to the toilet—were gaining in strength and stability.

Someone was talking in undertones behind the fabric curtain that screened off her bed. Contrary to the normal days, the room had a stream of visitors. Sounds of hurrying footsteps, hasty instructions and preparations.

'You've had a bath? You're looking gorgeous!' the doctor sat down on the bedside stool. 'They'll be arriving soon to take you away. This cloth bag contains your medicines. The dosages are given there clearly. Don't miss any of them. Your wounds are not fully healed. They may get infected again. Remember that I'm not there by your side to save you again.'

Was there more happiness or sadness in his voice? Seetha looked at him—the silvery white hair; eyebrows flecked with grey; thin lips hiding a warm smile; Seetha stretched and touched his fingers. They were soft and cool to touch. As usual, he covered her hands with his own.

'No one will even touch you hereafter. It was no minor campaign that was waged for you.' Seetha could not take her eyes off from that rare booming laughter.

Someone knocked sharply on the door.

'It's time!' The doctor rose to his feet. 'Wherever you go, stay safe!'

After stroking the top of her head, he went to the door.

From the other side of the curtain, peremptory queries in Turkish were met with serene answers. There was a familiar sounds of boots on the ground.

What are they saying? Will someone among them be in this group?

Seetha started to hyperventilate.

In a panic, she tried to call the doctor. He came running when he heard the ghastly cry.

'What, what happened?' Tense, he picked up his stethoscope.

Seetha clutched his hands in desperation. 'WHO? Who are they?'

Empathy filled the doctor's eyes. 'My child, none of these people will hurt you.'

Seetha rolled her head from side to side hysterically.

'None of the men who hurt you is in this group. Please trust me.'

The sound of a wheelchair could be heard.

'Is she ready?'

After helping Seetha back into the bed, the doctor stood up. A stately figure in uniform came into her sight. The insignia and medals on his uniform gleamed in the light streaming from the window.

After nodding his head to whatever the doctor told him in Turkish, the man approached her bed.

'Don't worry. You're safe.' Seetha looked disbelievingly at the huge paw that was stretched towards her for a handshake. Reaching into her space, he took her small limp hand and shook it once gently; then he disappeared beyond the curtain.

'See, he means no danger. His duty is to take you to your folks.'

Seetha nodded. Unable to bear the mental stress, she became nauseated.

'Easy . . .' the nurse helped her up. 'You need all your strength today. Do you feel any discomfort?'

'No,' Seetha whispered.

The military officer came in again.

'The judge is here to meet you. This is a concession made because of your present condition.'

A large man, dressed in civilian clothes, who had come in the wake of the officer looked at Seetha. When another two men joined him, the room suddenly looked crowded.

'You were taken into custody suspecting links with terrorists. Since during interrogation you were found to be innocent, it has been decided to release you.'

He spoke enunciating every word deliberately as if to ascertain whether she understood what was being said. One of his assistants proffered Seetha some documents.

'Please sign these.'

The judge stopped him, 'Wait!'

'Did you have any troubles while in the police custody?'

Seetha looked helplessly around to locate the doctor. He was nowhere to be seen.

'Please speak without fear,' the judge encouraged her.

'Why are you asking unnecessary questions?' the officer interjected. His harsh voice and uncontrolled body language scared Seetha.

'This is my duty, *bayım*. I've to record whether you have tortured her while in your custody. This is a case where even UN has intervened.' He spoke without lifting his eyes off the papers in his hand.

'Just do what you have been asked to do.' Men in uniform appeared from nowhere and pushed back the judge's assistants.

One of them turned towards Seetha, 'Do you have any complaints?' No sound emerged from Seetha's mouth.

'Do you have?' his voice deepened.

Seetha felt the man was looming over her like a giant and was going to eat her up. She covered her face with her hands.

'When she was arrested these wounds were present. Let her say if it's not so!' another officer said.

'If you intimidate her like this, how will she speak? All of you move out. Let me ask,' the judge said roughly.

'Why don't you do what you have been told to do?' the leader asked.

'No. My duty is not carrying out your commands.' He spoke without a hint of nervousness.

The officer was trembling with anger. He pulled out his pistol and pointed it at the judge.

'Do you still need to know about her injuries?'

The judge's mouth went dry. Seetha could see beads of sweat break out on his forehead.

'Speak! Do you?' the army officer screamed. 'If I shoot you dead here, no one's going to ask for an explanation from me. You know that, don't you?'

'No,' he spoke softly. His face had gone as white as paper.

'Take her signature on these documents and get lost from here.' He lowered the gun.

'These are the documents for your release. Sign them without a second thought,' the nurse whispered in Seetha's ear who was, by then, petrified with fear. The nurse took the pen from the assistant's hand and put it between Seetha's stiff fingers. Trembling, Seetha scrawled something resembling her signature. The assistant kept flipping the pages and showed her the places to sign.

'Over.' Showing relief, he straightened from his bent position.

The judge took the papers and nodded his approval.

'Time to go,' putting back strands of her hair in place, the nurse said.

Seetha saw the attendant approach with the wheelchair.

Along with Mibang and Piyush, Somasekharan was seated in the ambulance parked in front of the hospital. The place was deserted. Only the workers repairing the glass façade and the reception area that the protesters had wrecked were present.

'The hospital is functioning only partially. Only the existing in-patients are being treated,' Mibang said.

'They have really trashed the place,' Piyush said, surveying the area, astounded.

'The hospital refusing to treat the boy who was shot had provoked the students much. Imagine what we'd have done in their place.'

Mibang looked at Somasekharan as if querying whether his statement was correct. Somasekharan was not paying any attention to the conversation and was looking in the direction of the hospital anxiously.

'The decision was taken only yesterday. There must be a lot of paperwork. We saw the army brass go in. Don't worry . . .' Piyush tried to console Somasekharan, realizing the agony he was going through. Although Somasekharan tried to laugh it off, he did not succeed. Holding his head in hands, he had an emotional breakdown and started to sob. They looked at each other, unsure how to console him.

'Look, some people are coming from inside.'

Somasekharan looked up when Mibang said this. A group of people was coming out of the lifts. It had men in uniform and others in civilian dress. Behind them was a woman seated on a wheelchair pushed by an attendant. His face became flushed, and he leapt to his feet.

'Wait! Please don't be hasty. Don't move out of this vehicle,' Piyush stopped him. Somasekharan flopped back into his seat. He was unable to bear the formalities.

He was not paying attention to Mibang and Piyush shaking hands and making formal, polite conversation with the men bedecked with medals on uniforms that sported shiny brass buttons. He had eyes only for the scrawny, broken human being seated on the wheelchair.

He saw the doctor he had met during his visit standing beside the wheelchair. He was asking her something in between and caressing her head. Seetha was looking up and listening to him and replying.

The formalities did not take long. Mibang walked up to the wheelchair and holding Seetha's hand, gently helped her up. To apparently lighten the mood, he said something to the doctor, and both smiled. Taking slow, small steps, Seetha walked towards the ambulance. Each step she took seemed to be hurting her. Before she climbed into the ambulance, she turned around and looked as if saying goodbye. From behind the small group of stone-faced people, Dr Armağan smiled and lifted his hand as if in response to her look.

After sitting down slowly on her seat, only when she looked around did she see Somasekharan. Although her face went dark for some time, later she sat gazing out of the window showing no emotion. After saying their goodbyes, when Mibang and Piyush entered the ambulance, they were taken aback by the frigid atmosphere.

'Shall we start?' Mibang asked. No one responded. He gave a thumbs up to the police officer outside.

The ambulance started to move with armed police escort vehicles in the front and rear. The policemen shifted the barricades in front of the hospital and made way for the convoy.

There was less traffic on the roads. All along the route, small groups of students could be seen. Like the calm before the storm, the city of Istanbul stood with a long face.

Seetha continued to gaze out of the window to avoid meeting her uncle's eyes. Where were they taking her, she wondered. Suddenly, a familiar face on a poster by the roadside caught her attention. Who was that? She tried to rack her brains. Another poster with the same face flashed past. They seemed to be everywhere. A resemblance to Timur? No! It was Timur himself.

Seetha turned back to look at Mibang.

'Anything bothering you?' he asked with concern.

'The picture on that poster is my friend's. What's written on it?'

Mibang looked at Piyush. He felt it would be better to tell her the truth.

'He's dead. It's a call to participate in the protest march during his funeral.'

Seetha slapped her hands over her ears. She felt dizzy. Although she opened her mouth to scream, no sound came out. When he saw her keeling over with her eyes bulging, in one leap Somasekharan was by her side and held her up.

Seetha's transformation made everyone nervous. 'Shall we return to the hospital?' Mibang asked, his voice tremulous. He was well aware that the onus for ensuring that she had a safe passage out of Turkey lay solely on him.

'Can you stop the vehicle?' Somasekharan asked agitated. After gently laying her body on the seat, he sprinkled water from a water bottle on her face.

'Timur . . .' Seetha screamed, waking up from her swoon. 'You evil people, you are lying to me.'

Mibang was at a loss for words. He cursed the moment he decided to tell her the truth.

As she looked at, one by one, their downcast faces, Seetha realized what she had heard was indeed true. Their silence was eloquent. An impulse to smash everything in sight overcame her.

'I've to see him . . .' she pushed away Somasekharan who was trying to hold her close to him.

'For God's sake, please help me.' With folded hands she begged to the strangers in front of her. The manic look in her bloodshot eyes intimidated them. Mibang and Piyush looked at each other, unable to decide on the next course of action.

'We have to leave this evening for Delhi. The funeral would be over by now. It's not a sensible thing to go there now.' Piyush tried to reason with her.

'How will you take to me Delhi? Will you be dragging me by my hair?' snarled Seetha. 'I shall not come. Forget Delhi, or anywhere!' She was panting. 'I've lost everything. Now I have lost him too. If you won't let me see his body at least, you all will end up answering for my life,' she sobbed.

Somasekharan put his arm around her and held her close. 'It's a late evening flight. We still have time. If the funeral is not over, why don't we go there?' He gave the two men an appealing look.

'It can't work. We have a press conference at the consulate. That can't be changed. If we don't tell the world about Seetha's release, God knows what more losses we all will have to witness.'

'I've to go. How did he die? Did you all kill him? Bastards!' Seetha screamed at the top of her voice. She tried to feint and break loose from Somasekharan's grip.

'Please listen to me,' Mibang tried to persuade her. 'In all likelihood, there'll be uncontrolled violence at the funeral. The police have closed the roads. It's not safe for you to be taken there at this time and in this condition.'

'You are diplomats, aren't you? Any way that you can . . .?' Somasekharan asked expectantly. To see Seetha in that state and, at the same time, be helpless to come to her aid was insufferable for Somasekharan.

'Haven't you understood by now all that amounts to nothing in this country?' Mibang asked bitterly. He thought hard about what could be done at that stage.

'Let's go to the consulate and think it over,' Piyush suggested. He stole a glance at Seetha who was by then ranting incoherently. She moaned and pushed away Somasekharan as if she was demented. If she could, she would have smashed the glass of the ambulance and jumped out through the window.

The vehicles that overtook their slow-moving convoy were full of silent people with flowers in hand, who looked to be praying.

The ambulance was now driving on the bridge over the Bosphorus Strait. The consulate was not far off. Piyush let out a sigh of relief. The tension during the past few days had left him burnt-out. To add to that were the tears of this forlorn girl. He wished to be back in Delhi without further ado. He scratched his head wearily.

'I need to know where I am being taken. What right do you have to haul me off like this?' Seetha snarled again, her loathing apparent. Somasekharan kept trying to calm her down. However, she refused to listen to him and she kept whingeing in a monotone. Whenever they passed one of the posters with Timur's photo on it, she screamed with a strange sound from her constricted throat.

Piyush went and sat near Seetha. 'Please listen to me, Seetha.' He touched her arm with its swollen veins. It was chilly as if made from ice. 'You should let Timur's soul depart in peace.'

She looked up at him with her bloodshot eyes.

'If you participate in the funeral in this condition, the students will get provoked further. The police will attack them. There'll be more deaths. Youngsters like Timur will be shot and fall dead. Do you wish to see that?'

Seetha sat still. Tears were flowing down from her eyes that were fixed on his face. Piyush felt he was getting through to her.

'At certain times, we may not realize our love becoming a burden for those dear to us. This is one such moment. If you go to the graveyard now, Timur's cortège will turn into another tragedy. Would he want that to happen?'

Seetha remained still for a little while and then started to bawl. Somasekharan hugged her. He too was crying.

Watching Seetha recover her equanimity, a relieved Mibang presented Piyush with a smile of gratitude. He was at the end of his tether, unsure how to deal with the latest problem.

The ambulance turned into the road leading to the consulate. They saw OB vans had blocked the way.

Mibang vented his frustration, 'Damn! There's still an hour to go for the appointed time! Why are they here now?'

When they saw the convoy approaching, the photographers and videographers readied their cameras. The policemen jumped out of their vehicles and forced the OB vans to the sides, giving way to the ambulance. The police chased away photographers trying to shoot pictures of a weakened Seetha climbing out of the ambulance with the help of Somasekharan and entering the consulate.

'Don't let in *anyone* without my say-so,' Mibang ordered his assistant who had come running with his mouth agape at the sight of the ambulance.

'Sir, there are some people who have come to renew their passports, et cetera. What should be done with them?'

'Don't let in anyone new now. Those who are in, give them some excuse or the other and try send them away as soon as possible.'

Mibang followed Somasekharan who was moving with difficulty, holding up a collapsing Seetha.

'A room is ready. Let's go there.' A sofa that had been converted into an ersatz bed using sheets and cushions as pillows was in the room. Somasekharan gently laid Seetha's limp form onto the bed.

'Molae, please take some rest.'

'I'm not coming anywhere, uncle,' she pleaded, clutching his shirt-sleeve.

'You know that you'll not be forced to do anything that you don't want to. Let this press conference get over. Then we'll talk about this.'

He covered her with the sheet tenderly.

'Those morons wanted to drag you in front of the press. I didn't agree. Isn't it enough if I say what is there to be said?'

Planting a kiss on Seetha's forehead, Somasekharan went out. Watching the ceiling fan rotate, she lay like a lachrymose statue with unremitting tear glands.

Timur, where are you now?
Wherever you may be, I am with you.
I am sitting beside you, holding your icy fingers.

An old, dim-lit mosque made of stone with tall windows and carvings and cool interiors, smoky fragrance from incense, rise in front of Seetha. Shadowy mourners with their heads bowed are sitting around the imam who is seated next to the coffin, chanting the *Ṣalāt al-Janāzah*.

'Allahu Akbar.'

The recital of *takbeers* resound. They are repeated by quavering throats. The whiteness of the flowers on the coffin is blinding.

He is in peaceful repose. His face is wan. From his half-closed eyes, in between his lush eyelashes, he is watching!

'Timur!' Extending her hand, Seetha tries to touch him. She can't reach him. She stretches her hand even more. But he is receding.

'Now I don't have to wander about any longer in search of you. Be happy, dear one,' the frozen lips are moving.

They are moving away with the coffin. Way, way, off . . .

Seetha wailed.

'Timur . . . Timur . . .' she called out loud repeatedly in the hope that her calls may wake him up.

In her delirium, her febrile body shivered.

'Molae . . .'

A booming voice reached her as if someone was calling her from another world. She woke with a start, from a feeling that she was falling into an abyss. It was Somasekharan. She shut her eyes tightly out of vexation.

'Molae, please get ready, we've to meet the media people.'

'But uncle, you had said that you'd be handling them alone?

'It'd be better if you too meet them. Protests were held worldwide for you. All of them gathered here have filed stories in your favour. Shouldn't you be saying at least a couple of words to show your gratitude? They won't trouble you with many questions.'

Seetha sat up slowly. She felt dizzy. As she sat with her head bowed, he offered her the shawl in his hand.

'Here, cover your face with this if you feel the need.'

Seetha slapped away his hand in revulsion.

'Why should I cover my face? If you feel the need, cover yours.'

Somasekharan realized that he had dropped a clanger.

'The men who did this to me should be covering their faces. When I realized that I was pregnant and called amma for help, what she told me was that I was no one to her. Let her also go around covering her face. If there was someone who could have stood by my side, today, would I be in this condition?'

Somasekharan's head bowed out of mortification.

Straightening and arranging her clothes, Seetha stood up. Somasekharan followed her steps.

Loud applause started as Seetha entered the hall. She surveyed the crowd. The majority were bright-eyed and happy faces. Cameras flashed and kept flashing. After sitting down on the chair reserved for her, she looked at the media people as if querying what they wanted to know.

'We're happy, Seetha, that your release happened so quickly. Do you have anything to tell us about this?' When the hall fell silent, a woman seated in front asked.

'Thank you . . . my thanks to everyone who raised their voices for my sake.'

Although her voice was weak, she articulated it clearly.

'What are you going to do after your return to India?' A voice from the corner of the room.

'Who told you that I'm returning to India?'

Seetha looked at their faces, one after the other. Whispers could be heard going around among them.

'I'm going back to Barcelona. I've to complete my research.'

Seetha could see the media people getting perplexed. She assumed that the consulate press briefing would have been that she was being taken back to India. She looked at Mibang, seated next to her quizzically. He had gone pale.

Finally, he spoke up, 'The instructions received by me were that she should be taken back to India. We also need to consider Seetha's opinion on this. A final decision is yet to be made.'

'I believe I have the agency to take my own decisions. It's been proven that I have done no crime. We have a society in India that puts the blame on raped women and pronounce them as the culprits. I've no interest in returning there.' Seetha spoke leaving no one in doubt. She rose from the chair. She thanked everyone once more with folded hands and left the hall, holding Somasekharan's shoulder for support.

'I'm with you, all the way!' Somasekharan, who had been silent all the while, spoke while helping her into the bed. 'If Barcelona is where you want to go, that's where you'll go.' He tucked her in and pulled the sheet till under her chin.

'Try to sleep well for some time.' He left the room.

Seetha closed her eyes.

She must leave. Far away from everything!

Ashore

After circling over the sea once, the airplane started to swoop down like an eagle. The water had colour variations as if someone had flung blue paint into a deep green base. Ships that looked like pencil stubs and boats that resembled dots grew larger with every passing second.

'We've reached, haven't we?' From the nearby seat, Somasekharan craned his neck to look at the sights below them.

The two who were with her when she had taken off were no longer present.

Seetha touched her belly.

She felt the hollow feeling in the pit of the stomach just before the landing gear touched the ground. That alone was there. There was no hope that she could feel the throb of a tiny life or the wiggle of a tiny finger. The sprawling El Prat airport adjacent to the sea came into view.

Timur . . . when you decided to join me on that fateful day, is this what you had expected?

The plane landed with a bump. The small houses and trees by the side of the airport raced past and disappeared.

Somasekharan breathed a sigh of relief and pressed Seetha's hand. Although he started to say something, he fell silent when he saw her sad face.

He had only a small cabin-size bag. Evading others rushing to the luggage belt, two souls, deep in their private thoughts, walked slowly in the direction of the exit.

The airport buzzed like a giant beehive. Running at full tilt, jolly children were criss-crossing the concourses. To prevent them from crashing into Seetha, Somasekharan was on the watch for passengers pushing or pulling their stroller suitcases, busily reading the signage to get to their gates. Scared that he may lose her again, he held her hand tightly as she walked ahead as if in a trance.

From a distance they could see the crowds waiting behind the glass façade. As if a garden was floating and swaying in the breeze, the bouquets in the hands of the people were being waved overhead as they kept cheering. Somasekharan turned and looked back. A Chinese family trotted behind them. There was no one else. The gun-toting guards at the door too looked on, with an amused smile on their lips.

'Molae, do you know all these people?'

She lifted her head and looked. People were running towards the steel barriers.

Adriano, who always had a scowl on her face, was leading the charge. Maria was lingering behind with a bunch of white lilies. There was Montse, whose face was always buried behind a book. Many familiar faces beyond the barriers.

Seetha could feel her heart thumping and convulsing. She stopped, unable to move. *Without Timur* . . . She looked piteously at Somasekharan. If she could, she would have fled back into the airport. When he saw the helplessness and agony on her face, Marc, as if he had lost his patience, vaulted over the barrier, picked her up and held her aloft.

'Careful!' Somasekharan shrieked. He was no longer holding her hand.

Children showered them with flowers. They competed with one another to touch her, kiss her and hug her.

Somasekharan followed the parade of the joyous, cheering group of young people.

'Are you Seetha's uncle?' A sprightly middle-aged man offered his hand to Somasekharan. 'I'm Seetha's guide, Arnau. Come, we'll go together. Seetha will come with the students.' He led Somasekharan—who, pleased and thrilled, was watching the tumultuous welcome Seetha had received—to his car.

The radiant sun welcomed the group of students warmly. Others who were waiting outside came running. The whistling breeze, joining in the merriment, danced on the hems of their dresses and their hair.

There was a deafening roar. An airplane rose into the sky, its fuselage shining in the sun like a silvery fish. When it reached high above the sea, it dove into a bank of clouds like a kingfisher diving into water.

A young man standing at the corner of the car park and watching the excitement, could see Seetha's eyes leaping over her friends' shoulders and come searching for him.

'I'm here.' He lifted his hand and waved.

The salty breeze, a panacea for all wounds, caressed them and passed along.

Notes

Sur

1. Kurdistan Workers' Party [PKK] is an organization aimed at liberating Kurds from their life as second-class citizens. They claim breaking away from Turkey is not their objective, but attaining equal rights like any other Turkish citizens is. To counter systemic discrimination and human rights violations faced by the Kurds, they have adopted armed, guerrilla tactics. They are, therefore, considered as extremists/terrorists by the US and EU. However, in the fight against the Islamic State, the US and others have backed PKK's armed units.

Arman

1. The leader of the Kurds nationalists and now a political prisoner since 1999. Popularly known as Apo [uncle] he founded the Kurdistan Workers' Party [PKK]. Jineolojî or the Science of Women propounded by him advocating gender equality is the underpinning of Kurdish politics. Democratic confederalism form of self-governance in practice in the Kurdish regions of Syria is also his contribution.

Mustafa

1. Women's Protection Units of Kurdish militia.
2. People's Protection Units International of Kurdish militia.

Abdullah

1. Turkish identity card.
2. National Intelligence Organization, the Turkish Secret police.

Dewran

1. The north-eastern Kurdish dominated autonomous region of Syria.

Prison

1. Young uncle.

Rojava

1. A form of feminism and of gender equality advocated by Abdullah Öcalan, the leader of the Kurdistan Workers' Party (PKK) and the broader Kurdistan Communities Union (KCK) umbrella.
2. Syrian Democratic Forces is an armed militia of the rebels in North and East Syria, composed primarily of Kurdish, Arab, and Assyrian/Syriac, as well as some smaller Armenian, Turkmen and Chechen forces, militarily led by the People's Protection Units (YPG).
3. Older brother.

Mustafa

1. Association for Human Rights and Solidarity for the Oppressed (İnsan Hakları ve Mazlumlar İçin Dayanışma Derneği) is a Turkish non-governmental human rights organization.

Bahadir

1. Girl.
2. Sister.

Escape

1. Daughter.

Istanbul

1. Dear son.

Home

1. Maternal uncle.
2. Younger paternal uncle.
3. Elder brother.